CAMPO

THE FORGOTTEN GUNFIGHT

BY

BRYON HARRINGTON

EDITED BY

GARRY HARRINGTON

COVER ART BY

DYAN PAQUETTE

WESTERN HERITAGE DESIGN

www.westernheritagedesign.com

ISBN: 1453637842 EAN-13 - 9781453637845

Dedicated to

the participants of the Campo Gunfight
and the Gaskill Brothers Gunfighters
reenactment group.

"Pioneers have always been the stamina of civilization."

Ella McCain

Acknowledgements

CAMPO: The Forgotten Gunfight is a historical novel based on the true story of the Campo Gunfight that took place December 4, 1875 in the small California border town of Campo. In those days, Campo was a very important place as it was, for the most part, the only place to get supplies or services between Yuma and San Diego. The small town in 1875 consisted of a store, a blacksmith shop, a hotel, a grist mill, barns and stables.

The U.S. Army also had a telegraph office in Campo but it was manned by only a single telegraph operator. The town was owned by two brothers named Lumen and Silas Gaskill, two tough pioneers who settled in the valley in 1867. This story follows the Gaskill brothers, who themselves built the town along the Mexican border, and the *californios bandidos* who tried to rob the entire town.

It took over ten years to complete this novel. I joined the Gaskill Brothers Gunfighters reenactment group in 1992. I knew then that this was a significant gunfight in the Old West and the story needed to be told. It started slowly at first, going to historical societies and museums in the San Diego area, then branching out to Arizona and northern California, collecting anything I could about the people involved in this epic tale. I gathered articles from newspapers of the era. I also researched magazines, numerous web sites, government documents and periodicals, eventually accumulating a large amount of material for my own personal archives.

During this time, I wrote a storyline and then a rough draft, soon realizing that I needed to go back and list all the participants in the story and profile each one as accurately as possible. And then I started it all over again. It's amazing how, when you're doing something that you really love, time doesn't seem to matter much.

Over the years I spoke to many people in California, Arizona and Mexico. I thank them all for listening to me babble on about the gunfight and for any input they might have had about the affair. There are a few people who helped to make this story a reality and I would like to give them the credit that they all deserve, Epiphany Lopez and his wife, Lolie Lopez, Larry Freeland, David Chessmore, Billy Lang, Ella McCain, Ruth MacGill, Albert Simonson, Jane Kenealy, Gary Gorecki, Jim Hinds, William and Joan Waterworth, Carol Brooks, Jan Hedlun, James Gibbs and Billy Polk.

Also thanks to Dyan Paquette for doing such a professional job on the cover art and thanks to my brother, Garry Harrington, who edited this story, researched and wrote the Afterward, and for putting up with my stubborn pursuit of perfection. Thanks to you all.

Bryon Harrington
www.campogunfight.com

Chapter 1

SUMMER 1896, CAMPO, CALIFORNIA

A young cowboy levels his revolver and fires one shot straight and true, the bullet piercing the heart of an older man who crumples instantly in a dying heap in the dusty street. The slick-looking youngster then whirls his horse, spurs it sharply and is last seen galloping across the wooden bridge over Campo Creek and heading south toward the Mexican border just over the hill.

Dust hangs in the air along with the smoke of gunpowder, the sunlight filtering through the haze. Ed Aiken, visibly shaken by the ordeal, gets up from behind a rock and brushes himself off. His ears are ringing from the blasts as he looks first at the dead man and then at an old man, who is scratching away at the dirt with a hoe as if nothing had happened.

Still quaking from fear, Ed stammers, "W-w-why didn't you hide from those bad men?" Silas Gaskill stops digging and leans on the hoe; his hardened hands are folded across its handle as he silently watches a blacksmith come out of his shop and, along with his apprentice, walk warily across the wooden bridge to look over the dead man.

"Those men?" Silas says calmly. "Ed, *those* weren't bad men. The only thing you have to worry about with those kind is that they're bad shots," glancing at the spot where the dead man's wild shots had kicked up a clod of dirt between them.

"Bad shots! Well, one of them was a pretty good shot!" exclaims a still-frantic Ed, his heart racing wildly as he looks back at the dead man.

"Yeah," says Silas, "that he sure was, but this other guy here made it easy for him. Besides, if I'da watched those fools, that would've made me a witness and then I would've had to go all the way to San Diego to give my testimony and I don't have time for that."

As they talk, the blacksmith and his helper drag the dead man's body down the street and prop it up into a sitting position against the wall outside their shop. When they put his hat back on his head, he almost looks alive; just taking a siesta in the midday sun.

Aiken, however, can't take his eyes off Gaskill. Even though Silas is getting on in years, he marvels at the man's steely nerve. He could feel the strength the man still possessed the first time he shook his hand a few months ago when he arrived at this tiny outpost nestled in the hills about 50 miles east of San Diego, and little more than a mile from the Mexican border.

Silas is the type of man Aiken wishes he could be. But at just 22 years old, Aiken is a small man and prematurely balding. He knows little of hard work and fashions himself a businessman. And a savvy one at that. He felt he made a good deal when he struck a price with the Gaskills, Silas and his younger brother Lumen, to purchase all their many holdings in Campo for $8800, a town the two brothers built practically from scratch. There is the large, two-story stone store, a blacksmith shop, a house and a hotel, plus nearly 900 acres that include about 150 head of cattle as well as lots of pigs and some horses. That's not to mention the hundreds of bee hives as the Gaskill brothers were well-known for producing some of the finest honey in all of California.

But Aiken has no stomach for trouble. And the trouble today started in the saloon. The saloon that he had just built. He really wanted to quit the liquor business when he bought the stone store from the Gaskills. Before, there was no saloon, and the local men would gather to drink at the counter in the store. Aiken didn't think this was right, what with the rancher's wives coming to shop at the store, often with their children.

He was going to end the sale of liquor, but Silas had talked him out of it, telling him that cowboys would come from miles around to drink and gamble at the store. So, reluctantly, Ed had a doorway cut through the four-foot-thick walls and added the saloon.

So far, there have been a few fights in the saloon, but there had been no real trouble until this particular day. Aiken had seen the two men ride into town, neither of them familiar. The older one rode in first; a stocky man, but poorly dressed, with dirty clothes and bad teeth. He had arrived early in the day on a jaded gray mare that's still tethered out front. He bought himself a bottle of whiskey and immediately began drinking.

The younger one, probably in his mid 20s – "Not much older than me," thought Ed when he saw him – had ridden in only a couple hours ago. He, too, was dressed like a cowboy, but a little too clean, Ed thought as he gave him the once-over: clean shaven with a clean white shirt, his scuffed-up boots still showing some polish, and with shiny, silver spurs.

"Could be a gambler," thought Ed, as he'd seen a few come through now and again in his two short months in Campo, though they usually arrived on the stage from Yuma, on their way to San Diego to take the steamer to San Francisco.

Ed hadn't been paying them much attention until he heard a loud crash coming from the saloon and then heard the two men start arguing.

That's when Ed had come running for Silas, whom he had last seen working quietly near the blacksmith shop. "It's his problem anyway," Aiken thought as he hurried into the street, his eyes taking a moment to adjust to the brilliant sunshine of the beautiful spring afternoon. "Build this stupid saloon … I knew I should have quit the liquor part."

But Aiken lacks the backbone to do any such thing. Though he's now 65 years old with a long, full beard, Silas Gaskill `is a tough, hardened man despite being so tall and thin, and has never been someone to mess with.

Mostly, Aiken is just glad the elder Gaskill chose to stay on after the sale, as Silas said he'd remain in

Campo long enough to collect on the debts owed him and his brother by the area ranchers. Most of the store merchandise is sold on credit and repaid only when the ranchers sell a good crop or some calves or other stock. Ed is thankful that Silas stayed to help with the transition while Aiken got to know and earn the trust of the local ranchers, most of whom are sad to see the brothers go.

Aiken has enjoyed their conversations on the hotel porch each evening, listening to Silas talk about the early days of the great California gold rush.

Silas had earned the respect of the West almost immediately upon leaving his native Michigan in 1850 when he headed for the goldfields at the age of 21. He tried to sign on with a wagon train headed for northern California, but with just $17 in his pockets, he could not come up with the $200 the train boss demanded. Undaunted, Gaskill asked the man if he would accept his promise to pay the fare out of his first earnings upon reaching the gold diggings, adding that he was an excellent hunter and could keep the cooking pots full of deer and other game during the long journey.

The train boss agreed and Silas was such a good hunter that long before the wagon train reached California his debt was forgiven – entirely.

His hunting skills soon became very useful around the mining camps. One day, a rancher who lived nearby came into camp and said he would pay $50 to anyone who could kill a grizzly bear that had been preying on his cattle. The rancher had tried many times to kill the grizzly and failed, calling it Oso Diablo – the devil bear. Gaskill said he'd do it and several days later he returned to camp with the guilty bruin, collecting the $50 bounty and then selling the meat to the hungry miners for another $50. It was easy to find buyers with beef being so expensive and hard to get in the mining camps.

Silas soon realized he could make more money shooting grizzlies and other game than he could by panning for gold, and went on to make a good living at it, killing 302 bears by his own count.

"You've got to be one tough man to make your living killing grizzlies," Ed Aiken thought upon hearing this, "and Silas Gaskill is as tough as they come."

The commotion of the gunfight is now in the past and Ed thinks he should probably be getting back to the store, even though there are no customers in town. But Silas can see that Aiken is still unnerved by the minor skirmish, something he knows the new storeowner is going to have to put up with from time to time.

"Ed," he says, "you can't worry yourself about what just happened. You're gonna see a lot worse than them come through here. Why, I've seen a lot of bad characters in my life, a lot badder than those two. …"

"Well, yes," says Ed, "I have heard … about you and your brother Lumen … how you shot it out with the Chavez gang.…"

"That's right," Silas says, "now those men, *they* were a bad bunch. Especially Clodoveo Chavez and Cruz Lopez … they were probably the worst. They took over the gang after Tiburcio Vasquez was hanged up in San Jose. That was in the spring of 1875.

"Vasquez wasn't so bad," Silas continues. "Sure, he committed lots of robberies and led various gangs over the years, but he wasn't a killer. At his trial, it was never proven he had ever killed anyone, but they hung him for some killings anyway. Vasquez excelled at the art of robbing and was mostly just in it for the money. It was men like Chavez and Lopez who were the real killers, along with Vasquez's nephew Fedoro, who I killed myself, right over there."

Aiken's eyes bulge as he sees Silas point toward the blacksmith shop. His ears hang on every word.

"Yup, Chavez was a killer; he had no problem killing anyone who got in his way," Silas goes on. "And Cruz Lopez, he excelled in the art of killing … he *enjoyed* killing. Yeah, Lopez was in it for the killing."

Silas strokes his long, gray beard and stares silently into the past as he remembers back to that day more than 20 years ago.

"Go ahead, sit down on that rock, Ed, and I'll tell you the true story of the Great Campo Gunfight … for I was there myself. It happened on December the fourth, eighteen seventy-five, about 10 o'clock in the morning. Cruz Lopez led that attack, but this gang of bandits got its start when Clodoveo Chavez became the leader after the capture of Vasquez. Doesn't seem possible it's been over twenty years now…."

Chapter 2

EARLY SPRING, 1875

Clodoveo Chavez comes charging through the door of a little store located on the South Fork of the Kern River and presses a pistol to the head of Amos Scodie before the storeowner realizes what is happening.

"Manos arriba!" orders Chavez as he cocks the gun. "Hands up! If you don't want to die."

Seven other bandits follow their leader into the store; Scodie is quickly tied up, gagged and shoved to the floor. Then they start ransacking the place, locating the cashbox with its $800 inside and helping themselves to new clothes, hats and boots, stripping off their old clothes and leaving them in a pile. They even steal the candy jar!

A man named Jacoby comes out of a back room to see what the commotion is all about and he is quickly ordered to sit on the floor beside Scodie and is bound and gagged as well.

Scodie knows he is looking at the most feared band of outlaws left in California, the remnants of the Tiburcio Vasquez gang. Vasquez, he knows, is sitting in a San Jose jail awaiting the end of a rope after being convicted the previous month on two charges of murder. But it is this man, Chavez, who was Vasquez's right-hand man, who had taken credit for the murders and had publicly vowed to take revenge on the gringos if his doomed leader was not set free. In response to the threat, Gov. Newton Booth renewed efforts to see the $2,000 reward on Chavez's head collected.

Scodie had been warned that the bandits might be in the area. A couple days ago, he had been tipped off by a friendly looking Mexican who had bought a few items in his store. Said he had seen a "bunch of rough looking characters" holed up in a canyon not far away. "If I were you," this man named Raul told him, "I would gather all those horses you have running about in your pasture and put them safely in your corral." Good idea, Scodie had thought, thanking the man. "Da nada," Raul had replied as he left sporting a broad smile with slightly crooked teeth.

Now, Scodie wishes he'd taken more precautions, such as notifying the Inyo County sheriff. Too late for that now. The bandits are helping themselves to just about everything that isn't tied down, which at this point, means only himself and Jacoby.

The front door opens and a voice says, "*Jefe,* the horses are ready to move out. We can ride when you're ready."

"Gracias, Raul," Chavez replies.

Scodie quickly looks up to see a familiar face with crooked teeth smiling at him from the doorway. The man who had advised him to gather up his stock.

"No, thank Mr. Scodie, here," beams Raul. "That was nice of you to save us the trouble of rounding up your horses!" Rage flashes in Scodie's eyes at being so easily duped.

The bandits let out a laugh and head for the door. They've got all they came for. Chavez gives the order and they all ride off to the northeast. Scodie soon frees himself and forms a posse, and tracks the gang through Walker Pass all the way to Indian Wells, but gives up the chase there when they lose the trail.

Chavez and his gang continue to rob and pillage

lonely stage stations, ranches, travelers, freight wagons and stage coaches throughout the Panamint Valley over the next several months. On March 24, the gang holds up an isolated stage station in Little Lake, then four days later hits another several miles away, taking eleven fresh horses before disappearing into the surrounding hills. Even small towns aren't safe from Chavez's wanton attacks.

Somewhere along the line, he meets up with Cruz Lopez, who, along with a man named Jose Alvijo, are pulling off small robberies of their own up and down the Owens River Valley. Lopez and Alvijo, both ruthless killers, quickly find a place for their expertise in Chavez's band. Chavez sees Lopez as a great asset and it isn't long before he is one of Clodoveo's most trusted men.

Meanwhile, posses are crisscrossing the Panamint district searching for the elusive outlaws. But the only posse that really concerns Chavez is that of Alameda County Sheriff Harry Morse, who has promised the governor he will capture every last bandit; he was the one responsible for putting Vasquez behind bars and Chavez is next on his list.

Morse has become so good at his job that he almost single-handedly brought to justice some of the most-feared bandits of the day, such as the notorious Juan Soto in an incredible gunfight that left Soto dead and Morse a legend.

That duel in 1871 solidified Morse's reputation among the Mexican bandits as being invincible and earned him the nickname "El Diablo," – the Devil. Morse had tracked Vasquez all the way to Los Angeles the year before and was the one who tipped off L.A. County Sheriff William Rowland as to his whereabouts; it was only luck that Chavez escaped capture and now that the Devil is on *his* trail, he's taking every precaution.

"Two guards again tonight," Chavez tells his men as they camp by a small creek in the Inyo Mountains one night. They build their fire in a shallow depression so it can't be seen from a distance. It's been getting hot of late, and it's not because spring is slowly turning into summer. It's because they haven't been able to shake the posses that continue to hound them. But Chavez has an idea.

"Cruz, amigo!" he says, calling Lopez to his side. "Tomorrow, I think that we should split up. It's getting too hot for us to stay in this area much longer."

"Si," says Lopez. "I have been thinking the same thing."

"So this is what I want you to do," Chavez tells him. "In the morning, you take two men and ride west and I will take the rest of the men and the horses we stole and ride south. We are going to ride down to Old Mexico and try our hand there for a while. There's an old border town down there called Tecarte." (Today the town is known as Tecate.)

"Si, I have heard of it," Lopez says.

"Good," Chavez continues. "We'll meet up there in six or eight weeks and then plan our next move." He gets a bottle of whiskey out of his saddle bags and pulls the cork. "To a safe journey!" he toasts, and then takes a long pull. He hands the bottle to Lopez and he does the same.

Chavez, however, has more to this plan than he lets on. He has gotten to know Cruz Lopez very well and is confident that he will leave a bloody trail wherever he goes, which will take the heat off the rest of the gang. He knows a posse will follow the bloodiest trail. They sit around the warm fire and drink well into the night.

A wry smile creases Chavez's lips as he watches Lopez ride out of camp the next morning. With him is his cutthroat killer, Jose Alvijo, and another man named Ramos. They head west toward the Owens River, following a creek that flows through a small canyon to the valley floor. But sometime later, as they are coming out of the mountains, Ramos's horse missteps while crossing a rocky area and cracks a hoof.

"Maldito!" yells Ramos when he notices his horse is suddenly limping. Damn it. The other two stop and look back. Ramos gets off his horse and looks at the extent of the damage. "My horse is lame," he says. "Let me ride with one of you."

"No," comes Lopez's terse reply. "You're not going to tire out our horses. We might need to run and you would be a burden. You're on your own." Without a second thought, Lopez and Alvijo turn and ride off, leaving the stranded man to an uncertain fate.

The two bandits ride on, crossing the Owens Valley, and, turning their horses north to avoid some ranches, in a few hours come upon the Owens River. Walking their horses across some soft sand, they stop at the water's edge to let them drink. Just about that time, they smell smoke from a campfire and hear a voice coming from the other side of some bushes, just downstream.

"I think that we need to break camp, Mister Smith," they hear the voice say. "If we're going to find gold, then we need to look in the creeks coming out from the mountains."

Lopez and Alvijo silently dismount and tie the reins of their horses to the branch of a dead tree nearby.

“Mister Smith,” the voice says again, “you wait here and I’ll fill up the canteens and then we can get started.”

Cruz whispers to Alvijo, “I think there’s only two of them.” Cruz, with his left hand, pulls his pistol out of its holster. Alvijo pulls his gun too and the bandits creep up on the unsuspecting men.

“It’s going to be another hot day, Mister Smith,” the voice says again. “You want to take a drink of water before we go?”

Lopez looks through the bushes and sees a man filling canteens from the river, but he can’t see the second man because there’s a mule standing in the way.

“I said, ‘You’d better get a drink, Mister Smith,’” the man filling the canteens says, and the mule walks down to the river and gets a drink.

A smile crosses Cruz Lopez’s lips. He realizes that Mister Smith is a mule and the crazy old prospector is alone. Lopez and Alvijo push their way through the bushes and silently walk up to the man. The poor prospector looks up and sees the bandits standing there with pistols pointed at him. He’s wearing a gun, but he knows from the looks of these two he doesn’t stand a chance.

“Come up here!” Lopez orders the man and he reluctantly climbs the sandy riverbank. “You alone?” he asks the prospector.

“Yes,” the old man replies, “just me and Mister Smith here.”

Lopez looks at the mule and smiles again. “Toss your gun over here,” he instructs the man. The prospector complies and a grinning Alvijo picks it up. It’s an old, broken-down looking cap-and-ball Navy Colt. He throws it into the river.

"You find any gold?" Alvijo asks the frightened man. "No," responds the prospector, "not enough to amount to much anyways."

"Where is it?" demands Lopez.

"Mister Smith has it in his saddle bags," the old man replies.

"What else you got?" Alvijo says, giving the man a swift kick that knocks him to the ground.

"N-nothing. All I got is right here," stammers the prospector as he slowly gets up looking over the two desperados. "I know who you are." "What?" replies Lopez. "I, I, I know who you are; you're the left-handed bandit called Cruz Lopez. You robbed a stage up by Bishop." Cruz smiles; he loves to be recognized and he imagines himself to be famous someday, but now he has a problem.

Lopez looks around to see that they're still alone. "What we gonna do with him?" Alvijo asks. "Well, he knows who we are and we can't have him talking to no sheriff," Cruz replies, cocking his pistol and pointing it at the prospector. "No!" the old man yells as Lopez pulls the trigger and coldly shoots him in the gut. The miner drops to his knees, looks at the blood pouring out of him and starts to scream.

"No, don't kill me!" he begs. "I'll give you anything you want. Take my blankets … take my food. You can take Mister Smith, but please don't kill me!"

Alvijo smiles as he watches the man grovel, then points his gun and coldly shoots him, hitting him in the right arm. The prospector screams again and rolls over on his side, writhing in pain. Jose shoots him again, rolling him over once more, and the prospector is now crying and begging, “Please … please don’t kill me!”

Alvijo lets out a sinister laugh as he slowly draws the hammer back and pulls the trigger. As the ball blows the side of the man’s head off, the begging stops and the dead prospector falls face forward onto the riverbank. Now laughing wildly, Alvijo empties his six-shooter into the lifeless body.

Turning to Cruz, Alvijo says with disdain, “I can’t stand a man who begs for his life.”

“Si, amigo,” agrees Cruz, “it is a sorry thing to die like a coward.”

“Yeah,” says Alvijo, still smiling while he reloads his pistol.

Cruz walks over and grabs the prospector by the back of his shirt, drags him onto level ground and rolls him over. The two go through the miner’s possessions, but don’t find much. A nice sharp skinning knife and a pocket watch that doesn’t work. Lopez puts them in his saddle bags. Alvijo finds a small pouch of gold tied to the side of one of the mule’s packs. “Not much,” he says to Lopez with disappointment and puts it in his coat pocket.

They grab Mister Smith by the lead rope and he lets out a little bray and then follows them through the bushes to the waiting horses. The bandits mount up and ride south along the river.

Cruz knows this area well. His wife and kids live nearby, but he hasn’t seen them in more than a year. And now is certainly not a good time, even if he had the inclination. He doesn’t love his family anyway. Cruz Lopez don’t love nobody but himself.

Lopez knows that if they continue to follow the river, they will soon be near the town of Lone Pine, a town that lies to the east in the shadows of the tall fourteen-thousand-foot gray-blue jagged peaks of the Sierra Nevada. But at the foot of the mighty Sierras are some rounded granite foothills called the Alabama Hills. If there is a posse on their tail, Lopez knows that the best place to lose them around this area is in the Alabama Hills, so they cross the river at a shallow point and climb west into the dry, trackless hills. Lopez has hidden in these rugged hills many times and knows that it's unlikely anyone will be able to follow them there.

There's no better place around to ambush a posse, but just the same, the two take pains to keep their horses on the rocks as much as possible to help hide their tracks.

Suddenly, they come to a place where a split in the earth rises straight up about twenty feet and goes on like that for a considerable distance.

"What the hell is that!" Alvijo exclaims with surprise.

"I don't know what you call it," Lopez replies of the abrupt escarpment, "but it happened back in '72. The earth shook like it was the end of the world and ripped open all around here. It left wide trenches in some places and cliffs like this that go on for miles."

Alvijo has never seen anything like it before. "Were you living around here back then?" he asks.

"Yes, by the river east of Lone Pine," Lopez answers. "The earth shook so bad that it knocked me off my feet and pounded me in the gut so hard I couldn't even breathe. It flattened my house and almost killed my wife and one of my little girls. I had to dig them out."

"Wow!" Alvijo replies. "I can't believe that!"

"Well, it's true, amigo," Lopez continues. "The town of Lone Pine was almost totally destroyed and I think about twenty-five people were killed when their houses caved in. I haven't been back for some time; I wonder if the town has been rebuilt yet."

Alvijo stares in wonderment as they ride for miles deep into the forbidding hills before setting up camp at a spot where they can see back along their trail for a good distance. As Alvijo starts a fire where it can't be seen, Lopez pulls the packs off Mister Smith to see what the generous prospector has given them to eat. There's a bag of flour, some sugar, a little salt and a few other provisions, such as jerky and something that looks like hardtack. Cruz dumps the flour as neither knows how to bake anything. He puts some sugar in his mouth and grimaces as the sweetness reacts bitterly with his bad tooth. Not much here for two hungry bandits.

"Ever eat a mule?" Lopez finally says to his compadre.

"Si, very tasty," says Alvijo. He doesn't even look up from the fire as he hears Lopez cock his pistol and shoot Mister Smith in the head. The animal screams and bucks wildly for a moment, blood spewing from a gaping hole from the .44 caliber slug, before collapsing on the ground.

Lopez smiles. He loves to watch something die, whether man or beast. The mule thrashes its last and Cruz steps over it with the old prospector's skinning knife in hand. They cook up the back straps and gorge themselves before rolling out their saddle blankets in the soft, brown dirt and settle in for a rare peaceful night's sleep.

Well-rested the next morning, Lopez climbs up on a boulder and checks their back trail. He watches it for nearly half an hour – he can see down through the canyon for miles and is satisfied that no one is following them. They pack up and take a southerly route through the canyons, following one until they can see the valley far below.

They can see the small town of Lone Pine in the distance and they reach it just before sunset. Lopez looks around and is surprised that the town looks much the same as it had before the quake, being almost completely rebuilt and showing only a few signs of the disaster that befell it only three years back. The town is quiet and they put their horses up in the livery stable and find a saloon with whiskey and women. They will sleep with both tonight.

Lone Pine is a desolate town; there are some cattle ranches along the Owens River and some mines in the hills. But that's about it. The town itself consists of about fifty buildings, most of them adobe. There's a saloon, a hotel, a blacksmith shop, a small store and some houses here and there. But no sheriff. The nearest law is miles away and this is one of the reasons Lopez has come to this place.

But there is another reason Lopez has ridden to Lone Pine. On the outskirts of town, there is a small store, one of the only buildings to withstand the great earthquake because it was made of wood. The storekeeper there was a man Lopez disliked very much. The last time he was there, about two years ago, the man called him a "dirty Mexican" and told him not to touch any of the merchandise. "Leave them alone unless you pay for them first," he remembers the man telling him.

Well, Cruz Lopez is not the sort of man you say that to, but the store was full of customers that day and Cruz was alone … but the words were seared into his memory.

"I hope this man is still there," Lopez is thinking

as he tells Alvijo about the storekeeper during breakfast the next morning. "You want to have some fun today?" he says with a hurting smile, slightly hung over from the whiskey. "Si, amigo," replies Alvijo as a smile comes quickly to his hurting lips as well. Alvijo takes out his pistol, checking it to see that it's fully loaded. Lopez does the same and with a crooked smile still pursed on his lips, says, "Let's go."

They retrieve their horses from the stables and slowly walk them down the street to the store. There's a mangy-looking dog barking in front of the small building, bringing the storekeeper to the open front door. He sees the two men, Mexicans he notices, probably the same two who stayed in the hotel last night. He heard about their ruckus, drinking wildly and carrying on with the whores. He hopes they are just here to water their horses at the trough and then will be on their way.

Without looking at the storekeeper, Lopez reaches up and pulls the brim of his hat down a little to shield his face. No sense letting this gringo recognize him. The storeowner looks down at his dog, which is no longer concerned with the strangers, and similarly, he turns and steps back into the store while wiping his hands on his dirty apron.

"Ready, Jose?" whispers Lopez. "Si," says Alvijo quietly. "This is going to be fun, no?" "Si," replies Lopez, his face curling into a momentary smile as he follows Alvijo into the store. The storekeeper, now behind the counter, looks up long enough for the bandits to see the disgust for them etched on his face before the man returns to the newspaper he is reading. They walk closer and when the man looks up again, Lopez allows himself a mental chuckle when he realizes the man does not recognize him.

This man he has wanted to kill for some time is now right in front of him, unaware of his impending fate. The familiar adrenaline rush of death suddenly starts to course through Lopez's veins … that good feeling he always gets before he is about to kill somebody.

"I would like to see them spurs, senor," Lopez says politely, nodding his head toward the wall behind the shopkeeper. The man turns, and as he reaches to lift the spurs off the nail from which they are hanging he hears the cocking of two pistols behind him. The storeowner wheels around as fear instantly grips his body.

"Why, you, you, you can't…," stammers the storekeeper, unable to finish his sentence.

"Can't what?" snarls Lopez, the smile returning to his lips. "Can't touch this? Can't touch that? Can't touch the merchandise?" He laughs, and then, raising his voice, adds, "What? I can't touch your precious spurs?"

Lopez reaches over the counter and grabs the storekeeper by the scruff of his hair and slams his face into the counter. Blood splatters from his nose and mouth.

"Remember me?" Lopez continues as he steps around the counter still holding the storekeeper by the hair and slamming his head back into the wall. "A couple years ago I was here …" Lopez goes on, but stops when he sees the look of recognition join that of fear on the man's bloody face.

"Yes, it is me you sorry ass son of a bitch. It is me, the great Cruz Lopez, who is going to kill you." Still holding the man by the hair, Lopez throws him to the floor, and then, as the storekeeper lifts himself onto his knees, the bandit delivers a powerful kick to his gut, rolling the man onto his back.

The storekeeper looks up at Lopez as Cruz points his pistol at the man's face. "Hasta nunca," Cruz says as he pulls the trigger. The bullet strikes the man just above the right eye, snapping his head back to the floor.

Alvijo goes to the window and pulls the curtain aside just enough to see a small boy running away down the street. "Cruz, amigo, we will have company soon," he yells to Lopez, who doesn't seem to hear him. The killer is still enjoying his handiwork, the storekeeper's legs still twitching.

"It only takes one bullet to kill a man," Lopez says without looking up. He lets out a laugh almost instinctively. "Yes, it only takes one bullet to kill a man."

Alvijo interrupts Lopez's fun with urgency in his voice. "Cruz, there's a boy, a muchacho; he ran away to get help. We must get out of here."

"Si, si," says Lopez. "Look for the cash box and I'll get some supplies and things." Cruz grabs a burlap sack and starts to fill it. Alvijo moves quickly around the counter and slips on the fresh blood draining from the storekeeper's head, falling and banging his knee. "Chingas!" he curses, rubbing his aching knee as he gets up and locates the cash box.

They look out the doorway and all is quiet. Even the dog has run off to hide. So they mount up and start to ride. Lopez is all happy now. He takes a swig from the bottle of whiskey he grabbed in the store and says, "Vamos, amigo. We ride south now and join up with Chavez."

Laughing wildly, they spur their horses and gallop off in a southerly direction.

Chapter 3

Jack Kelly is dreaming. All his life he has been dreaming. Dreaming of being someone important, someone to be looked up to. His parents had that dream for him too. They had been among the lucky ones to have booked passage to America after surviving the Great Potato Famine, only to be evicted off their land like so many others in Ireland in the 1840s.

Upon their arrival at Ellis Island in 1852, when Jack was barely two years old, his parents had moved them to Boston where in the mid-1800s nearly one quarter of the population was Irish. But, growing up on the streets of Boston, Jack saw the hatred of the Irish, even though his uncle had pulled in a favor so that his father could get onto the police force which had been created in 1854.

Now 25, the modestly built Kelly, with sky-blue eyes and blonde hair, tries to make the best of things in this wayward outpost of Campo. He would like to be as brave as his grandfather was when he stood up to the absentee English landlords who stole his family's land, but he couldn't even stand up to the bullies on Boston's South Side who used to take particular pleasure in picking on him.

To listen to Jack Kelly, you might not know he is in reality a coward. He tried to disprove this fact by joining the Army, but it didn't escape his commanding officers, who quickly found the perfect military position for him: He was assigned to the Army Signal Corps where he was trained as a telegrapher.

As the lone soldier stationed in this small town, Kelly feels he fits in no better than he did on the streets of

Boston. Oh, sure, he has gotten to know most of the folks, telling himself and anyone who will listen of the strategic importance of the Campo Army telegraph station. In essence, the telegraph line is important. It connects the Army outposts from Prescott in Arizona territory south to Phoenix and then to Tucson where it turns west going all the way to the Pacific coast in San Diego. Another telegraph line in San Diego runs up the coast to San Francisco and then still another heads east all the way to Washington, D.C. The line between Prescott to San Diego was built in 1873 and it only took one hundred and sixty seven days to build four hundred and seventeen miles of telegraph line.

So as he hears the distinct "clickety, click, click" of an incoming wire, Kelly imagines it's a critical Army communiqué from Washington or some other sort of important business. But as he begins writing down the message, he realizes it's simply a telegram for Lumen Gaskill, co-owner of the store which houses his tiny office that contains only a small desk and a sleeping bunk in a forgotten back room.

He calls out to him through the open door that separates the telegraph office from the rest of the store. "Lumen," he hollers while continuing to write down the message. "Click, click … click. Clickety, click…. Click."

Lumen steps into the back room and looks over Kelly's shoulder. "It's here!" Jack says, knowing that at least to Gaskill, this will be big news. "It just arrived this morning on the *Ancon*."

Lumen reads the telegram: *"To Campo station. Stop. From Steiner and Klauber. Stop. Steamer Ancon arrived this morning from San Francisco. Stop. Manifest list checked, confirmed that one porcelain bathtub with claw feet is on board. Stop. Expect it to be unloaded today and will be ready to ship to Campo. Stop. Request freight arrangements. Stop. Klauber. Stop."*

"Well, it's about time," Lumen exclaims. "Sure is," agrees Jack, "it's been, what, six months?"

"More like eight," replies Lumen. "I can't believe it's really here. Eliza will be so pleased.

"Jack," Lumen tells him, "send back a telegram. Tell Klauber to send it on the very next freight wagon coming to Campo … and tell him that I want to know when it's going to arrive."

"Okay, Lumen," Jack says. He smiles at Lumen as he begins to click away at the telegraph key. "Click, click … click." Jack knows what this means to Lumen, and more so to his lovely wife, Eliza, who has been especially kind to him, often inviting him to dinner.

Lumen and his brother had just finished building the two-story Campo hotel, having worked on it for most of the year and two weeks ago they had the grand opening. Mrs. Gaskill had a nice, modern bathing room built into the hotel where they planned to put the porcelain tub, ordering it, they thought, in plenty of time from a warehouse in San Francisco. But it had been on back order until now. She had wanted guests to have a little luxury in the hotel, since they would still have to use the wooden outhouse, located out back, for their other business.

All excited, Lumen runs out the door and down the street. "Eliza," yells out Lumen as he bounds up the front steps of the hotel. "Eliza, it's here, it's finally here!"

His wife is upstairs fixing up a room that was just vacated by a guest from the night before. With her is Vi Price, a black lady that Mrs. Gaskill hired to run the hotel, whom they affectionately call "Auntie Price." A rather large woman, Price likes living in Campo, where she is well-received by the townsfolk. And the dry, comfortable climate of the town, located at 2,500 feet, has allowed her to pretty much forget the rheumatism that had forced her west, freed by the unspeakable war too late to save her husband, who had succumbed in the sweltering cotton fields of southern Mississippi.

"She's so wonderful," Eliza Gaskill is always saying of Auntie Price. "Why, I couldn't run this place without her."

Lumen rushes into the room at the top of the stairs. "What's here, dear?" asks Eliza as she and Auntie Price tuck the corners of a fresh linen sheet onto a bed. "The tub!" exclaims Lumen. "It's arrived by steamer in San Diego."

She embraces her husband of nearly nine years and says, "Oh, Lumen, that is just the best news! When will it be here?"

"It will be put on the next freight wagon coming to Campo," he says. "I told Jack to find out when it will leave San Diego."

"Oh, Lumen, this is wonderful!" Eliza replies. "Yeah," agrees Lumen, "I can't wait to take a hot bath in that tub."

"No," she says, "not just the tub, the whole town. It's so wonderful here in Campo … you and Silas have accomplished so much in our seven years here … the store, the blacksmith shop, the hotel, our beautiful house, the barns and stables … the mill, the bee ranch … the cattle business. It's all come together, just like you said it would."

"Well," Lumen says, taking it all in, "when Silas

and me looked at this place back in '68, we could see that it was a good move to buy the store in Milquatay Valley, it being on the San Diego to Yuma road and all. And with a lot of hard work and a lot of luck, we could see right off we could make a good go of it here."

"I love you, Lumen," says Eliza with an endearing smile.

"I love you, too, dear," replies Lumen. "Ya know, I'm not doing this for me; it's for us, Eliza, us and our little boy … for Walter and his little brothers and sisters who ain't even born yet."

"I know, darling," Eliza says, starting to cry softly on his shoulder.

Auntie Price has remained politely silent taking it all in, but now she's rolling her eyes. "Why, now, you two lovebirds!" she exclaims. "My, my, why don't you just find yerselves a room! A body would think you was just hitched," she adds as she walks into the hallway and heads down the stairs.

"Now that sounds like a might right idea," says Lumen with a wink.

"Not now, dear," she says with a coquettish smile and a hint of a blush. "You'll have to wait till later!"

"I'm going to hold you to that," Lumen says as he gives her a squeeze and heads for the door himself, "but right now I've got to get back to the store."

He happily bounds down the stairs and is out the front door, leaving her as breathless as she was the day she met him up in San Bernardino.

Standing on the porch, Lumen is rethinking Eliza's words. "She's right," he says to himself. "We *have* done really good here." He never thought he'd be able to say that at just 32 years of age.

"Bang, bang, Yer dead, mister," is the next thing Lumen hears as he steps off the hotel porch.

Lumen turns and looks, and a smile creeps up his face. "Looks like ya got me!" he exclaims as he grabs his stomach, wobbles and falls to the ground with a dying groan. Then he starts laughing as his six-year-old son Walter runs up and jumps on his back, holding the toy wooden gun that Lumen had whittled for him out of a piece of twisted cottonwood.

"I got you!" the proud boy laughs, and then Lumen grabs him and starts tickling him and says, "And now I've got you!" They're both laughing and rolling around in the dirt. "Okay, okay," Lumen says after a moment. He gets up and lifts the boy to his feet and says, "Now look; you're all dirty." Brushing Walter off, he adds, "Your mother will have our hides if she sees this."

Lumen then remembers where he's heading. "C'mon," he says, "we've got to see if we have any customers yet."

As they enter the front door, Lumen sees that he does; a man and a woman are already standing at the counter. "Howdy, Simon," says Lumen as Simon Miller and his wife turn to greet him. The Millers are an older couple in their 50s who own a small ranch a few miles east of town. "How have you been?" adds Lumen politely as he extends a hand to the rancher, then tips his hat in the direction of Mrs. Miller and says, "Mornin' ma'am."

"We've been just fine," says Simon Miller. "Got out a bit early this morning. Missus here needs some sewing things and I've got a small list here of other things," as he hands it to Lumen, "like nails for nailin' some barn boards back on. Them damn Santa Ana winds that blew last week 'bout blew a corner of my barn away."

"Yeah," Lumen agrees, "them east winds sure can blow hard at times when they get a mind to."

"Yup, damn them winds," Simon repeats before remembering something else he forgot to put on the list. "You know, lately I've seen a couple large flocks of quail around the ranch, so add a couple boxes of shotgun shells to that list, too."

"Sure thing," Lumen says as he begins to gather up the items on the list.

"And how are you, little man?" Simon says to Walter, who has been hidden from view behind his towering father's legs.

"Jus' fine, sir," Walter says politely.

"And how's your ma?" Mr. Miller asks.

"She's fine too, sir," responds the boy.

"Good, good," says Simon, pleasantries concluded. "Now Lumen," Mr. Miller says as he turns to the father, "it's been a good summer … enough rain to put the grass up tall and keep the cattle fed. And now I've got some fat beeves to sell, or I'll swap you some, and pay off what I've charged this summer."

"Well, I reckon we can take some of your beeves, Simon," says Lumen, "but let me ask Silas about it first. He'll want to ride out and look them over."

"That's no problem," Mr. Miller agrees. "Tell Silas he can ride out anytime."

"Okay, I'll tell him," Lumen says. "Here's your order, and the sewing things are in a little bag in here, ma'am," looking at Mrs. Miller.

"Thank you, Lumen," she says. "Have a nice day."

"Likewise, ma'am," he replies as the Millers leave the store and Walter runs off to play.

Silas Gaskill walks out of the blacksmith shop and tips his hat in the direction of the Millers as they drive away in their wagon. Though Silas is now 45 years old – thirteen years older than Lumen – he is still strong and lean, an older version of his brother save for the close-cropped beard. He picks up a large wrench and starts to unbolt a wagon wheel. He wrestles it off and rolls it over to the blacksmith shop and leans it against the door jamb. He looks up and sees his brother walking toward him.

"Morning, Lumen," he says, turning his attention back to the wheel and the broken axle.

"It's here!" Lumen says a bit excitedly.

"What's here?" asks Silas without looking up.

"The bathtub!" replies Lumen. "Well, it's not here in Campo, but it's in San Diego. Just arrived by steamer this morning."

"Good," says Silas as he continues to work on the wheel. "When they going to send it up?"

"Don't know yet," answers Lumen. "Kelly's supposed to find out. Oh, and Simon Miller was just in the store and says he's got some fat cows and he wants to settle his account."

"We'll have to see them first," interrupts Silas. "What's he owe us anyway?"

"Got a copy for you right here," says Lumen, anticipating his brother's question. "Two-hundred-eleven dollars and thirty-two cents."

"All right," says Silas. "I'll ride out there and take a look at them."

"That's what I told him," Lumen says as he turns back toward the store.

Silas looks at the axle and thinks to himself, "About busted in half. I'll have to make a new one," and begins removing it from the wagon.

Chapter 4

The adrenalin rush of a fresh kill is still flowing through Cruz Lopez's veins as he and Jose Alvijo ride quickly out of Lone Pine. Lopez expects that a posse will soon form to give them chase, but he doesn't worry too much about what he knows will be little more than a bunch of dirt-poor ranchers, who won't stick to his trail too long, even if they can find it.

For now, he is happy. Very happy.

Cruz could never get it. "Why work your whole life away, work yourself to the bone, and for what?" he often thought to himself. "Those ranchers, they work mostly for nothing."

Lopez usually doesn't even bother robbing them; except for some horses, they don't got much else … no money, no gold. About all they ever got is some food, "and they'll give you that … stupid ranchers." Cruz is lost in thought as they ride south, passing to the west of what looks like a big, dry lake. They slow their horses to a trot in order to discuss their situation.

Alvijo is the first to speak. "Cruz, they are sure to send a posse," says the younger of the two. "Si, I know, Jose," acknowledges Lopez, "but it will take them a little while. They are not going to ride off into the desert without first getting some supplies together".

"Yes, I think they will try to catch us," Alvijo reasons. "We grabbed plenty of food at the store … enough for a week or more … we only have four canteens of water, but we can refill them at the river."

"Si, that is true," Lopez says, "but if the posse closes in on us, without more water we will be stuck riding near the river."

"You are right," realizes Alvijo, scratching his stubbly beard. "That would not be good. That would give the posse an advantage."

"Yes, it would," agrees Lopez. "If the posse gets too close, I want to turn to the east and drop down in to the great valley of death."

"Bueno," says Alvijo, "but we will need a lot of water if we're going to go to that bad place, or we will be the ones to die."

"We will need extra water, and extra horses," adds Lopez. "I have ridden through the death valley before. It's the hottest in the summer" when the temperature can reach 130 degrees or more. "But we can make it through with the extra horses and water," Lopez continues. "Still, we may have to ride four or five days until we find some more water. I know where to find some springs in the canyons and we must travel mostly at night if we can." Fortunately it's only a couple of nights shy of the full moon.

Lopez thinks for a moment as they continue to head south.

"For now, I think we should follow this road," Lopez finally says. "Stop anyone we find and take from them whatever we need. Hopefully, someone we come across will have lots of water … a coach or a wagon if we get lucky. If anyone is out here, they will be sure to have water.

"With enough water, we can survive in Death Valley," assures Lopez, "and if the posse gets too close, if they want to catch us so badly, they will have to follow us to hell to do it.

"And only I know the way!"

Lopez laughs at his own words.

"Si, that is a good plan, amigo," says Alvijo.

When the sun is directly overhead they come across a lone traveler and easily get the drop on him. He's riding a large bay horse with a white blaze. They order him to get off the horse, then they take his gun and tell him to start walking. Why waste a bullet when the sun may do the job just as well. But first they take his boots, which they will toss in the bushes a short ways down the trail. No sense making his long walk a comfortable one.

The man wisely removes his boots, deciding to take his chances with the desert rather than these desperados.

Lopez and Alvijo ride hard for a while until they find a high place to stop and rest. From here, they can see over their back trail for miles … no sign of a dust cloud following them.

Cruz looks over his new horse. "A nice saddle," he thinks, but then notices an even bigger prize: two full canteens tied to the saddle horn. In the man's saddle bag, Lopez finds some food: a couple apples and some jerky wrapped in a cloth.

They decide to rest a while and eat some of the jerky. Then Alvijo pops to his feet as he notices a dust cloud coming toward them from the south.

"Look, we have more company," says Alvijo as he points at the approaching party. "Bueno, Jose," says Lopez, "it looks like a stage coming and we are in a good place to ambush it."

"Okay," says Alvijo, "but how should we do it?"

Cruz thinks for a moment as he looks around, hatching a viable plan.

"I'll stay here," he tells his companion, "and when

they get close, I will try to flag them down. You take my new horse and your horse and go hitch them out of sight. Then you hide in them rocks up there," pointing to an outcropping close by. "When the stage passes, I will wave it down and when it stops, they will see just a man and his horse. And while they are busy looking at me, you will get the drop on them from behind."

Alvijo likes the plan. Especially the part about him not being the bait.

"I will do it," Alvijo says, grabbing the two horses and walking them to a good hiding place behind some trees. Then he climbs up the small slope and hides behind some rocks.

It doesn't take long for the stage to come into view, but since Lopez is sitting on the side of the road in the shade, the coach's driver doesn't see him immediately. He's tipped off to his presence only when he notices a lone horse tied to a small bush. Lopez quickly observes that there is no one riding shotgun, a good sign as the coach slows and stops about 20 feet away.

"Need help, mister?" the driver calls out. A couple of passengers stick their curious heads out the windows of the coach, but see just the lone traveler.

"Yes, I do," says Lopez. "And you have been good enough to come along to help me," he adds while standing up, which is Alvijo's signal.

"Manos arriba! Hands up!" yells Alvijo from his perch on the cliff. The driver turns to see two pistols pointed in his direction and gives a quick thought to a hasty escape, but just as he's about to slap the reins on the horses' backs, he looks back at Lopez and sees he's now got his pistol out and he's got the drop on him too.

"Whoa, whoa, whoa," he says to the horses as he

settles them down. They can sense that the driver is nervous and are about to bolt. Meanwhile, the passengers duck back into the coach and Lopez hears a pistol cocking from inside.

"You had better send it out, amigo," Lopez says, "or we will shoot you all," waving his pistol toward both sides of the road, giving the impression that the two bandits are not alone.

"They have us surrounded; give it up or you'll get us all killed," comes another voice from inside the coach. Two pistols are thrown out the window and the driver tosses down his sidearm as well. Cruz picks them up and puts them into his saddle bag.

He looks at the driver and orders him down from the seat. "Everybody out and hands up," he yells to the passengers. The door swings open and three men emerge, their hands held high. Alvijo climbs down from the rocks and covers Lopez as he searches the men's pockets. He takes a plug of tobacco from the shirt pocket of the driver and finds a few coins and a watch in his other pockets.

The passengers all are well-dressed, not men willing to die over a robbery, thinks Lopez, who gets no resistance as he searches their pockets, finding some more money, another watch and a folding knife. Turns out they are mining engineers on their way to Virginia City to work for the Comstock. He climbs on top of the stage and starts rifling through their luggage, but finds mostly mining instruments, which he throws to the ground. No use to him.

Climbing down, he cuts a horse off the team and Alvijo fashions a hackamore bridle and puts it over the horse's head. Finally, Cruz finds what he's looking for tied to the back of the stage: four large canvas water bags, all full. “Better than gold,” Lopez says to himself.

He packs them and the other things on the horses, which Alvijo has retrieved from hiding. He swings up into the saddle, and then covers the four men so that Alvijo can do the same.

“I want to thank you gentlemen for your kind hospitality,” says a chuckling Lopez to the men, still holding their hands over their heads.

“You’ll hang for this,” the driver says as he disdainfully spits out a big wad of tobacco juice in the bandits’ direction. “Robbing the stage is one thing, but horse stealing? They will hang you for that for sure if they catch you.”

“Ha, ha, ha,” bellows the cocksure Lopez. “You tell them that if they want to hang the great Cruz Lopez, they will have to follow him to hell to do it … ha, ha, ha … right, amigo.” Alvijo, too, is now laughing, and adds, “Si, al infierno. Ha, ha.”

“Vamonos,” yells Lopez, as he spurs his horse, wheels and gallops off with the brown bay in tow. Alvijo fires his gun into the air and the passengers scatter. Grabbing the lead rope of his new horse and laughing wildly, he spurs his horse and gallops off following Lopez south down the road. They stay on the road for most of the rest of the day, swinging off to the east just before sundown, looking for a tall mesa from which they can look over their back trail.

As they work their way through the increasingly thickening brush, they find what they’re looking for. A tall mesa from which they can see back for miles. They see nothing.

The butte is a good place to camp for the night and Alvijo starts to gather twigs to kindle a fire. “Looks like we aren't going to be followed after all," he says. But Lopez is more cautious. He walks over and with his left foot scatters the small pile of kindling Alvijo has stacked in a circle. Lopez says, "No fire tonight," and nothing more. "Okay, Cruz," says Alvijo apologetically, thoughts of a hot meal quickly chased away by his grumbling stomach.

They hear some coyotes yipping off in the distance, chasing a rabbit perhaps, Cruz imagines. Lopez pulls the bottle of whiskey he grabbed at the Lone Pine store from his saddle bag and takes a long pull, then hands the bottle to Alvijo. No hot meal, but the next best thing to warm your bones, thinks Alvijo, who takes a swig himself and passes it back.

"It's good to relax after such a busy day," says a pleased Lopez and the two sit and drink without speaking as they watch the sun go down. Suddenly, Alvijo jumps up and points out across the blackness of the desert. Out there, miles away, right on their back trail, they see the light of a flickering campfire.

"That's the posse, I believe," Lopez says, "about three … four miles back. Might even be Morse, if he hasn't given up yet."

"What should we do?" asks Alvijo.

"Get some sleep," Lopez decides. "Even with this moon, they can't track us through the chaparral in the dark, and if they've got lanterns, we'll see them coming. Tomorrow before sunup we will circle around the back of this mesa and ride east. We will watch our back trail and if we see them following, well, by then I think we will be near many canyons that will lead us into the valley of death.

"There are many old Indian trails that lead to the

bottom of them canyons," he goes on. "We can drop down into the valley as long as we swing north of the Panamint Mountains. If the posse is foolish enough to follow us down there, we will lose them in the sandy dunes. The winds will hide our tracks."

By mid-morning, they see the telltale dust cloud behind them and Lopez starts looking for a trail. In a short while, he finds what he's looking for. An old Indian path leads into a side canyon heading for the valley floor far below.

Sometime after noon, not having the convenience of stopping for a quick midday meal, the two bandits cross a salt-encrusted dry lake bed. It's hot as hell and even though they're not pushing them, their horses are sweating hard.

Alvijo spots a small pool of water in the middle of the lake bed and says, "Ah, it must have rained not too long ago down here; we can finally water the horses."

"Not here!" clamors Lopez. "This water is poison, full of alkali. We will have to wait until after we cross. I know of some canyons on the other side and some of them have small springs in them. If we get lucky, we will find one, and we can rest there."

Lopez leads them south across the dry lake bed as the shadows grow long and the sun finally goes down. The temperature, however, does not, at least not right away, and the wind picks up. Finally they come to the mouth of a small canyon that Lopez thinks looks familiar.

In the moonlight, they ride up it and after a short while they come to a small palm oasis. Lopez knows that the palm trees grow only because there is water somewhere near the surface. They dismount and turn their horses loose. Already sniffing the cooling air, the horses walk directly to a small creek among the shadows and begin drinking gratefully.

The water bubbles up out of the ground and collects in small pools, flowing one into another for about 50 yards before disappearing in a small bunch of tules. There, the water sinks back into the sand, reclaimed by the desert.

"No good if the posse catches us boxed up in this canyon," Lopez says, "though I doubt they're still on our trail. Let's drink up, fill our canteens and water bags, and move along."

Alvijo says nothing as he begins filling the canteens. When they are finished, they retrace their path out of the canyon to the valley floor and with refreshed horses ride all night. The wind blows up a might and Lopez decides that a little taste of blowing sand is better than a showdown with a posse. "They could never track us in this," he thinks to himself, guided by the light of the full moon.

Knowing that they have lost the posse the two bandidos ride on for a few nights. Sleeping during the day, they ride south into the Mojave Desert and still moving mostly at night they eventually arrive at the small town of San Bernardino.

Having lots of money from their plunders, they find a room at a boarding house on the outskirts of town that is run by an old Mexican lady. There, they clean up before riding into town.

For the next few weeks they live it up, spending most of their money on whiskey, women and song. They eat at the finest restaurants. But soon, some people in town are starting to talk about these two Mexicans who have so much money and no viable explanation as to where they got it. That's when they know their welcome has worn out.

Riding off early one morning they head south again, skirting several small towns as they make their way toward the Mexican border and the town of Tecarte where they are supposed to rendezvous with Chavez and the rest of the gang.

Continuing south, they come to an old stage station called Warner Springs. Cruz knows where they are now and they settle in for a quiet night and a hot meal. In the morning they ride on south and in a couple of days as they near the Mexican border they come to a trail seldom used by the local gringos and for good reason: it's aptly named Horsethief Canyon and leads straight south into Mexico.

There is no better place to run stolen horses across the border than through Horsethief Canyon, a desolate ravine far from any ranches, with steep walls and several small side canyons for bandits to hide out in if a posse suddenly should appear. It is well-known by area ranchers that bandits are frequently found here, so they wisely avoid the place.

Lopez and Alvijo are riding slowly when they come around the corner along a small creek and are surprised to see a bunch of men with sombreros on their heads, sitting on a couple of logs passing around a bottle of tequila. Everyone at once reaches for their pistols, but then big smiles come over their faces: it's the rest of their own gang.

"Amigos, you made it!" yells out one bandit when he sees the travel-weary pair.

Clodoveo Chavez is sitting on a rock, relaxing in the shade of a giant oak tree, when Lopez and Alvijo ride in. He's about the only one not surprised by the reunion. He figured they would be along in a week or two if nothing distracted them, or they didn't get hung or shot.

Chavez looks up and gives the two a quick once-over as they ride into camp. "Amigos, good to see you," Chavez says between drags on a hastily rolled cigarette. "Git down off those horses and we'll have a drink and you can tell us about your long journey."

Lopez and Alvijo climb down and hand their horses over to another gang member. He leads them off to a small makeshift corral off to the side with some horses in it – horses they had stolen on their ride south that will soon be driven across the Mexican border.

Another hands them a bottle of tequila and Lopez, and then Alvijo, take long pulls of the golden liquid. Cruz wipes his mouth and smiles, shaking off the dust of a long ride as he does so.

"Very good," he says, looking at the half-empty bottle in his left hand. "I haven't had tequila in some time. Nothing but the gringo's whiskey," he adds, before gulping down another drink and handing the bottle back to Alvijo.

Cruz tells them about their ride, looking around as he does so to see whether he recognizes all the bandits in camp. Besides Chavez, there is Francisco Albitrio, a small, quiet man whom Cruz has always liked: a follower and not a leader. To his left is Garcia Alvitro, a new member of the gang about whom Cruz knows little other than he goes by Poncho. Along with his pistol, he carries an old musket bayonet in a sheath worn on his side. He's wanted for murder in Los Angeles, Lopez seems to remember. And then there's Fedoro Vasquez, the nephew of the great Tiburcio Vasquez, their former leader whom

Chavez was unable to save from a hangman's noose in San Jose.

"He's a mean one," thinks Lopez, reminding himself to never let his guard down around him. You always keep a close eye on someone who is a fast gun like Fedoro. And now with a point to prove too. "He thinks he has to live up to the Vasquez name," Lopez tells himself.

The bandidos drink and laugh heartily at Lopez's story. Chavez is delighted as he listens. Cruz did exactly what he wanted him to do and got away with it. And tomorrow they will be in Mexico. He then fills in Lopez and Alvijo on what had happened to them since they had parted.

"We rode south fast," Chavez says. "And we stopped and hid out in the Mojave Desert for a few days. We robbed a couple of miners near the Salt Lake trail." If there was any posse following them, they had lost their track by that time. Then they headed south again and robbed a stage station in the town of Helendale near the Mojave River.

"Helendale?" Cruz exclaims. "We skirted that place when we came out of the desert."

"Good thing you did," Chavez replies. "They probably wouldn't have given you a very good reception if you had." All the bandidos laugh.

Chavez tells them about the other things that happened and everyone toasts their good luck. When they're done, Chavez clears his raspy throat and addresses his men.

"Amigos, listen up," Chavez begins. "Tomorrow we will ride to Tecarte and you muchachos will bring the horses we've stolen from the gringos down into town and then south to the Mendosa rancho. Soon, I will be riding to Arizona. There has been a large gold strike in the northern part of Sonora; there are many mines on the Mexican side.

"I want to go and have a look for myself. If things look good, I think we will move the gang over there for a while and rob us some mining payrolls and gold shipments like we did in the California gold camps."

"Si, si," echo the bandits excitedly.

"Fedoro, you will sell the stolen horses to Mendosa and bring the money and the men back to Tecarte," continues Chavez, who wants to test the loyalty of the younger Vasquez now that he is leader of the gang.

Fedoro offers no resistance to what he knows is a job any of the gang can manage. "Si," is all he says.

"Good," says Chavez. "I'm going to get some rest now. Cruz, you and I will be leaving before daylight, going to Tecarte ahead of the others. Two guards tonight."

"Si, si," the men reply.

Chavez finds himself a place to bed down, spreads out his bedroll and goes off to sleep to the sound of an owl hooting off in the distance.

Chapter 5

Clang. Clang. Clang.

Silas Gaskill bangs on the red-hot metal as he turns it over on the anvil. After a few blows from the hammer, he dips the hot metal into a bucket of water. It cools quickly with a hiss, allowing the blacksmith to take a look at his progress.

He's making a pair of barn door hinges for the Cline ranch.

The metal is still too thick on the hinge that he's working on and it needs more heat, so back into the forge it goes. He wipes the sweat and grime from his brow as he waits for it to get hot again. A shadow passes in front of his eyes and Silas turns to see the figure of a man standing in the doorway, silhouetted by the brilliant sunshine streaming into his blacksmith shop. He squints.

"Bonjour, Monsieur. Gaskill," says the man and Silas relaxes as he knows immediately who it is. "Good day to you," the visitor adds in his unmistakable French accent.

"Hello, Frenchy," says Silas. "What brings you to town?"

"Oh, just picking up zee mail for Senor Ynda," he responds, holding up a stack of letters for his boss, who owns a sheep ranch in the small town of Las Juntas, just across the Mexican border southeast of Campo.

No one seems to know Frenchy's real name, only that he's been around for quite a few years now, working as a sheepherder on the Ynda rancho. There are various stories about how he got there, the most prevalent being that he was a sailor who jumped ship in San Diego some years back.

Silas knows Frenchy hasn't stopped by just to show him the mail. "Whatcha got there?" asks Silas, noticing a shoulder bag that appears weighted down by something heavy.

"M'sieur Silas, I have got something to show you," Frenchy says, reaching into the bag and pulling out some hand-sized white rocks. He gives one to Silas, who takes it in his large, leathery hands. "I found zee rocks like these laying on zee ground below a small hill," Frenchy explains.

"I followed zee rocks up the hill and I came across a large piece, no, chunk of this white rock sticking up out of zee ground. I broke off these here and if you look real close, you can see there are zee gold flakes,' he continues, growing more excited as he speaks.

"Yes," says Silas, "yes, they are. Let's step out into the sunlight and take a better look at these." Once outside, Silas sees Frenchy's light iron-gray horse tied to the hitching post, and holds the rocks up into the sunlight in order to look them over more carefully. "Well, the white part of the rock is quartz," he says almost immediately, "and quartz *is* considered the mother of gold." As he says this, he takes out his pocket knife and scrapes at one of the rocks. The gold flakes in the quartz crumble under the pressure from the knife blade. Just as he figured.

"Sorry, Frenchy, it's not gold," Silas reports.

"Not gold?" says Frenchy, not surprised, but ever hopeful.

"Nope," concludes Silas, "nothing but iron pyrite. Fool's gold, Frenchy." Silas saw plenty of fool's gold back in his prospecting days in northern California and now he lets out a little chuckle, remembering how often the greenhorns arriving from back East would make the same mistake that Frenchy has.

"Fool's gold," Frenchy sighs. "Fool's gold. So I'm not going to be a rich man, just a poor old fool."

"Don't fret none, Frenchy," consoles Silas. "Iron pyrite has fooled many a man. You've just got to keep looking. There *is* gold out there somewhere and someday, someone will find it. And it could be you, Frenchy.

"Here, take a look," he adds, stepping closer to the Frenchman. "See, if it was real gold, when I scraped it with my knife like this, the blade, well, it would have dented it, because real gold is malleable, and it's very soft.

"Iron pyrite, on the other hand, is hard and crumbly, see?" he continues, showing him how it disintegrates under the knife's blade. "Gold is also very heavy, the heaviest rock out there and that's why it's able to be panned in the creeks. There's fool's gold in the gravel beds too, but when you pan it, it will wash away well before the gold does."

"Mon Dieu," says a disheartened Frenchy as he takes the worthless rocks back from Silas. "Someday soon, I must find gold. I will need to find lots of zee gold, for I think that is the only way I will ever see my homeland again. To strike it rich, and to return to France a wealthy man, that is my dream.

"But," Frenchy continues, "time erases dreams and I don't think I will have the time to ever get back home, for I am getting to be an old man. I don't think that I will ever see France again."

"Well, Frenchy," says Silas, "these rocks didn't turn out to be the right ones, but the only thing for you to do is to keep looking. In your line of work, you travel through a lot of desolate places. And you're grazing your sheep on relatively unexplored ground; someday you just might stand a chance of finding something. As good a chance as anyone."

"Have you heard about the rich gold strike about thirty miles southeast of Tecarte, near Japa?" Silas asks.

"Oui," Frenchy replies, "I have heard. About two years ago, some men from San Rafael found zee gold in the creeks and then they found rocks like these with gold in them coming out of the mountains."

"That's right," Silas says, "But do you know what they found first that led them to believe that gold might be present?"

"No," Frenchy replies.

"They found some small holes dug in the ground on a bench above a creek," Silas says. "Old holes, some of them washed in with gravel. It was the Spaniards who probably dug them; they were here more than a hundred years ago and they were very good at finding gold."

"So you look for these old holes?" Frenchy asks.

"Yes," Silas says. "You want to keep a eye out for old diggings, as that can lead you to a nice strike. No one goes about digging holes for nothing; the bigger the hole, the better your chance is of maybe finding something really nice. But remember, the Spaniards didn't find it all and sometimes when they did find a nice strike they covered it up when they left so no one would discover it and maybe they could come back sometime later and work it some more."

"So how do you find a mine that they covered up?" Frenchy asks.

"Well, sometimes you can't," Silas says, "but the

bigger the mine, the bigger the tailing pile that they left. The tailing pile is the rocks that they had to remove to get at the gold vein and it is probably somewhere near the mine, usually downhill from it as they would never carry it uphill."

"What do tailings look like?" Frenchy replies.

"They are rocks that are broken and vary jagged," Silas answers. "There will most likely be a lot of them in one area and they will look out of place; sometimes in a pile and sometimes just a bunch of rocks on top of the ground spread out down a hill. Lumen and I saw lots of diggings and tailing piles up in the mother lode."

"Then I will keep an eye out for them," Frenchy says. "And if I find some, I will bring them to you, M'sieu Gaskill, for I trust you to be fair with me."

"Thanks for the trust, Frenchy," Silas replies, "but don't trust too many people when it comes to gold; most men would sell their mother for it. If you do find a nice strike, I will be fair with you and I will help you make something of it. We can draw up a partnership and I've got the capital to get it off the ground, so if you do find some gold don't tell no one but me."

"Okay, M'sieu Gaskill," Frenchy says. "If I find some I will bring it only to you."

"Good Frenchy," Silas replies. "Like I said, you are out in desolate places and you just might find some yet."

"You are right," Frenchy says, suddenly upbeat again. "I *will* keep looking, and who knows? I may find it yet. Thank you, Merci, M'sier Gaskill. I have taken enough of your time … next time, maybe I will bring you real gold."

"I hope you do, Frenchy," says Silas as he shakes

the man's hand. "Good luck!"

Silas walks back into the shop and notices that the forge is no longer glowing. He tosses in a shovel full of coal and pumps the bellows until the glow is fiery red again.

Next door in the store, Lumen is reading the newspaper. Even though the issue of the San Diego *Union* is two days old, having come only this morning on the stage, it's still fresh news in Campo, since Jack Kelly hasn't received any new telegrams from San Diego in a few days.

"Says here there's been a shooting down at George Webb's ranch," says Lumen to Thomas Cameron, who owns a nice spread not far from Campo and is in town this morning to get his horse shod. While in town, the tall, lean Scottish Highlander, with a short, red beard, thought he'd catch up on some gossip, pick up any mail he might have and maybe toss back a drink or two in the store.

"Oh, yeah?" inquires Cameron. "Hadn't heard about it. What's it say?"

"According to this, a sheepherder got killed at the Alpine Ranch. One of George Webb's boys shot him in the head," Lumen says as he reads the front-page article. "It appears that he was seen looking through their windows at night and when they confronted him, Warren Webb pulled a gun and killed him."

"Well, serves him right," says Cameron.

"Maybe so," offers Lumen, "but the paper says the sheriff is going to hold an inquest into the matter anyway."

"I know George Webb and his boys," interrupts Cameron. "George raised them to be honest, God-fearing and respectful of others. If that's what they say … then that's how it happened.

"That's what I think," he adds as he takes another shot of whiskey.

"I know the Webbs too," replies Lumen, "and I think you're right and that's what the inquest will find, I reckon."

Cameron changes the subject as he pours himself another shot. "So, how's the new hotel doing?" he asks, perhaps a bit more interested since his own sweat – well, a little of it anyway – went into its construction as Thomas works for the Gaskills on occasion.

"Just fine," says Lumen. "We've had fifty-one paying guests already and that bathtub I told you about, since we put it in I don't think it's been empty yet. And the water heater Silas built has been steaming ever since."

"Who's been stoking the fire?" adds Cameron, more to continue the conversation than to satisfy any pressing curiosity.

"Miss Price," says Lumen. "She's been a wonder. We couldn't run the hotel without her."

"Yup, you're lucky there, Lumen," says Tom as he pours yet another drink. Enough small talk, he thinks. After five shots, Cameron now has the courage to speak his mind in front of the younger Gaskill. He's glad he's talking to Lumen; it'd probably take a whole bottle of whiskey for him to tell this to Silas.

"You know, Lumen," begins Cameron, searching for the right words, "you and Silas have got so many hives on your east side, that them durn bees are swarming my cattle troughs."

"Bees need water too," interrupts Lumen.

"Yeah, well, as I said, them durn bees you raise

don't know how to swim very good and my cattle are getting fat drinking up all those drowned bees," Tom replies.

"Well, then," says Lumen, beginning to laugh, "if we're fattening up your cows at our expense then we should get a cut …."

"A cut?" exclaims Cameron. "You Gaskills get a cut of everything around here as it is!"

"C'mon, Tom," replies Lumen, trying to settle the rancher down. "Silas and me, we're just trying to make a decent living."

"Yeah, I know," says Cameron, backing down. "I'm just joshin' with ya, Lumen," he adds, though not too convincingly, thinks Lumen, as he watches the man down another drink in one gulp and then use his shirtsleeve to wipe away the sweat that has been beading up on his forehead.

If there had been any mounting tension between the two, it is broken instantly as the door opens with a slam and Walter runs in. "Pa! Pa! Pa!" the youngster yells without looking at Tom Cameron. "There's a rattlesnake in the woodpile. Miss Price told me to come getcha …."

"Slow down now, boy," Lumen says back. "Are you sure it's not a gopher snake?"

"No, Pa," exclaims Walter. "I saw it myself. It's a big, red rattlesnake! And it almost bit Miss Price! You know, Pa, how she's afraid of snakes."

"Oh, she's deathly afraid of snakes," Lumen says, nodding to Tom Cameron.

"C'mon, Pa," urges Walter, tugging on his father's shirttail. "We've got to kill it!"

"All right, I'm a'comin'," Lumen says as he grabs his shotgun from behind the counter. "You comin' with us, Tom, or are you gonna stay here and watch the store?"

"No, I think I need to be going home now," Cameron says, and, reaching for the whiskey bottle on the counter, adds, "Put this on my account, please."

"Okay," Lumen says, fighting back a smile since he knew the answer before he asked the question. He hesitates a moment to open the books and adjusts the ledger, much to Walter's disapproval. "C'mon, Pa!" the boy yells again, still tugging on his father's shirt.

Thomas Cameron says a curt goodbye as he unties his horse from the hitching post, mounts up, gives his horse a quick giddy-up, and starts to trot out of town without looking back.

Before he barely gets across the bridge, he hears the report from Lumen's shotgun. "Another dead snake," he says to himself, "that's good … another dead darn rattlesnake." He pulls the cork from the whiskey bottle and takes another long drink.

"Snakes. They scare the hell out of me too," he thinks as he puts the cork back in. "I'm glad nobody could tell."

Chapter 6

Clodoveo Chavez is up early, well before daylight. Another restless night sleeping on the hard ground. Such is the life of a bandito, he is thinking. Always on the move; always another weary day in a hard saddle; and always an uncomfortable night on the rocky ground. Chavez cannot even remember the last time he slept in a real bed; well, one that did not belong to a saloon keeper anyway.

He walks over to the campfire, which had gone out sometime during the cold, long night. He kicks at the embers with his foot and sees the faint red glow of the coals that survived the night. He reaches for some dry tinder, sets it in the middle of the coals, and blows softly into the fire pit. Immediately, a flame rekindles, and Chavez grabs some small twigs and adds them to the mix.

The fire comes to life and the twigs begin to burn; Chavez savors its warmth, rubbing his cold hands over the flames. Even though they are this far south, the October nights are still cold in the desolate mountain valleys east of San Diego.

He adds some larger sticks and the fire flares up nicely. He puts on some coffee and smelling that, the rest of the men slowly begin to stir. Finally, Cruz Lopez wakes and gets up from his bed, which is nothing more than a saddle blanket laying on the ground, with his saddle for a pillow and his bed roll for a blanket.

Stretching his stiff limbs, Lopez joins the other men around the growing fire.

"Coffee, amigo?" Chavez offers Cruz.

"Si, some coffee, por favor," Cruz replies, while

shaking the leaves and sticks from his hair. He takes the tin cup in both hands, warming them as he downs half of the scalding brew in one gulp, quickly clearing his head of the tequila from the night before.

As the men drink their coffee, Chavez gives the day's orders to his men. "Si, si, *jefe,*" they say in unison. All, that is, except Fedoro Vasquez, who stands silently off to the side. This does not escape the attention of Clodoveo Chavez. He has been keeping a wary eye on the nephew of their former leader. Fedoro is a very fast gun and a very dangerous killer who idolized his uncle, but it has been seven months now since Tiburcio met his fate at the end of a rope in San Jose.

"He is getting too bold," thinks Chavez to himself. "He wants to be a leader like his uncle. I may have to kill him someday. We will see.

"But," Chavez considers, "it's nice to have two cutthroat killers around here like Vasquez and Lopez … each leery of the other. Someday they are going to try to kill each other and when they do, they will be too busy shooting at each other to shoot at me."

For a moment, the thought comforts Chavez. Then the first faint rays of daylight creep into the depths of Horsethief Canyon and Chavez is brought back from thought. "Cruz," he says to Lopez, "let's saddle up and get on the trail. I want to get to Tecarte sometime in the afternoon. I know a place there where we can get a good meal and a soft bed. A soft bed with some nice, pretty senoritas. I think you would like that, no?"

"Si, si," says Lopez with a wide grin. "I would like that. Let's go!"

Cruz decides to saddle up the big bay horse with a white blaze that he took from the lone traveler near Lone

Pine and the two bandits ride down the trail that follows Pine Valley Creek, a small, bubbling stream that winds along the canyon floor among groves of tall oak trees. Neither man speaks as the sun climbs in the cloudless sky. Soon they come to where Pine Valley Creek flows into the larger Cottonwood Creek, which flows in from the left, having completed its long run from the base of the Laguna Mountains. Cottonwood Creek flows from a place called Buckman Springs, then crosses Morena Valley and drops into a steep canyon before swinging west through Hauser Canyon where it joins forces with Pine Valley Creek.

Here it turns south and flows directly into Mexico and a few miles west of the border town of Tecarte, where it flows into the Tijuana River Valley. There is no better route through which to run stolen horses from California to Mexico.

Chavez and Lopez stop here to rest their horses and let them drink from the clear, cold water. Now that he's getting this close to Mexico, Chavez is beginning to relax a little and he and Lopez can talk more easily.

"Cruz," Chavez begins, "things were a little hot for us up in the north, no?"

"Si, amigo," Lopez responds, thinking about that posse that chased him and Alvijo out of Lone Pine. "Very hot up there with that diablo Morse running around," he adds.

"That's why I think we should take the gang and drift east to Sonora," Chavez continues. "There's a new gold strike over there and maybe we can make something of it. Kind of what we did up north. Rob us some mining payrolls and gold shipments. Lead the posse on a wild chase. Lose them on some well-hidden trails we will have already scouted out and then disappear back into the hills to a safe hideout."

Lopez likes what he hears. "Si, that is a good plan," he says with a smile on his face, "but I think we will need supplies and things. A wagon full of them … food, water, blankets and more guns and ammunition. And more men."

"Yes, I agree," says Chavez, having already given thought to this. "We will need these things, as you say. We will find plenty of men in Tecarte, and the other things, we will have no trouble getting them. I have a friend who lives near Tecarte who should know where to get them.

"But right now I am hungry and I remember a small ranch down the creek a ways," he says. "We will stop there and see if we can get a bite to eat." It is not uncommon in the West for ranchers to feed travelers, usually for a small fee, but often for nothing.

"Si, I am starving too," admits Lopez, whose dinner once again came out of a bottle the night before. "How far is it to that ranch?"

"Maybe a mile or so," Chavez figures, "and then after that, it's only about another mile to Ol' Mexico."

"That sounds good, *jefe,*" Lopez replies, as he scratches behind his left ear and finds a small tick. "Chingas," he curses as he squeezes the small insect between two fingers and pulls the tick off, leaving the head buried deep in his skin. Showing it to Chavez, he flicks it away and says, "I hate the damn things."

"I got to agree with you there," Clodoveo replies, feeling a little itchy himself.

They ride on down through the canyon, going slowly, not wanting to run into someone who might get the drop on them. The sun has been up for a while, warming the bottom of the canyon, which at this point narrows dramatically. Lopez looks off to the side of the trail and sees a large rattlesnake coiled on a rock, warming itself in the sunshine. It's no threat, being ten feet off the trail, and the horses fail to notice it. Around the next bend, Lopez spots another off to the right under a bush, and then another one.

"Sure are a lot of rattlers around here," Cruz says to Chavez. "I just seen three."

"Si, I've seen four myself," says Chavez, chuckling.

As they ride out of the canyon, it opens up and they come to a well-used trail. They turn south again, and follow it for a short distance before they can see a ranch house, a small barn and stables ahead of them. Stopping the horses behind a patch of tall brush, they watch the ranch house quietly for several minutes. They see smoke drifting out of the chimney. The small stable only has one old horse running loose in it. This is a good sign.

"The men must be away," Lopez says to himself. He sees an easy target and that good, familiar feeling begins to warm him all over. That feeling he gets every time he's about to kill something. Chavez sees it too.

"Easy, amigo," Chavez tells him. "We are here just to get a meal."

Lopez looks at Chavez and sees that he is serious, much to his disappointment.

"Okay, *jefe*," Lopez shrugs. "Let's go. I am hungry too."

He gives his horse a quick kick and slowly they ride toward the ranch house. They are spotted by a pair of watch dogs, who come running toward them barking, alerting all to their arrival. Chavez holds his horse back as it tries to shy away from the approaching dogs. Lopez whips one of them in the face with his reins; the dog yelps and runs away. Lopez smiles.

Virginia Sheckler hears the barking dogs and looks out the front window. She sees the two riders approaching and calmly she tells her 14-year-old son, Claude, to go and get the shotgun from the bedroom. The boy obeys without question.

Mrs. Sheckler has a bad feeling. From the direction from which they are coming, she guesses that the two men have ridden out of Horsethief Canyon, and she knows the sort of men who ride from that direction. A lot of bad men have ridden through in the past and the Shecklers have always known how to handle them. But her husband, Ben, left for the day, going to the town of Potrero to help a neighboring rancher witch a well. She has never been alone without her husband when some rough-looking bandits happened by, and as these two get closer, she thinks she recognizes one of them. The man on the right looks a lot like a notorious bandit she has heard about.

Actually, Mrs. Sheckler is *not* alone. Today, she has a house guest, Laurie Whittacker, visiting from San Diego for a few days and naïve to the ways of the wilderness. She is unaware of any danger.

"Laurie, get away from the window," Mrs. Sheckler says calmly but sternly to her friend. "And take off that necklace and hide it."

"Why?" asks Mrs. Whittacker, instinctively touching the expensive gold necklace with the small rubies embedded in it which adorns her milky-white neck. She curiously steps toward the window to take a look for herself.

“Laurie, I said get away from that window!” Mrs. Sheckler says more urgently. “Do as I say. I think those men are bandits.”

“Bandits!” exclaims Mrs. Whittacker, clutching again at her necklace.

“Yes, and if they’re who I think they are, they are the worst ones,” says Mrs. Sheckler, “so go and hide that necklace and don’t go near the windows again.”

Mrs. Sheckler then turns to young Claude, who is holding the shotgun. She takes it from him, checks to make sure that both barrels are loaded with buckshot, and hands it back. “Claude, I need you to go hide in the bedroom and watch out through the curtain. But don’t let them see you, okay?”

“Yes, ma,” the boy says to his mother, going into the bedroom and crouching below the half-open window.

Mrs. Sheckler takes the lever-action rifle down off the pegs on the wall beside the stove and leans it beside the front door. Then she composes herself, takes a deep breath, and goes out to meet the visitors.

The two bandits notice that this woman coming to greet them is not the same one they just saw peeking out the window.

“Buenos dias,” Chavez says.

“Good morning to you, too,” Mrs. Sheckler replies.

“Is your husband at home?” inquires Chavez.

“Not at the moment,” Mrs. Sheckler tells them. “The men are not far away, repairing some fences. Can I help you?” she asks.

“Si, senora,” Chavez continues. “We have been on the trail and were wondering if you could spare a couple of lost vaqueros a meal."

"Yes," she says. "I have some rabbit stew on the stove. If you would tie off your horses beside the barn, I will serve you each a large bowl.

"It will cost you two bits each, please," she adds, holding out her hand. It takes all her courage to keep her hand from shaking as the bandits pull a couple of coins out of their pockets and hand them to the woman.

"Go and seat yourselves at the outside table over yonder," she says, pointing to a table and bench next to the barn that Ben had built just for such occasions.

"Muchas gracias, senora," says Chavez politely.

Mrs. Sheckler turns and returns to the house, while the bandits tether their horses and go and sit down, as requested.

"The men are fixing fences?" Lopez says doubtfully. "I think that is a lie."

"Si, amigo," replies Chavez, "that is probably a lie, but we can't be certain."

They stop talking as they see Mrs. Sheckler approaching with a couple of bowls, two spoons and four tortillas. Cruz is so hungry, he can smell the hot stew as she sets it on the table before them. "Gracias," he says.

"Yes, gracias," adds Chavez, "it smells very good."

"You are both welcome," says Mrs. Sheckler. "I expect that you gentlemen are very busy and probably will be on your way as soon as you finish, so I won't keep you from your meal. You can just leave the bowls on the table and I will get them later."

"Gracias, ma'am," Chavez says. "Si," nods Lopez.

As Mrs. Sheckler turns and walks to the house, Lopez watches her slim figure disappear through the doorway. "Nice looking woman, no, amigo?" Cruz says as he dips a tortilla into the stew.

Claude Sheckler watches his mother return to the house from his hiding place below the bedroom window. He also sees the way that one of the men is staring at her. "You just try and mess with my mother and I will shoot you," the boy thinks as he touches the shotgun's hammers with his thumb and sees that they are still on the safe-cock position. At the same time, a slight gust of wind blows the curtain back a little. Claude ducks quickly out of sight, hoping he hasn't been seen. But out of the corner of his eye, the ever-alert Chavez catches the face of a boy, and the glint of the shotgun's double barrels through the open window. He says nothing and keeps eating, scooping up another mouthful of stew with his folded tortilla.

"Clodoveo," says Lopez finally, "it would be *so* easy to take this ranch. And two women, we could have some fun, no?"

"No!" Chavez says sternly. "We have business in Tecarte. And I don't want no gringo posse crossing the border and following us there."

"It would be so easy!" interjects Lopez again. "The men are gone…."

"Not all the men," Chavez interrupts as he finishes his stew. "In the back window there is a boy, a muchacho, with a double-barrel shotgun, and I think the lady might have a gun too."

"Si, jefe," pleads Lopez, "but a boy? What could he do to us?"

"Cruz," says Chavez, "*any* man with a shotgun is very dangerous, even a boy who knows how to use one. The boy who likely shot the rabbits that are in the stew you just ate. That boy is a dangerous foe and I think he could easily get one of us, maybe both of us.

"No, Cruz, today we smile and ride away and thank them for their hospitality," he concludes.

The two get up and walk to the hitching post on the side of the barn to get their horses. As they swing up into the saddle, Chavez yells, "Muchas gracias, senora," and they ride on toward the border.

After a while, Lopez breaks the silence.

"So what *would* you do?" Lopez asks.

"What do you mean?" replies Chavez.

Lopez rephrases the question. "What would *you* do if someone got the drop on you with a shotgun?"

"Well, Cruz," Chavez says, "if you throw up your hands, they will take you and probably hang you from the nearest tree."

"So what is the alternative," Lopez inquires further.

"The alternative," Chavez says, "is simple. You die like a man, amigo … You die like a man."

Chapter 7

San Diego County Sheriff Nicholas Hunsaker rides into Campo on a broad-chested buckskin mare with one white stocking. Silas Gaskill is working at the forge in his blacksmith shop, but hears the easy gait of the horse coming down the road and steps to the door to see who the visitor is.

"Howdy, sheriff," Silas says as Hunsaker dismounts and ties his horse to the hitching post out front.

"Hello, Silas," responds the sheriff. "How ya doing?"

"Just fine, Nick," Silas replies. "What brings you way out here to Campo?"

"Well," the sheriff begins, "I'm riding out to Jacumba Station. You've probably heard that Pete Larkin has been losing cattle to some of the Indians living out there."

"Yup, we've heard," Silas replies. "Some of them have been killing his cattle, taking the meat and feeding their families."

"Well, Pete sent me a letter asking me to look into it," Hunsaker continues. "Damn Indians. Waste of my time. I hate having to do this. You know, a couple months ago I had to ride all the way from San Diego to Temecula … not once, but twice! … to evict a whole tribe of Indians who were squatting illegally on the Temecula Ranch property."

"Yeah, we heard about it in the paper," Silas says.

"And now I have to ride all the way to Jacumba to deal with more Indians," bemoans Hunsaker.

"Well, sheriff, you're in luck," Silas replies. "This

wagon here is Pete Larkin's, and one of his ranch hands, McFall Pearson, is in the store talking with Lumen. I think he will probably be leaving in the morning."

Silas sees a man walking out of the store. "Here he comes now."

"Afternoon, sheriff," Pearson says in greeting.

"Hi," the sheriff replies, trying to remember if he's met the man before. "I hear you're going to be driving that wagon to Larkin's ranch in the morning."

"That's right, sheriff," Pearson replies, with a look toward Silas, "That is, if it's ready to go?"

"It will be ready," Silas promises. "Just got to put the wheel back on."

"Okay, then," Pearson says, "I'll be leaving about sunup if you want to ride along."

"Yes, I would like to," answers the sheriff.

"Is this about the Indians stealing Mr. Larkin's cows?" McFall inquires.

"Yes," replies Hunsaker. "I got his letter and I'm on my way out to look into it."

"Good," says McFall. "Pete will like that." After a brief pause, Pearson adds, "Well, I've gotta go now. I'm staying the night out at John Williams' ranch and I'll be back come sunup."

McFall gets on his horse and rides out of Campo.

"Seems like a good fellow," the sheriff finally says, having determined he's never met the man prior to today.

"Sure is, sheriff," says Silas, "as good as they get. He's going out to the Williams ranch because he's going to marry John's oldest daughter on Christmas Day."

"Well, good for him," the sheriff responds, then changes the subject. "So, where can I spend the night,

Silas?"

"You can stay in the new hotel if you like," he replies. "We've got plenty of rooms available tonight, two dollars a night, including dinner."

"I guess I just might do that," the sheriff says. "So how *is* the new hotel?"

"Just fine," Silas replies. "It's been a real boon to Campo. Auntie Price will be cooking up her famous Southern-fried chicken tonight, so you're in luck if you're going to be staying."

"I guess I came out here on the right night," Hunsaker says. "Can I stable my horse with you?"

"Sure, sheriff," Silas says. "I'll get one of the boys to take your horse over to the livery stable and feed it and put it up for the night."

Silas turns toward the barn beside the blacksmith shop. "Charlie!" he yells. Charlie is one of Tom Cameron's sons.

"Yes, Mr. Gaskill," comes the reply as Charlie emerges running from the barn's side door.

"Would you put the sheriff's horse in the stable and give it a couple of forkfuls of oat hay?"

"Sure, Mr. Gaskill," the boy answers, but he doesn't move right away, instead looking down at the street. He scuffs the toe of his boot as he kicks at the dirt, catching Silas's attention.

"Is there something you would like to say?" Silas asks.

"Uh, yes, Mr. Gaskill," Charlie manages. "It's payday."

"Payday!" exclaims Silas. "You sure?"

"Yes, sir," the 12-year-old replies sheepishly.

"Go on, then," Silas says, letting out a grin that is

meant for Hunsaker and not the boy. “Put up the sheriff’s horse and then go and see Lumen in the store and he will settle up with you.”

“Thanks, Mr. Gaskill,” Charlie says as he unhitches the horse and heads for the stable.

Silas puts away his tools and he and the sheriff walk over to the store. They are met at the door by Jack Kelly, the telegraph operator.

“Hi, Silas,” Kelly says, and then sees Hunsaker and adds, “Oh, hello, sheriff,” seeming surprised to see him. The sheriff doesn’t have need to come to Campo often.

“Hi, Jack,” the sheriff returns as they shake hands. “How’s the Army treating you?”

“Army?” Jack replies quickly. “What Army? They stuck me way out here in the middle of nowhere, all by myself.”

“What’s the matter, Jack?” Silas interrupts. “Don’t you like Campo?”

“Yeah, I like Campo all right,” Kelly admits. “The weather is darn-near perfect, most of the time, that’s for sure, but I need more than tumbleweeds and cows. I need a little socialization with my sweetheart. We’re getting married on the twenty-first of December in San Diego.”

“I have heard about that,” Hunsaker replies. “Seems like all you young folk are tying the knot these days. I saw your future missus in town just the other day….”

“You did?” says Kelly excitedly. “What was she doing?”

“Oh, she was down by the wharf talking with some sailors,” Hunsaker replies. He and Silas let out a laugh, but Kelly is mortified and then angry when he realizes the sheriff is teasing him.

"That's not funny!" Kelly declares sharply.

"Sorry," the sheriff says, cracking a smile. "I couldn't help myself. I know Miss McNaley is a proper woman, a fine woman and will make you a good wife. I saw her at the dry goods store picking up some things."

"That's better," a relieved Kelly says. "You gents don't know how I wish I was stationed at San Diego or San Francisco … or even Sacramento. Anywhere but Campo."

"Just think, Jack," adds Silas, not as quick as the sheriff to give up on the teasing, "you might get lucky and get stationed at Yuma someday."

"That's not funny either!" says Jack. "You two are some real jokers. Well, I …."

Just then the telegraph begins to click.

"Well, I … gotta go," Kelly says as he runs into the back office to take down the message.

Just then Lumen Gaskill walks up to the store, having skipped out for a moment to run over to the hotel. "Sheriff, good to see you," Lumen says with his hand extended.

"Good to see you too, Lumen," responds Hunsaker. "How's Mrs. Gaskill?"

"Never better," replies Lumen. "The hotel's open; you staying the night?"

"I reckon I might," Hunsaker says, "that is if I can get a heapin' helping of Miss Price's fried-chicken dinner!"

"Sure, sheriff," Lumen says. "We only have one other guest this evening and we got plenty.

"Walter!" Lumen yells.

"What, Pa?" Walter replies from somewhere in the

back of the store where he's been playing. Walter likes to toss pebbles through the open trap door into Campo Creek, which runs through a sort of culvert directly under the store.

"Run over to the hotel and tell Auntie Price that there'll be another guest this evening," Lumen instructs his son.

"Sure, Pa," Walter says, running out the front door toward the hotel.

"And tell her to put out an extra plate for dinner!" Lumen yells as Walter disappears up the street.

"See you all in a little while," Silas says as he steps toward the door himself. "I've got to go put that wheel back on Pete Larkin's wagon, else you and McFall won't be able to leave in the morning."

Only Lumen and Hunsaker are left in the storefront. "So, you want a drink?" Lumen asks. "Sure," replies Hunsaker, wondering what's taken so long. Lumen steps behind the counter, grabs two shot glasses and fills them to the brim with whiskey.

Each takes a glass, nods at the other as he holds it up and downs the shot in one gulp.

Lumen is first to speak. "So, what's happening with that shooting out at the Alpine Ranch?" he asks the sheriff.

"Well, it was George Webb's son, Warren, who did the shooting," Hunsaker begins. "The man he killed was a local sheepherder, a 19-year-old Frenchman named Pasqual Beilles. I sent one of my deputies to the Webb ranch as soon as we heard about it. Deputy Miller got the coroner to ride out there with him and they held an inquest and found it to be justifiable homicide. I got signatures on the inquest from men like William Flinn,

Adam Beaty, John Harbison and others. They all said it looked like self-defense to them."

Lumen pours them each another round.

"But I think there might be more to it than that," the sheriff continues after he and Lumen finish the drink. "Miss Everheart, the new school teacher, is staying at the Webb ranch and she's a very pretty young lady. I think these two young boys were competing for her affection and it got out of hand. Anyways, it's out of my hands now. The district attorney is investigating and if it goes to trial, well, that will be his decision and not mine."

The lad, Charlie Cameron comes into the store and walks up to the counter where the men are talking. He waits for a pause in their conversation before addressing Lumen.

"Mr. Gaskill," the boy says, "here is my time card. Silas told me to give it to you to settle my pay."

"Okay," Lumen says, taking the card, which is little more than a scrap of paper Charlie has been using to keep track of his hours. Lumen pulls his ledger book from underneath the counter and flips it open to the page with the bookmark in it. "Here you go. Two dollars and twenty-five cents," Lumen says, handing him a couple silver dollars and one bit.

"Thanks, Mr. Gaskill," Charlie exclaims as he puts the money in the breast pocket of his vest. He turns and hurries toward the door. "I've gotta be getting home now," he says. "Pa will be worried if I'm late for dinner."

The young Cameron already has his horse, Lady Bell, saddled and tied to the hitching post in front of the store. He unties the reins, then puts his left foot in the stirrup and has to reach hard to grab the saddle horn as he swings into the seat.

“Let’s go home,” he says to the mare, and Lady Bell immediately follows his command and starts off on a trot toward the Cameron ranch.

“Tom’s got a good boy there,” the sheriff says as he watches him ride out of town.

***

Later that evening, the sheriff is having dinner with the Gaskill brothers and another man, the lone other guest at the hotel, who will be riding to San Diego in the morning. He gets up upon finishing his meal and excuses himself, saying that he has to get an early start tomorrow.

Vi Price comes in to take his empty plate away, and as she does so, Sheriff Hunsaker exclaims, “Miss Price, that had to be the best fried chicken I’ve ever tasted.” The brothers agree.

She smiles and says, “T’wern’t nothing. Just an old recipe passed down by my mammy from hers. But thank you kindly just the same.” As she clears away the dishes, Lumen gets up and pulls a box of cigars out of a cabinet. He extends it toward Hunsaker.

“Sheriff?” he offers.

“Why, thank you, Lumen,” he says as he takes one. Silas and Lumen each take one too and Lumen puts the box away. The men light their cigars with a candle set on the table as Silas pours each a shot of whiskey.

“You boys are just too generous,” the sheriff adds as he tosses back the shot. “But, Silas, there’s one thing I’ve got to ask you about and I don’t know quite how to put it.”

“Well, sheriff,” says Silas, grinning at his brother as if they have already prepared themselves for what they are about to hear. "Just go ahead and say what's on your mind. That would be the best way to do it."

"Okay," Hunsaker begins, "it's just that, well, you see, a while back a gentleman came through San Diego and happened into my office. Said his name was Frank Millay."

Silas and Lumen sneak a look at each other at the mention of the man's name. Hunsaker pretends not to notice.

"This here Frank Millay claims his brother was shot and killed in Mendocino County back in '65 by a man named Silas E. Gaskill. He said that this Gaskill fellow paid one thousand dollars bail and then fled the county. That was ten years ago. This Millay heard about you living here in Campo and he thinks you're the wanted man."

The pause that follows becomes almost uncomfortable.

Finally, Silas takes a long puff off of his cigar and speaks.

"Sheriff, I don't know nothing about this affair," he says. "There are men with the same name roaming all about the West. I think that this man, Millay, has made an honest mistake and has confused me with someone else."

"That's right, sheriff," Lumen quickly adds. "Lots of men use any name that suits them. In one town they call themselves Mr. Smith and in the next town they're Mr. Jones, or whatever. We see men traveling through Campo sometimes who don't use their real names. It's obvious, but we don't question it none. Ain't none of our business."

"Yeah, that's true," says the sheriff, "it could be just an honest mistake. But if I remember right, you boys came to Campo about seven years ago and came down from the north somewhere, right?"

"Yeah, we did," Silas replies, a bit agitated that the sheriff is continuing to press the issue. "We have been all over northern California, and parts of Nevada too, but that don't make me no murderer."

"You're right, Silas," Hunsaker says. "It could be someone else he's talking about. It's not my jurisdiction up in Mendocino County anyway, and I have never got a sworn warrant or even a wanted poster or nothing…."

"That's right," says Lumen, a little hotly. "Silas has never killed anyone and nobody's gonna say any different. You just remember this sheriff," he adds with a look that could burn a hole through the sheriff's forehead, "we take care of our own here in Campo."

The veiled threat is not lost on the sheriff. "Yes, you do," replies Hunsaker, not used to being talked down to. "You take care of things real good out here along the border. Doing real good, some people are saying, maybe a little *too* good."

"What are you trying to get at now?" demands Silas, not used to being trifled with even by someone wearing a badge.

"Oh, nothing," Hunsaker continues. "It's just that some folks around here are saying that Campo Cattle Company has more than doubled its cattle holdings in the last two years and no other rancher has even come close to doing that. You and Lumen been buying some beef somewhere?"

Silas has heard enough. "Damn you, sheriff," he replies hotly, "you know as well as anyone that Campo Cattle Company is a success because we know how to run a cattle ranch and we've got plenty of water and the best grass for twenty miles around...."

"Yeah," adds Lumen, "you tell them people to just mind their own business...."

Hunsaker is feeling ganged up on, and for good reason. "Easy now, gentlemen," he tells the riled-up brothers. "I'm not making any accusations here. You Gaskills are highly regarded citizens around here and it will take more than just rumors to get the law involved.

"It's getting late," Hunsaker says as he fumbles with his pocket watch. "I must be retiring to my room if I'm going to ride with Mr. Pearson at sunup. I take it that my horse will be ready?"

"It will," says Silas curtly.

"Good. Then thank you for a wonderful dinner. Good night, gentlemen," Hunsaker says as he gets up and leaves the dinner room. After they've heard his footsteps reach the top of the stairs, Lumen looks at Silas with concern on his face, perhaps a little scared even.

"Don't worry, little brother," Silas says as he pours each of them another shot. "The sheriff was just fishing. He don't got nothing.

"Cheers," he adds, as they clink glasses and gulp down another shot of amber liquid.

Chapter 8

Clodoveo Chavez and Cruz Lopez ride slowly down the main street of Tecarte, a small town in a little valley just over the Mexican border, about ten miles southwest of Campo. They stop in front of a small livery stable and look down at a large man taking a siesta in a rickety chair leaning against the building.

"Last time I was here, you had a much larger chair, Manuel," says Clodoveo Chavez to the man, who has his sombrero pulled over his face against the midday sun.

Manuel, who runs the livery stable, recognizes the voice immediately and by the time he rights the chair and removes his hat, his puffy cheeks are stretched into a broad grin.

"No, Senor Chavez, this is the same chair," admits the balding man. "I am afraid it is me who is larger. You see, my wife is too good a cook…."

Chavez smiles. "Well, you either need a new wife or a new chair," he replies with a laugh. "Or, perhaps, both!" This brings a chuckle from Lopez as well.

"Well, unfortunately, Senor Chavez, I can afford neither," replies Manuel with a sigh.

Manuel can't help but notice that all of the men in the street are watching, and all of them have removed their sombreros upon hearing Chavez's name. In Tecarte, almost everyone has heard of Clodoveo Chavez and they all give him total respect.

"Can I get anything for you and your amigo?" Manuel asks the bandit.

"Yes, Manuel, I would like you to feed and brush

down our horses," Chavez says, "and then give them some water … but not too much water, you hear?"

Chavez takes out a gold coin and flips it to Manuel, adding "and keep the horses out of sight."

"Si, senor, you can count on me," says Manuel, looking at the coin and then around at the men in the street as he discreetly puts the gold piece in a safe place. "More than two month's wages," he thinks to himself as he buries the coin deep in his breast pocket. He takes the horses' reins and leads them into the barn.

Lopez looks around and then says to Chavez, "Not much of a town."

"Big enough, amigo," Chavez counters. "Let's get a drink in the cantina. I have a good friend, Romulo Gonzalez, who lives near here. He used to ride with us back in '73 when Vasquez was our leader. Those were the good days, when up in the north there were still good places to hide out.

"But now, I'm afraid, we have worn out our welcome in Alta California, for a while anyway," Chavez continues. "Tonight, we will stay in Tecarte and have some fun and make our plans for the goldfields in Sonora."

"Si, jefe," says Lopez as he and Chavez walk down the dusty street to the cantina. When they enter, it is dark and musty. The stench of tequila and stale tobacco hangs in the air.

The patrons of the bar have already heard that the famous bandit is in town and they instantly recognize which of the two Chavez is. With his large frame, rugged looks and that jagged scar on his cheek, and with the way he carries himself, it's easy to recognize Clodoveo Chavez.

"Senor Chavez, it's a pleasure to meet you," the closest man says with a slight bow. He also bows to Lopez. The patrons know that you don't offer to shake hands with men such as these if you don't know them very well, not unless they offer their hand first.

Lopez loves this part of being an infamous bandit. The part where he sees the fear in peoples' eyes when they are recognized. It's better to see fear in their eyes than respect, he has always said, because with fear you also get power.

"Amigos," Chavez says, waving his right hand in the air, "a drink for everyone!"

Everyone cheers as Chavez throws a few gold coins on the bar; the bartender hurriedly scoops them up and then gathers glasses and begins pouring drinks for the house. Chavez notices two men seated at a table in a dark corner in the back of the bar and walks over to them.

"We will be sitting here," he says to the men, and the two men quickly gather their drinks and get up. "Si, si, Don Clodoveo," they say in unison as they move to a table in the front of the bar.

Another man comes out through a doorway from behind the bar to see what the sudden commotion is all about. As he looks around, he sees Chavez already sitting at the back table.

"Clodoveo!" he says with a grin, his hand outstretched. "Pedro, good to see you," offers Chavez as he stands up and shakes the bar owner's hand. "And this is mi amigo, Cruz Lopez."

"Si," says Lopez as he too stands and shakes Pedro's hand.

"Good to see you … both of you," Pedro tells them. "If there is anything I can get for you, just let me know."

"Gracias, my friend," Chavez says. "I knew we came to the right place. I will need a place for my men to stay for a few weeks, a place big enough for us all." Pedro nods as Chavez continues. "And tonight Cruz and I will need the company of two of the prettiest senoritas in all of Mexico."

"But, of course," replies Pedro. "The finest girls, I know where to get them for you and your amigo."

"And one more thing," Chavez adds. "Do you know if my friend, Romulo Gonzalez, is still living around here?"

"Si, he has a small rancho a few miles southwest of here," Pedro replies.

The words are good news to Chavez. "Can you send a rider to get him and tell him to meet me here tonight?" he asks Pedro, though the request is phrased more as an order than as a question.

"Si, I will send someone immediately," Pedro answers. "Will that be all for now?"

"Si," responds Chavez, "we will let you know if we need anything more."

Cruz pours them each another drink. Clodoveo reaches into his pocket and pulls out a small pouch full of coins and tosses it onto the table, adding, "And I don't want anyone else to know that we are here, comprende amigo?"

"Si, jefe, I understand," Pedro says as he reaches for the pouch.

Just then, Cruz Lopez slams his left hand down on the pouch. "You hear of any strangers about," Cruz says, "you be sure to let us know."

"Si! Si!," a startled Pedro says as a lump rises in

his throat. "I know of everything that happens in town. I will let you know right away." Lopez eyeballs him real hard and lifts his hand off the pouch. "You had better," he warns. Pedro says, "Si," again and picks up the pouch, bows slightly and walks away, stopping only to give his bartender instructions about how to treat his new guests.

"I don't trust him," Cruz says to Clodoveo. "I don't trust him either," Chavez replies, "but we will need people like him and the best way to get their loyalty is to pay them well and to make them fear you.

"Look what happened to Tiburico," continues Chavez, "turned in by someone he trusted. When there's a reward on your head, you can afford to trust no one."

"Si," agrees Lopez as he lifts another glass to his lips.

Suddenly, the door to the cantina flies open and Chavez and Lopez both instinctively draw their pistolas and swing the barrels toward the commotion in the front. Four drunken vaqueros stumble into the cantina, pushing and shoving their way to the bar. Chavez watches them closely. They shout to the bartender to bring them some tequila. Lopez, too, is keeping a wary eye on them and quickly sizes them up. A smile creeps to the corners of his mouth. He watches them continue to push the other customers away, looking for someone to pick on. "These men are drunk and mean," Lopez says to himself, " just let them try that with us."

But the four men do not see the two bandits sitting in the darkness as luckily their eyes have not yet adjusted from the brightness of the street. They turn back to the bar and demand another drink.

At about the same time, two other men, both in their early 20s, and neither with a horse, are walking down the street outside. Alonzo Cota and Rafael Martinez are sheepherders for a man named Cenac and they have been watching over his flock for the past four months. Finally, enough wool has been sheared for them to get paid and the two friends have two weeks off, heading home to see their families.

Cota has come to Tecarte to see his father and mother, sister and little brother. His sister has four small children; they're his only living relatives. Martinez is just passing through Tecarte on his way to see his sweetheart, Maria, who lives with her parents on a small rancho on the outskirts south of town. She is the most beautiful senorita for many miles around and Martinez is going to marry her someday. He is a good-looking, well-built young man and Maria is all he ever talks about.

"My sweet Maria," he says to Cota, "what will she think of me? A poor sheepherder … we have just worked for many months and what did we get?"

"Not much, amigo," agrees Cota, patting his small pouch.

"Si," says Martinez, "I need to make much more before I can marry my Maria. I will need to buy a small rancho, build a casa, and buy some cattle, a few goats and one or two horses.

"How much would that cost?" he asks his friend.

"I don't know," Cota replies, "but I do know that you will never make that much money working for Cenac." By now, they are standing in front of the cantina. "C'mon, let's go in and have a drink. That will make you feel better."

"No," says Martinez. "I must save all that I can and give it to Maria's father, to show my good faith and my support for the family."

"Don't worry, amigo," Cota chuckles, "I will buy you a drink." He puts his arm around Martinez's shoulder and steers him toward the cantina's door. "C'mon, what harm can come from one drink?"

But they can see that they are in trouble the moment they walk in. The vaqueros all turn at once and focus their bloodshot eyes on the two newcomers.

"Ah, what do we have here?" the nearest vaquero says. "I don't know," says another as he comes closer to look the men over, then turns and adds, "but they smell like sheep!" The vaqueros start laughing.

In the back, Chavez turns to Lopez and says, "Cruz, watch this. This just might get interesting."

Lopez looks up and a smile returns to his lips as he anticipates the spilling of blood.

"We don't want no trouble," Martinez says to the vaqueros.

"Trouble?" the first vaquero says. "You bring that sheep stink in here and you don't want no trouble? Well, you got trouble!" Three of the vaqueros start to encircle the pair.

"Yeah," says the second one again, "I hear you sheepherders just *love* their sheep … baaa … baaa." They all laugh again.

"Yeah, I bet your girlfriend is a sheep," adds the first vaquero as he steps in front of Martinez. More laughter.

Martinez is now enraged. Nobody calls his girl a sheep. Not his sweet Maria. He takes off his hat and tosses it onto the nearest table and cups his left hand to his ear as if he didn't hear the slurred speech of the vaquero.

The vaquero leans closer to Martinez and repeats louder into his ear, "I said, 'Your girlfriend is a …'"

That's as far as he gets before Martinez quickly balls his right hand into a fist and slams the man in the chin with an uppercut that smashes the vaquero's jaw and knocks out several bloody teeth. Martinez sees the man's eyes roll back so that when he falls to the floor, they have no color; all that is showing is the white part. Martinez knows that this man is out of the fight.

The vaquero on the right starts to throw a punch, but Martinez easily ducks it and hits the man with a left to the gut and a right to the face, knocking him over backwards. As he does this, Cota blindsides the third one, who is busy watching his amigos go down. With a tightly closed fist, Cota splits the man's right eye wide open and blood splatters all over. The man screams, and Cota punches him two more times in the face and the man falls to the floor in a heap.

Meanwhile, the fourth vaquero, who has remained at the bar, starts to pull his gun to shoot Cota, but Martinez sees this and grabs a chair, smashing it over the man's head. The man crumples to the floor and the pistol slides toward Cota, who quickly picks it up and covers Martinez. But he needs no help. The man that was hit in the gut is starting to get up and Martinez kicks him hard in the face, breaking his jaw with a crack and knocking him senseless to the floor, blood gushing from his mouth.

Martinez reaches down and pulls a gun out of the man's holster, but there is no further attack. The rest of the patrons are silent, glad to see the bullies get their due. Four men lay sprawled out and bleeding on the floor amidst knocked-over and broken chairs. The bright late-day sunshine streams through the doors, illuminating the settling dust caused by the sudden ruckus.

After what seems like a long pause, two men start

clapping in the back of the cantina. Cota and Martinez look back, but in the dark corner all they can see are the silhouettes of two men sitting at a table.

"Bravo. Bravo, amigos. Very good fight," says Chavez loudly. "Come, share a drink with us."

They look around again and see that there is no further trouble and put the pistols in their belts. They walk back to the rear table and as their eyes adjust to the darkness, Cota's begin to bulge as he recognizes Chavez.

"Senor Chavez, if them were your men, we did not know," an apologetic Cota blurts out. "We are very sorry."

When Martinez hears Chavez's name, he too becomes instantly concerned.

"No need to apologize to me, amigos," he says to the pair with a raspy laugh. "I would not ride with men like these. I was about to throw them out of here myself when you two came along and took care of it for me. Sit and share a drink with me and my friend, Cruz Lopez."

That's another name that both of them have heard before.

Cota can't believe he's about to have a drink with two of the most famous men in all of California – Alta or Baja. Martinez is just as much in awe. "This is Clodoveo Chavez," he says to himself, "the famous bandit leader, the one who rode with Tiburcio Vasquez!"

Like all Mexicans, the legend is well known to Martinez. He plays the rest of it out in his head. Vasquez was a folk hero in these parts, robbing and killing gringos, so the story goes, mostly in northern California, for more than 20 years before his capture and execution earlier this year. And before him, it all started with the legendary Joaquin Murrieta, who was killed by Capt. Harry Love of the California Rangers in 1853. Martinez had listened intently as his father and grandfather told him their stories when he was a boy.

The two sheepherders each pull out a chair and sit down with the famous bandits.

"My name is Alonzo Cota, and this tiger here is Rafael Martinez," Cota says in introduction.

"Mucho gusto," Chavez says as he and Lopez shake their hands. Nice to meet you.

Chavez yells at the patrons to drag those "stinking vaqueros" out into the street and to tell them not to come back in here once they wake up. "Si, si," the men say as they pick up the vaqueros and head toward the door.

"That was a good fight," Chavez says, turning back to the two men seated in front of him. "Four against two, and they had guns and you didn't."

"Si," says Martinez, still worried about further trouble, "maybe we should give them their guns back," starting to take his from his belt.

"No," says Chavez, "you keep them. When them hombres wake up, they will be angry; besides, they are lucky to be alive. If they had tangled with us, they would not have been so fortunate.

"So, to lose a gun, that is a small thing, no?"

"Si," says Cota, "and we might need these guns." He looks at Martinez.

"That's right," Lopez cuts in. "It takes many punches to kill a man, but it takes only one bullet to kill the same man."

"Si, si," they all agree.

"More tequila," Lopez yells to the bartender, "and two more glasses too!"

"So," asks Chavez, "are you two from around

here?"

"Yes, for the most part," says Cota, the spokesman for the two. "I'm on my way to see my family. They live near here. And Rafael, he has a girlfriend and her family lives nearby. He is on his way to see them. We have been working on a sheep ranch all summer and we have got two weeks' leave."

"A sheep ranch?" says Chavez. "You might as well be working for nothing."

"That is true," Cota sighs. "We didn't get paid very much for our time."

Just then, two pretty young girls walk in through the back door. The bartender sees them and points to the two bandits. "I'm sure those are the men you have come to see," he tells them.

The girls giggle and head toward the back of the room.

"Come," Lopez says as he reaches out for the one he wants, the fatter of the two. He grabs her by the arm and sets her upon his lap. The other moves toward Chavez; she has heard many stories about this bandit and is glad she will be the one who will please him tonight.

"If you would like," Chavez says to the two men, "I can get both of you a woman too."

Cota smiles and Martinez blushes. "Thank you, senor, but not for me, not tonight," says Cota. "Me and my friend must be going soon. And as I said, Rafael here already has a sweetheart of his own and he is going to marry her."

Lopez chortles at hearing this. "Well, amigo, if you want some milk, you don't have to buy the whole damn cow," he says, laughing as he gives his girl a little squeeze that makes her giggle again. They all laugh at this.

"But she is such a sweet cow, hey Rafael?" Cota teases his friend and they all laugh again. All except Martinez, whose face is now beet red.

"That's okay," Chavez says to him. "Go to your sweetheart, but before you leave, I want to make you an offer. I could use a couple of men like you two, if you're interested, of course. For the right man, the rewards are beyond your wildest dreams, amigos."

Cota and Martinez are stunned. They can't believe they're being offered a position in the most famous gang in all of California. There is no greater honor they can imagine. But they respectfully decline.

Chavez laughs and downs another shot. "Well, you two think about it," he says. "The offer's still open if you want it."

"Thank you," Cota says, rising from his chair. "C'mon, Rafael, it's getting near dark and we should get going."

Martinez nods as he too rises to leave.

"You muchachos be careful," Lopez says as they turn. "Those vaqueros might have woken up with a desire for revenge and could be waiting for you out there."

"We will," Cota says as he and Martinez head for the door. They stop and look outside to see that the street is empty. They check their new guns to make sure they're loaded and, nervously, they walk out into the street and turn south out of town. Little did they know that when the four vaqueros woke up and were told about Chavez and Lopez, they had already high-tailed it out of town, not planning to come back.

Back in the cantina, Chavez and Lopez are beginning to have some fun with the girls, laughing and drinking. They call to the bartender to have dinner brought to them, a huge feast, for they are hungry. All they have eaten all day is the rabbit stew at the Sheckler ranch. The bartender leans through the door behind the bar and tells the cook to hurry up a meal.

A short while later, a couple of old women come out with two large platters full of food, plates of carne asada, rice and beans, and tortillas. The bandits hungrily dig in.

"This is good, no?" Lopez says with a mouth full of food. "Si," Chavez replies.

By now it is almost dark. A lone rider comes into town and ties his horse at the hitching post in front of the cantina. He's wearing a wide-brimmed sombrero and a long serape, covering a pistol that is snuggly fit into a well-worn holster. As he heads toward the steps, he throws back the right side of the serape, exposing his pistol.

As he enters the cantina, the bartender is busy lighting the lanterns and the flickering light is reflecting eerily off the walls. The cantina is almost empty now, save for some commotion in the back corner. The man walks toward the bar, stops, and looks around. His entrance has not escaped notice.

"Romulo!" comes a yell from the back. "My amigo, we are over here," Chavez continues, waving his friend toward their table.

"Clodoveo, my old friend," Gonzalez says as he walks to the back to greet the men.

"It's been a long time," Chavez says as he gets up to give the man a hearty slap on the shoulders.

"Si," says Gonzalez, "it's been since Tres Pinos, no? We had some good times there, huh?"

"That we did, my friend," Chavez recalls. "It's good to see you."

"And the same here," Romulo replies. Chavez then introduces him to Lopez.

"It's too bad about Vasquez," continues Gonzalez. "He was a great man."

"That is for certain," Chavez answers. "He taught me just about everything I know about this business."

Romulo picks up a glass and pours himself a shot of tequila and offers a toast to the gang's former leader. The three clink glasses and down a shot in Vasquez's honor.

"Is it true," Gonzalez inquires, "that when they hung him, his last words were 'Pronto?'"

"Si," Chavez reports. "that was what he said all right. The gringo sheriff asked him if he had any last words and all Tiburcio said was "Pronto!" Quickly!

"That was a sad day," Chavez continues. "We wanted to rescue him, but there was no hope. The sheriff had fifty armed men all around the jail in San Jose and there was no way to get him out alive. He knew it too. He would not have us risk the lives of so many of his men for his own. A brave man."

Chavez takes another bite of food.

"So, after that I took over the banda and we have ridden a bloody trail to avenge him," Chavez goes on. "But now our trail is too hot up north so we have come down to Mexico to see what opportunities might befall us here. I have heard about a big gold strike down in Sonora."

"Si, that is true," confirms Romulo. "There are some very rich mines in that area, I am told."

"Well," Chavez says, "I'm planning on putting a

large gang together and riding down to Sonora and relieving some of those miners of their wealth."

All three men laugh.

"That's not a bad idea, amigo," says Romulo.

"But I will have to find some more men first," Chavez continues. "Men who are good with a gun."

"How many men?" asks Gonzalez.

"About six to ten or more if you could find them for me," Chavez answers.

"Si. I know of some good men," Romulo replies, "and maybe they will know some more."

"Good, good," Chavez says, wiping his chin with one hand and shooing some flies off his food with the other. "And then we will need to equip this small army … we will need more guns, ammo, food, cooking supplies, tents, blankets and warm clothes, what with winter coming on. And we will need wagons to haul everything."

"Hmmm," ponders Gonzalez, scratching the stubble on his own chin as he thinks for a moment. "I know of a small town, just across the American side of the border about only ten miles from here … a town called Campo," he says. "It is owned by two gringo brothers with the name of Gaskill …."

"Gaskill?" blurts Lopez while taking a bite of food, accidentally spitting some of it out as he does so. "I remember a few years ago up north, near Hangtown, a man by that name sold a silver saddle that I had lost to him in a card game. A nice saddle that I had a saddle maker inlay with silver conchos. I told this man named Gaskill, or Gaskell, or something like that, that I would pay the debt, but he done and sold my saddle anyway. I have always wanted to see this man again."

"Well, maybe it is one of them," Romulo replies.

"I heard that they came down to Campo some six or seven years ago and pretty much built the entire town themselves. I know they came from up north somewhere, but I'm not sure where. Anyway, they have a small store, a blacksmith shop, a new hotel and a few houses scattered about … that's about it. And no sheriff either.

"It would be as easy as Tres Pinos!" Gonzalez adds, laughing as he gives Chavez a slap on the shoulder.

"That sounds like just what we're looking for," Chavez says. "I think we will rob this town called Campo, bring everything that we steal back here in wagons and then we will ride for Sonora."

"Si," says Cruz. "I like that plan. We will have enough men. We will take such a small town easy enough."

They all laugh.

Suddenly, Gonzalez remembers something he knows will interest Chavez, who is busily downing his dinner. "Clodoveo, I have some information I think you will appreciate," he says.

"What is it?" demands Chavez.

Gonzalez smiles. "I know where Don Antonio Sosa is!"

Chavez drops his spoon on his plate. "No, you don't!" he says. "You're just pulling my leg!"

"No, my friend, I am serious," Romulo replies. "I know where he lives and can tell you where to find him."

"That *is* good news," Chavez decides. "I have wanted to kill him for quite some time. Where is that dog?"

"Not far," Romulo says, "down in San Rafael, about thirty miles south of here. I can show you…."

"No, not me," interrupts Chavez. "I will be riding

off for a few weeks, but you can show Cruz here; he's my second in command."

"Si, I will show Cruz how to find him," Gonzalez says. "I know what it means to you to kill this man."

"Why?" asks Cruz. "What did he do?"

"He killed a good friend of mine," Chavez replies. "Several years ago, he rode jefe of a posse and when they caught my friend, they just hung him up from the nearest tree and left him for the vultures.

"I vowed someday to avenge his death," Chavez says, "so Cruz, I want you take some men and go down to San Rafael and kill this man for me. And not quickly either."

I would *love* to," replies Lopez, his body already coursing with that good feeling just at the thought of killing.

"Settled, then," says Chavez. "In the morning, I will be riding for Arizona. I will be back in about five, six weeks or so. Cruz, you take the horses that Fedoro and the others are bringing down from Horsethief Canyon and take them to the Mendosa ranch to be sold. Then ride with Romulo to San Rafael and kill Sosa for me. When I get back from Arizona we will all meet up back here in Tecarte and then we'll raid Campo."

"Sure, jefe, I will take care of all of it," Lopez says. "No problem," adds Gonzalez.

"Well, then, gracias, amigos. I must be going to bed then," says Chavez as he squeezes his whore. She giggles again. "It will be a long ride tonight," he says, looking at the girl, "and a longer ride in the morning." He lets out a laugh as he puts his arm around the girl and guides her toward the door to the side room, and then out the back door to the rooms Pedro has reserved for them.

"Buenos noches," say Lopez and Gonzalez as they watch Chavez weave across the floor. "Buenos noches."

Chapter 9

Rafael Martinez and Alonzo Cota aren't taking any chances. They're walking down a back street in Tecarte, not wanting to run into the drunken vaqueros again. They still can't believe what happened in the cantina, being invited to join the Chavez gang. And by Chavez himself, no less.

"What do you think, Alonzo?" asks Rafael.

"I can't believe it!" Alonzo replies. "That was Clodoveo Chavez. Right here in Tecarte! And to be asked to join his gang, well, no one is going to believe it."

"I know what you mean, amigo," adds Rafael. "Chavez is the most famous person I have ever met. But we can't join his gang...."

"Why not?" Alonzo cuts him off.

"Because they are *killers*," replies Rafael, "and we are not, that's why!"

"I guess you're right," Alonzo shrugs. "But just think of it, the glory of riding with these men. I have heard the stories all my life. About the great Tiburcio Vasquez, who took over the gang after Joaquin Murrieta was killed."

"Yes," adds Rafael, "I have heard the stories too. Joaquin and his gang started robbing and killing gringos back in '49. That was after his brother was killed – the gringos hung him for something he did not do. At first, Joaquin rode to avenge his brother's death, but I think after a while, he rode for the money and the glory."

"Si," Alonzo says, "you are probably right. But what a life to live ... to ride free like the wind and not to have to work like a slave for no man. Like we just did for

Cenac. You want to see what a working man gets, look I'll show you."

Cota reaches into his pocket and produces a few small silver coins.

"Four months labor and this is what a working man gets," he says in frustration.

"I know," Rafael says, "but it is an honest man's labor. Do you think you are ready to live the life of a bandit?"

"Maybe not," Cota agrees as they continue to walk, turning a corner onto the main street leading south out of town, the vaqueros nowhere to be found. "But I do know that Joaquin Murrieta was a great man…."

"But," Rafael interrupts him, "do you know what happened to him when the gringos caught up to him in '53?"

"Yes, I remember that story well," Alonzo continues. "He was ambushed by Capt. Harry Love and his posse. They tried to capture him alive, but when he tried to ride away, they shot Joaquin in the back. They killed him and his lieutenant, 'Three-Fingered' Jack.

"Then Capt. Love took a long knife and cut off Joaquin's head," Cota adds, mimicking the motion of a slice of the throat. "And they also cut off the hand of Three-Fingered Jack, put both the head and the hand in large pickle jars, filled them up with brandy and took them back to the governor of California for the $1,000 reward.

"And last I heard," Cota continues, "that gruesome jar with Joaquin's head in it is still sitting in a store window in San Francisco for anyone who walks by to see."

"Don't you see?" says Rafael. "*That* is the life of a

bandit and that was the life and death of Joaquin Murrieta."

"Aaah, but," counters Alonzo, "look at the man who started up his own gang after the death of Joaquin. Tiburcio Vasquez wasn't caught until last year and the gringos were lucky to capture him then. So he rode the bandit's trail for about …" he continues, trying to add the years in his head and his fingers, "oh, about twenty years."

"Yes," says Rafael, "but I heard that he spent a few years in prison in the '60s and they caught him and hung him in the end."

"Well, that is true," replies Alonzo, "but I don't think they will hang Chavez. Did you see how big and strong a man he is? I don't think the gringos will ever catch him."

"They will, eventually," concedes Rafael. "Someone will put a bullet in him. Like Cruz Lopez said, 'It only takes one bullet to kill a man,' even a man like Chavez."

"Well, I hope not," says Cota. "I really liked him. You know, my sister will never believe that I spoke to him."

"We will need to hide these guns someplace," says Rafael. "I can't show up at Maria's house with a gun." "That is true," Alonzo replies. "I know a good place just up ahead."

They come to a rocky outcropping beside the road. "Up here," Alonzo says, climbing up the rocks to a small cave. "We can put them in here and then cover them with small rocks." Rafael hands up his gun and Alonzo puts the guns in the hole and covers them up.

"Nobody will find them here," he says. The two

friends continue on down the road and soon they arrive at the front gate of the casa of Alonzo's family. "Come in and help me verify my story," he asks Martinez.

"No," Rafael replies, "you're on your own. I have to get to Maria's before it gets too late. Her father, Senor Estrada, would frown on that and I have to keep on the good side of him. As Maria's father, I have to show him the respect that he deserves. He is a good man and a man of God."

"Well, go on then," Cota says, "go and see your beloved sweetheart and I'll stop by and see you manana."

"Okay, amigo, see you tomorrow," replies Martinez, patting his friend on the shoulder as he turns to continue down the street.

Cota stands for a moment to watch him. "He is really a nice friend," he thinks as he watches Martinez turn onto the dirt path that leads to the Estradas. "He will make Maria a fine husband."

Rafael Martinez's heart is now racing. He can see Maria's house up ahead. The outside lamp is lit, hanging on a hook by the front door. And he can see light coming from inside through the open windows.

He can't believe it! He hasn't seen Maria in four months! She will be so surprised to see him.

The dog starts barking as he gets closer, alerting those inside to his approach. Martinez sees someone pull the curtain back and look outside; then the curtain falls back and almost as quickly the front door bursts open.

"Rafael!" exclaims Maria as she runs into his waiting arms. Her long, black hair glistens in the light of the just-risen moon. She is the most beautiful girl that Martinez has ever seen.

"Maria," he says as he squeezes her tightly, "I

love you!"

"I love you too, Rafael!" she says back to him. "Oh, Rafael, I knew that you would be back soon. I prayed to God to send you back to me! Oh, thank you, Lord," she adds as she holds him tightly, wanting to kiss him so badly, but knowing that by now her father must be watching them.

And she is right. As they turn toward the door, the entire Estrada family is watching. Manuel Estrada is a small, thin man, but is still a strong man despite his 58 years of age. He is a devout Catholic and is raising his children the same way. He likes this young Rafael Martinez, but he doesn't think he is the right man for his Maria. He knows his daughter loves this rough, naïve young man and that she is at the right age to marry, and was hoping that in his absence she would find someone better, someone from a more-respected Catholic family, and forget about this young man.

But his eyes tell him this is not the case. She has waited patiently for Martinez's return and he can see the love in her eyes as he watches his daughter hold tightly to this sheepherder's waist.

"Oh Lord, what should I do?" he says to himself. "Should I forbid this young man from seeing her? Or should I take him into my flock? Maybe in time, with your guidance, Lord, I can turn this wild, young lad into a good, decent, respectable man of the church."

"Father," Maria says smiling, "look who has returned!"

"Yes, I see," Manuel replies. "And how have you been, young man?"

"Just fine, sir," he responds politely. "I have been given two weeks' leave by Senor Cenac. He has paid me for my labor and I would like to give it to you, sir," he adds, holding out the small pouch for Sr. Estrada, "to hold it in trust, for someday I wish to marry your daughter and we can use this money to help build our own rancho."

"I like you, Rafael," Sr. Estrada says as he looks into the pouch, "but this is not very much money. I will hold it for you, if you would like, but if you want to marry my Maria, and give her a proper home and raise a family of your own, you will need much more money than this."

He looks into the bag again, as if to count the money, but can plainly see that the pouch contains little.

"This would not even buy you a cow," he continues. "You will never make enough money as a sheepherder to get the things you need. I'm sorry, my son, but I feel you will never be sovereign enough for me to give you my daughter's hand in marriage."

Martinez is deflated and Maria is near tears as the words hang in the air.

"But, sir," replies a chagrined Rafael, "I can find other work. I will work hard."

"Father!" cries Maria. "But I love him and I want to marry him!"

"I am sorry, my child, but that is the way of the world," Sr. Estrada replies, "and it is the way of God. And you must obey your father." He turns to Rafael and changes the subject. "Young man, you must be hungry. You can come in and have some dinner and you may spend the night and sleep in the front room. In the morning we will talk more about this."

He turns and walks into the house.

"Oh, Rafael!" exclaims Maria again, clutching Martinez even tighter as she continues to cry. "I love you!"

"I love you too, Maria," he says again, lost for words.

"But what can we do?" she asks. "My father won't change his mind easily."

"I know," Rafael says, "but I will change his mind. I will make enough money. Don't worry, my sweetheart, I will do whatever I have to so we can be married."

Not far away, Alonzo Cota is at his family's house. After dinner, he and his sister go for a walk. Her name is Rosaria Sanchez and she is four years older than Alonzo and has four children of her own between the ages of 2 and 10. They all live with their parents since her husband, Francisco, was killed. He was a teamster who drove a wagon twice a month from Tecarte to Ensenada, a small seaport village on the Pacific Ocean about 75 miles to the southwest.

He was a big man, and mean, and even meaner when he drank, which was most of the time. He didn't treat Rosaria very well; sometimes he would come home drunk and beat her for no reason. And the kids too. So Alonzo didn't like him much. He had thought about killing the man himself, so he didn't grieve when Rosaria's husband was killed in a knife fight in a cantina in Ensenada about a year ago.

Although he was mean to Rosaria and the kids, he did keep food on the table and a roof over their heads. So now, without the meager money her husband earned, hard times had left Rosaria with no choice but to move back into her parent's small home.

Rosaria does what she can to help out. She sews and makes blankets and weaves baskets that she sells to the man who owns the small store in town.

They walk quietly for a while and then Alonzo breaks the silence.

"The Chavez gang is here in Tecarte," he blurts out.

"No," she exclaims, "I don't believe you!"

"But it's true," Alonzo says. "Clodoveo Chavez, the famous bandit, is in Tecarte right this very moment, him and his lieutenant, Cruz Lopez. They're drinking in the cantina and that is where Rafael and I met them."

"The Chavez gang here in Tecarte?" Rosaria replies with alarm. "Do you think they are going to rob the town?"

"No, no," replies Alonzo disarmingly. "I think they're just hiding out. Chavez offered to let me and Rafael join the gang."

"You said 'No,' I hope," Rosaria says, hanging on the reply.

"Yeah, we told them no, but he said that if we change our minds, we could join up later," Alonzo responds.

"Alonzo!" she says. "You don't want to be a bandido, a wanted man, do you?"

"No," Alonzo says, "I don't want that," then after a pause adds, "but just think of the money. And what it could mean to our lives. Rosaria, see here," showing her his coin pouch, "this is all I earned for four month's labor working on a sheep ranch."

Five silver coins are all he can show her. "I want you to have these," he says as he hands her the pouch. "This is for you and the muchachos."

"Thank you so much," she says to Alonzo. "You are the best brother I could ask for. But," she pleads, "promise me that you won't join the Chavez gang."

"Don't worry, my sister," he says. "If I do, it will be only for long enough to make some money so we don't have to break our backs no more trying to make a living."

"Alonzo, I don't want to lose my oldest brother," Rosaria interrupts.

"You're not going to lose me," he shoots right back, a bit angrily. "I can take care of myself." He wants to tell her about the drunken vaqueros, but knows she will disapprove. He's surprised she hasn't scolded him already for just going into the cantina in the first place.

He thinks maybe he's said too much already. Rosario can't shake the feeling of dread that has come over her with what he's told her already.

"God, I hope so," she thinks. "He will make the right choice. God, please help him make the right choice."

Chapter 10

It is misting lightly, as the sun begins to rise to find Silas Gaskill and his brother, Lumen, riding along a mountain trail. They are out looking for some of their stray cattle. They come to a clear-flowing creek and stop to let their horses drink.

"You know," says Lumen. "This here is Cottonwood Creek. An old Indian told me a while back that about ten years ago a miner was living down here and panned himself up a few buckskins full of gold."

"Could be," replies Silas. "Cottonwood Creek starts up at Buckman Springs where two creeks come together. The Buckmen creek is the smallest and joins in from the west, but the larger branch … I think it's called Kitchen Creek, it flows down out of the Laguna Mountains and I would bet there's some gold to be found coming down from there.

"You know," Silas adds, "Frenchy the sheepherder stopped by the blacksmith shop the other day and he had some quartz rocks that he found."

"Yeah?" Lumen replies. "Did they have any gold in them?"

"No," Silas says, "but they were full of iron pyrite."

"Well, with that and a nickel you can buy a shot of whiskey," laughs Lumen . "We've seen that before; did you tell him it was fool's gold?"

"Sure," Silas says. "I hated to though; I could see he was all excited about it. But I told him to keep on looking. I also told him what to keep an eye out for as he's grazing them darn sheep of Ynda's in lots of remote places down below the line. He just might come across something someday."

"He might," Lumen adds, "but I don't think he would know gold if it bit him in the backside."

"You're probably right there," Silas replies, "but who knows? He might find an old digging or a nice outcropping of quartz with some color. I told him if he did find something to bring it to us and to keep his mouth shut. It's a longshot, I'll admit, but he is already out there in the hills and it ain't much work for him to keep an eye out. For most men, though, it's a lot of work, prospecting for gold," Silas continues, "and most men don't ever find enough to amount to much anyhow and when they do, they go and spend it all gambling and drinking and whoring. I've seen it all before too many times to count."

"What do you think about the Julian mines?" Lumen asks as they wade their horses across the creek and ride slowly down the trail.

"Some of them are producing some mighty high-grade ore," Silas says, "and a few of the mine owners will become rich men, I think, now that the courts have settled the land title dispute and the greedy Cuyamaca land grant owners have lost their claim to the lands in the Julian district."

The sun has broken through the mist and is warming up the morning very nicely. The trail leads them up onto a large, flat rock beside the creek. They look down at the rock to see small, round depressions ground into the bedrock here and there.

"Grinding holes," Silas says in way of explanation as he and Lumen dismount to take a closer look. "As you know, the Indians made these holes grinding acorns and other nuts and roots for food."

"Yeah," Lumen replies, "That hole must of took some time to make, It's got to be at least eight inches deep, and look at all the pottery shards. It looks like someone broke them here not too long ago."

"More likely they shot them," Silas observes. "I hear that some of the Campo boys like to come out to places like this and look for the pots and use them for target practice. Look," Silas points, "there's some shell casings over there."

Lumen looks and sees a bunch of brass shell casings littering the ground.

"Disrespectful little bastards," he says. "Some of these pots are very old and should be left alone."

"That's true," Silas replies, "but boys will be boys and I guess they're too tempting a target for them. It's a shame, though," he adds. "I bet these pots will be worth something someday. I found a cave full of them up in Jacumba a few years back … they're probably all gone by now too."

"Look!" Lumen says as he bends over and picks up a small, shiny black object off the ground. "An arrowhead," he says, holding it up for Silas to see.

"Yup," he says, looking it over. "This one is made of obsidian … nice one too … you could find a handful of them if you look around long enough." He hands it back to Lumen.

"I think I'll give it to Walter," Lumen says as he tucks the arrowhead into his shirt pocket.

"Well," Silas says, surveying the canyon, "I think we should go down here a ways. If there's any cattle in this canyon, that's where they'll likely be. Down below a spell the canyon opens up into some small meadows where they might find some grass to eat."

The brothers get back on their mounts and ride downstream.

***

Back in Campo, Eliza Gaskill is minding the store. There are two customers in the small building, Mr. and Mrs. Cline, who own a nice ranch about three miles northeast of town.

"Where's Lumen?" Charlie Cline, who is also the town's justice of the peace, asks her.

"Oh, he went out riding with Silas this morning to look for some stray cattle," explains Eliza.

"Well," Cline says, "tell him that I want to talk to him. One of my boys stopped at the Sheckler ranch yesterday and young Claude told him that Clodoveo Chavez, the Mexican bandit, and another man stopped by their house the day before last. They asked for breakfast and left riding south. Didn't cause no trouble, thank the Lord, as Mrs. Sheckler was home alone with another woman visiting from San Diego and only Claude was with them.

"If this is true," Cline continues, "we should warn the area ranchers to keep an eye out for them and to keep their horses in the stables at night."

"Oh, my," says Eliza, "is that the notorious bandit that I hear the men sometimes talking about?"

"Yes, it is," replies Charlie, "and if them bandits are around here, we all need to take precautions."

"Well, I will certainly let Lumen and Silas know when they return," Eliza promises.

"I think that we should send Sheriff Hunsaker a telegram and let him know about it too," Cline adds.

"The sheriff came through town just yesterday," Eliza counters. "I think he's out at Pete Larkin's ranch in Jacumba right now."

"Okay," Cline says, "when he comes back by let him know about the bandits then. They probably rode down south of the line anyway, but we should be on our guard just the same."

"If the sheriff rides back through we will tell him," Eliza says.

"How much is that large bag of flour?" says Mrs. Cline, who has been walking around the store browsing while her husband has chatted with Mrs. Gaskill.

"The large bag is two dollars and fifty cents," says Eliza.

"Oh, my," Mrs. Cline exclaims, "that's expensive. Can I save money if I buy two of them?"

"No, I'm sorry, Mrs. Cline," Eliza apologizes. "It's the shipping costs that make it so expensive. If you would like, you can ask Lumen, but I don't think he'll sell it any cheaper."

"That's okay," Mrs. Cline says, "we need it anyways. We also need ten pounds of sugar, a sack of salt, ten boxes of yeast powder, two bottles of vinegar, one box of pepper, four bars of coldwater soap and Charles needs a couple boxes of pistol caps and powder and balls."

Eliza listens intently to the list. "I think we have all that in stock," she says as she busies herself readying the order.

"So, how's the hotel doing?" asks Mr. Cline.

"Couldn't be better," says Eliza, looking up for a moment from the scales where she is weighing out the sugar. "Auntie Price helps me with the guests and all. I don't think I could run it without her."

"Well," Mr. Cline lauds, "we hear that it is the best hotel in all of rural San Diego County."

"Why, thank you," Eliza replies proudly. "That is quite a compliment." She finishes boxing up the order. "Will there be anything else?"

"Why, yes," Mrs. Cline replies, "I almost forgot to ask if we have any mail."

"No, not today," Eliza Gaskill says, looking into the Cline's mail box. Mrs. Cline picks up the box from the counter while her husband grabs the sacks of salt and flour from the floor.

"Have a nice day," she says to Eliza as she opens the door of the store for them.

"Same to you folks," she says as they leave. "Bye, bye now."

Chapter 11

Clodoveo Chavez awakens early and gets out of bed. He draws the curtain back and sees the alleyway is all quiet. The eastern sky is a faint pink announcing the arrival of a new day. Quickly dressing, he opens the door and looks back. The girl he spent the night with stirs, but doesn't awaken. He never did catch her name. He usually doesn't, though they all know his.

Chavez heads straight for the stable, where he sees Manuel waiting for him with his light colored palomino already saddled. He flips the man a small silver coin and says nothing as he mounts up. Manuel wants to thank the man, but just nods appreciatively instead.

Chavez rides slowly east out of Tecarte, heading for Arizona. He has told Lopez that his plan is to scout out the Sonora mining operations, but he also hopes to hole up for a while. He has been on the run ever since that devil Morse made things too hot up in central California months ago, and as the sun's first rays warm his face, he thinks it would be nice to sleep in the same place two nights in a row for a change.

He stays well south of the border as he heads toward Yuma, "No need to be seen near Campo," he thinks, only turning north when he's sure he's well past the place.

He finds a trail that turns north and he rides along it for a while, reining up only when he sees a small ranch ahead. He doesn't know it, but it is Jacumba Springs, the ranch owned by Pete Larkin, the place that the sheriff has just visited, leaving only yesterday. Looking the ranch over for a while, Chavez decides to go around this place;

it's good instincts like that, mixed with a little luck, that have kept him alive for so long.

He backtracks a few hundred yards, rides a mile east and then turns north a bit and shortly he comes upon the Yuma road, at the top of Devil's Canyon. Here, the landscape changes drastically; the gentle slope he's been riding all day now drops off into a abyss that looks like it might be from another planet.

Dropping off down through the gorge, Chavez can't believe that someone actually built a road through here. He looks up and can see giant boulders on the steep canyon walls; most look like they're about to come crashing down at any moment.

Just as it is nearing sundown he rides out on the edge of the road and, looking off the rim, he can see a small rancho. There's a cooking fire burning in front of the house. He can see a woman tending the fire.

Hot food would be welcome. Looking the place over, he can see that there's a spring or a running creek nearby because he can see some desert palm trees growing off to the side of the adobe house. "Quiet, out-of-the-way place," he thinks as a smile comes to his lips. "Just what I need," he says to himself and in about a half hour is riding up to the ranch.

"Hola," he yells from about a hundred yards off.

Dogs start barking and a man comes out of the house, stops and looks him over for a second, waves him in and turns and walks back into the house.

***

"Chavez!" Lumen Gaskill yells. "Are you sure?"

"Yes," replies Eliza. "The Clines said that Chavez

and another man had eaten breakfast at the Sheckler ranch."

"What do you make of it?" Lumen says, turning to his brother. "Could be true," Silas replies. "We haven't heard anything in over a month now about Chavez and his gang. Last thing I read was that he was up in the Panamint area … Ridgecrest, Lone Pine, up around there somewhere."

"Who's Chavez?" asks Jack Kelly as he walks in from the telegraph office in the back room, having overheard the conversation.

"A bandit from up north," Lumen replies, "and a bad one at that."

"Oh," Kelly suddenly remembers. "I think I did see something about him in the *Union*."

"What else did they say?" Lumen asks his wife. "Well, that's about it … Ben wasn't home, she had a friend visiting from San Diego, but she told her to hide in the back room. Claude was at home; she gave him a shotgun and told him to watch from the bedroom window."

"Sounds then like it's true," Silas says. "If the sheriff rides back through from Jacumba, we should tell him about it, and we should also tell all the ranchers in the area to keep an extra eye on their stock."

"We should do the same thing," Lumen replies. "Let's bring in some of the cattle a little closer to town just to be on the safe side. If that bunch is really around here then some cows or some horses are bound to come up missing and they usually will go for the easy ones first."

"You're right, Lumen," Silas says. "I'll tell the Cameron boys tomorrow to go out and move them in a little closer and to keep an eye out for tracks or the like. Best to be on the safe side.”

Chapter 12

Chavez leaves the small ranch before sunup. He slept under a palm thatch roof on a bunk made from sticks with some straw thrown over it.

"A meal and a sore back is all I got," he says to himself as he rides off toward the east. And the toothless old tipo had the nerve to charge him a silver dollar at that! "Just wait and see what I do to you," Chavez muses, "if I ever see you again."

He rides on down through the steep rocky gorge, rounds a bend at the canyon's mouth and is hit directly in the face by a hot, fiercely burning sun rising in the east. As he looks across the flat, sandy, windy inferno, he's glad that he stole a large water bag and filled it and his bota bags at the spring before he left.

"It was probably worth the dollar after all," he thinks as he sets off riding out onto the forbidding wasteland. He follows the road as best he can, losing it from time to time because of the blowing sand. Two hot days later he rides up over a small hill and can see the green ribbon of trees and bushes lining the Colorado River. The road leads on and soon he can see the ferry landing. This narrow gorge is the only place south of the Grand Canyon where a ferry boat can cross the Colorado River. It is called the Yuma Crossing.

Chavez stops at the landing and sees that the ferry is on the opposite side of the river, which here at the narrows is less than a quarter-mile away. The pull rope becomes taut and the boat starts across the Colorado in his direction. It'll take a good ten minutes to make the crossing.

Chavez climbs off his horse and sits down in the shade and watches the boat, which is really nothing more than a raft with a pulley system. He can see three men pulling hard on the rope as the raft battles the strong current. He can also see two passengers, each with his own horse. When they get about halfway across, Clodoveo can see that they're both gringos, are well-dressed and have fine-looking horses and saddles.

"Could be lawmen," he thinks and he pulls his sombrero down a little bit and undoes the leather strap looped around the hammer of his pistol. He's still sitting in the shade when the boat comes ashore.

The gringos walk their horses off the ferry and mount up, and Chavez notices that they pause a little bit to give him a look over before riding on. Or is he just imagining things? Chavez gets up and walks his horse down to the ferry. He's the only one waiting.

Looking at the three men on the raft, he sees that two of them are young, so he figures correctly that the older one chewing tobacco is the pilot and directs his question toward him. "How much to cross?" Chavez asks.

"A dollar fer you and two dollars fer your horse," cackles the man. "Unless of course you want to swim across," laughs the man, spitting tobacco juice that is the same color as the muddy water of the mighty river.

Clodoveo reaches into his vest pocket and produces three silver coins with such little hesitation that the pilot is momentarily surprised. Mexicans aren't usually so eager to part with their money, he thinks suspiciously. He's ferried thousands of them across the river in his day, and this one looks about as mean as they get, he reckons.

"Let's get going, then," the pilot says, seeing no

other customers. Chavez walks his horse onto the boat's platform and hands the pilot the coins on his way past. "Hold him steady," he tells Chavez of his horse, and then says to his two employees, "Heave to."

The rope tightens and the two men start to pull the boat across the river. Chavez steadies his mount and then ties the reins off on the railing once he sees that the horse is comfortable. He leans back on the rail and looks back at the two gringos, who are riding over the crest of the hill, not looking back.

"Bueno," Chavez thinks, but then his thoughts are interrupted by the pilot. "You from around these parts?" He turns and looks down at the inquisitive pilot, who is much shorter than he is, and about ten years older, with wispy, curly red hair and a receding forehead. And one of those annoying high-pitched voices that sounds like two alley cats having it out.

"No," is all that Chavez says and he turns back toward the river.

"A stranger, huh?" carries on the pilot, not getting the hint. "That's okay, mister. We get lots of strangers around here. Say, that's a nice palomino you got there."

Chavez doesn't look at him or even answer.

"Not a talker, eh?" the pilot says as he spits the large wad of tobacco over the railing. "Suit yourself," he says, grabbing his pouch for a fresh chew. "Me? I like to talk," he adds, starting to pull on the rope with the other two now that the boat has entered the main current. "Yup, I talks to myself if I have to," he adds.

The pilot keeps jabbering away and Clodoveo tries to block it out. But then the pilot says something of interest to him. "They're gonna build a prison up there on that hill," the pilot says, nodding toward the Arizona side.

Chavez now gives his attention to the man.

"Yup, a big prison to house all the bad men of the territory. Gonna make the prisoners build it themselves, stone by stone." The pilot lets out a little laugh.

Chavez turns and looks at the hill, which sticks out into the river, kind of like a peninsula. There are large granite outcroppings on both sides of the river here, causing the Colorado to narrow significantly. That's why the ferry was built on this spot back in 1849; thousands of men heading to the goldfields crossed here in those days.

As the ferry reaches the other shore, Chavez unties his horse and disembarks without saying a word.

"A prison!" Chavez ponders as he rides past the hill. "That's not for me. I'll never be one of the poor souls who will be sent there, most of them probably to die." He laughs to himself. "Suckers," he thinks. "I know I will never see the inside of a prison," for he has vowed never to be taken alive. He will not be taken like Vasquez; he will die fighting before he will give up. He prefers a bullet over a rope.

He rides on into Yuma, sticking to back streets and riding slowly, with his serape draped around him. He does not want to be recognized in this town. There is a $2,000 reward on his head – dead or alive.

Carefully, he makes his way down a side street. He stops behind a small adobe house, climbs off his horse and removes the saddle. He then leads his horse into a small stable. He's been here before, but not for a while. He knocks at the back door and hears footsteps on the other side. The door opens an inch and Chavez sees the barrel of a pistola pointed at him. He stares at the gun barrel for a moment and then the door swings open wide and he is greeted with a big hug and ushered hastily inside. The door is shut quickly, but not until after the man has given the back street a once over.

"You are taking a great risk to be here. There have been men in Yuma looking for you," hisses a concerned Ramon Ramirez. "But it sure is great to see you, amigo," he adds, breaking into a smile.

"You, too, Ramon," says Chavez, who has used the Ramirez home as sanctuary in the past. "I have been careful."

He has known the Ramirez family for many years, or more correctly, they have known him. Ramon's mother grew up with Chavez's mother in California before the gold rush panned out and the Ramirezes moved to the border town to be closer to their family south of the border.

There is obvious concern in the household that Chavez has arrived, but he assures them he will not be staying long.

"I am here for only one night and will be leaving at first light," Clodoveo tells Mrs. Ramirez, whose hair is a lot grayer than he remembers from his last visit a few years ago. She goes into the kitchen and begins preparing a meal for their guest.

The front door opens and Ramon's son, Juan, walks in and places his hat on a hook by the door. "Look who's here!" Ramon Ramirez says, and Juan turns and breaks into a big smile. "Clodoveo!" he shouts and hurries over to shake his hand.

"Hola, amigo," replies Chavez in greeting to the young man, who is in his early 20s and five or six years younger than himself. "But, please, when I come around here I wish for you to call me 'Jose,'" he instructs them. "Jose Espinosa."

With a bounty on his head, Chavez feels it will be safer to have an alias in these parts.

"Si," Ramon says, patting the visitor on the back. "Jose it is. Would you like to sit at the table, Jose?"

Juan pulls out a chair for him and Clodoveo sits down. Chavez knows the young Ramirez looks up to him greatly. Maybe someday he'll ask him to join the gang, he thinks. It's nice to have unquestionably loyal people surrounding him. In the future perhaps....

Mrs. Ramirez returns and places a hot meal in front of him. These are good people, Chavez thinks. He knows he is safe here and will enjoy the rare opportunity to sleep in a warm, comfortable bed, Not on the hard ground or in some flea-infested whorehouse like in Tecarte.

In the morning, he saddles up early and says goodbye. He is given a bag of food by Mrs. Ramirez, who refuses his offer to pay for it. "No, you are always welcome here. I know how much your mother worries about you."

His mother! He has not given her much thought in a while. No time, he thinks. He thanks them again and leaves quietly. He purposely does not tell them which way he is heading. No need to give a bounty hunter a way to find him, he reasons.

He swings southeast for half the day, parallel to the border, then crosses a series of small sand dunes. The wind is blowing a bit from the east and he pulls out his bandana and ties it around his face to ease the bite of the sand. He doesn't mind, though, knowing the wind will soon cover his tracks and no one will be able to follow him.

He turns to the north and heads for the Gila River,

where he's certain there are a lot of small ranches spread out to the east along its banks. Perhaps he can befriend a rancher and hopefully find some work … maybe breaking some horses or rounding up strays. From here, he can ride down across the border and have a look at those gold mines he's heard about.

Sometimes the perfect hideout is in plain sight, he tells himself with a sly laugh.

Chavez knows he is getting close to the river. His horse can smell the water and wants to run. Chavez wisely pulls back on the reins and keeps his horse at a slow walk. Chavez always wants to keep his horse fresh, so he can outrun a posse if the need arises.

He looks up and sees a small dust cloud in the distance. He is now in a place where there are some small hills and he rides to the top of one for a better vantage point. He ducks behind some bushes and waits for a moment. Soon, he sees a stage coach come over a distant hill and disappear down the other side. From here, Chavez can also see the river, which winds along in a westerly direction.

Like the river, the stage is also heading west. It looks like a Concord coach and he can see that it will pass by him only a short distance ahead. Chavez can't help his excitement. After all, he is a bandit, and it's usually pretty easy to get the drop on a stage coach. Even when you're alone.

But it would not be good to hold up this stage, he decides. He's only a day's ride from Yuma and a posse could be back here to look for him by tomorrow afternoon, and he has hidden his trail well. "No, I will not rob this stage," he tells himself, but he does ride ahead a bit to be closer to the stage when it passes.

He grabs his horse by the reins and slowly walks it ahead, careful not to raise any dust and give his position away. Shortly, he sees the stage road just ahead and hides his horse out of sight and climbs a little knoll overlooking the road.

He sees the dust cloud coming closer and soon can hear the stage, which rounds a corner and heads toward him. He can see the driver and a man riding shotgun. A couple of men with rifles could take care of him, he thinks, but, aah, this would be so easy from here. The element of surprise always makes all the difference.

But he remains perfectly still as the stage rides past. He can see the passengers in the coach; four men and one woman – and a pretty woman at that, he thinks. But he lets them pass and when they are out of sight, he thinks out loud, "They never knew the danger they were in." He then lets out a little laugh, but catches himself, and rechecks to make sure there are no other dust clouds in sight.

He climbs back on his horse and continues to ride east for a while. He knows he must find a place to cross the road without leaving any tracks and after a few miles he comes to a place where the ground is hard pan. It is old sedimentary rock that was once the ocean floor. It was lifted up over millions of years until it got exposed to the surface. Then the wind and the summer monsoonal rains scoured the rocks, leaving them swept clean of sand and dirt, with only a small bush able to grow out of a crack here and there.

"This will do," he says to himself, and soon the road is well behind as he turns north again.

He picks a wash that gives him an easy ride down to the river. At the riverbank, he stops and looks things over. His horse really wants to get a drink now and Chavez has to fight with him a little to hold him back. “Easy now,” he tells him, “I’ll let you drink in a while. We will camp here and tomorrow we will cross the river and follow it. Then we will have much water to drink.”

After letting his horse drink a little water, Chavez finds himself a campsite up away from the river and settles in for the night. It’s a beautiful night, warm and still, as only a night in the southwest desert can be. It seems like he can touch the stars. “What are they?” he thinks, something he has wondered about ever since he was a little boy. Chavez watches some small bats flying around.

His mind wanders back to his childhood and the words Mrs. Ramirez said this morning. He remembers how his mother had wept the last time he rode off. He told her not to cry, that he would be back someday, but she feared otherwise. “No, you will not be back,” she cried. “You will be killed. You will die an outlaw’s death.”

Now he thinks she is probably right. He’s got a $2,000 reward on his head and that’s a lot of money. He has to be careful, ever cautious. Never can he relax, even for a moment.

Suddenly, in the darkness he catches a glimpse of movement behind a bush off to his left and in one smooth motion, he quickly draws and cocks his gun. Something has moved in the shadows; he can’t make it out, but something is behind a small bush. It moves again, and Chavez’s keen eyes make it out to be a coyote, crouching behind the bush watching him.

Chavez points his gun at the coyote, which doesn’t move, not knowing if it has been spotted yet. Chavez is hungry, having eaten only the warm biscuits and some jerky given him by Mrs. Ramirez this morning. He has some beans and rice, but he would have to cook those, and he dares not start a fire. It could be seen or smelled for miles. It'll be jerky again.

He would welcome some fresh meat, but even he has never eaten a coyote, and to fire off a shot is unthinkable.

"No, senor coyote, I will not kill you," he says to himself, "for I am just like you." He smiles.

A Chinaman once told him that when a man dies, he gets reincarnated and comes back as an animal. "I would like to be a coyote," thinks Chavez, "yes, a lonely coyote. That would be the animal for me."

Chavez hears another coyote yip from off in the distance and the one behind the bush turns and silently scampers off to join the others.

"Yes, I would be a coyote," Chavez thinks again as he drifts off to sleep.

The next morning, he saddles up and lets his horse drink some water, but not too much. "You always have to be ready," he tells his horse again, stroking its neck. He crosses the river, which is only a few feet deep here, and turns north again.

"No good riding this close to the river," he thinks, "where I'd be more likely to come across someone."

He rides for a while and eventually starts to see small ranches off toward the river. He has seen a lot of cattle since yesterday, many with different brands.

After another night without a hot meal, he is awoken the next morning by the rumbling of his own tummy. That afternoon, Chavez comes upon a couple of cowboys driving some cattle and he rides up to where they can see him. He waves to them and they cautiously wave back as he rides up to greet them. He sees that one is tall and lean, with skin that has seen too many years in the sun and wind. He watches the other one, who is smaller and younger, from the corner of his eye as the man maneuvers around his flank to cover the older one.

The first one just sits and stares at Chavez, saying nothing.

Chavez smiles, and asks, “Who is the owner of this ranch, senor?”

“It is Charles Baker’s ranch and you are trespassing,” he quickly replies. “You’d better have a good reason to be here, mister. We’ve got orders to run off trespassers. The hard way ….”

Chavez stops listening as he turns his horse slightly so he can see the second cowboy. He notices that he has his hand on his pistol grip. “I could outdraw him,” Chavez thinks to himself. “The man is wearing gloves! A good gunman, a really fast gunman, always takes off his glove on his gun hand. It slows you down too much; you can not feel the hammer. … You must know precisely where the hammer is and you feel for it with your thumb. And you also must have complete trigger control.”

A man with a glove on loses much of his trigger control and may even discharge the weapon early, shooting himself in the leg or the foot.

“No, a real gunman would never keep on a glove,” Chavez concludes, “maybe on the other hand for fanning the hammer, but not on his gun hand.”

While the first man continues to talk, Chavez continues to size up the situation.

“If it comes to shooting,” he decides to himself, “I will shoot this second man first. The first man won’t be a problem … his hands are still on his reins and resting on his saddle horn." He notices the first man has finished with his warning.

"Well," Chavez replies, smiling friendly, "the hard way … let's hope it does not come to that. I would like to speak with Senor Baker. My name is Jose Espinosa and I'm looking for work as a ranch hand."

"Mr. Baker is at the ranch right now," the first cowboy says, "and that's where we're going, so if you want to speak with him, you can ride along with us."

"Si, si," Chavez says. "Gracias, amigos." Chavez falls back and off to the side a little as he follows the first man. The land is open enough here so he can ride out of the dust the cattle are raising. The second cowboy takes position on the other side and Chavez can see that he's watching him closely.

The sun is going down by the time they reach the ranch house. The ranch owner sees them coming and notices that a stranger is with them. He comes out to see who it is. Chavez introduces himself as Jose Espinosa and the owner says, "I'm Charles Baker," shaking his hand. Even though the man must be in his 60s, Chavez notices he has a powerful grip. A grip gotten from decades of hard work, he reasons.

"I lost some horses down by the border," Espinosa explains. "I'm about out of food and I'm looking for a place to work for a time until I can round them up."

He can see Charlie Baker sizing him up, mulling it over.

"I can break caballos or repair fences or just about any ranch work. I've been a vaquero all my life," Espinosa adds.

Chavez can see Baker's brow unfurl and he knows he's passed muster. "Sure. Be glad to have some extra help," Baker says to him. "Got lots of work and lots of grub, but I'm short on spending money so I can't pay you nothing."

"That would be all right," Espinosa agrees. "I might stay for three or four weeks."

"That's fine," Baker replies. "The bunkhouse is right over there. Supper is at the ranch house an hour after dark and work starts early. Breakfast is at sunup."

"Gracias, Senor Baker, I appreciate it," says Espinosa.

Baker turns to one of the other two men. "Joey," he says to the older cowboy, "show Jose here where he can keep his horse."

"Sure thing, Mr. Baker," he says, and then turning to Espinosa adds, "Follow me."

***

The next day, a man arrives at the Baker ranch, a man who works for King Woolsey, who is one of the largest cattle ranchers around these parts and also owner of some of the stage stations along the Gila River. Luis Raggio has been instructed by Woolsey to deliver some cattle to the Baker ranch: four bulls to be added to the breeding stock. He drives them in and puts them in a large pen.

He then rides up to a man working on a fence nearby, and even from behind, he recognizes Clodoveo Chavez instantly. The two had grown up together in Monterey County south of San Francisco and while they weren't exactly best friends, they knew each other well. All the *californios* of Mexican descent did.

Raggio is one of the few men who knows that the scar on Chavez's face came from being kicked by a horse when he was 15 years old, and not from some knife fight as one would suspect. Raggio was even there the day it happened.

"Clodoveo, what a surprise!" Raggio exclaims. "I didn't know you were around here?"

At the mention of his name, Chavez's hand drops to his gun. He turns quickly and is as surprised to see Raggio as his childhood pal is to see the bandit.

Chavez then looks around to see if anyone could have heard him being addressed by his real name. Satisfied, he turns back to Raggio and says quietly, "It's good to see you, Luis, but I'm going by the name of Jose Espinosa now."

"Oh, I'm sorry, Clodoveo," says Raggio, quickly realizing his mistake and apologizing again as Chavez glares at him. "Yes, yes, it's Jose. I will remember."

"Good," says Chavez. "You better."

"So, uh, Jose, I haven't seen you in a few years," Raggio inquires, fully knowing the answer.

"Well, I've been kind of on the move these last few years," Chavez says. "You know, business and all."

Just then, Charles Baker rides up to the two men and can see by their expressions that this is not their first meeting. He turns to Luis, whom he's never met, and asks, "You the man that Woolsey sent with the bulls?"

"Si, Senor Baker, I'm Luis Raggio and the bulls are in that pen over there." Raggio points to a corral next to the barn.

"Okay, good," Baker says. "Let's go take a look at them." He spurs his horse toward the corral. As he does, he hears Espinosa say to Raggio, "Luis, come back and talk to me before you leave."

"I will," Luis says as he climbs on his own horse

and follows Mr. Baker.

"This could complicate things," Chavez thinks to himself. "Luis knows way too much about me." He knows he could trust Luis when they were kids, but he didn't have a reward on his head then.

Down at the bull pen, Charles Baker likes what he sees. "Yup, just like Woolsey promised. Good stock," he says, looking the bulls over. "Si, senor!" Luis replies. "Mr. Woolsey brought them down from his ranch up near Prescott, twenty-five in all. These four are the best ones."

"Good," says Baker. "Tell Woolsey I'll take 'em."

"I will, Mr. Baker," Luis says. He gets back on his horse and trots back over to where Clodoveo, er, Jose is working on the fence still.

"Aah, Luis," Chavez begins, "you know it is good to see you."

Luis is a little nervous at the tone of Chavez's voice, but replies, "Same here."

Chavez steps closer and lowers his voice. "You know," he says, "that I can't afford to have anyone find out my real identity."

"Si, of course," Raggio concurs. "I won't tell anybody. Not a soul, I promise."

"Good," Chavez replies. "I don't want to have to worry about you. You are my friend. I'll trust you to keep my secret."

"You're my friend too," Luis replies. "You can trust me."

"Okay," Chavez says, "but just remember, I'm very serious about this."

Luis manages a smile and in a hushed voice says, "Clodoveo, I would do nothing to harm you. You are like a brother to me."

“Si, we had some good times growing up together, no?” Chavez says to him.

“Yeah,” Luis recalls, trying to remember one that didn’t involve Chavez bullying him or one of the other smaller boys. “Like the time we stole that bottle of whiskey from that gringo? He was passed out on his porch and you snuck up and took the bottle right out of his hands!”

“I remember,” Chavez smiles. “Then we got so drunk down by the creek that you fell in.”

“Yeah, that was the first time I ever got drunk,” Luis laughs, so drunk that he only has a vague recollection that Clodoveo actually pushed him in. But he’s not about to bring that up now. “Those are fond memories,” is what he says instead.

He notices Clodoveo relax a bit as they talk and that is a good thing, Raggio thinks. “I think I can trust you,” Chavez finally says to him. “I’d like you to come riding with me. Can you get a few days off and come with me down toward the border?”

“Sure, I guess,” Raggio replies warily.

“I’ve got some horses down there that I, uh, lost in a thunderstorm,” explains Chavez, “and I need to go and see if I can find any of them. It will take me another day to finish this fence. How about the day after tomorrow?”

“Okay,” says Raggio. “I’ll see you then, but I’ve got to be getting back to Woolsey’s ranch now. He’s expecting me.”

Luis mounts up and, remembering Chavez’s warning, says, “Goodbye, Jose. I’ll see you in two days.” He spurs his horse and it bolts across the yard, past the corner of the barn and heads down the road out of sight.

“Phew!” thinks Raggio, breathing a little easier

now that he's beyond the wary eye of Chavez. He slows his horse, but can't slow his mind. He plays out the events of the past few minutes, trying to figure out what it means.

"Chavez, right here at the Baker ranch," Raggio thinks to himself. "A man with a $2,000 reward on his head."

Raggio's heart is racing wildly and he still can't quite catch his breath.

"Two-thousand dollars!"

Raggio kicks his horse now and rides quickly down the familiar trail toward Woolsey's Agua Caliente ranch.

"Two-thousand dollars. My God, two-thousand dollars."

Chapter 13

A fast-moving stagecoach comes bouncing into the town of Campo. It pulls up in front of the store, scurrying some chickens that have been scratching at the dirt in the street. Often customers leaving the store will lose a few kernels or seeds out of the heavy bags they are carrying and the chickens are always there to clean up the mess.

The driver throws the brake on the mud wagon and the stage jerks to a stop. The door opens and a tall, wiry man steps out and stretches his weary limbs. A twelve-plus-hour stagecoach ride east from San Diego over the foothills of southern California can be a tiresome affair.

"Uncle Silas! Uncle Silas!" yells a boy to the man getting off the stage. Silas Gaskill turns around to see his nephew, Walter, running up to him. Walter has been playing among the rocks off to the side of the store. He's got a stick in his hand, pretending it's a rifle.

"Hi, Walter," Silas says as the boy runs up, "Whatcha hunting for?"

"Bears!" exclaims the six year old. "I'm shooting grizzlies just like you and Pa used to. I got me one up in them rocks and I'm going to go up there and root him out of there."

"Well, good luck," says Silas, "but you just keep an eye out for rattlesnakes when you're playing up in those rocks, you hear?"

"Yes, sir," promises Walter, who turns and runs back toward the rocks, yelling, "Look out Mister Bear, I'm coming to get you."

Silas smiles. "Walter is a good kid," he says to himself. "Wouldn't it be nice to have one of my own? Maybe I should find myself a new wife and have some children. I'm already 45 years old; I better do it before it's too late.

"Maybe if I could find the right woman. Maybe I *should* start a family," he continues to think. "Hell, I could still live to see most of my grandchildren get born…."

"Here you go, Silas," someone says, interrupting his thoughts. He turns around and sees the stagecoach driver handing down his carpet bag from atop the stage. He takes it and says, "Thanks, Jeb. You know, I don't think you missed *any* of the bumps this time."

"No, not a one!" Jeb replies as he spits out a squirt of tobacco and manages a half-serious smile. "I got 'em all, just for you … no extra charge."

"Thanks again," adds Silas, as he turns and walks up the steps of the store. Inside, he sees Lumen and Jack Kelly sitting at a table playing poker for matchsticks. Lumen's pile is very large and Jack's pile is very small. Silas steps through the door, propped open by a smooth stone from the creek, and walks in.

"Howdy," Silas says to the men, who return the greeting. "Looks to me that you're losing, Jack," he says to Kelly.

"Yup, I swear he's cheating," Jack says, "but I just can't prove it."

"That's because I'm not," Lumen lets out with a laugh. "If I really was cheating, then I would've had all your matchsticks long before now."

"Well, you might be just about to have them all," Jack concedes, as he looks at his cards one more time and then slides the rest of his sticks into the pile in the middle of the table. “Call,” he says. “Two pair … tens and deuces. What do you have?”

“Sorry, three ladies,” Lumen delights, laying them down in front of him and letting out another laugh as he pulls the rest of the matchsticks over to his pile.

Jack throws his cards down on the table in mock disgust. “See what I mean?” he says. “It happens every time I play him.”

“Any word about the Chavez gang?” Silas asks.

“No, not that I’ve heard of,” Lumen replies. “It’s been real quiet; too quiet and I don’t like it.”

The men look at each other somberly.

“So,” Lumen says, turning to Silas, “did the sheriff have anything to say to you?”

“No, Lumen, not a peep,” replies Silas, setting down his carpet bag next to the counter and reaching for a shot glass and a half-empty bottle of whiskey.

“Good, then,” says Lumen. “So how did the beekeepers’ meeting go in town?”

“About as I expected,” says Silas. “We got to the meeting right after the Webb trial got out. John Harbison had to testify at the trial and then we all went over to Horton Hall and had the meeting. It seems that Harbison has had a lot of his apiaries destroyed by cattle or sheep lately, so he wants to change California’s ‘no fence law’ so he can fence in the apiaries that he’s got on public land.”

Kelly is listening intently. Of all the Gaskills’ dealings, he knows the least about the beekeeping business, which just might be the brothers’ best source of income. They have become by most counts one of the largest sellers of honey in all of southern California and perhaps even the country.

"Right now," Silas continues, "the law gives rights only to owners of cultivated land. Only they are able to collect on damages caused by free-ranging cattle and sheep. Harbison passed around a petition to change the law to include beekeepers who are keeping bees on government lands, and then to be able to fence in their apiaries.

"There were a lot of people there and some of them asked me what I thought about the 'no fence law,'" Silas goes on. "They all know we are on both sides of the issue, being both large cattle ranchers and beekeepers."

"That's true," says Lumen. "So what did you tell them?"

"I told them that we really don't have much trouble keeping our cattle out of our apiaries. And if we did have trouble, we would simply move the cattle or move the colonies. Anyway, we all agreed that we should form a San Diego Beekeepers Association. I was appointed to the sub-committee. We drew up a memorandum to be circulated for signatures and most everyone signed it.

"Harbison was so busy shaking hands with everyone that I didn't even get to talk to him after the meeting," Silas continues. "But I did stop over at Steiner and Klauber before I left. Klauber told me that they received all the honey we freighted them last month … seven-hundred and fifty-two pounds of honeycombs and thirty two barrels of honey. He's going to ship it to San Francisco on the steamer and sell some of it to other shippers there, then ship the rest of it by rail back East … New York or Boston, maybe.

"When he gets back, he'll deposit our share into

our bank account and then will wire us the amount we received from the sale so we can enter it in our ledgers."

Silas finishes the story and can finally knock back the drink he has poured.

"Good," Lumen says. "That's over two-thousand pounds of honey and combs we have shipped to San Diego this year. So I guess now is the time to go and build us some more hives. Get them ready and then in the spring, maybe we can put out another two hundred more or so.

"And we've already got some good rain this fall," Lumen continues, "and if the weather keeps going like this into the winter, we should have plenty of wild buckwheat blossoms come spring. Should raise honey production by about ten to twenty percent next year, I reckon.

"What do you think, Silas?"

"Sounds about right," he replies. "Klauber told me he can sell just about all the honey we can ship him. I'll get the lumber together to build the apiaries. I know a new place we can put some … on government land … over past the west end of Hauser Canyon there's a nice valley backed by a big mountain. I found it hunting last spring. The whole mountainside is full of buckwheat bushes and I think we could put a couple hundred new hives out there. Or maybe two colonies with a hundred each, about a mile apart."

"Sounds good," Lumen replies. "We'll need to spread them out as much as we can to get the most honey from our hives as possible."

So far, Kelly has remained silent, listening intriguingly to the conversation.

Finally, he can't control himself. "Why is this wild

buckwheat so important to making honey?" he blurts out.

"It's because," Lumen replies, "the wild buckwheat blossoms make some of the best honey in the world. And that's what makes San Diego County honey so special, because we've got the best climate for them to grow them. And sage blossoms, clover and others. … But, you see, you don't always get a lot of buckwheat honey every year. In order to get a lot of buckwheat blossoms, you really need a wet winter, to really get the bushes flowering."

"Yeah," adds Silas, "you won't get a lot of wild buckwheat blossoms if you have a dry winter. During dry winters, the next summer you will get mostly sage and clover honey, and maybe not even much of that. Oh, it's still pretty good honey, but you won't get as much and it won't be as good as the wild buckwheat."

The door of the store opens and Lumen's wife, Eliza, comes in.

"Hello, sorry to interrupt you gentlemen," she says as she walks in, "but Lumen, have you seen Walter?"

"Well, yes, I guess he was in here about a half hour ago," Lumen says, "but I thought he went back home."

"I saw him," Silas says. "He was playing in the rocks behind the store when I got off the stage about twenty minutes ago."

"Oh, thank you, Silas," she says. "C'mon, Lumen, let's go find the little scalawag."

He grabs her hand and leads her toward the door.

"Don't worry, dear, he couldn't have gone far," Lumen says.

"Yeah," says Silas, "he's just got a grizzly bear cornered up there somewhere. Nothin' to worry about."

But, of course, he's not a parent, least not that's he's aware of.

"Walter! Walter!" he hears from the street as Lumen and his wife look for the boy.

"I guess the apple doesn't fall very far from the tree," Jack Kelly observes.

"What do you mean?" asks Silas.

"Well," Jack replies, "you and Lumen used to hunt grizzly bears up in the north, right? I heard that you two killed a lot of bears. More than anyone else has ever done."

"Well, that's true," says Silas, "I shot a lot more than Lumen, though. I got to California in 1850, but Lumen didn't get here 'til '57. And he was still young then.

"But, you're right," continues Silas, "I reckon that Walter, he's got hunting in his blood. Just like Lumen and me. Our dad taught us to hunt at an early age, and at about nine or ten years old we were carrying rifles of our own, hunting and bringing down big game. It won't be long before Walter is ready to learn himself."

"So," Jack says, "how many bears did you kill up north?"

"Myself?" Silas says, thinking, "I guess I killed a might over three hundred. I sold the meat in the gold camps. The miners needed the meat to eat, beef being too expensive for most of them. I made more money hunting grizzes than I ever made panning for gold."

Kelly shakes his head in amazement. "Hunting grizzly bears sounds too dangerous for me," he says.

"It can be," says Silas, "if you don't know what you're doing. You want to kill it in one shot, which is hard to do if you don't know how. All we had back then were muzzle-loading rifles so I liked to carry two fifty-caliber Hawkinses, just to be on the safe side. Most of the time I would drop them with one shot and that is the key to safe grizzly hunting. That, and you got to hunt downwind of where you expect to find them darn brutes. If he can smell you, you won't be able to get close enough to put a bullet in him.

"And even if you do, he will know where you are and just might get you before he dies," Silas continues, remembering many a close call. "Even when you place the shot carefully, and get him through the heart, he can still live for up to a minute or so. And that is all the time he needs to kill you."

Kelly shudders.

"So, you've got to wait for the shot," Silas goes on, "one that you know that you can make, one that will take him down quickly. And if he don't go right down, and he don't know where you are, you might be able to get a second shot into him…."

Kelly can't contain himself. "Did you have many that didn't go right down?" Jack asks excitedly.

"Sure," Silas says, "I had to trail many a wounded bear. That can sometimes be a scary thing. They like to head for a cave or a thicket or swamp or something like that … anything they can hide up in. And they will wait for you to come in and get 'em."

"Whoa," says Jack, "what do you do then?"

"Wait them out," says Silas. "You certainly don't go stomping right on in after them. You check the wind, see which way it's blowing. If a grizzly can smell you, he will know for sure right where you are and be ready for you. And you only follow his trail when the wind is in your favor. If the wind is not in your favor you can circle around him, try to get him from behind. But the main thing is to wait him out; you don't need to hurry, he'll be there when you get there. There are not too many other animals out there that'll chew on a grizzly bear."

"How about the ones that stayed to fight?" questions Kelly.

"Well, that was what the second rifle was for," Silas continues. "And if that weren't enough, I would head up the nearest, tallest tree. One big enough that a grizzly couldn't tip over or chew through."

"Wow," says Kelly, "did things like that really happen to you?"

"Sure," Silas replies, "every now and again. You know, once a grizzly chased me up a tree and kept me there all night and well into the next afternoon."

"How'd you get down?" asks Kelly.

"Well, the grizz was a monster brute," Silas recalls, "well over a thousand pounds, at least. I had put two good shots into him and it didn't seem to affect him at all. I just had time enough to drop my guns and climb a good, tall oak tree. I was lucky one was nearby that I could jump up and just barely grab the lowest branch and swing up to another branch and climb up to a safe perch. Well, that bear was so mad … it tried to climb the tree … it clawed at it … and it dug at the ground and tried to root up the tree. I knew I was safe as long as I stayed up there.

"He stayed down there rooting and clawing until after dark and all night long I could hear him breathing and moving around a bit, so I knew he was still there," Silas continues. "I didn't dare sleep at all. Then as the sun came up I could see him laying on the ground about twenty feet from the tree. He would look up at me, get all mad again, and root and snarl and try to climb my tree.

"After a few hours, he started to get bored and wandered off a bit. I waited a while and then decided to try to retrieve one of my guns. But every time I'd get to the bottom limb, that bear would come a'chargin' back, sending me scurrying back up the tree like a squirrel."

Silas laughs as he remembers his plight.

"Well, finally he left and I made it to the bottom branch. I waited a while, thinking he was hiding waiting for me to come down, but when he didn't come back I decided to take a chance. I could see my second Hawkins rifle – the one I tied a sling to – on the ground about ten feet from the bottom of the tree. I knew if I could just get that gun and get back up into the tree again, I'd be able to reload and shoot the bear when it returned.

"After waiting on the bottom branch for about half an hour or so and still no bear, I jumped down to the ground, slung the Hawkins over my shoulder and scrambled back up that tree."

"And the bear didn't come back?" Jack asks.

"No," Silas replies. "I reloaded that Hawkins and waited for the bear to come back. It started to get on toward late afternoon and it still didn't come back, so I figured that it had gone somewhere else, so I climbed down from the tree and started looking around. After I loaded my other gun, I searched around and I found the blood trail and checked the wind. It was in my favor, so I quietly followed the trail and shortly I found the bear dead in a little thicket."

"Wow," says Jack again, "the grizzly was dead?"

"Yup," says Silas, "it had lost so much blood it bled out, I reckon."

"We found Walter!" Silas and Jack look up to see Lumen coming back into the store. "He was playing right where you said he was Silas."

"Good," says Silas. "Well, Jack, I've got to get over to the blacksmith shop and see what needs to be done. I'll see you later."

"Amazing," Kelly says again, shaking his head and talking more to himself than to Silas. "I'll see you later, too."

Chapter 14

It's late afternoon in Tecarte. Chavez rode off to Arizona a week ago. The stolen horses that had been kept in Horsethief Canyon were brought into town around noon by Fedoro Vasquez, Alvijo and Alvitro. Four horses were missing and still somewhere in the canyon. Cruz Lopez had found a nice stable on the outskirts of town to keep the horses in, one that was out of the sight of any curious eyes. He is not too happy about the missing horses.

Five bandits are in the cantina drinking and having a good time. They are sitting at the back table, the same one that Chavez and Lopez had taken over. They are alone in the cantina except for three men who had entered a few minutes ago and are standing at the bar having a drink, talking quietly amongst themselves.

The bandidos are getting drunk and a little loud. Two of the three men at the bar recognize them, having heard earlier in the day that the gang was in town, and they wisely mind their own business. The third man doesn't know any of the bandits, but like everyone in the Southwest in the 1870s, Benito Garcia has heard the legendary stories of the famous Chavez gang.

Garcia is on his way back to his ranch in a little valley south of Las Juntas after delivering a wagonload of honey to San Diego and he has stopped in Tecarte to visit his cousin Pablo and his friend Jorge. Of course, that means a stop in the cantina for a drink.

"Tequila, por favor," Garcia says a bit too loudly to the bartender as they all notice the commotion coming from the table in the back. "Shhh!" says Pablo to Benito under his breath. "Talk quietly. If those men are part of the Chavez gang as I have heard, we don't want to draw any attention to ourselves. They are very dangerous men."

"Si," adds Jorge, "very dangerous men. Have you not heard of them?" he asks Benito.

"Si," Garcia whispers, sneaking a peek in their direction. "Certainly I have heard of them; who hasn't? But I did not know they were anywhere near here. I thought they were up north robbing the gringo towns and stagecoaches there."

"Yes, that is what we thought too," answers Jorge. "We don't know why they are here. Some say they are hiding from the gringo posses who are looking for them."

"Well, let's have a quick drink and get out of here then, while we still can," says Benito, not wanting any trouble either.

They all toss down their shots of tequila and the first two start for the door. But as Garcia pays the bartender for the drinks and turns to follow, he overhears one word from somewhere in the back of the room that nearly stops him dead in his tracks: "Campo."

Instead of following the other two out the door, Garcia stops for a moment to strike a match on the wall and calmly takes three quick puffs on a cigar to bring it to life. As he does so, he listens carefully to the conversation going on in the back of the room.

"We are going to rob the Campo store," he hears another bandit say in a drunken slur, "and we are going to kill all of them gringo bastards." "Si, si," all the other bandits chime in. They all begin to laugh as Garcia steps through the door into the darkening street to join the others.

"So, they are going to rob Campo and kill

everyone in town," Garcia says to himself as he takes a long draw on his cigar. The words race through his mind a second time. "I must ride ahead and warn Silas. He had helped me before and I must help him"

He walks over to the hitching post where Pablo and Jorge are waiting.

"So, you still going to stay the night?" Pablo asks his cousin.

"No, I don't think so," Benito replies. "I can still make a few miles before nightfall, so I think I will be on my way."

"Well," Pablo says, a bit surprised, "you know you have a place to stay anytime you come to Tecarte."

"Gracias, Pablo," replies Garcia, "and if you come near my small rancho, you will always be welcome. And you too," he adds, turning to Jorge.

"Gracias," Jorge says. "I might just take you up on that someday."

Benito climbs up on the wagon seat. "Well, amigos, I must be going," he says as he unties the reins and slaps them gently on his horses' backs. "Adios."

The wagon lurches gently forward and Benito turns back and waves as he disappears around the corner and heads out of town.

"I thought he was going to spend the night?" Jorge finally says to Pablo, a bit confused.

"Si, me too," Pablo replies. "Maybe the Chavez gang being in town scared him off. Anyway, I don't think we should go back in the cantina tonight. I've got a bottle of tequila back at my house. It might be safer to go back and drink there, don't you think?"

"Sounds good to me," agrees Jorge, giving a quick look back to the cantina and the danger within. "Let's go."

Back in the cantina, things are getting heated as the bandits continue to drink.

"That's right, when Chavez gets back we will ride into Campo, rob the town and kill anyone who gets in our way," Lopez says again, as if the whole idea was his.

"When is Chavez going to return?" asks Vasquez.

"In about four weeks or so," Lopez replies, downing another shot of tequila.

"So what did he say for us to do until then?" Vasquez goes on.

"I am going to bring those horses," he says, waving in the direction of the corral the stolen horses are being kept in just outside town, "and I am going to take them down to the Mendosa rancho in Las Hurtos and sell them. And while I'm doing that, you and Alvitro here will go back to the canyon and round up the missing horses and any strays that you can find and bring them back here."

Vasquez, clearly irritated, cuts Lopez off. "Why don't I bring the horses to Mendosa?" he demands. "After all, Chavez told me I was to be the one to do it, remember?"

"Well, he changed his mind," Lopez shoots right back. "Anyways, he left me in charge and that is what I am telling you to do."

"Left *you* in charge?" Vasquez shouts out. "I'm not taking any orders from you. You're not *my* boss. If anyone should be left in charge it should be me. I am Fedoro Vasquez, the nephew of Tiburcio Vasquez and this was his gang. He was the leader for over twenty years and I have been in the gang for longer than anyone else except Chavez."

"Maybe so," Lopez counters, "but he told me before he left, right at this very table, to take command in his absence."

"Well, we will settle that when Chavez comes back," Vasquez states boldly.

"Why not settle it right now?" Lopez fires back.

Vasquez looks at Lopez and sees that his left hand is under the table, probably with a pistol in it, he reckons. He glances at Cruz's buddy, Alvijo, whose hand has just slowly dropped to the butt of his pistol.

"Bad odds," Vasquez thinks. "Very bad odds."

"No," Vasquez finally says, "we will wait for Chavez to come back. I'm going out to check on the horses."

"Yeah, you do that," Lopez says as Vasquez turns his back on the killer and grabs a bottle of tequila off the bar as he walks toward the door, all the while wondering if he's about to get shot in the back. But he hears no report as he steps through the cantina door into a street that is now dark. He turns and walks down the street toward where he knows the horses are being kept.

Back in the bar, Lopez says to Alvitro, "So what about you?"

"What do you mean?" Poncho asks, a bit alarmed.

"Whose side are you on?" Lopez demands. "You and Vasquez have been hanging around together ever since you joined the gang."

"Si, that is true," Alvitro says, "but I'm not going to take sides here. This is between you and him."

"Good," says Cruz, "you are a wise man. Don't let me down and I won't have to kill you."

"Ha, ha, ha," Lopez and Alvitro laugh together as if it were a joke, but both know otherwise.

"I won't let you down, Cruz," Poncho replies.

"Let's have a toast," Lopez offers. They grab the bottle in front of them and each takes a long, hard pull.

Outside, Alonzo Cota and Rafael Martinez are walking up the main street of Tecarte wearing the pistols they took from the vaqueros the week before.

"So we both agree," Cota says, and Martinez adds quickly, "Yes, I agree. It is the only way for us to get some money. Enough money so I can marry Maria. And I will do anything to marry Maria."

"That's right," Cota says, "there is no other way. And we will do it just long enough to make what we need and then we can get out."

"Sure," Martinez replies, "but what should we do now?"

"Well," Alonzo says, "we need to find Senor Chavez and ask him if he still wants us. And the best place to do that is to go back to the cantina and see if he's still there."

"Okay," says Rafael nervously.

They continue up the street and can see a dim light coming from inside the door of the cantina. Muffled voices also come from somewhere inside. They stop out front, still not sure what they'll do next.

"Here it is," Alonzo says, adjusting the pistol in his belt. "Are you ready?"

"Sure," swallows Rafael with trepidation in his voice. "Let's do this."

They walk cautiously inside and the place is empty except for the din they can hear coming from the back.

"Hey, look," they hear Lopez yell from the back table. "This is the wildcat that was in that fight I was telling you about, and his partner," Lopez says to the other two men. "Hey, amigos, come back here."

Cota and Martinez recognize Lopez, but notice that on this night he is drinking with two other men, not Chavez. They walk back to where the men are sitting.

"You should see these boys fight," Lopez tells Alvijo and Alvitro. They all shake hands. "You should have been here that night," Lopez continues. "These two knocked out four armed vaqueros right here in this cantina with their bare fists."

"Oh, it was nothing," offers Cota, "Rafael here did most of the work."

"Si," says Lopez, "that he did, and what brings you two back here?"

"We are looking for Senor Chavez," Cota says.

"Ahh," Lopez replies, "so you have decided to join our gang, huh, amigos?"

"Si," both say at once, looking at each other quickly for reassurance.

"Well, Senor Chavez is away for a few weeks," Lopez tells the men. "He left me in charge and if you would like to join the gang you have to talk to me."

Cota and Martinez look at each other again. They had hoped to speak with Chavez himself.

"Well, if the offer is still open, we would like to join," Alonzo finally says.

"Si," adds Rafael, "we want to make some real money for once in our lives."

The three bandits let out a little laugh.

"And so you shall," Lopez says. "The offer is still open. We need some good men and if you are willing to ride with us to Sonora, you will find what you seek. There are gold strikes down there producing a lot of gold and we plan to raid some of the shipments and miners' payrolls.

"We will make a lot of money," Lopez continues, "but to share in the spoils, you will have to do exactly what Chavez and I say at all times, comprende?"

"Si, si, we will," both reply.

"Good," Lopez says. "We have a small job to do and if you would like, you can ride along with us."

"But we have no horses," Alonzo interrupts, and then wishes he hadn't.

"No problem, amigos," Lopez says with a smile. "We have a few extra mounts that you can use, and some old saddles if you need them."

"Great," Alonzo replies, relieved that Lopez took no offense to his intrusion. "What do you think, Rafael?" he asks his friend.

"Sounds good to me," he says.

"Then it is settled," Lopez decides. "You two meet us at the old stable down by the creek tomorrow at sunrise. We need to move some horses to a rancho about twenty miles distant and then we will ride to San Rafael to do Chavez a favor."

"We will be there," Cota tells the bandits. "Right, Rafael?"

"Si, you can count on us," Martinez assures them.

They turn and walk out of the cantina. Once in the street, Martinez turns to Cota and says, "Well, God help us now."

Chapter 15

Benito Garcia drives his wagon at a normal pace out of town even though his heart is racing wildly. He can't believe it. "The Chavez gang! Right here in Tecarte!" he says out loud, and then catches himself, looking behind him. He can't afford to draw attention to himself with Chavez and his deadly crew right here in Tecarte. Leaving this late, with darkness falling, had not been in his plans but he has to warn Silas Gaskill about what he has overheard.

"They're going to rob the Gaskills' store," he says under his breath, ignoring the urge to look behind him again. "I must warn them."

Almost in a panic, he realizes his team has sped up and he reins them back, trying to think more clearly about what he is doing, his heart still beating wildly.

He figures that he can get a few miles or so out of town before dark. It's a clear night, and if the sky stays fairly bright, he can drive the horses for a while, and when it gets too dark, he reasons, he'll stop to make camp and then get started again at first light. He figures that'll put him in Campo by 9 a.m. at the latest.

Benito drives his team as long as he can and then stops where the road crosses a small creek. A good place to camp, he thinks, with good water and some good grass for the horses. "This will do," he says to himself.

He takes care of the horses and then cooks himself a small meal. It's a cold night, but he lets the fire go out quickly and he shakes out his bedroll in the shadow of a big rock, where he can't be seen. And after a long, uncomfortable night, that's where daylight finds him –

cold and wet from the dew, and exhausted from getting almost no sleep.

After a yawn and a stretch, Benito shakes the dirt off his blanket and rolls it up. Then he hitches the horses to the wagon, picks up camp without taking time for breakfast and drives off toward Campo, just across the border to the northeast.

He doesn't want to somehow get overtaken by the bandits, he thinks over and over again as he pushes the horses harder than they're used to. The day is bright and clear and by the time he arrives in Campo at around nine o'clock it's getting warmer and the temperature has already risen to about 75 degrees.

Garcia stops at the outskirts of town. Campo is such a peaceful little village, he thinks. Looking at it now, it's hard for Benito to imagine the horror that is about to befall this place. He sees black smoke rising steadily from the chimney of the blacksmith shop.

"Looks like Silas is already at work," Benito says to himself as he gently slaps the reins on the backs of the horses, which brings the team into town at a slow walk, so as to raise no alarm.

He sees Silas come out of the blacksmith shop rolling a wagon wheel. He has the wagon with the one missing wheel with the axle up on blocks and he rolls the wheel over and starts to mount it onto the wagon. Out of the corner of his eye, Silas sees Benito Garcia sitting in his wagon looking around.

The sight doesn't sit right with Silas. Garcia was a friendly enough guy when he was last here about three weeks ago, thinks Silas, but he's acting strangely now. "Oh well," Silas says to himself, "if he needs something he will stop over and ask."

Benito gets down from his seat and ties the reins off on the brake lever. He slowly and cautiously walks over to Silas.

"Buenos dias, Senor Gaskill," he says in greeting.

"And buenos dias to you, Benito," Silas answers without looking up as he wrestles to get the wheel back on the axle. "How are you doing?"

"Fine. Just fine," offers Garcia unconvincingly.

"Well, you don't look fine," Silas says with a glance at the man. "Looks like something's gotcha spooked. Your face is pretty white for a Mexican."

"Si, si," Benito says nervously. "Silas, I need to speak with you."

"Sure, go ahead," Silas says. "Is it about your wagon?"

"No, no," Benito says, "the wagon is fine. Silas, this is very important. Can we go into your shop? I don't want to be seen."

Silas stops work on the wheel and stands up. "Yeah, okay," he says, realizing something serious must be wrong. "Come with me," he says, as he wipes his hands on a rag and steps inside the shop. He walks to the back bench where nobody can hear their conversation.

"Watcha got in your craw, Benito?" he asks Garcia.

"Silas, you must not tell anyone that it was I who told you this, you've got to promise me," Garcia begins.

"Sure, you've got my word," says Silas. "This sounds serious."

"It is, Silas, it is," he says. "I was in the cantina in Tecarte yesterday afternoon just before dark and I overheard a group of men that were identified to me as the Chavez gang planning a robbery…."

“The Chavez gang!” interrupts Silas. “So it *is* true. There were rumors around that they might be in this area. Chavez and one of his men were seen at the Sheckler ranch a week or so ago asking for breakfast.”

“Well, there were five of them in the cantina,” Garcia continues, “and all drinking heavily. I heard one of them say they were going to rob Campo….”

“Rob Campo!” Silas interrupts again.

“Yes, that’s what he said,” Garcia goes on, “and then another one said that they would kill anyone who got in their way.”

“Holy cow! Son of a bitch!” exclaims Silas in disbelief.

“It’s true, Silas,” Benito replies. “I heard those very words myself.”

“Did they say when they was coming?” Silas asks.

“No, no,” replies Garcia, “I dared not stay to hear any more. I left as soon as I could and came straight here to warn you.”

“Well, Benito, I’m glad you did,” Silas says. “I gotta tell my brother about this right away and get the town prepared. They might strike today.”

“I know, Silas,” Benito says, “but I do not want anyone to know that it was me who brought you this information. Those banditos, the Chavez gang, are very bad men and they would come after me for sure.”

“You’re right there,” says Silas. “So what would you have me do?”

“Well, if you could just let me get out of town before you give the alarm, that would help some,” Garcia requests.

“All right,” Silas replies.

“Gracias, amigo,” thanks Garcia.

"No, thank *you*," Silas says back to him. "Benito, I know the risk you're taking and I really appreciate it."

"Thank you," Garcia says again. "You helped me out the last time I was here and I owe you for that. Now I must go back to my little valley in Mexico.

"Good luck, Silas," Garcia says as they shake hands. "I hope you men can handle them. I only saw five of them in the cantina, but I would bet there will be more."

"Me too," Silas says. "Thanks to you we will be ready."

Benito hurriedly returns to his wagon and in a minute he's out of sight, leaving town going east on the road to Jacumba – away from Tecarte and hopefully away from the bandits.

* * *

Luis Raggio arrives at the Baker ranch at 9 in the morning. Chavez is already waiting for him and eager to get on the trail. He doesn't like to be kept waiting. It's a perfect day for riding as it's not too hot and the wind hasn't started to blow yet. They ride south for the rest of the day, making only small talk as they work their way through the Mohawk Mountains.

By nightfall, they are very near the border and decide to camp there. Luis looks for some firewood, and except for some dry greasewood in the wash, there's nothing much around. He walks up a small hill and on the other side, atop a small 20-foot cliff, he finds a long ironwood branch.

Ironwood is so dense that it won't burn very well unless you break it into small pieces. It might have been sitting here for 50 years or more, he thinks, but it's far too heavy for him to drag back to camp. Instead, he manhandles the branch over to the edge of the cliff and pushes it off. The old, dry branch shatters into small pieces as it hits the rocks below.

"Hmmm," Raggio thinks, "this just might work!" Luis chuckles at his ingenuity and makes his way down to retrieve some of the shattered pieces. When he returns, he finds that Clodoveo already has a fire going, so Luis simply adds the pieces of ironwood to the flames.

In about half an hour the fire is burning so hot that they have to move back to keep from getting scorched. Luis pulls out some jerky to go with the hot coffee they have just made. He also brought some bread and a jar of honey. They devour the whole loaf and then lean back against a rock to talk a spell.

"You want some more coffee?" Luis asks. "No," Clodoveo replies, "I'll just drink what I've got."

After a moment, Luis finally works up the courage to ask Chavez the question he's wanted to since he first saw him at Baker's ranch two days ago. "So, tell me what happened to Vasquez?" Luis asks. "How did he get captured so easily?"

Chavez had been wondering how long it would take Luis to get around to asking about Vasquez.

"He got set up by a man called Greek George," Clodoveo replies. "Tiburcio was messing with his woman and he turned him in for a cut of the reward money, that's what I think. I'll kill that bastard if I ever see him again."

"So it was the sheriff in Los Angeles that got him, not Morse?" Raggio asks.

"That devil Morse tracked us all the way to the hills outside Los Angeles and we didn't even know it,"

Chavez explains, "and I tried to convince Vasquez we were hanging around Greek George's too long. But he wouldn't quit this woman.

"Morse might have got all of us, cuz he found out where we were," Chavez continues. "Someone tipped him off. But he took the information to Rowland and that skunk double-crossed him. He told Morse his information was unreliable and sent him back north. Seems Rowland already had made a deal with Greek George. Rowland was too yellow even to do the job himself. He sent his deputy and five other men instead and they surprised Vasquez and shot and wounded him."

"You weren't with him then?" Raggio inquires.

"No, me and another man rode out a couple days before that," Chavez says. "But when I heard Vasquez was in jail, I turned back and went to see him."

"No!" exclaims Luis. "You went to visit him in jail? How'd you pull that off?"

"I just put on a disguise, walked in the front door and asked to see him," Chavez explains, letting out a big laugh along with Raggio. "He was quite a celebrity, you know, and everyone went to the jail asking to see him. I just waited until I knew that Rowland was not there and his deputies didn't recognize me. They searched me and let me right in."

Chavez and Raggio laugh again at the stupidity of the gringos.

"So what'd he say?" Raggio inquires further.

"At first he didn't recognize me either," Chavez says, "and we got a good laugh out of that. He said he noticed when they brought him in that there was a wanted poster for me on the wall and I must've walked right past it on the way in!"

Chavez and Raggio laugh even louder.

"I told Vasquez that I would get the gang together and bust him out," Chavez goes on, "but he told me, no, that he was certain he would get clear of the charges, since it was Abdon Leiva and Romulo Gonzalez that killed those men at Tres Pinos, not him. He said not to risk it.

"Then a few days later, he was put aboard a steamer for San Francisco and we never knew he was gone until it was too late," Chavez adds. "So we got on our horses and rode north as fast as we could, but we couldn't outride a steamer. By the time we got there, he was already locked up in the San Jose jail. Me and two others put on disguises and snuck into town to see what we could do, but the jail was guarded so well, we knew that we had no chance."

Raggio is listening intently as Chavez continues.

"They found him guilty of murder even though he never killed no one. I didn't know what to do, so I dropped a note in the Wells Fargo Express letterbox in Hollister saying it was me who did all the killing in Tres Pinos and that I would take my revenge if they strung up my captain. But it didn't have no effect and you know the rest."

"I heard Vasquez took it like a man, right to the end," Raggio adds.

"That's right," says Clodoveo. "When they put the noose around his neck, he had only one word for the gringos: 'Pronto!'"

Chavez was in Hollister that day last March getting drunk with old friends and lamenting the death of his jefe. He was actually seen crying in sorrow at the loss of his friend. Chavez hadn't even cried that day the horse kicked him in the face.

"That was a sad day when I heard that they had hung him," Chavez says, "but I promised I would make the gringos pay for it dearly and I have kept my promise."

Luis has noticed that Chavez is walking with a slight limp since the last time he saw him, and asks about that too.

"Oh, that?" Chavez replies. "That happened at Kings Ferry." He laughs about it now. "We had just about the whole town tied up, but then some men came in and started shooting, so we had to make our escape," Chavez recalls. "But we had left our horses on the other side of the bridge they'd just built, because we didn't want anyone to hear us coming, and some rancher shot me in the knee when I made a run for it."

They talk for hours – or at least Chavez does. Raggio mostly listens. But the fire has now died down to ashes and they turn in for the night.

The next day, they ride on and don't find any sign of the horses Chavez claims to have lost. The ride takes them below the border into Sonora and Chavez asks Luis what he knows about the gold mines down there.

"Not much," Luis says, "but there's a lot of them popping up in this area, despite all the trouble."

"Trouble?" Chavez says, unaware of this news.

"Well, apparently the Yaqui Indians are stirring up a lot of trouble and the Mexican army has been sent in to put them down, but that hasn't done anything to stop the mining."

That's all Chavez wanted to hear. "Good," he says, "that's very good."

After a few more questions about the mines, they turn around and ride back across the border. Chavez never mentions the missing horses again. “Strange,” Raggio thinks, “all this talk about the mines.”

* * *

Silas decides to give Garcia ten minutes before he tells Lumen. He goes to the back of his shop and gets out his shotguns – two .12-gauge, double-barreled muzzle-loading caps-on-nipples types with hammers. He dry fires the caps to get rid of any moisture that might be present and determines everything is in firing order, then drops the hammers down on both guns to the safe-cock position. He then carefully reloads them, and hides one of them in a handy spot by the front door. He keeps the one in his hands as he steps into the sunshine and looks around town.

The street is quiet. No one had seen Garcia come or go.

“It’s a good place to defend,” Silas thinks to himself as he looks around Campo as if it’s the first time he’s ever seen the place. “Them rocks in the middle of town, we’ll put some men with rifles hiding up in them, and then some lookouts up on the hills overlooking town.”

Silas spots Jack Kelly coming out of the store. The telegraph operator stops and lights a cigarette which he pinches between his lips. He fails to see anything unusual as Silas approaches him carrying a shotgun.

“Seen Lumen?” Silas asks Kelly. Jack exhales some smoke so he can respond. “Yup, in the store,” he says, gesturing with his thumb over his left shoulder.

Silas says, “Come on in Jack. This concerns you too.”

"Me?" queries Kelly, shocked that anything to do with the Gaskills would concern him. "What is it?"

"You'll see in a minute," Silas says as Kelly turns and follows him into the store where Lumen is standing behind the counter writing in the ledger book. He sees right away Silas has something on his mind, but is busy with the books.

"Hi, Silas," he says, "just a minute. I'm bringing some accounts up to date…."

Silas cuts him off. "We might not have a minute," he exclaims.

"What? What do you mean?" Lumen says.

"I think that the rumors about the Chavez gang are correct," begins Silas. "I just got a report that they're down in Tecarte right now and planning to rob Campo…."

"Noooo!" interrupts Lumen. "Who did you hear that from?"

"Well, I promised I wouldn't say," Silas replies, "but I think that the information is credible and we should get prepared. I don't know when they're planning to attack but it could be anytime, so we need to get ready."

"What do we have to do?" asks Kelly, despite a huge lump in his throat.

"Tell all the ranchers that bandits are in the area and prepare to defend Campo," Silas replies.

"But the Chavez gang?" interrupts Kelly, "they're the baddest bunch in all of California. You said that so yourself. Shouldn't I send a telegram to the Army. Maybe they would send some help."

"No," Lumen says. He knows that the Army would have to send troops from Yuma, or maybe even from San Francisco on a steamship, and that could take days or even a couple weeks, and that's if they sent troops at all.

"No, we've got to get ready and be able to protect ourselves on our own," Lumen decides. "And we've got to hide some guns where we can get to them quickly when the fighting starts."

"I've got my Army Colt," Jack says, trying to remember where he last saw it. "It's an old cap-and-ball, but it shoots good."

"Okay," Silas replies, "but if it's been loaded for more than a week or so," which he's sure it has – knowing Kelly, it's probably been months since he's fired it – "then go out back, shoot the old loads, clean it up real good, then dry fire some caps and load up some fresh chambers."

"Why?" says Jack. It's a question that tells Silas why Kelly was assigned to the Signal Corps as a telegraph operator instead of fighting Indians up in the plains of Montana or the Dakotas.

"Because," Silas says in exasperation, "the old loads might not be reliable anymore and when the Chavez gang shows up, do you want a gun that you can't depend on?"

"That's right," Lumen adds, "and yell 'fire in the hole' real loud before you shoot off those old loads so we'll know it's you and not the bandits doing the firing."

"Okay," Jack says as he hurries off through the door to the telegraph office to get the revolver, which last he knew was in the top right-hand drawer of his desk.

"Amazing the Army ever took that boy," Silas says while Lumen gets out some guns from behind the counter and starts checking them over. Some need to be cleaned and some just need to be loaded.

"I got my four old double-barrel shotguns, two percussion rifles and my needle gun and three or four pistols," Lumen reports.

"You going to depend on that needle gun?" Silas asks his brother. "It fouls after a few shots."

"Not if you know how to use it," Lumen shoots back. "It'll blow a hole clean through a man at five hundred yards."

"I wish we had a Winchester rifle, or even a Henry," says Silas. "We need all the firepower we can muster."

"We got all the firepower we will need," Lumen says, "and there's plenty of men around Campo who will bring their Winchesters with them. Plus, we got plenty of ammo stocked up in the back of the store there," he nods.

"Yeah, you're right," Silas says, and then he spins quickly to his left and reaches for one of the shotguns as he hears the doors to the store burst open.

But it's just Andrew and Zachariah Elliott, two local boys about 15 and 16 years old. They live nearby and had been sent to the store by their mother to fetch some flour and other baking goods. They are alarmed, though, at the sight of the Gaskills' arsenal.

"What's wrong, Mr. Gaskill?" Zach, the older boy, asks Silas, who is in front of the counter.

Silas is quick to respond. "Well, howdy boys, you're just the two lads we were looking for." Good boys, these two, he's thinking. They'll do just fine.

"Us? What do you mean?" Andrew replies.

"Boys," Silas says, "we've just learned that the Chavez gang is in Tecarte right now and that they're planning to rob Campo."

Silas didn't think the boys' eyes could get much

bigger than they did at the mention of the Chavez gang, but they doubled in size when he mentioned the raid on Campo.

"The Chavez gang?" they both reply at once. "You mean the bandits that rode with Vasquez?"

"Yup," Silas says, "one and the same. And we have just heard that they have set their sights on Campo and they could show up at any minute. We need you two boys to ride on out to the neighboring ranches and warn everyone and to have them send some help if they can to defend Campo."

"Sure, Mr. Gaskill," they both say again.

"One of you boys ride east and the other ride north," Silas instructs, "and tell everyone you can find. And boys, you two be careful. We expect them to ride in from the south, but them killers could come into Campo from any direction."

"Okay, Mr. Gaskill," they say, running out of the store and jumping on their horses and riding swiftly away, forgetting all about their mother's flour.

"Well, let's get ready," Silas says to his brother. "They could arrive at any time."

Then, from out back, they hear a yell. "Fire in the hole!"

Chapter 16

Rafael Martinez and Alonzo Cota arrive at the old stables by the creek before dawn. Lopez is already there. He's got two horses culled from the herd for the boys to ride and has them tied to a hitching post.

"Them two horses are for you," he says to them. "You will find some old saddles and bridles in the barn over there," he adds, pointing to a dilapidated shed beside the corral. "You each pick one and get saddled. We ride soon."

"Si, gracias," they say in unison. They walk into the barn and find five old saddles in the small tack room; each picks one that looks like it will hold together. They each grab a horse, saddle up and get ready to go.

"We may well be sleeping on the trail for the next few days or so," Lopez says to them. "Do you have bedrolls?"

"Si," says Alonzo.

"Then get them tied on and let's get going," Lopez says without waiting for more of a reply.

As the two secure their bedrolls, Alvijo rides up. "You two ready?" he asks.

"Si," they reply.

"You know anything about driving horses?" Alvijo asks them.

"Enough," Cota replies. "We can do it."

"Muy bien," Alvijo says, "then one of you boys ride flank on the left and the other on the right. Keep them together and heading in the right direction. Cruz will ride up front and lead the herd and I will follow up in the rear."

“Si, senor,” Martinez and Cota say.

“Don’t let them run,” Alvijo adds, “but you got to keep them moving fast enough so they don’t stop to graze all the time. We will keep them moving for a couple of hours or so and when we find a creek with good water in it, we’ll let them drink a little while and then move them out again.”

Simple enough, they think.

Lopez, who is sitting on his horse by the corral gate, yells impatiently, “Vamos! Let’s move them out.”

“Si, jefe,” says Alvijo, used to being cut short by Lopez. Alvijo leads his horse to the gate, throws it open, and walks his steed around to the back of the corral. The horses start to move out of the corral and, flanked by Cota and Martinez on each side, instinctively fall in line behind Lopez.

They have been driven so long – some all the way from central California – they all know the routine by now and it’s an easy drive all morning. By late afternoon, they come to a small box canyon with some grass in a small meadow. It looks to Cruz like a good spot to spend the night, so he leads the herd in and they set up camp at the opening to the canyon.

Cruz pulls some jerky out of his saddle bag and hands it around.

“It is not much, but it’ll have to do for tonight,” he says to the greenhorns. “You two did okay today,” he tells them. “Tomorrow, we will bring the horses on to the Mendosa rancho and sell them. Your cut will be small, of course, because you didn’t help steal them and bring them down from California.”

“Si,” Cota says almost automatically, “we understand.”

"Good," says Lopez, "I like men who understand."

Cruz gets out a bottle of tequila, pulls out the cork, and takes a long drink. He hands the bottle to Cota and turns to Martinez.

"So, Rafael," he says, "you still going to marry that sweetheart of yours?"

"Si," Martinez says, his face lighting up at the thought. "Maria is the woman that I love and I will do anything for her."

Lopez cuts him off with a loud, "Ha!"

"Do anything for a woman?" he says disdainfully, nearly spitting out his second drink of tequila as he laughs. "Boy, you've got it all wrong, amigo. A woman should do anything for *you*."

Cota takes the bottle back from Lopez, downs another drink himself, and passes it to Martinez. But Rafael turns it down, so Cota hands it back to Lopez instead.

"Me?" says Lopez, taking another swig. "When I see a woman I want, I just take her and have my way with her. I don't ask her if she wants me … that doesn't matter. And when she no longer pleases me, and I've taken my pleasures from her, I cast her aside like a chicken bone.

"After all, after you have eaten all the meat, you throw away the bones, right?" Lopez adds with a roaring laugh as he takes yet another drink and hands the bottle to Alvijo.

Martinez and Cota glance at each other. They don't know what to say to Lopez; what to make of these brutally appalling men.

Finally, Martinez dares to speak. "But … if you love her … you would not treat her this way, right?" he asks Lopez.

"Love!" bellows Lopez. Alvijo starts laughing too.

"Love! Why, the only thing that I have ever loved is myself," Lopez exclaims, laughing loudly the whole time, "and sometimes I don't even love me." He grabs the bottle back from Alvijo and takes another long pull.

He wipes his chin with the sleeve of his jacket and changes the subject.

"There is one other thing that I do love," Lopez adds, "and that's a good fire. It's going to get almighty cold tonight, so you boys go out and bring in some firewood before it gets too dark and get us a real nice warm fire going."

"Okay," Cota says almost automatically. "Come on, Rafael, there's a dead oak tree down by the creek." They get up and start toward the water.

"So," Cruz says to Alvijo, "what do you think of our new recruits?"

"They might be good fighters in the cantina," Alvijo says, "but these two are not hardened men like us, amigo. I will like to see how they react to the sight of death and blood and gore."

"Well," Lopez replies, "when we catch up with Sosa, you will get your chance. I talked to Romulo Gonzalez last night and he told me how to get to Mendosa's rancho. We will sell him the horses and in a couple days, Romulo will ride down and meet up and ride with us to help us find Sosa.

"Ha, ha, ha," laughs Lopez, feeling a little bit of that warm feeling he gets.

"I cannot believe there are men such as that," Martinez says to Cota as they look for firewood.

"I know!" agrees Alonzo, as mortified as his friend. "He's a hard one for sure."

"Hard one! He's mucho loco!" Martinez exclaims. "What are we getting ourselves into!"

"Shhh," cautions Cota. "Quiet down a little; we don't want them to hear us. So they're a little loco, what did you expect? That they were altar boys or something? No, they're hard men, the hardest no doubt, but this is our only chance, so let's not mess it up.

"Remember, we are going down to Sonora and rob the rich mines there," Cota continues. "We will ride with them long enough to get a lot of money and then we will quit and ride home rich men. And then you can marry Maria."

"You're right, I guess," says Martinez, "but if Maria's father ever finds out!" He shudders at the thought.

"How's he going to find out?" Cota asks. "We will be way down in Sonora; he could never find out. You tell him we hit a small gold strike and sold out to some rich man and that's all he will ever know."

"But … Maria?" replies Martinez. "I will have to tell her."

"I wouldn't," Alonzo says, "but that's up to you…."

"But I don't want to live a life that's a lie," Rafael interrupts, "and Maria, she would never understand. She would think that I sold my soul to the devil and then I don't think that she will ever marry me."

"So we stop at the mission on the way back and give confession," Alonzo offers, "and then we come back rich miners from Sonora. You marry Maria and I'll buy my little rancho and be able to support my sister and her children. And maybe find a little wife of my own…."

"Sounds like a tall tale to me," says Rafael. "Do

you really think that it's going to come out that way?"

"Why not?" Alonzo inquires.

"Because," says Rafael, "we could get killed, or worse."

"What could be worse than that?" Cota asks.

"If we get caught, we might get hung," replies Martinez. "How would you like it if a posse caught us and hung us from the nearest tree?"

"Not very well," Cota agrees, "but I'm not planning on getting caught. If things get too hot, we can always just sneak away by ourselves and disappear. We'll probably end up being poor sheepherders for the rest of our lives."

"That's not very funny," Rafael says.

"Not very funny," Alonzo agrees, "but it's true. Riding with the Chavez gang is the only way out for us, so let's not ruin it and just do everything they say, agreed?"

"Agreed," Rafael offers sheepishly. "I guess we're in it now. Let's find some wood and get back before they wonder what's keeping us."

There's a dead oak tree right in front of them and broken branches lie on the ground all around them. They pick some up and hurry back to the camp.

* * *

Back in Campo, it's like someone just stuck a stick in a hornets' nest. The whole town has come alive and there's people carrying guns running about every which way. A tall Kumeyaay Indian rides an old mare into town with a Sharp's rifle in his hands. He stops at the hitching post in front of the store.

Silas Gaskill looks up from the front porch, where he's matching up guns with ammunition. "Hello, Captain Billy," he says to the Indian. No one seems to know why he's called Captain and Silas has never bothered to ask. About all Silas knows about him is that he was born south of the line but never seems to want to go back there.

"Howdy," Captain Billy replies. "I just got word about the Chavez gang coming this way and thought you might want another gun close about."

"We sure do," Silas agrees. "Tie up that horse behind the livery stable and go over to the hotel. Vi Price has some chicken stew on the stove. Eat up and then come back and find me."

By the time Captain Billy returns a half hour later, Silas has figured out how best to use the Indian.

"I think we can use you as a lookout up on that hill," Silas says, pointing to a high hill to the northeast. "We already got someone up on that other hill," he adds, pointing to it too, "and we're going to send out some more men to watch from other hills along the border too.

"But I want you up on that hill," he says again pointing to the one to the northeast. "It's got the best view of the border and you've got the best eyesight of anyone I ever met. If you see them a long way off, come on down and give the alarm. If they are too close to town for you to get down here, fire off a shot with that old Sharp's to let us know they're coming so we won't be surprised by them killers."

"If that's what you think's best," Captain Billy says. "I'll get my horse and head up there now."

Almost immediately, McFall Pearson comes riding into town like a man who is obviously used to being in the saddle. Both he and his horse are out of breath.

"Hi, Silas, I just got word and came riding in as fast as I could," Pearson says.

"Good, we can use all the help we can muster up," Silas says. "Them outlaws haven't showed themselves yet, but with all of us here guarding the town, I think it'll be the end of the Chavez gang if they show up here now."

"Yeah, looks like you've got everything covered here in town," Pearson says, looking around as he ties his horse off on the hitching post, "but what about the other ranches in the area? What if the bandits don't come to Campo? What if they only plan to rob some of the outlying ranches instead?"

"We thought of that," Silas replies. "We're getting some men together and are going to send out scouts to watch from some of the mountain peaks overlooking the trails near the border. If they come across, we'll know about it and we will hunt them bastards down."

"Think they might already have crossed?" Pearson asks.

"They might have," ponders Silas. "All we know for sure is that they were in the Tecarte cantina yesterday afternoon and they were talking about raiding Campo."

"How many men do you expect they'll have?" Pearson continues.

"We don't know for sure," Silas replies. "We do know there were only five men in the cantina talking about the raid, but it reckons that there'll be more than that when they get here."

As he talks, McFall walks over and slides his Winchester Model 1866 lever-action repeating rifle out of the scabbard strapped to his saddle. "Well, I brought my '66 and it holds seventeen rounds in the magazine and one in the chamber," he adds, holding the rifle proudly in front of him for Silas's inspection.

"Where do you want me?" he adds.

Silas looks at the rifle and thinks for a moment. "How 'bout you put your horse in the stable and join the guys hiding up in them rocks," Silas says as he points to the boulders near the center of town. "Hide up in there and keep a lookout and in a couple of hours we will send up some men to relieve you."

"Okay," Pearson says, grabbing a box of cartridges from his saddle bag, filling his pockets, then checking the chamber of the rifle to make sure it's loaded. "All set; see you after sundown, Silas."

"Come to the hotel for some supper," Silas says, "and thanks for coming."

Pearson gives him a wave, puts his horse away in the stable and then disappears as he climbs up into the rocks.

A good man to have on your side, Silas thinks to himself as he walks into the store to find Lumen standing behind the counter. Five other men are trying to get ammunition from him.

"We're almost out," Lumen repeats to the men, "one box of .44 Henrys left and it's two dollars and ten cents."

"Two dollars and ten cents!" exclaims the man.

"That's for a box of fifty rounds," Lumen says in defense of the price.

"But we're here to help you," says another man. "You should be giving us the bullets for free!"

"I'll tell you what," booms Silas from the doorway, turning everyone around. "All the bullets you put into the bandits are free. You pay for the ones that miss."

The men do not think he's funny.

"Ah, you Gaskills probably just made up the whole story about the Chavez gang just to sell ammunition," one of the fellers says.

"You boys believe what you want," Silas says as he walks around the counter, "but if you go around spreading rumors that aren't true, you'll have to deal with me."

"Oh, sorry," says the man. "I was just joking around a little. Meant no harm by it. You can count on us."

"Okay, then," Silas says, "I need you boys to pick a building in town to watch from. Two men to a building and keep out of sight. If you see them ride into town, wait until I give the signal to open the ball. We want to make sure it's the bandits and not some poor vaqueros riding through."

"Okay, Silas," says one of the men and they all grab their rifles and head for the door to find places to hide.

"What do you think?" Lumen asks once the men have gone.

"We'll be all right," Silas replies. "Even if twenty bandits show up, I think we can handle them. You did stow away enough ammo for the two of us, didn't you?"

"Of course," Lumen says, "we've got plenty for ourselves. Any more men show up to help?"

"Yeah, McFall Pearson rode in and Captain Billy is here, too," Silas says. "I gave them each a place to watch from."

"Good," Lumen says, "them are two good hombres. And one of the others told me John Williams is on his way in to town. I'll keep him in the store with me; you'll be in the blacksmith shop and the others are all up in the rocks or in the buildings. I think that anyone who rides into Campo to rob us are going to be caught in a crossfire that none of them will survive."

"Yup, I agree," Silas says. "All we need now is for them to make their play."

With that, Silas turns and walks out the front door.

Chapter 17

RETURN TO SUMMER, 1896

Ed Aiken, the man who bought the Gaskills' store, is mesmerized by Silas's story. He hasn't budged from the rock he's sitting on, the same one he was hiding behind only a couple hours earlier when the drunken cowboy was killed. It's a good thing it's a quiet day at the store and his wife is tending the counter, he's thinking, because he wouldn't want to have to interrupt Silas to go wait on a customer.

But just then they hear Silas's name being called and they look up to see Silas's wife Catharine walking toward them. "Oh, there you are," says Catharine as she finds her husband of 14 years leaning on a hoe under the pear tree. "What are you two men up to on such a beautiful afternoon?"

"Silas was just telling me the story of the Great Campo Gunfight!" exclaims Ed Aiken.

He's a lot more excited about it than she was when Silas first told her the story years ago. She thought it was all kind of grisly; but that may have been more from her Philadelphia upbringing.

Then she notices the dead man leaning against the blacksmith shop; she had heard the shots earlier and had been informed that a drunken cowboy had been killed, but assumed the body had been removed by now.

"Someone should get that man out of the street," Catharine remarks. "I'm sure someone will," Silas replies.

"Soon, I hope," she says. "That man doesn't

deserve to be treated like that." But Silas replies, "Oh, he got what he deserved."

"Well, if you say so, my love," she relents. "I'll leave you two gentlemen alone then."

"What did you want me for, dear?" Silas inquires. "Oh, just checking on you, old man," she replies. "I'm not so old!" he says with a smile. They both laugh and she turns and walks back toward the house.

Ed Aiken can see how much she cares about her husband.

"Now, where were we?" Silas asks. "Oh, yeah, I remember. While we were getting ready in Campo, over in Arizona…."

STANWIX STATION ARIZONA

NOVEMBER 23,1875

The desert winds are blowing fiercely, whipping up sand into a blinding sandstorm. Blowing it into the eyes of William Clark Colvig as he opens the door and quickly ducks into Stanwix Station, one of the many stage stops on the road from Yuma to Tucson.

"Goddam," Colvig exclaims as he shuts the door, blocking out the howling winds. He then removes his hat and beats it against his clothes to knock the sand off. "It's really blowing out there."

"Blowin' harder than a Southern Baptist preacher

on Easter Sunday," proffers King Woolsey, the keeper of Stanwix Station, who is sitting at a table filling his pipe with tobacco.

Another man is stirring a pot of stew that's slowly bubbling on the woodstove off to one side. "I doubt the stage will show up at all today," says Harry Roberts, a big man with a bushy beard, as he gives the full kettle another stir.

"I reckon not," says Woolsey. "If I was driving that stage, I would have stayed in Yuma if I'd seen this one a'comin'. If they don't show up by tomorrow we'll send a telegram to Yuma and see if they left yesterday or not. If they did, we'll send someone out to look for them."

"So, what do you think, Mr. Woolsey?" asks Colvig.

"About what?" replies his boss, looking up from the table.

"About Chavez!" Colvig shoots back immediately. "Do you really think Luis is right?"

"I wouldn't doubt it at all," Woolsey says, "not that Luis Raggio is the most trustworthy man I have ever had the privilege to meet. Very far from it. But, if he says he knows beyond any doubt that a man who calls himself Jose Espinosa is really Clodoveo Chavez, the wanted outlaw, then I'm pretty sure I'd believe him. After all, him and his brother Vincente and Chavez all grew up in the same town near Hollister, so they've known Chavez all their lives. I don't think there's any mistake."

"So, what are we going to do?" Colvig interjects at his first opportunity.

"I'm gonna do nothing," Woolsey responds, not the answer Colvig was hoping for. "I've got my two ranches to run and my stage stations to run and I'm a fairly wealthy man. So, I'm not going to do anything. Not that I'm afraid, mind you," he quickly adds. "It's just that I've already had my share of adventures in my life. Running down renegade Indians and outlaws here and there, but that was a long time ago. This is not any business that I want a part of.

"But if I were you," Woolsey adds, looking directly at his hired hand as if to give him the courage, "I'd take the Raggio brothers, and maybe Harry here, and go on down to the Baker ranch and collect on that two-thousand-dollar reward."

A lump rises in Colvig's throat at the thought of taking Chavez without Woolsey's help. "Do you think the four of us can take a man like Chavez?" he asks.

"Sure," Woolsey replies, "if you can get the drop on him. All you've got to do is wait it out … surprise him in the bunkhouse or something. Don't even tell Charlie Baker what you're doing until later.

"And after you take him – dead or alive – you bring him straight to Yuma and send a telegram to the sheriff in Los Angeles for the reward."

"You think it could be that easy?" queries Colvig, more than a little apprehensive at the thought. "They say Chavez has killed more men than Custer's killed Indians."

"But he's still just a man," Woolsey says, "and all men can be killed. What you got to do is get close enough to surprise him, but that won't be easy. You see, a man like Chavez, he's got good instincts. He couldn't have lived as long as he has otherwise. So you got to catch him off guard, when he's the most vulnerable. That's the only way to get the drop on him and then you got him."

Roberts has been listening silently in the corner since the beginning. "I'll help you," he finally says, "but I don't want to kill no one if I don't have to."

"Okay," Colvig says, relieved to have someone he can trust with him, not that he has any real reason to distrust the Raggios. "Good," he adds, "I don't want to kill him either, but I will if he won't surrender."

He turns to Woolsey and asks, "Do you think Luis and Vincente will go with me and Harry?"

"Why don't you ask them yourself, Bill. I think I hear them coming in for dinner now," Woolsey replies.

Just then, the door opens to the howling winds and the Raggio brothers hurry quickly inside, taking off their coats and shaking off the dust. Luis is in his mid 20s, while Vincente is only 17, having come down from Hollister about six months ago to join his brother.

"Howdy," says Luis, glancing at the stove to see that dinner's ready. "Just a might breezy out there today."

"Yeah, we noticed," replies Roberts. "It was about the time we saw a crow flying east but a'headin' west …"

The Raggio brothers let out a laugh.

"Ain't funny!" Roberts shoots back. "It happened."

"So," King Woolsey says, "Bill here has got something to ask you boys."

"What is it?" Luis asks, turning to Colvig.

"Well … um … it's … um … it's about Clodoveo Chavez," Colvig finally stammers out. "Do you really think it's him?"

The Raggio brothers give each other a quick glance, knowing what Colvig has in mind, a thought that has not escaped their minds either.

"Sure it's him," says Luis. "I spoke with him the day after he arrived and we went off riding together for a couple days down south toward Sonora too. I have known him since we were little muchachos in the hills outside Hollister. Vincente was just a baby then. I know his mother and his brothers and sisters. I remember the day he got that scar on his face. He got kicked by a horse. He was lucky it was just a glancing blow or it would have knocked out all his teeth. His face was a mess for quite a while."

"Yup," Vincente adds, "he's had that bad scar on his face ever since I can remember. There's no mistake it's him."

"There's a two-thousand-dollar reward on his head," Colvig replies, "dead or alive."

"We know," says Luis, again making quick eye contact with his brother. "We were thinking about that too, but Chavez knows us as well as we know him. I think if we were to go gunning for him he might sense it and probably would kill one or the both of us. I reckon if we're going to take him, we'd need some help."

"I'll do it," Colvig says matter of factly. "I'll capture Chavez, but you three will have to be the ones who bring him to Yuma to collect the reward, and then we'll split it four ways even. Is it a deal?"

For the third time the Raggio brothers glance at each other. "Yeah, it's a deal," Luis says.

They all turn to Harry, standing by the stove with a big spoon in his hand.

"Sure thing," agrees Harry after a slight hesitation. "We'll go collect the reward and bring your five hundred dollars back to you."

"Good, then it's settled," Colvig says. "Five hundred dollars will help me a lot. That'll be enough money to put down on a small spread of my own."

"Well," says Woolsey, who has been listening

intently, “whatever the reason, I say all you got to do is wait him out and take him when he has his guard down, and if he resists any you may have to kill him. And you can expect he ain’t going to go peaceably.”

“What if he’s not alone and there’s more of his gang with him there at the Baker ranch?” Colvig asks Luis.

“I’m pretty sure he’s alone,” Raggio has determined. “The other two cowboys at the ranch have been working there for much longer, far as I can tell. I think Chavez is there because he’s hiding out or something. I spent two days with him … we rode south across the border. He kept asking me what I knew about those gold strikes down in Sonora. I think maybe he’s planning something down there.”

“When did you see him last?” Colvig asks.

“Last week,” Luis answers.

“Hmmm, then I think we’ll need to check to see if he’s still there,” mulls Colvig.

“That’s true,” Harry says. “We need to know if he’s still there and how many others are at the ranch.”

“That sounds like a good plan,” Luis says. “When do we want to do it?”

“The sooner the better,” says Colvig, “before someone else recognizes him and gets the same idea.”

“Or he gets spooked,” Woolsey interjects. “He won’t stay at that ranch for long. I’d lay money down on that.”

“Okay,” says Colvig, “then Luis, you’ve got to ride down there and see if he’s still there as soon as the sand stops blowing.”

“It’ll probably die down by sunup,” Woolsey says. “Enough talking. Harry, give me some stew. I’m as hungry as a horned toad on an old ant hill."

***

It's just before midnight in Campo and the streets are quiet. The Gaskills are getting anxious and almost wish the Chavez gang would strike soon and get it over with. It would be a short fight, they think, if the outlaws showed up now.

The men who had been watching from up on the hill were called down after dark; no sense leaving them up there as it clouded up in the late afternoon, so there's no moon tonight.

Four men remain outside guarding the town. It's so cold that it was decided to rotate the guards every two hours. Most of the others are sleeping either in the hotel or in a nearby building. The fire is burning bright in the fireplace of the hotel. Four men are getting ready to relieve the guards.

Silas hands a cup of hot coffee to McFall Pearson. "Drink it down," Silas says, "it's pretty cold out there."

"Yeah," Pearson replies, "so cold that I don't think those bandits will attack us before sunup."

"No, I don't think they will either," Silas says, "but we can't get caught with our pants down. You all know what the Chavez gang did up in Kings Ferry?"

"Sure," says John Williams, "they robbed the entire town."

"Not just that," continues Silas, "but they snuck into town and tied up thirty-five or forty people and held them at gunpoint while they robbed the town blind."

"That's right," adds Pearson. "It was only luck that a few men came into town and surprised the bandits and drove them off."

"But that was when Vasquez was leading the gang," Williams says. "Do you think Chavez is bold enough to try the same thing here?"

"Why not?" replies Silas. "Chavez is a cold-blooded killer … not as smart as Vasquez, but more brutal."

"I agree," Pearson adds. "I heard he was the one who killed the three men in Tres Pinos, not Vasquez. It was Chavez and Romulo Gonzalez."

"That's right," says Silas, "and that's why we can't let our guard down for a minute."

The men finish their coffee and grab their rifles and shotguns, checking them over as experienced frontiersmen do. Confirming they're loaded, the men put on their warm coats and step out the door into the cold night air.

***

The next day, the sandstorm that had blasted through Stanwix Station is only a memory and the stage had rolled in by mid morning, about fifteen hours late, but safe and sound. That afternoon, Luis Raggio had ridden to the Baker ranch to make sure Chavez was still there and still alone. He made up a story that he had been sent out looking for some stray cattle that had wandered off during the sandstorm, and felt convinced that his unexpected appearance didn't alarm the bandit. To make sure, he had left him a little gift.

The following morning, Chavez awakens to find it very cold in the bunkhouse at the Baker ranch. The woodstove has burned itself out during the night. His head is throbbing from drinking too much whiskey the night before. He gets up, putting on his boots and accidentally kicking over the empty whiskey bottle on the floor. Outside, it's a beautiful sunny day. The sun has been up for about half an hour and the day is warming nicely. He opens the door to find it's a lot warmer outside than it is in the bunkhouse. He walks over to the water trough and splashes some water on his face. The cold water is invigorating.

"Strange," Chavez thinks to himself about the night before. Luis Raggio had been there, stopping by for an hour or so, and then leaving after it got dark. He never could have reached the stage stop before midnight in the darkness and he knew it was going to be a cold night.

"Something is not right," Chavez says to himself. Raggio was acting strangely, but he can't put his finger on it. "He rode in and out in the same direction," Chavez is thinking, "but he really didn't have a reason to stop by. Said he was looking for some strays, but he didn't have any with him. And he left this bottle of whiskey. I wouldn't have done that if I was riding out into a cold night."

An uneasy feeling that Chavez can't explain tells him it's about time to be moving on. "I've been here too long and I should be getting back to Tecarte before Lopez gets in too much trouble," he thinks to himself. "Besides, I've already got what I came for."

The gold mines in Sonora are full of gold and he has already found some nice trails leading to twisted lost canyons to hide out in. He thinks he might rob the gold shipments and then hide out in Arizona. That way the Mexican posses will likely give up the chase at the border.

“Si,” he decides, “in a few days it will be time to go. But today I’ll help Mr. Baker dig the foundation to his new house. It will be good to have a friend in the area in case something goes wrong in the south.”

“Jose,” yells one of the other ranch hands. They’re heading toward the stable to mount up for a day working on the range. “Your breakfast is getting cold.”

Chavez splashes some more water on his face and heads to the main house for breakfast.

Chapter 18

Luis Raggio, William Clark Colvig and Harry Roberts are riding along the Gila River on the trail from Stanwix Station to the Baker ranch. Luis's brother Vincente is bringing up a wagon behind them. They left an hour after sunup. Luis had arrived last night around midnight with the news they were hoping to hear. Not only was Chavez alone, but he was alone with a bottle of whiskey, courtesy of Luis.

The sun is out and the day is quickly warming up. The 16-mile ride will take several hours with a wagon.

"Let's stop and let the horses rest for a while and get a drink," says Luis, more tired himself than the horses after riding half the night and getting little sleep, his nerves not allowing him any shuteye.

"We might need to run them later," he adds.

"What do you mean?" replies Colvig. "Why might we have to run the horses?"

"Well," Luis says, "what if we are able to take Chavez alive? If we do, and Chavez has any of his gang close by, I figure they will not let us just ride off with him and collect the reward. We might be in a running gun battle and then we will need fresh horses, don't you think?"

It was a contingency Colvig hadn't thought of.

"King Woolsey said all we'll have to do is sneak up on him and take him by surprise," replies Colvig. "He didn't say nothin' about no running gunfight!"

"You won't have to worry about that," Luis points out. "You'll be riding back to Stanwix Station. Me, Vincente and Harry, we're the ones who'll be taking the risk getting Chavez to Yuma, that's how I see it. Whether we take Chavez dead or alive, word's gonna get out and someone is going to be out looking for us and we'll need to be ready."

"That's right," Harry says. "This is risky business and we need to be ready for anything, so when we take Chavez, we need to get out of there as quick as possible and bring him to Yuma. And there's another thing that we haven't thought about yet."

An increasingly irritated Colvig dismounts along with the others to let the horses drink. How can there be so many things they neglected to consider, he thinks. Finally, he says, "And what would *that* be?"

"Well," Harry replies, "what do you think Charlie Baker might do if we go and gun down one of his hired hands?"

"You're right!" Colvig agrees. "I don't think he'll like us coming on his ranch and shooting someone down and letting us just ride away."

"Don't worry about Mr. Baker," Luis interrupts. "He already has seen how Chavez and I know each other. I think he'll believe me when I tell him that his hired hand is really the most-wanted outlaw in all of California."

"I hope so," Colvig replies. "I don't want no misunderstandings. We gun down the man he knows as Jose Espinosa, then someone might want to stretch our necks."

"We don't have to worry about that," Luis says, again trying to calm Colvig. "Chavez told me last night that there are only two other cowhands working at the ranch right now and they're both going to be riding out around sunup. He also told me that he was going to be working all day with Mr. Baker on a new house he's building on the other side of the river.

"Since Chavez and Mr. Baker know neither of you two," Luis continues, "you just ride up slow and easy like. That shouldn't alarm either of them."

"So what we gonna say when we get there?" asks Harry.

"We will tell them we have been on the trail a long time," Colvig answers, "and would like to know if Mr. Baker has some provisions that he would sell us. We tell him we are hungry and will pay for a meal. You keep Baker busy and I'll take Chavez when I get the chance."

"Okay," Harry says, "I can do that, but don't wait too long. I can't talk forever."

"Once we cross the river, you two had better ride ahead of me," Luis says. "I need to stay out of sight, because if Chavez sees me, the play is up."

"I know," Colvig replies. "You stay far enough behind so you're out of sight, but close enough so that you can come a'runnin' when I give the signal."

"What's the signal?" Luis asks.

"It'll probably be a gunshot," Harry says.

"Yeah, but let's hope not," Colvig adds. "I want to capture him alive if I can, then I'll just yell for you. You guys be ready; I don't want to be left to fight him on my own."

"Don't worry, Bill, we won't let you down," Harry says. "Now let's get back on the trail before the fox leaves the henhouse. If we don't dally, we'll be there before noon. Let's go."

The three bounty hunters get back on their horses and with a gentle kick of their heels and a subtle pull on the reins, they get moving again. It is a little before noon when the three arrive just east of the ranch. Looking over the valley, they can see Baker's house and corrals on the north side of the river. Out across the south side they can see the construction under way on a new house about 200 yards above the riverbank. It doesn't look like much yet; some adobe bricks are stacked on one foundation about three feet high so far. Others are drying in racks nearby.

"You know where to cross over, Luis?" Colvig asks Raggio. "Yeah, follow me," he replies, leading them down into the green thick brush that grows along the river.

Luis leads them to a trail that brings them to a shallow place to cross, only about two feet deep with a hard bottom, and at least fifty feet across. Once on the other side, they ride downriver hidden by the thick undergrowth. Soon they can see the worksite.

"Okay, Luis, this is about as far as you should go," says Colvig. From their concealed location in the brush, they scope out the site. They are more than 200 yards from the house and they can see two men digging in a trench. Other than that, all seems quiet.

"Looks like they are putting in more of the foundation for the house," Colvig says to the other two.

"So, how do you want to do this?" asks Harry, who seems to be sweating more than the heat of the day would dictate.

Luis gets out his revolver and looks it over, making sure it's loaded and ready to go. The other two do the same. Harry Roberts puts a sixth round in his Colt, fumbling with it as his hand is shaking slightly as he tries to align the bullet with the chamber.

"We just ride on up like we said," Colvig answers. "It looks all quiet enough. You ride in about fifty feet ahead of me, Harry; it'll look less imposing that way."

Harry grabs the bandana tied around his neck and uses it to wipe the sweat from his brow. "Okay," he says with a slight crack in his voice, "let's do this."

The two men ride out of the brush and head slowly and deliberately toward the house in progress. Chavez and Baker are digging a small trench about two feet deep and two feet wide where a foundation of rocks will be laid. Two of the sides are already laid and have a short adobe wall sitting on them. A split-rail fence runs just behind the house attached to a small shed.

Jose Espinosa looks up and his wary eye catches the two riders shortly after they emerge from the bushes. "Look, Mr. Baker, two riders," says Espinosa. "Anyone you know?"

"I can't tell yet," says Baker, as the midday sun and the rider's wide-brimmed hats have their faces in shadow. But the same goes for the riders. From this distance, Colvig and Roberts can't tell which man is which. It's not until they get to within 50 yards that it becomes evident which man is Chavez, recognized first by his powerful build.

"I wonder what they want, Jose," Mr. Baker says to Espinosa.

"Trespassing, most likely," says Espinosa, who can now see that both men are *americanos.* "Want me to run them off?"

"No, Jose," Baker replies. "It's nothing to worry about. Riders pass here all the time. We'll see what they want."

Jose says, "Okay," but Chavez casts an eye about for the nearest pistol, which he sees hanging on a fence post about 15 feet away. It's Mr. Baker's gun. His own, he realizes, is hanging on one of the adobe walls at least

25 feet away.

Colvig and Roberts stop about 20 feet from the men.

"Can I help you gentlemen?" Baker asks.

"I hope so," Harry says. "Sorry to come in unannounced, but we could think of no other way. We have been on the trail a long time and was wondering if we could buy some provisions. And maybe a good meal. All we've eaten in a week are some scrawny jackrabbits. We've got money to pay you."

"Well," says Mr. Baker, "we don't have anything with us here to eat, but we can check over at the main house," nodding at the building on the far side of the bank. "Why don't you get off those horses and set a spell. In a little while I'll ride over and see what I can spare."

They say thanks and Harry climbs down and goes over to shake hands with Mr. Baker, introducing himself and trying hard not to look at Chavez. Colvig gets off his horse and begins rubbing its front leg as if there's something wrong with it. Chavez remains in the ditch, watching Colvig only somewhat cautiously.

Roberts pulls out a small wad of bills and is asking Mr. Baker what kind of provisions he may have for them to buy. The small bundle of cash catches the attention of Chavez and his eyes linger on it just a moment too long. Colvig sees Chavez look away and in one smooth, quick move pulls a shotgun from the scabbard attached to his saddle.

"Hold it right there!" Colvig says forcefully as he steps clear of his horse, thumbing back the two hammers. Chavez turns quickly and sees Colvig holding a double-barreled shotgun pointed right at his midsection no more than 15 feet away. His first thought is the prophetic words he said to Cruz that day at the Sheckler ranch.

"What is this?" Chavez exclaims as he steps back and takes a quick look behind him at Mr. Baker's pistol, which is still a good 15 feet away.

"Put up your hands. You're under arrest!" yells Colvig again as he sees Chavez look around desperately.

"But you've got it all wrong, senor!" exclaims Chavez, trying to talk his way out of his predicament. "There's some kind of mistake."

Colvig isn't falling for it. "You do what I say," he barks. "You're the bandit called Chavez. If you try to run, I will shoot you."

Never before has Clodoveo Chavez been so aware that this might be his final minute on Earth. Never before has he let a man get a drop on him like this.

"I guess my mother was right," he thinks. "The only chance I've got is to get to that pistol."

He looks back again and sees Mr. Baker's pistol hanging there only 15 feet away – 15 *long* feet. "It might as well be a mile," he thinks, "but it's my only hope."

Quick as a cat, Chavez jumps up from the trench and out of the corner of his eye sees the man with the shotgun swinging it in his direction. He ducks as the shotgun roars and the buckshot hits the fence post inches above his head, blasting it into splinters.

Surprised, he looks up and sees the pistol is now only a few feet away, nearly within his reach, he thinks, and he lunges for the holster. Just then, the shotgun roars again, and this time it finds its mark, the buckshot catching Chavez squarely in the back, bowling him over and smashing him into the fence.

He hangs on to the top rail for a moment, looking up at the clear blue sky. It has never looked so blue. As he hangs there, looking at the brilliant sky, he thinks, "Wow, dying don't hurt at all, no, not at all." And then the blue sky turns to gray and then to black as he slides down the fence and slumps to the ground.

Just like that, Clodoveo Chavez, one of the most notorious bandits the West has ever seen, is dead.

"You got him! You got him!" exclaims Harry as he rounds the corner of house. He grabs Chavez and rolls him onto his back.

"It's him, right?" Colvig asks, shaking like a leaf in an autumn breeze. "Tell me it's him."

"It's him," calls out Luis Raggio as he comes riding up in a gallop. "You shot the right man."

Colvig is so nervous that he has to sit down.

A stunned Mr. Baker, recognizing Raggio, demands an explanation to what he just witnessed.

"We shot the bandit, Clodoveo Chavez," Luis tells him. "We tried to take him peaceably, but he went for his gun. You saw that."

"That's not Clodoveo Chavez," Mr. Baker states, "that's Jose Espinosa from California."

"No, he's not," Harry and Luis tell him at the same time.

"He's Chavez all right," Luis adds. "I've known him all my life."

Harry looks the body over. "Yup, he's dead all right. What do we do now?"

"We wait for Vincente to come up with the wagon and then we take him to Yuma like we agreed," Luis says.

Colvig gets up off the ground and looks at his handiwork. "I tried to take him alive…."

"We know," Roberts says. "We saw what happened; so did you Mr. Baker."

But Baker, looking down at the lifeless body, still believes that an innocent man may have been killed. "What do you mean he's a bandit?" questions Baker again. "This man is Jose Espinosa and a guest at my ranch. You men had better be able to prove yourselves."

"We can," Luis assures. "Me and my brother Vincente grew up with Clodoveo Chavez in the Hollister area and we knew him very well."

"Is that so," Mr. Baker says, becoming slowly convinced.

"Yes, it's true," Luis insists. "He was only going by the name Espinosa because he was wanted for murder in California. Our plan was to arrest him and turn him in, but he went for his gun. Bill here had no choice but to shoot him."

"It's the truth," Colvig adds.

Baker looks at the men and looks at the body of a man who seemed like a hard worker, not a desperate killer. Finally he says, "Well, I believe you, Luis. I saw how you two knew each other when you saw him here that first time a couple weeks ago. So I gather there's a reward on his head?"

"That's right," Luis replies, "and now we need to take the body to Yuma and show it to Sheriff Werninger. And then we will send a telegram to Los Angeles and see about the reward."

"All right," Baker says, "but I'll tell you boys, I don't like bounty hunters sneaking around my ranch."

"We're sure sorry about this," Harry tells Mr. Baker, "but it was the only way we could think of to get him."

"I can see it your way," Baker says, "but you'd better get that body off my ranch as soon as possible. I don't want any more killings on my ranch either, do you boys hear me?"

"Loud and clear," Harry says apologetically as he and Luis drag the body into the shade and cover it with a blanket. "My brother Vincente is coming with a wagon soon," Luis tells the ranch owner.

Mr. Baker looks at Colvig, who is as white as a ghost and looks like he's about to get sick. "You okay, there?" Baker says to the man. "Yeah," Colvig says, "it's just that I've never killed a man before." "Well you have now," Baker interjects, "and a man like him probably has lots of friends. You're going to have to watch your back now for the rest of your life."

Colvig looks into Mr. Baker's eyes and knows that he is right, already dreading what he has done.

Suddenly, Vincente and the wagon come into view after having crossed the river.

"Okay," says Luis. "Let's get this over with."

Chapter 19

It's raining lightly in Campo – a cold rain, the kind that stiffens the joints and settles into the bones of the men guarding the small village. Captain Billy is sitting in the entrance to a small cave high in the rocks on the hill overlooking the town. From this vantage point, the Indian can see clear across the valley all the way into Mexico.

He looks down the hill and can see Silas Gaskill working his way up through the brush and rocks along the side of the hill. "He must be looking for me," he thinks, so he gives a little whistle. Silas hears it and looks up to see Captain Billy sitting in a nice dry spot out of the rain.

He waves to him and Captain Billy raises his hand in acknowledgement. Silas scrambles up the steep slope and climbs under the rocks into the little cave to join the Indian out of the rain.

"Hello, Silas," says Captain Billy. "Come to relieve me?"

"Yeah," Silas replies, a little out of breath from the climb. "You've been up here since sunup."

"That's okay," says Captain Billy, "I'm used to sitting around and watching things."

"Well," says Silas, "it's a little after noon and I thought that you might be getting hungry. I don't know if anyone's told you or not, but today is Thanksgiving Day and Vi Price and my sister-in-law, Eliza, have been working since early this morning putting together a feast that would do a king proud. They got roast goose, sweet potatoes, squash and corn and turnips, pumpkin and apple pie and the best-smelling bread that you ever sniffed in your life."

"Well, now, you don't say," says Captain Billy salivating. "It's been a mighty long time since I've had a chance to chew on vittles like that."

"It's all there waiting for ya down at the hotel," says Silas, settling in and leaning back against a rock. "I already had myself all I could muster and there's plenty more. The women folk are going to have dinner ready all day for the men guarding the town."

"Well, thank you now, Silas," replies Captain Billy. "I think I'll just take you up on that offer."

Captain Billy gets up from underneath the overhanging rock marking the entrance to the cave and begins to shake out his cold limbs. "You think that Chavez bunch is going to show themselves soon?" he asks Silas.

"Sooner or later they will," replies Silas without hesitation. "I just wish they'd get it over with."

"I hear ya," says Captain Billy in agreement. "This waiting gets old." It's been several days now since they were first tipped off about the attack and he has heard some of the men talking about the whole thing being just a rumor. "Maybe you should just get some boys together and ride on down to Tecarte and round up them ruffians and get it over with," the Indian suggests.

"I thought of that too," says Silas, "but we can't make the first move, not over the line anyways. If they don't show themselves by tomorrow, I think we will send a spy down across the border and see what's happening down there."

"I'll go if you want," Captain Billy offers. "I can get in and out of Tecarte as well as anyone. But I'm a wanted man on that side of the line. I don't tell anyone this, but I once killed a man down there who killed my brother, and I haven't been back since."

"I knew you didn't like to cross the line," says Silas, "but I didn't know why. Your secret is safe with me; we can find someone else."

"No, I'd be glad to do it," Captain Billy insists. "I know all the back trails to Tecarte; don't worry about me, I can do it. Now I think I'll go on down and taste some of them vittles you been talking about. I ain't had a Thanksgiving feast before, but I heard about 'em though."

"Well then," Silas says, "I reckon you're in for a treat. Take as long as you want and send someone else up here after a while. Till then I'll watch over things."

Captain Billy smiles as he turns and walks down the steep hill. He gets to the hotel and even before he opens the door he can detect the wonderful smells coming from inside the building. He opens the door and is greeted immediately by Eliza Gaskill.

"Come in, please, Captain Billy," she says. "Silas told me he was spelling you up on that cold hill and that you'd be down for dinner. It's ready whenever you want to eat; just let us know."

"Thank you, ma'am," Captain Billy says politely. "It sure smells almighty good. I'll take some now if you would, please."

"Coming right up," Eliza responds as she turns and heads for the kitchen.

Captain Billy looks around and sees five guns leaning by the door – three rifles and two shotguns. He can hear people talking and walks down the hallway and into the dining room and it's no surprise that he sees exactly five men sitting at the dining room table eating dinner – Lumen Gaskill, Charles Cline, John Williams, Simon Miller and Thomas Cameron.

"Could have gotten every one of your scalps," Captain Billy says with a laugh. "You left all your firepower back by the door."

The men stop eating for a moment and let out a rousing laugh.

"Come on in, Captain Billy," says Lumen Gaskill. "We don't need to worry about getting sneaked up on in here. We've got seven men guarding the town and two up on that hill, plus Silas up there where you were keeping watch."

"That's okay," Captain Billy says, "but I think I'll just keep my old Sharp's handy anyhow," holding up his .50-calibre rifle.

"Do whatever you like, my friend," Lumen offers with a sweep of his hand. "There's a whiskey bottle and a glass over on that shelf; just help yerself, that is, if you don't have an objection, Charlie."

Charlie Cline, as justice of the peace and closest thing to a lawman in town, knows just as well as Lumen that offering whiskey to Indians is against the law. But Captain Billy ain't your typical Indian, having adopted most of the white man's ways.

"I reckon we can all look the other way," Charlie Cline replies. "After all, you've been the one sitting up in those rocks in the rain all day," he says to Captain Billy, "so go ahead and warm your bones." Everyone else concurs.

"Thank you, gentlemen," Captain Billy says politely as he heads to pour himself a glass. "It certainly would take the chill off."

The old Indian listens in as the men return to their conversation.

"As I was saying," resumes John Williams, "we're

going to have the wedding at my ranch. It's going to be on Saturday the 25th, Christmas Day. The women folk are doing all the arrangements and all. It's going to be quite an affair and everyone's invited. Bring your kids too and after the ceremonies we'll have a grand dinner and dance all night. I've hired Mr. Eagle to play the fiddle …"

Captain Billy can hold his tongue no longer. "Who's getting married?" he interrupts.

"Well, it's my daughter Alemeda and McFall Pearson," replies John Williams. "I couldn't ask for a better son-in-law than McFall."

"That's for sure," says Thomas Cameron. "McFall Pearson is as fine a man as I've ever met."

Just then, Eliza Gaskill enters the room with a large platter of food. "Here you go," she says as she hands the heaping plate to Captain Billy. "Oh my," Captain Billy exclaims. "Is this all for me? I've never seen so much food on one plate before."

"Yes, it's all for you," says Eliza Gaskill with a smile. "Everyone else has already eaten."

"Well then, thank you, ma'am," Captain Billy says as he takes off his hat and hangs it on a hook on the wall, then sits down with the other men at the long table.

Before Captain Billy can take his first bite, Jack Kelly runs in with a piece of paper in his hand. "Lumen, a telegram just came from Sheriff Hunsaker," Kelly says urgently as he hands him the paper.

Lumen opens it and reads it aloud. *"To Gaskills, Campo Station. Stop. Got message about threat of bandits. Stop. Advise Cline, justice of the peace to organize posse of citizens to protect Campo and surrounding ranches. Stop. Keep apprised. Stop. Hunsaker."*

Lumen folds the paper in half and looks up. "That's it," he says.

"That's it!" exclaims Charlie Cline. "He's not going to send us any help?"

"Well, from a legal standpoint he really has no other choice," offers Lumen in defense. "The bandits are in Mexico and until they cross the line he has no authority over them."

"I still think he can send us some help," retorts Charlie. "As justice of the peace I think that the more help we get the better off we are."

"We really don't need any more help," replies Lumen. "We can take care of ourselves; we've got the men and firepower to handle a sizable force should we need to. We'll be okay."

"What I'm worried about," adds John Williams, "is how we're all going to stay here and protect Campo when we all got our own ranches to tend to. With winter on the doorstep, we got a lot of chores that are not getting done sitting here."

"That's right," echoes Tom Cameron. "I'm lucky I got my boys doing the chores for me, but some of the others will have to make do some other way."

"I know," Lumen says almost apologetically. "We know that you can't stay in town indefinitely. If the bandits don't arrive soon we'll have to disband. Just give us a few more days if you can."

"You won't need that long," Captain Billy says with a mouth full of sweet potatoes and holding a goose leg in his left hand. "Me and Silas already talked it over and if those ruffians don't show themselves by tomorrow afternoon, I told Silas I would ride down to Tecarte and have a look around … maybe ask a few questions."

"That's a good idea," Lumen says, "but you'd better be careful. That Chavez gang is ruthless, just a bunch of no-good killers. If they get a whiff of what you're up to …"

"Don't you worry none about me," says the Captain. "I was born on that side of the line before the line was ever drawed. I have a lot of friends there and I can speak the language. No one's going to bother with me." Captain Billy secretly hopes that's true. "I'll go down and find out if the Chavez gang is around or not."

"That *is* a good plan," Lumen reiterates, and all the other men agree. "Well, it's time for me to spell some of the others," Lumen adds as he rises from the table and excuses himself. "I'm going outside for a while." He puts on his hat and coat and walks up the hallway toward the front door, where he bends down to grab his needle gun. As he does, he looks out the window of the front door.

"Great," he thinks to himself, "it's still raining." He opens the door and feels the swirl of wet, cold air curl around him as he walks out into the empty street.

***

"Ha, ha, ha," laughs Cruz Lopez as he staggers around a big room with a nearly empty bottle of tequila. He's at the Mendosa Rancho about 15 miles west of San Rafael, Mexico. And once again he's drunk.

Juan Mendosa, the owner of the ranch, is a wealthy man in his elder years and he didn't get his wealth by being an honest man. That's not the way it works in this part of the world. Mendosa made his fortune by moving stolen horses and cattle that come from the north to buyers much deeper into the heart of Mexico.

He changes the brands with a running iron and then resells them to just about anyone – the Mexican army, revolutionaries, Yaqui Indians. It doesn't matter to him as long as they pay the price. Being the middle man has been very lucrative for him over the years. He now has a nice spread, a large ranch house and 15 or so vaqueros working for him. A bunkhouse, barn, corrals, stables and a small blacksmith shop dot the property.

"I like your rancho," Lopez slurs as he talks to Mendosa while warming himself beside a six-foot-tall stone fireplace.

"Si, it's nice to be comfortable in your older years," replies Mendosa. "That's why I built this place. You need to think about that Cruz, my amigo." In the couple of days Lopez has been his guest, he has come to like this man, despite his obvious character flaws. Lopez reminds him of his younger years, although, of course, Mendosa has not seen the bandit's ruthless side yet. "After a while you will get tired of being chased by lawmen and posses and then you'll want to settle down," Mendosa tells him.

Lopez gives the words some thought, then replies, "That is true, but I don't think I am quite ready to retire yet." He laughs loudly and then staggers as he takes another long pull from the bottle.

There's a knock at the big front door and it opens. In out of the cold and rain walks Romulo Gonzalez, dripping wet and shivering.

"Romulo!" says Mendosa in greeting. "Come on in my friend. Come in and get warm by the fire."

Gonzalez takes off his wet serape and hangs it on the hook by the fireplace to dry.

"It's so good to see you," Mendosa says, not

having seen the man in nearly a year. "Same here," says Romulo as he extends his hand to the ranch owner. "You got any more of that," Gonzalez says to Lopez, pointing to the tequila. Mendosa, seeing that Lopez has the bottle down to its last swig, offers Romulo a bottle of his own and walks across the room to a cabinet. He grabs a fresh one for both of them.

"What are you doing riding out in weather like this?" Mendosa asks Gonzalez. "We thought we might not see you until the morning."

"We have business we must be attending to in the morning," explains Romulo, "and when I rode in, one of your men told me that I might find my friend Cruz in here."

"Si, I'm here," Lopez says, swaying a bit as he leans against the rocks that make up the side of the fireplace.

"Yes, I see," glares Gonzalez, a bit dismayed that Lopez is as drunk as ever. "You going to be in good enough shape to ride in the morning?"

"Sure," Lopez replies, "I'm always ready to ride. Just show me where my horse is and point him in the right direction."

They all laugh at this one, especially Lopez.

"So, then," Romulo says, pulling the cork from his bottle and taking his first pull of the night, "we will ride over to San Rafael in the morning."

"Si, manana," Cruz says. "I will be ready to ride in the morning."

"Good," replies Romulo, "then we can take care of that favor for Chavez and get back to Tecarte. He should be back soon and then we have that other business to attend to." He takes another long pull from the bottle.

"Where are the other men?" he asks. "They're drinking in the bunkhouse, I think," says Lopez. "Okay, good then," Gonzalez says. "I will put my horse in the barn and find a spot to sleep in the bunkhouse, if that's okay with you, Senor Mendosa."

"Si, Romulo, anytime," says Mendosa. "You don't even have to ask. You are always welcome here. They've got some food cooking over there so just help yourself."

"Gracias, amigo," replies Romulo. "See you in the morning. Buenos noches."

Gonzalez grabs his still-wet serape, wraps it around him, opens the door and heads back into the cold, wet night, bottle in hand.

Chapter 20

Don Antonio Sosa is excited despite the cold, damp morning at his rancho just outside the small Mexican village of San Rafael. For several weeks he's been looking forward to a trip to San Diego to take care of some pressing business. First he must meet Henry Leclaire at the store of Louis Mendelson in San Rafael, as the portly man will ride with him on the journey.

Sosa can see the concern on the face of his wife of 16 years as he kisses her goodbye on the front steps. "Don't worry, my love. I'll be back as soon as I can and if you need anything, send one of the boys to San Rafael or to the Flores's casa; they are good neighbors and they will help."

"I'm not worried about *me*," she says, "I am worried about *you*. You're the one that's going to be out on the trail for many days and nights and it's so cold this time of year. And you could get caught out in the rain."

Sosa thinks how lucky he is to have such a caring wife. And beautiful too, as she is ten years younger than him and still has a youthful figure despite having borne him six children.

"I've been on the trail many times in the past and I'll be alright," he says with a smile, patting his holster, which holds a Colt Army model black-powder six-shooter, the same one he used to carry when he was the governor of the entire territory.

He hugs and kisses her one more time as the children look on. "You boys look out for your mam'a, you hear?" he tells them. "And help her out and do your chores."

"Si, Papa," the older boys say.

He gets into the little two-wheeled buggy and looks back at his family and smiles. Then with a "ya" and a crack of his whip, the two horses jump into a trot and just like that he's on his way.

Sosa is a happy man. Though now 52 years old, he is still strong and lean. As a young man, he had many adventures traveling all over the Baja peninsula and northern Mexico. He made some good connections in the right places, good enough to get him appointed to a term as governor a few years back. He earned a good amount of money, but also a lot of enemies. Because of this, he had to move his family around a lot.

But seven years ago he took his small fortune and retired from politics, buying his little spread and settling into the life of a rancher. "I've got a wonderful life," he thinks to himself as the horses instinctively follow the road to San Rafael, about a 20-minute ride. He has a small herd of cattle and lots of other smaller stock, mostly goats, sheep and chickens. He also has a work horse, some riding horses and two fine horses that are now hitched to his buggy. He loves these horses and takes good care of them.

Next thing he knows he's pulling up in front of Mendelson's store in San Rafael. He sets the brake and steps down. The cold, damp morning now shows signs of improving nicely; the sun is burning through the fog, radiating its warmth.

"Buenos dias," a man says to him and he turns to see a short, stout man standing in the doorway of the store. A carpet bag sits at his feet.

"Hello, Henry. Buenos dias to you too," Sosa says in reply. Mr. Leclaire's name is really Alphonse, but everyone who knows him calls him Henry.

"I think we chose our departure day wisely," Sosa continues. "The weather's about to break and I think we'll have sunshine following us all the way to San Diego."

"I sure hope so," Leclaire responds, placing his carpet bag in the back of the buggy next to Sosa's. "That rain last night really came down hard for a while and I was getting nervous."

Sosa smiles. "No need to worry, my friend," he says. "You're lucky to live here in this beautiful place, as are we all. We call it, 'Terra del Dios.'"

"Yes, I have to agree with you there," Henry says. "This is the land of God and we are all blessed to live in a place such as this."

A man walks across the street; he nods hello to the two men as he passes and enters the store.

"Come inside, Mr. Sosa," says Henry. "Mr. Mendelson wants to see you before we go." "Okay," Antonio replies and the two men enter the store. Louis Mendelson is behind the counter doing some paperwork and the only other person in the store is the man who just entered before they did. He's off to the side looking at some blankets.

Mendelson looks up and says, "Senor Sosa, so glad to see you. Please come around to this side of the counter." Sosa walks over and opens the small swinging door that separates the store from behind the counter. They shake hands and Sosa replies, "And it's so good to see you again too, Louis."

Mendelson looks over at his lone customer and asks him if he needs any help. Rafael Martinez looks up from the pile of blankets he's been pretending to look over. "No, no, senor, I was just looking at these blankets," he says.

"Well, if you need any help, just give a holler," Mendelson tells him. "I've got some business in the back. Come, come," he says, motioning to the two men to follow. "I've got something to give you to take to San Diego."

They walk down the small hallway to the back room where a small office is set up. There is a small iron box bolted to the floor with a padlock on it. Mendelson takes a small key from his pocket and opens the safe.

Martinez hears the creak of the safe door and moves closer to the hallway so he can hear what the men are saying.

"Henry, here is the money I want you to bring to Steiner and Klauber," he hears Mendelson say. "Give it to Abe Klauber. There's six hundred dollars in gold coins in this bag. This covers what I owe them and then some. And get a receipt. And also give him this list of some more supplies that I want them to freight out as soon as possible, hopefully before the end of the year if they can."

"I will, boss," Leclaire assures.

"And this is for you, Antonio," says Mendelson as he turns to Sosa and hands him some papers. "These are documents about a land trust that I have an interest in north of the border in San Diego. If you would carry them with you and deliver them to J.S. Mannasse and Co., which is two doors south of the Wells Fargo Express office, I would be greatly in your debt."

"That's no problem," Antonio tells him. "I have some business with them also."

"Well then," says Mendelson, "I have asked the right man. I will, of course, pay you for your service."

"That's not necessary," Sosa replies. "As I said, I

have to go there anyway. It would be my pleasure to help you."

"Thank you, Don Antonio, you are very kind," Mendelson says. "When are you leaving?"

"Just as soon as we can," Sosa replies. "I think if we can get on our way soon, we will be at my friend Trinidad Seseno's casa by noon and can stop for lunch. I need to see him before I leave and then we will be on our way again in the afternoon. We should be in San Diego in three days and if God be with us, be back here in two weeks' time."

"Good, then, have a nice trip," Mendelson says, satisfied with the itinerary. "I'll see you as soon as you return, and Henry, do be careful with that gold."

"Oh, I will, sir," Leclaire says, clutching the bag in both hands and holding it tightly to his chest. Mendelson closes the safe with a creak and secures the lock; the three men walk back up the hallway into the store just in time to hear the front door close.

"Oh, I forgot I had a customer," Mendelson realizes too late. "I hope he didn't steal anything." He looks around the store quickly and all seems in place. "Well, gentlemen, I bid you a safe journey," he says, shaking hands again with Sosa as the two men walk out of the store into the warmth of the street.

Sosa marvels at the beautiful day that has unfolded. "Perfect," he says, "the weather is going to be with us. I think we are going to have a wonderful trip to San Diego."

They climb aboard the buggy and Sosa puts the papers that Mendelson asked him to deliver into a small trunk, along with the pouch containing the gold. Then he places the trunk between the two riders and ties it securely to the seat.

"Let's go," he says to the horses and lightly cracks the whip over their backs, and the buggy begins to move. Sosa pulls hard to the left on the reins and the horses obey, turning the little buggy around in the street, and with a "ya" the horses break into a trot and they're on their way north.

***

Cruz Lopez is sitting under a large tree nursing an even larger hangover than usual. Every once in a while he leans over and vomits small amounts of yellowish bile that leaves a wretched taste in his mouth. He's been throwing up all morning.

"You going to live, amigo?" teases Romulo Gonzalez, who along with Jose Alvijo and Alonzo Cota is waiting for Martinez to return from San Rafael.

"Yeah, I'll live," sneers Lopez. "I just drank a little too much last night."

"I'll say," Gonzalez replies. "A *little* too much? Amigo, you drank two bottles of tequila! You were as drunk as a burro that wandered into a pile of pulque pulp!" Gonzalez and Alvijo let out a laugh that draws a dirty look from Lopez, bringing the laughter to an abrupt halt. Even Cota thought this was funny, but he dared not laugh at Cruz Lopez, especially when he's in such a sour mood.

"Look!" Cota suddenly says, pointing south. "Rafael is coming back." Martinez is riding fast, heading to where he left his compadres a couple hours before. He had been appointed to ride into town to find out any news about Sosa. He rides up and climbs off his horse.

Lopez sits up, still holding his head. “So, what did you find out?” he barks.

“Very much, amigo,” Martinez says excitedly. “I saw Sosa with my own eyes and he is leaving San Rafael at this very moment!”

“What do you mean, ‘At this very moment,’” demands Lopez. “Where’s he going?”

“I mean, I saw Sosa at the dry goods store and he and another man are leaving in a buggy for San Diego. They are on the road this very moment; they left town right after I did, but they were headed on the northwest road and they’re stopping for lunch at the house of a man named Trinidad Seseno. Then they’re leaving for San Diego in the afternoon.”

“I know of this man,” says Gonzalez of Seseno. “I know where he lives – about seven or eight miles out of town on the road to Tecarte.”

“He’s in a buggy, you say?” Lopez asks Martinez.

“Yes, a two-horse buggy with another man who works for the storekeeper. And I heard them say they’re carrying six hundred dollars in gold with them.”

“Gold!” exclaims Lopez so loudly that he groans at the pain echoing in his head. It takes a moment for him to recover from the pounding. “What else did you learn?”

“Just that they were leaving right away, so they should already be on the road ahead of us,” Martinez reports.

Lopez can’t believe their good fortune. He turns to Gonzalez and asks, “Is there any way to get ahead of them without being spotted?”

“Sure,” Romulo replies. “If they’re stopping for lunch. We can follow them and then swing wide of Seseno’s house and ride on ahead and find a good spot to wait for them."

Lopez splashes some cold water on his face from a small creek flowing nearby and savors the cool feeling. "Good," he says, "then let's go." Cruz gets up and they all swing up onto their mounts. "Vamos," yells Lopez again as they break into a fast trot toward the Tecarte road.

***

Back in Campo, Jack Kelly comes running out of the telegraph office and yells to Lumen and Silas, who are standing over by the blacksmith shop with a few of the other men. Captain Billy is on his horse, about to leave for Tecarte to see what he can find out about the bandits.

"Lumen, Silas, you've got to see this!" Kelly yells as he runs up to them with a piece of paper in his outstretched hand.

"What is it?" Lumen asks.

"Just came off the telegraph line from Yuma," Kelly says. "It's about Chavez."

Lumen quickly grabs the slip of paper and begins reading it aloud. *"To San Diego, from operator Yuma station. Stop. November the twenty-six, eighteen-seventy five. Stop. Clodoveo Chavez, notorious California highwayman who was lieutenant under Vasquez and most daring of gang killed yesterday at Texas Hill, Arizona, by man named William Clark Colvig while attempting arrest. Stop."*

The men in the street begin murmuring about the news.

Lumen continues to read the telegram. *"Colvig and three others with him employed by King S. Woolsey, keeper of Stanwix Station. Stop."*

Lumen is stunned. "Holy Moses, Silas, what do you think of this?" he asks his brother.

"Well, if it's true, then I'd say our troubles are over," Silas resolves.

"What about the rest of the Chavez gang?" Captain Billy asks. "They're still down in Tecarte, last we knew."

"I suspect you're right, Billy," says Silas, "but I don't think they'll try anything without Chavez. He was the only one bold enough to rob Campo. Without their leader, I'd say the rest of them will probably disburse and ride for the hills. Let's call in the rest of the men and see what they think about it."

Silas grabs his shotgun and fires into the air. "Come on in men," he yells, "we've got something to tell you!"

The men start gathering around and Lumen and Silas tell them the shocking news.

"Good, that's what I say," offers John Williams. "Me, too," adds Simon Miller. "Without their leader they won't amount to much. They positive it's him?"

"Well," says Lumen, looking at the telegram again, "it says here that it was Chavez who was killed."

"What do you think he was doing over in Arizona?" asks McFall Pearson.

"I don't know and I don't much care," decides Silas. "If he's dead, then I say good riddance."

"Here, here," all the men reply. "What should we do now?" Miller asks.

"Well, I guess with the latest news we don't need to guard the town like we were," Silas says, "but I still think that we shouldn't let our guard down. I know that most of you men need to get back to your ranches and I guess any of you who need to leave should go."

"But what if they still try to rob Campo?" asks Williams.

"We still have enough people in Campo to put up a fight," says Silas, "and if a few of you can stay for a couple more days just to be sure, then I think we'll be alright."

"I'll stay," says Captain Billy, sliding off his horse, relived that he doesn't have to cross the line after all. "No need for me to ride down to Tecarte now anyways."

"We'll stay too," a couple of the other men say.

"Good, then," says Silas. "The rest of you can go home to your ranches and if we hear anything important, we'll send someone out to inform you. And men, I want you to know that Lumen and me really appreciate you coming to help out like this."

"Don't you worry about that none," the men say. "We're all neighbors here and we know you'd do the same for us."

"Well, thanks anyway," Lumen adds. "But we really never did have anything to worry about. The U.S. Army was kind enough to station their best fighter right here in Campo!"

Jack Kelly smiles, knowing he's being picked on.

"Yeah," adds Silas, "Jack here could take on all of them bandits by himself, couldn't you, Jack?"

"Yeah, sure," smiles Kelly, playing along for the moment.

"And look," continues Silas, "Jack is so 'bad' that he doesn't think he needs to carry his pistol to whip them bandits."

The men all chuckle as they look and see that

Kelly is not wearing his sidearm.

"So," Silas says to Jack, "just where *is* your gun?"

Jack feels for his gun belt, but finds it's not there and sheepishly says, "Well … I don't know!"

All the men laugh uproariously and Kelly's face turns beet red as only an Irishman's can. "It's … it's in my office," Kelly blurts out.

"Sure, Jack," someone says and they all laugh one last time.

The men start to disburse and Lumen says to Silas, "What do we do now?"

"Well," says Silas, "we park our shotguns where they will be within easy reach so we can get them in a hurry if we need to and then we get back to business as usual."

"That's it?" says Lumen. "Yeah, that's it," replies Silas as he turns and walks toward the blacksmith shop. "I've got lots of work to catch up on," he says as he walks inside, puts coal in the forge and gets some kindling to light it up with.

***

The five bandits have no problem following the little buggy; the tracks are unmistakable in the fresh mud in the road from the deluge of the night before. It's not long before Romulo Gonzalez suddenly holds up a hand.

"We will need to go around," he announces to the others. "The Seseno ranch is just ahead; if we go around that way," pointing to the right, "we should be able to circle around without being seen and then come back to the road."

"Si," says Lopez, feeling a little better now. "Let's

go."

The men follow Gonzalez and after they're past the Seseno's, they make their way back to the road. "Stay out of the road," Lopez warns them. "I don't want them to see our tracks in the mud and get suspicious."

They continue on for a mile, riding off to the side of the road until they reach a place where the road narrows as it passes a large rock outcropping that is only about 50 feet wide, where a normally dry stream bed cuts through from the left. By this hour, there is only a trickle running through it from the rainstorm.

A good enough place for an ambush, Lopez thinks. "We will hide here," he says. "Cota, you climb up on that hill a ways and find a good place to hide and watch for them."

"Okay, jefe," Cota replies.

"And stay up there," Lopez adds. "I don't want them to see you coming down."

Alonzo nods, gets off his horse, hands the reins to Martinez and starts to climb the small hill.

Lopez looks over the situation. "It is a good spot," he proclaims. "We can hide the horses over there behind those bushes," he says to Gonzalez. "Two of us will hide on this side of the road and the other two over there and then we'll catch them in a cross fire."

"Cross fire?" Martinez says to himself, a bit confused. Then he looks at Lopez and sees that the bandit is checking his gun to make sure it's loaded. Martinez starts to figure out this isn't going to be a simple robbery. "He's going to kill them!" he almost says aloud, then catches himself. A jumble of thoughts races through his mind in a millisecond. "What am I doing here?" "What will Maria say?" "I don't want to kill anybody."

He doesn't hear Lopez when he tells him to hide the horses.

"Martinez!" yells Lopez a second time. "What are you waiting for? I told you and Jose to take the horses and hide them over there out of sight."

"Si," Martinez says, but he just stands there looking at the ground, unable to move.

"Rafael!" yells Alvijo, "don't just stand there. Grab those reins and follow me."

"Huh? Oh, okay," Martinez finally says and follows Alvijo into the bushes to hide the horses.

Lopez and Gonzalez formulate a simple plan. "We wait until they get far enough into the pass that they can't turn around quickly and then we come out – two on each side – and take them," Lopez says, adding a cruel laugh at the thought of what's to come. He is happy now. The hangover has suddenly been replaced by that good feeling that's coming over him again, the anticipation of the kill.

When Alvijo and Martinez return from securing the horses, Lopez instructs them to hide on the other side of the road. "Over there," he says, gesturing with his pistol. "Hide real good and when they come, watch me and when I give the signal, come running out and we'll stop them."

"Okay," says Alvijo grinning. Martinez can only nod as he's still lost in a whirlwind of thoughts.

An hour passes and nothing. Lopez is getting anxious. His head is beginning to throb again. But that all changes when suddenly he hears a call from Cota up on the hill. Lopez looks up and sees him pointing down the road. Lopez looks in that direction and can see a horse and buggy coming.

"Hey, get in position," he yells in a muffled voice

to the others. “They’re coming.” It doesn’t take long for the buggy to come around the corner into the small pass.

Don Antonio Sosa sees Cruz Lopez stand up from behind a rock. “What the …?” he thinks, and then sees the pistol in Lopez’s suddenly steady left hand. “Highwaymen,” he says to Henry as he sees the three others emerge from their hiding places, all brandishing guns. Sosa sees they’ve got the drop on him and he can do nothing but pull back on the reins.

“Amigos,” Lopez says to the riders, “we have been waiting for you.”

“What do you want?” Sosa replies sternly.

“Want?” bellows Lopez in a sarcastic snarl. “Well, since you are asking, senor, I will start with that gold you are carrying.”

“Gold? What gold?” Sosa replies evasively.

“Don’t be a fool with me,” Lopez warns, “or I’ll blow a hole through you right now and get it myself.” He cocks his pistol and points it in Sosa’s face. That’s enough for Sosa.

“No, don’t,” he says. “It’s right here.” Sosa unties the trunk from the seat and gives Henry a look as he does so. The fat little man has his hands up and is shaking in fear. Sosa throws the box to the ground at Lopez’s feet.

“There,” he says, “take it and go. But I warn you that I am the former governor of the territory and I will get a posse and hunt you down….”

“You will, now?” interrupts Lopez with a derisive laugh. “And just how are you going to do that when you’re dead?”

Sosa can see that this man is not fooling. In a panic, he slaps the reins hard on the two horses’ backs and the buggy lurches forward. Alvijo has to leap out of the way and barely misses being run over, falling to the ground.

Lopez wasn't expecting Sosa to try to flee and can snap off only a hurried shot. The bullet just misses Sosa, but strikes Henry Leclaire in the left side of the head. The unfortunate man dies instantly and falls in a heap out of the right side of the buggy and lands at the feet of Martinez. The shocking sight of the fat man flopped on his back with a gaping hole in his head is surreal to him.

Martinez is snapped quickly back to reality by another explosion, this one from the gun of Gonzalez, whose wild shot misses the buggy but strikes the horse on the right in the side, lodging in its left lung. The horse, though, doesn't falter as the buggy, skidding wildly, rockets down the trail as Lopez and Gonzalez empty their guns.

"Jose! Rafael! Get the horses, pronto!" Lopez yells as he quickly reloads his weapon. Alvijo scrambles up from the ground and yells, "Si, jefe!" and runs into the bushes and returns with the horses.

"Get the gold out of that trunk and follow us," Lopez orders Alvijo and Martinez. Then he and Gonzalez jump on their horses and gallop off after the wagon.

Alvijo runs over to the trunk and opens it. "The gold!" Jose exclaims with a big grin as he turns to Martinez, who is still standing looking at the dead man. Alvijo ignores him and ties the pouch to his belt and begins rifling through the rest of the box. Seeing nothing but papers and not knowing how to read anyway, he sees little value in them and scatters them to the wind.

He tosses the trunk into the bushes and grabs one of the arms of the dead man and tries to drag him from the roadway. But despite the slick mud, Leclaire is still too heavy and he tells Martinez to help him. But Martinez doesn't respond.

"Rafael, grab his arm! Let's go!" Alvijo yells to him. Martinez mindlessly does as he's told and they drag Leclaire into the bushes. Meanwhile, Cota slides feet first down the hill upon which he was hiding and gets some cactus needles stuck in the palms of his hands as he falls backward. The sight of Cota is a relief to Martinez, but there's no time for conversation.

"C'mon, let's go," Alvijo tells the two friends, handing them their reins. They quickly mount up and ride after their compadres.

Sosa is slapping the reins wildly on the backs of his horses. He's been scared before, but never like this. "Such lifeless eyes," is all he can think as he relives the previous 60 seconds in his mind. Sosa has been in a few gunfights in his days, but never has anyone got the drop on him like Lopez did. "There's no doubt that man was about to kill me," he tells himself.

The road is now starting to climb, winding over a small hill. Something is wrong with the horse on the right and it's starting to falter. Looking closer, Sosa sees there's blood coming from its left side. The horse is starting to slow, blood frothing from its mouth.

Sosa knows that it's not going to last much longer and surely the highwaymen are right on his tail. He sees a road that cuts off to the right. It's not much more than a trail, but it might be his only hope. He needs to get off the road and into the chaparral, the tall brush that grows in the dry, desert hills. He might be able to hide in the brush and make an escape after dark.

It's too late, though. The two pursuers come up quickly. Sosa slaps the horses even harder with the reins, then pulls them to the right and they obey. But the turn is too hard on the muddy road and the wounded horse stumbles and loses its footing, collapsing to the ground in a dying gasp. The buggy skids to the left and tips, throwing Sosa hard to the ground.

Sosa starts to get up but only makes it to his knees before Lopez and Gonzalez are upon him, guns drawn.

"Throw that pistol over here," Lopez orders as he jumps down from his horse. Sosa can only do as he's told.

"What do you want with me?" Sosa demands of his captors, who are soon joined by the other three, riding up from behind.

"Well, gov'ner," Lopez replies with a hideous laugh, "we are only here to do a favor for a friend."

"A friend?" a confused Sosa inquires. "Who is this friend?"

"That does not matter," Lopez tells him. "The only thing that matters is that you are about to die."

Martinez is overwhelmed by the thought that this man, who never did anything to Lopez, is about to be killed – shot in cold blood while on his knees. But then Martinez becomes even more horrified as he watches Lopez put his gun back in his holster and pick up a rock the size of a coconut from the ground.

"No! No!" exclaims Sosa, who tries to get up from the ground. But before he can, Lopez kicks him hard in the face, knocking him onto his back. Blood gushes from his mouth.

"You son of a bitch!" Lopez yells as he smashes the rock on the top of Sosa's head. It's only a glancing blow, but it knocks him senseless. Then Lopez lifts the rock high and brings it down on the man's head with the full force of his body, crushing his skull like a ripe melon.

But he's not done. Once more he lifts the stone above his head and brings it down with abandon. Over and over Lopez smashes Sosa in the head with the rock until his skull cracks open and half of his brain comes spilling out.

Martinez is mortified and he turns and falls to his knees, puking into the bushes, retching at the nauseating sight.

But Lopez is still not through. Cota now is spellbound as well as he watches the killer pull out a big knife. He cuts deeply into the dead man's throat, slicing him from ear to ear. Blood is everywhere.

"Take that, you son of bitch," Lopez yells maniacally and then throws the body to the ground. "That was for Chavez!"

Lopez's eyes are wild as he steps back, admiring his handiwork.

Gonzalez steps in and quickly goes through Sosa's pockets. He pulls out a billfold, some cigars and a folding knife. He pockets the knife and cigars and hands the billfold to Lopez, who puts it in his own pocket without even looking at it.

Lopez then notices Martinez, heaving again by the side of the road.

"What the hell are you doing over there?" he yells at Rafael. "Get your ass up and be a man!"

Martinez gets up quickly and wipes the vomit off his face with his shirtsleeve. "Yes, senor," he stammers. "I … I was just surprised by it all, that's all."

Lopez lets out a grunt. "Yeah, sure," he says, turning his attention quickly to Alvijo. "You get the gold?" he demands.

"Si, jefe! right here," Jose says smiling, holding up the pouch.

"Good," Cruz says, "then let's get out of here."

"That would be a good idea," Gonzalez adds. "I've got to live near here and I don't want to be seen in this area."

"What about the other horse," Alvijo says, pointing to the horse standing nearby, still hitched to the buggy.

"Leave it," Lopez says. "Everyone for miles around would recognize it. It would draw too much attention."

"Si," Alvijo agrees as they all mount up and ride off quickly to the north.

After a short while they slow to a fast walk and Lopez can see that Martinez is still as white as a newborn sheep. "I don't know about you, Rafael," he says, shaking his head. "Did you not expect this?"

"I am sorry," Martinez replies, "it was my first time."

"Okay," Lopez says. "I'll let it go … this time."

Lopez digs his large spurs deep into the side of his horse and it bolts ahead.

"Let's go," he yells. "We've got to get back to Tecarte."

Chapter 21

It's a beautiful late-November morning in Yuma and Juan Ramirez is working at the livery stable cleaning stalls as he does every day. The young man looks up and sees a wagon coming into town, flanked by two armed horsemen. This would not be unusual if not for the 30 or more people following it as if it was a parade. Most of them are Mexicans and something in the back of the wagon is causing quite a commotion.

Curiosity getting the better of him, Ramirez ducks under a fence rail and trots over to take a look. He isn't expecting to see the horror that awaits him. His idol, the great Clodoveo Chavez, is lying dead as a doornail in the back of the wagon. His face, covered by flies, is contorted in a frozen grimace.

Stunned, Ramirez stumbles backward, falling to the ground. His sombrero tumbles off and is kicked a few feet away by one of the followers. He scrambles to his feet, retrieves his hat and runs off to find his father. As he turns the corner on the dirt street, he can see his father saddling a horse to go duck hunting in the marshes south along the Colorado River.

"Papa!" he hears his son yell as he comes running up the street. "Papa!" yells Juan again as he approaches the Ramirez home fully out of breath.

"What is it, my son?" his father asks, seeing a concern on Juan's face he does not recognize.

"It's Chavez!" Juan exclaims. "He's dead!"

"Dead?" replies Ramon Ramirez, the words zapping him like a bolt of lightning. "How do you know this?"

"I just saw him!" Juan exclaims. "He's lying dead in a wagon that's just coming into town."

Ramon unhitches his horse and pulls himself up into the saddle with the unthinking agility of a man much younger than his 62 years. "Go and tell your mother," he tells Juan and turns the horse quickly and gallops off down the street in the direction of the growing commotion.

He finds the wagon stopped in front of the sheriff's office. Yuma County Sheriff William Augustus Werninger is standing at the front door of his office scratching his whiskers as he looks over the chaotic scene.

Ramon Ramirez ties his horse off to a hitching post and runs over to the wagon, where sure enough, the body of the man he considered like family lies dead in the back.

Even though he has seen the telegram sent from Stanwix Station, the one which was sent on to Campo, the sheriff still steps forward and demands all official-like, "Who among this calamity can tell me what the hell's going on here?"

Luis Raggio maneuvers his horse in front of the crowd and addresses the sheriff from the saddle. "We have in the back of this wagon the body of the California outlaw Clodoveo Chavez," Raggio begins. "He is wanted in Los Angeles for murder. We tried to capture him alive, but he resisted arrest and was killed trying to arm himself to make an escape."

"I see," says Werninger, stepping into the street to get a look at the body himself. The crowd, now suddenly silent, parts as he does so. He looks at the body. "Clodoveo Chavez, you say? I've heard of him."

"But you've got the wrong man!" Ramon Ramirez

hears himself blurt out. "That man is not an outlaw; that is Jose Espinosa and I have known him for years."

"No, it's not!" Luis and Vincente Raggio both say almost at once. Harry Roberts is suddenly not so certain. "You said you were sure about this!" he says sharply to Luis Raggio under his breath.

"I am," Luis reassures him and the others. "This *is* Chavez, the wanted man. He sometimes goes by the name Jose Espinosa; that is his alias. He calls himself by that name."

"Do not believe him, sheriff," Ramon Ramirez says as his son joins him by his side. "The man in this wagon is Jose Espinosa."

"Si," adds Juan, out of breath, not quite sure what his father's getting at, but going along with it. "This is Senor Espinosa," he adds. The crowd is getting angry again.

"Well," says the sheriff, looking at the Raggios, "seems like we've got a little problem here."

Werninger turns to a man nearby. "Charlie," he says, "go get the coroner and tell him to get over here right away. And find Deputy Thomas. I need him here too." Charlie immediately runs off down the street, his hat in his hand.

"Now you three," the sheriff says, gesturing to Roberts and the Raggios, "tie off them horses and come into my office. You've got some explaining to do." They do as instructed. "And you too," Werninger adds, looking at the Ramirezes. "You come in too."

Werninger turns to the crowd still standing around the dead body and says, "Don't nobody touch nothin' till the coroner gets here, do you hear me? And I mean nothing!"

"Yes, sir, sheriff," one man says. "I'll watch him for you."

"Good," the sheriff says as he turns and follows the others into his office and shuts the door.

"Well, gentlemen," he begins, "just until we straighten this out, I would like you to remove your firearms and put them on that table over there."

"Sure, sheriff," Harry Roberts replies. "We don't want no trouble with the law."

"Well," Werninger continues, "we're just going to see about that. I want the whole story – from the beginning."

The three bounty hunters take off their holsters and place the guns on the table.

"Sheriff, my name is Luis Raggio and this is my brother, Vincente," begins Luis. "And this gentleman with us is Harry Roberts. We all work for King Woolsey over at the Agua Caliente Ranch out by Gila Bend…."

The three tell their story, about how Luis grew up with Chavez in northern California, meeting him at the Baker ranch, riding with him into Mexico. And about Bill Colvig shooting Chavez and not wanting to come to Yuma with the body.

"Smart man," the sheriff interrupts. "If he's the shooter, then how can I get a'hold of him?" "He's at Stanwix Station," Roberts says. "He won't go anywhere until he hears from us."

"You had better hope not," the sheriff says. "This is a serious matter and if you shot the wrong man then someone is going to answer for it."

The deputy, Billy Thomas, comes hurriedly through the front door.

"The coroner's here," Thomas states. "He wants to

know if he can move the body."

"Sure, Billy," says the sheriff. "I want an autopsy done as soon as possible. And tell the coroner to go get Doc Loring. I want him to view the body too."

"Okay, Will," the deputy replies as he heads right back out the door.

"So," begins Werninger again, now turning his attention to the elder Ramirez, "you say you know the dead man as Jose Espinosa."

"Si, that is true," says Ramon Ramirez as his son nods in agreement. "He has been a friend of the family for years and I know him to be a good man, not an outlaw like these men claim. He was here in Yuma just three weeks ago. He said he was looking for work in the area. He's a vaquero by trade."

"Well," says the befuddled sheriff, "there's certainly going to have to be an inquest held to sort this one out. So until then," he adds, turning back to the others, "I'm going to have to place you three under arrest."

Harry Roberts gives Luis Raggio a heated look as the sheriff gets up and grabs his jail keys.

"Do any of you boys have any more weapons on you?" the sheriff asks them. "Guns or knives or anything?"

"I've got my boot knife," Luis Raggio says, reaching down and then putting it on the table with the guns.

"That better be it," the sheriff warns. "If I find out later that any of you boys have anything else, then it's going to go hard on you."

"Sure, sheriff, we understand," Luis Raggio says. "That's all we have."

"Then I've got to lock you boys up for a while," the sheriff says. "In there," he adds, nodding toward the open cell behind them. Once they're inside, the sheriff shuts the door and locks it, placing the keys on a peg next to the woodstove against the far wall. Then he turns back to the Ramirezes.

"You are Ramon Ramirez, you say, and you live here in town?" he asks the older man.

"Yes, sheriff, and this is my son, Juan," he says.

"Good, then," the sheriff replies. "I will need you to speak to the jury once we get it impaneled, so I would like you to stay close to town for now."

"We will," the father and son say in unison.

The Ramirezes head for the door just as it opens again. Deputy Thomas re-enters. "Doc Loring is on his way to the coroner's office," Thomas reports. "Are these the men who killed him?" he adds, looking at the three anxious faces in the jail cell.

"Yes. And no," Werninger replies. "If these men are telling the truth…."

"We are, sheriff, we are!" insists Luis Raggio.

"We'll see," he says. "Anyway, as I was saying Billy, the man who did the actual shooting didn't want to come in. He's holed up at Stanwix Station. Apparently works for King Woolsey."

"Are we going to ride out there and get him?" Thomas asks.

"No, not yet anyway," answers the sheriff, grabbing some paper from the top drawer of his desk and writing something down. "Take this over to the telegraph office and send it to Sheriff Rowland in Los Angeles. He knows this Chavez and maybe he's got a good description of him."

“Okay,” the deputy replies, grabbing the note and heading out the door again.

Down the street, Ramon and Juan Ramirez are walking their horse home. “I can’t believe it,” Juan exclaims with tears in his eyes. “Clodoveo is dead!”

“I know, my son,” says Ramon consolingly, “but it’s true and nothing we can do will bring him back.”

“So what *can* we do?” Juan asks his father.

“We can get revenge,” Ramon Ramirez says. “It won’t take that gringo sheriff long to figure out that Jose and Clodoveo are the same man and then they will let them bounty hunting bastards out of jail and they will probably get the reward.”

“But we heard them say the man who killed him is at Stanwix Station?” Juan says.

“Yes, a man called Colvig,” Ramon says. “Take my horse, Juan,” he adds, handing the reins to his son. “Ride out to your cousin Pepe’s ranch. Tell him what has happened and that we need some men with enough rifles and horses to ride to Stanwix Station. We will leave tonight and go pay this man Colvig a visit.”

“Si!,” exclaims Juan, jumping on the horse.

“I’ll be ready to leave when you return, so hurry,” Ramon adds.

“I will, father!” Juan shouts as he gallops off.

Ramon Ramirez watches for a moment, then turns the street corner. “My wife will be taking this pretty hard,” he thinks. “I must take time to console her.” But mostly he’s thinking about his rifle hanging on the wall. “I will need to oil it and load it up,” he thinks, “and then we will go and get our revenge!”

Chapter 22

Early that evening, Juan Ramriez arrives back in Yuma with Pepe and three of his cousin's best men, all packed and ready for a long trip. Pepe had never met Chavez himself, but had heard all the stories of the famous bandit from his uncle and knows how fondly they thought of him.

"This gringo will pay dearly if we get the chance," Pepe promises his uncle upon arriving at the Ramirez home. "So how do you want to do this?"

"I've been thinking about it," Ramon explains. "I think we should ride on the road as far as we can get without being seen. Then we turn north until we get to the river, follow it and come in from the west. We hide our horses and sneak up on the place. There's a creek that has cut a gulch alongside the station and we can ride in that gulch and get pretty close without being seen.

"We'll come in at night and when the sun comes up, we'll make our play," he continues.

"That sounds like a good plan," Pepe says. "Si," echo the others.

"Okay then," says Ramon. "We‘ve got a lot of miles ahead of us so as soon as it's dark, be ready to ride."

***

Not far across town, the inquest is just getting started. Despite the late hour, a jury of 12 men has been seated in the courthouse. They are viewing the body, which by now has turned black and is starting to bloat and smell. Best to get the viewing out of the way first.

Edgar G. Smith, the coroner, starts by describing the entry wounds and their effects upon the body. “Fifteen in all, eleven in the left lung, four in the right,” he testifies matter of factly. “One of them ended up in the heart. Killed almost instantly. Shot in the back from a slight angle. At close range, I’d reckon.”

Then Smith gives a description of the body. “Height, five-feet, ten-inches tall; weight, about one hundred and eighty pounds; black, short-cropped hair,” he begins. “A close-cut beard. A scar on his right cheek extending from the eye to the lower jaw. And a scar on the right leg near the kneecap.”

That done, the coroner pulls a heavy sheet over the body and motions to some men in the back to help him carry the table the body is lying on out of the courtroom. “That’s about it,” he says as he walks out.

Then Sheriff Werninger takes the stand and tells the jurors how the stories of the men in his jail and those of the Ramirezes differ and how he first was informed about the affair when he had heard about the telegram sent from Stanwix Station, and that he had sent a telegram to the sheriff in Los Angeles to get a better description of Chavez.

But Werninger admits he’s yet to hear back from Los Angeles, so it’s decided to reconvene the inquest at 10 o’clock the following morning.

***

By the next day, things have returned to normal back in Campo. Silas can be heard pounding a piece of hot metal on the anvil. Clang, clang, clang. The sounds reverberate throughout the small village. Lumen is in the hotel finishing his breakfast.

"Now don't you fret none," Lumen tells his wife, "we can take care of ourselves."

"But, dear, what if the telegram was wrong," she replies. "What if those cutthroats come in and raid us anyway?"

"Captain Billy is still up on his hill watching over things," Lumen reassures her. "He will let us know if anyone's coming. If they do come, I want you and Walter and Auntie Price to go to the house, get my needle gun and stay out of sight. Don't come out until I come and get you."

"Okay, honey, we will," she says, "but I'm still scared."

"Everything will be all right," assures Lumen again, this time adding a hug for good measure. "Silas and I can handle them. I just want you off the street if anything happens, okay?"

"Okay," she says.

"I've got to go open the store now," Lumen says. "I love you, Eliza," he adds, kissing her on the forehead.

"I love you too, Lumen," she says, clutching him tightly.

"C'mon Walter!" Lumen yells up the stairs.

"Just a minute!" he hears Vi Price yell back. "I'm tying his shoes."

Moments later Walter bounds down the stairs two at a time and is standing next to his father.

"C'mon, boy, let's go open the store," Lumen says to him, and the two women watch the father and son walk down the porch and head toward the store next door, Lumen's hand around his son's shoulder.

"That boy is going to be just like his father," Vi Price says. "I know," Eliza replies, "that's what's got me worried!"

***

Cruz Lopez and the others are almost back to Tecarte after a hard ride, that good feeling still rushing through his veins from the killings of the previous afternoon. They've been riding a series of switchbacks, working their way up over a small group of mountains into the Tecarte valley.

It's getting dark and with no moon lighting up the desert landscape, the trail is getting too hard to follow and Lopez decides to hold up for the night. It's a warm night for late November, fortunately, and it won't be too unpleasant for them to sleep under the stars.

"Hold it up, amigos," he says when they reach a small, flat area. "We'll camp here tonight and ride into Tecarte in the morning."

They're all tired anyway as it's been hours since they last gave the horses – and themselves – a rest.

Cota isn't even off his horse before Lopez orders him to go find some firewood. "Si, jefe," he replies as he turns his horse. Accustomed now to keeping an eye out for firewood around dusk, he remembers seeing a fallen tree just a little ways back. He figures he can throw a rope around it and drag it back to camp.

There's some good grass growing nearby and Cruz tells Martinez to take the saddles off all the horses and to graze them.

"Si," Rafael says, still in shock about what took place the day before.

Alvijo clears some brush away from a flat, sandy area and builds a fire pit using a circle of stones. Lopez sits down with his back to a rock.

"Aaahhh," he says. "I needed to get out of that saddle."

"Si," says Alvijo as he plops down against another rock.

"I could sure use a drink of tequila right now," Lopez adds.

"Me, too," says Alvijo, both knowing they have none.

"How much gold did we get yesterday?" Lopez asks his friend.

"A very nice pouch full," answers Alvijo proudly as he takes it off his belt and tosses it to Cruz.

Lopez holds the bag in one hand, bouncing it up and down a couple times trying to ascertain its weight. "Nice," he concludes. "Let's split it up."

He unties a dirty bandana from his neck, spreads it out on the ground and pours the contents of the bag onto it. The bright gold coins glisten in the pale light of the setting sun. Romulo looks at the gold and his eyes light up. He hasn't seen this much gold since he rode with Vasquez back in '73.

That was the day he was chased by a posse and barely escaped. He was saved from a hangman's noose only because of the border. When he crossed into Mexico, the posse gave up the chase and he was a free man. Since then, he has never crossed back over the line and has no plans to do so again.

Martinez comes back and sees the shiny yellow coins spread out on the bandana. A week ago, he would've been staring at a fortune, but now he's appalled that two men's lives can be worth so little. Cota returns, dragging a dead oak branch behind him just as Lopez has finished divvying up the booty. He gives Alonzo and Rafael about $50 each – a bigger cut than they deserve, he's quick to tell them – and divides the rest with Jose and Romulo.

Cota looks it over with amazement. He has never held so much money at one time before. But Martinez reacts differently. He clenches his fist tightly around the coins, not wanting to look at them. He can almost feel the coins heating up, burning a hole right through the palm of his hand.

"The devil's money," he says to himself. "What am I going to say to Maria? Or her father? How am I going to explain where I've been? Or how I got this money?"

Still, he walks over to his saddle and drops the coins into his saddle bag.

"Not much to eat tonight, amigos," he hears Lopez announce. "You'll have to make do with whatever you've got."

It doesn't matter much to Martinez anyway. His stomach is still tied in knots and he could never have eaten anyway. For one of the bandits, at least, it's going to be another long, cold night.

Chapter 23

The bandits saddle up and hit the trail early the next morning. They are quite hungry, having not eaten in nearly two days, and can't wait to get back to Tecarte and put a stop to that constant grumbling. But at least they slept well.

All except Martinez, that is. He didn't sleep a wink, unable to get the horrible events of the last two days out of his head. "Oh, God," he says to himself, "how did I get myself into this? I will never do this again, I promise, Lord."

It doesn't take long for the five bandits to ride down into the valley when suddenly Martinez, riding in the rear, speaks up. "Amigos," he says, "I will meet you later in town. I need to see Maria, and her father's house is down that trail," pointing to the fork on the left.

Lopez pulls his horse's reins sharply to the left and spins around in the trail. Riding up to Martinez, he challenges his new recruit. "So, you going to leave your friends now, huh, Rafael?"

"No, no, senor," Martinez replies, realizing he's spoken too boldly. "I just want to see Maria for a short while, that's all."

After an awkward few moments, Cota speaks up too, and says, "I would like to see my family too, if that's all right with you, jefe."

Lopez turns his horse slightly so he can see both of them. "Sure, sure," Lopez says, forcing a smile, "you two should go and see your families. That is a good thing. But let me warn you – do not say anything about our ride these last few days."

"No, no, amigo," they both say.

"Because if you do," Lopez continues, "not only will I do to you what I did to Sosa, but I will do it to your loved ones too. I hope you understand me, amigos. I'm not fooling around; this is a very serious business we are in."

"We understand, Cruz," says Cota. "We will talk to no one about this."

"Good," Cruz replies. "Chavez will be back soon and when he does, we'll be getting ready to go to Sonora and get some real gold. We've just got us one little job to do before we go and I will need both of you for it. So you men take a couple of days to see your families and then meet up with us at the Tecarte cantina in two days, comprende?"

"Okay," the two say. "In two days. At the cantina. We'll be there."

They pull their reins and with a little kick they trot on down the road to the left.

"And don't forget you're riding my horses!" Lopez yells after them.

When they get out of earshot, Cota says to his friend, "I am sorry, Rafael. It's my fault I got us into this."

"No, it's not," replies Martinez. "It's just as much my fault. I don't know what we were thinking. How could we have gotten into a mess like this? We will be wanted men. How can I marry Maria now?"

"But, Rafael," says Cota to his friend, "no one saw us when they killed those men. The bodies might not be found for days, or even weeks."

"That doesn't matter," Martinez knows. "I was seen in San Rafael. In the store."

"Well, there's nothing to tie you to the two dead men," Cota says, "except this gold. So let's hide it somewhere real good, maybe that place where we hid the guns before. It's not far up ahead."

"Si," says Rafael. "I do not want this gold no more. It's got blood on it and I don't think I could ever spend it without remembering how I got it."

"I hear you, amigo," Alonzo replies. "Let's hide it away and figure out what to do with it later. Remember, we have to meet back up with Lopez and the gang in two days."

"I know," acknowledges Rafael, "and that's another thing. If we don't meet up with them and ride for Sonora they will kill our loved ones. Do you really think that Lopez would do that?"

"You saw how loco he is," Cota replies. "I think he will do as he says. I wish there was another way, but I think we will need to stay with them until we get to Sonora, or some place far off, and then we can look for a way to escape."

"I guess so," Rafael says. "What do you think Lopez meant when he said we've still got one little job to do?"

"I don't know," Alonzo replies, "but whatever it is, I bet we won't like it."

The two are coming to their hiding place among the rocks. They hide the guns and the gold and agree to meet back at this spot in two days.

Rafael Martinez has never felt a hurt like he feels now. A pain that he can't describe, but one that he feels from head to toe. But mostly it's in his gut. He wants to be sick, but he hasn't eaten since the day before yesterday.

As he turns the last corner, he sees smoke rising from the chimney of Maria's house. Her brother and sister are playing in the front yard, but the Estrada's dog sees the horse and rider before they do and starts barking.

No turning back now, Rafael tells himself. The door opens and he sees Maria's mother looking out. He figures they won't be expecting him to be riding a horse and probably won't recognize him. Then Maria looks out and screams, "Rafael!"

She runs out and he dismounts just in time for her to throw her arms around his neck. "Maria!" he says, taking her into his arms and holding her tight. "I love you so much!"

"And I love you, Rafael!" she replies as she kisses him on the lips. Rafael is surprised and looks to see if her father is watching.

"Father's not home," Maria says, her beautiful smile momentarily rescuing Martinez from his torment. "He is helping Senor Juarez in Tijuana and won't be back until tomorrow."

"But … your mother?" Rafael stammers. "She is watching."

"Don't worry about her," Maria says with a wink. "She won't tell Father. She knows that I'm a grown woman, old enough to be married."

Rafael smiles. All the hurt that he was feeling has just been melted away. Holding this beautiful woman in his arms is all he's ever wanted. He squeezes her tightly. To Martinez, she is worth more than all the gold in Sonora.

"Maria," he says, "I love you more than anything in the world. And I want to be the one who marries you."

"Oh, Rafael," she says, "we *will* get married, even

if father disapproves. I will run away with you if I have to." She looks him deep in the eyes. "God has made you for me and me for you. Father will come to see that and he will have to approve."

Rafael sees the commitment in her eyes and knows that she is telling him the truth. "The truth," he thinks. "It is I who is living the lie." He pulls her close, trying to hide his lying eyes.

"Rafael," she finally says as if noticing it for the first time, "you're riding a horse!" Looking closer, she adds, "And you look like you've been on the trail.

"What have you been doing?" she asks naively, teasingly poking him in the ribs.

"Aah, Maria," he says, fumbling for his next lie, "I've got a new job!"

"A new job!" Maria exclaims as her eyes light up. "What is it? Tell me about it!"

"Yes, my sweetheart, I've been working for a rancher in Ensenada," he replies, wincing inside at his torrent of lies.

"Oh, Rafael," Maria gushes. "I love it down there by the seashore. How I love the sound of the waves. And the white birds flying overhead."

"That might be it," thinks Martinez to himself. The answer to this nightmare. "I could get the gold and take Maria to Ensenada and we could get married down there. Lopez would never know that's where we went and in a week or so, the gang will be riding for Sonora and maybe even get themselves killed. Then we wouldn't have to hide from them."

Thinking it through, Martinez quickly dismisses the notion. No, that would never work, he realizes. He just told Maria he has a job in Ensenada and what is she going to think when she finds out he has no job? And how's he going to explain how he came across $50 in gold? He has already told too many lies.

"Tell me about your new job, Rafael?" she asks, and Martinez feels the noose drawing even tighter. "Are you a vaquero?"

"Yes, yes, dear, I am a vaquero," he hears himself say. "I have been working on a small rancho in the hills. This horse belongs to my employer. I have only two days and then I must return to work."

"Oh, Rafael," beams Maria, "that is so wonderful! Father will be so pleased." She turns around and sees her mother standing in the doorway watching them. Taking Rafael by the arm and walking toward the small house, she says, "Mother! You won't believe this! Rafael has a new job working for a rancher!"

"Is that true, young man?" she asks him.

"Yes, senora," he immediately replies. Maria's mother looks him in the eye and she sees him glance away as he answers.

"Rafael has to return to work in two days, Mother," says Maria. "Can he stay with us until then?"

"Yes, I believe it will be okay," her mother says, "but it is your father who will decide and he won't be back until tomorrow, so you will have to ask him then."

"I will, Mother," says Maria as she escorts her love through the front door. "Come, Rafael, you must be hungry."

For the first time since he arrived, Martinez can tell the truth. "Thank you, Maria, I am starving."

Maria's mother watches the young couple closely as they go through the door. "Something is not right here," she says to herself. "This boy is hiding something."

She doesn't know what it is, but she knows he will never get it past her husband.

"Come, children," she says to the little ones, still playing in the yard. "I might as well feed you your lunch too." Picking up some firewood, she brings the children inside and shuts the door.

***

The telegraph is clicking away in the back office of the Campo store. "Click, click … click … clickety, click." Jack Kelly is furiously writing down the message.

"Is it about Chavez?" yells Lumen from the other room, where he's got the trap door open and is sweeping dirt into the creek below.

"Yes," Kelly replies. "It's from the sheriff in Los Angeles. Hold on a minute."

Jack scribbles down the remaining words as they come off the wire. "Click … click, click."

"Here it is," Jack says as he emerges from his room and hands the message to Lumen.

"To operator Yuma station. Stop," Lumen reads. *"Los Angeles sheriff's reply to Yuma County sheriff's request for identification on Clodoveo Chavez. Stop. Chavez height five-feet-ten, weight about one-hundred-eighty-five, dark complexion, thin beard, circular scar on right cheek from outer corner of eye toward nose, good white teeth, walked a little lame from previous gunshot wound in leg. Stop. W.R. Rowland, sheriff, Los Angeles County. Stop."*

Lumen re-reads the message and then says, "I guess that his identity has not been proven yet."

"You think he's still alive then?" Kelly asks

anxiously.

"No," Lumen says, "I think they got the right man. Anyway, with a description like that, it won't be long until we know for sure." Lumen hands the copy back to Kelly, who goes back into his office to send the message on to Yuma.

"Yup, it won't be long," Lumen says to himself as he walks back around the counter and checks the hidden shotgun to make sure that it's ready to go if he needs it.

***

As Lopez and his compadres ride up the main street in Tecarte they notice three familiar horses tethered in front of the cantina. The tall Appaloosa belongs to Fedoro Vasquez and the shorter buckskin mustang is Poncho Alvitro's. The other mustang, the one that is mostly black, is ridden by Francisco Albitrio.

"That is good," thinks Lopez to himself. "If Vasquez tries to start something, Francisco would side with me. That leaves Vasquez and maybe Alvitro." Cruz looks and can tell that Alvijo and Gonzalez are thinking the same thing.

"Come on, amigos," he says, dismounting. "I am hungry."

The three bandits enter the dark cantina and as their eyes adjust to the light, Lopez can see three men sitting at their usual table in the back. The one facing them looks up.

"Cruz, you have returned!" says Fedoro Vasquez, pretending to be pleased by Lopez's arrival.

"Si," utters Lopez with little more than a grunt. "It was a good ride. We sold the horses and you three will get your split."

"That's right," Vasquez replies, "and do not try to short us none either."

"Go to hell, Fedoro," Lopez snaps back. "I've got all the money right here, but now I think I will wait to split it up until Chavez gets back."

"Chavez is not coming back," Vasquez replies. "He's never coming back."

The words stab at Lopez like a dagger in the night. "What do you mean?" he demands loudly.

Gonzalez, too, steps forward and demands an answer.

"Chavez is dead," Vasquez reports. "He was killed in a place called Texas Hill, Arizona, about three days ago. We just found out last night."

Lopez is staggered. "How do you know this?" he demands again, even louder.

"It was in the San Diego newspaper. Pedro told us," snaps Vasquez, pointing to the owner of the cantina, who has been standing off to one side listening. Cruz wheels around as Pedro steps forward out of the shadows.

"Si, it is true," Pedro says almost apologetically. "A friend of mine stopped by the cantina yesterday afternoon. I know him very well. He had just ridden from San Diego and said the whole town was talking about it. It was in the newspaper; he had brought a copy of it as he can read English and he read the story to us. I am very sorry, senor."

Romulo wipes a tear from his eye and asks, "How'd it happen?"

"It said he was working at a rancho and someone recognized him and tried to collect the reward on his head," Pedro tells them.

But Lopez needs to know the details and presses the old man.

"How … did … he … die?" Lopez demands in a low, drawn-out voice. For him, this is the most important question.

"He was shot in the back by a man with a shotgun while he was trying to reach his pistol," Pedro says. "It was hanging on a fence post."

"A shotgun!" Cruz thinks to himself, immediately recalling their conversation that morning at the Sheckler ranch and the chilling words Chavez said as they rode away with only a meal. It seems like forever before he speaks again.

"He died like a man," Lopez finally says, "but this man who killed him, he will not be so lucky. His days are numbered because I'm going to kill him myself. But I will not waste a bullet on such a pig as this. I am going to cut his heart out and stuff it down his throat!"

"Si, si!" yell the others. All except Vasquez.

Pedro goes and gets three bottles of his best tequila and some glasses and puts them down on the table. "These are on the house," he announces. "I think you hombres may need a drink or two."

Jose and Francisco open the bottles and start filling up the glasses. Lopez looks over at Vasquez, who is staring him down and has his right hand under the table. Gonzalez notices it too.

"So, Fedoro," Lopez says, "Are you going to shoot me from under the table?" thinking that's what he would do to him.

"No, Lopez," he replies as he slowly stands up with his hand near his gun, ready to draw. "Not from under the table. I can take you, though, and I'm ready to prove it."

The other men scramble to get out of the way, knocking over some of the glasses in the process. Romulo and Jose are ready to draw down on Vasquez. Fedoro can see that he's going to be outnumbered once again if he tries to make a play.

The cool Lopez hasn't even put his hand near his gun yet. "Fedoro," he finally says, "I'll give you a chance to live. You accept that I am now the leader of the gang or me and my men are going to cut you down right here."

"You and *your* men?" Vasquez scoffs. "I've been riding in this gang since my uncle was the leader. He started this gang and the leadership should rightfully fall to me."

"No, it doesn't," Lopez replies. "Clodoveo left me in charge and I'm staying in charge."

"That's right," Alvijo pipes up. "I was here when he said that."

"And I was here also," says Gonzalez. "Chavez was my friend and he said that Lopez is the leader."

"And you, Francisco, what do you say?" Lopez asks of the newest member in the room.

"You are the leader," he wisely decides. "I have no problem with that."

"And you, Poncho? Are you going to back Fedoro's play?" Lopez inquires.

"No, no amigo," he says. "I told you I wouldn't get involved in your business. This is between you and Fedoro."

"So, then," Cruz says, as his left hand slowly moves toward his gun, "you're all alone Fedoro. It's your move."

Fedoro looks around. He can see that it would be

suicide to make a move now. He knows he's a faster draw than Lopez, and is confident he can beat him, but the others would surely gun him down before he has the chance to taste his victory. Today is not the day.

"Okay," he says after a long pause, "you're the leader now. But don't think you're going to treat me like some stupid mule. I've been in this gang longer than any of you and I'm to be treated with respect."

"Of course you are," Lopez assures him. "You have earned that."

"All right, then I'm with you," Fedoro says, extending his right hand toward Lopez. Cruz looks him straight in the eye as he slowly reaches out and shakes hands with Vasquez.

"You better mean that, Fedoro" says Lopez with little empathy. "You better mean that."

The standoff averted, Lopez turns to the bar and yells, "Pedro! We're hungry! Bring us some food! Pronto!"

Chapter 24

In Yuma, the second day of the Chavez inquest is just getting under way in a jammed courtroom. It seems like every Mexican in town is there, lining the back walls and spilling out into the hallway.

The Raggio brothers and Harry Roberts are brought in by Deputy Thomas and seated before the jury. The first witness called is Luis Raggio. After being sworn in, he tells how he and his brother grew up near Hollister along with Chavez and have known him for most of their lives. He remembers how Chavez got that scar on his face, not from some gruesome bar fight as most would think, but by being kicked by a horse.

He goes on about how he recognized Chavez at the Baker ranch and how the outlaw recognized him, too, and swore him to secrecy that he was really Jose Espinosa and not the most feared bandit in all of California. And about how they all planned to capture him for the reward money, but had to kill him when Chavez refused to give himself up.

When Harry Roberts takes the stand, he tells how it was Colvig who did the shooting. “He ordered Chavez to throw up his hands, but he went for his pistol instead and Bill had to shoot him in the back,” Roberts testifies. “It was self-defense.”

As Harry goes through the details, Sheriff Werninger looks up and sees Charlie Baker push his way into the courtroom. His timing is just right, and the sheriff nods to Charlie to take a seat. A young vaquero in the back row sees the man and humbly vacates his seat so Baker can sit down.

Next, Doc Loring is called to testify. He gives a physical description of the body, describing the wounds and the likely cause of death. It's all very professional and well-detailed, much like what they heard from the coroner the night before.

Vincente Raggio is called forward, and he also tells about how he and Luis grew up with Chavez, though admits he didn't know Chavez as well as his brother since he is nine years younger – and about how they decided to arrest the bandit and take him back to Los Angeles for the $2,000 reward.

Excused, Vincente Raggio takes a seat as Sheriff Werninger retakes the stand. He testifies that he observed the body as it was brought into town by the defendants and about the telegram he had sent to the sheriff in Los Angeles asking for a detailed description of Chavez. He tells the jury that he has now received a reply from Sheriff Rowland and the description that he sent matches precisely the features of the deceased man known as Jose Espinosa and Clodoveo Chavez.

The jury foreman asks him if there is any other evidence to add or witnesses to hear from. Werninger says he has no further evidence, but did have three more witnesses, except two of them were unable to be located when he went to their house that morning.

"A man named Ramirez who lives in Yuma was present when the body was brought into town and he and his son were the only two claiming the deceased was Espinosa and not Chavez," Werninger explains. "I told them both not to leave town, but when I went to their house this morning, Mrs. Ramirez told me both her husband and her son were away and she didn't know when they would return."

The defendants give each other a quick look, unsure what this latest news means, but they know it's probably not good. But they don't have long to think about it as the foreman asks the sheriff who his other witness is.

"It's Charles Baker," the sheriff says, and the Raggios and Roberts spin around in surprise, not having seen the rancher sitting in the back of the room. Baker is sworn in and seated. The foreman asks him for his testimony.

Baker tells his side of the story, about how this man who called himself Espinosa came riding into his ranch a few weeks ago asking for work – and about how he had come to know and like the man, considering him honest and hard-working. But then he adds about how the man seemed to know the Raggios and that Espinosa had told him they were old friends of his and that they had all grown up together in the same place in California.

Baker then tells about the day of the killing, about how he and Espinosa were working in a trench on his ranch when two men rode up and asked if he could spare some provisions. He identified Roberts as one of the men, but it was the other man, he said, that got the drop on them – and how he had tried to take Espinosa alive, but Jose had gone for a gun, which was hanging on the fence post. "That's when the guy they called Bill shot him in the back," Baker says.

The foreman decides that he's heard enough and excuses Baker, announcing that the jury will render its verdict at 2 p.m. The jury reconvenes a two o'clock sharp. The prisoners are led in and seated at the far table and listen intently as the foreman rises to read the decision.

"I, Will Barney, foreman of the jury, hereby

announce that the inquest into the death of a man named Jose Espinosa has found that he came to his demise by being shot by a shotgun held in the hands of William Clark Colvig in the county of Yuma, Arizona Territory, on the twenty-fifth of November, eighteen-hundred and seventy-five. We also find that this man named Espinosa and the California outlaw Clodoveo Chavez are one and the same man and that the death was justifiable and in self-defense," reads Barney.

Looking up, he adds, "Sheriff, you can release the prisoners."

The Raggios and Harry Roberts are overjoyed, whooping and hollering. Getting up, they start slapping each other on the shoulders. "I told you not to worry," Luis Raggio tells Roberts. Luis turns and shakes the sheriff's hand and some of the jurors too.

"So, sheriff, does this mean we can take possession of the body and be on our way to California?" Luis asks Werninger. "I guess so," the sheriff replies, "but I don't know how you're going to get it to Los Angeles in any condition to get the reward."

Luis thinks this over for a second as he knows the sheriff is right, and then suddenly sees Doc Loring walking out the door and gets an idea.

"Doc! Doc Loring!"

***

It is now getting late at the house of the Estrada family. Maria's father has returned home and the family is eating dinner.

"So, young man," Sr. Estrada says to Rafael. "I am told you have found employment down in Ensenada."

"Yes, senor," Martinez replies. "It's only a temporary job for now, but my employer was kind enough to lend me a horse and give me time off to come and see Maria."

"I see," Sr. Estrada says, trying to hide his suspicion. "But you've only been gone a week since you were last here. How did you impress your employer so quickly?"

"Well … I … I have known him for some time and he has just asked me if I would like to work for him," Martinez explains. "Only temporary for now."

"Oh, Rafael!" Maria beams, "I bet you could work hard and maybe someday be a ranch foreman. How grand! What do you think, Father?"

Manuel Estrada looks at his beautiful daughter and can see how hopelessly in love she is with this boy and now he wishes he had put a stop to this long ago. He also can see she has not questioned a single word of his story, but he isn't buying any of it. If Rafael really did go to Ensenada and only had a week to do it, then whose horse did he ride down there on? And then he worked for this rancher and after just three days was given his leave and a horse so he could go visit his girlfriend two-day's ride away?

"I doubt this story very much," he thinks. But then again, the saddle Martinez has is about worn out, not the type you'd expect to draw the attention of a horse thief. Rather more like one you'd maybe let someone borrow if you were to lend them a horse.

"Maria," he says to his daughter, "I expect that if Rafael applies himself to hard work and accepts Jesus Christ as his savior, then I feel that he may make something of himself someday.

"Don't you think so?" he adds, looking Rafael dead straight in the eyes.

"Uh, yes, yes, senor, I believe I can," Rafael manages to say with a choked voice. "And I do accept Jesus as my savior," he quickly adds.

"Then, my son, if you truly do, then you understand that it is the daughter's duty to obey her father," continues Sr. Estrada. "And respect his wishes. If you have a good job in Ensenada, Rafael, then I am glad for you. But you still can't marry my daughter until I give you permission. And you will have to prove yourself to me before I can permit it."

"Oh, Father!" Maria exclaims. "He will, he will!" Maria grabs Rafael's hand under the table and squeezes it tightly. "Won't you, Rafael?"

"Yes, Maria," Rafael says. "Yes, I will."

***

The following morning, the sky is starting to show the first signs of the coming day. Ramon Ramirez and the others are in position in the rocks about 100 yards in front of Stanwix Station. They rode up the wash a couple hours ago and hid their horses just to the south, planning on a quick getaway after they are done with their business.

It has gotten cold and Ramon is shivering as the temperature has dropped about 10 degrees in the last hour, a common occurrence on clear, moonless nights in the desert. It had been decided that Ramon will be the one to open the attack and he's waiting for the right moment.

Everything is dark inside the station house, but then the bushwhackers notice a faint light coming from inside the adobe building. King Woolsey has just woken up and lit a lantern in the kitchen, and now turns his attention to lighting the pot-belly stove so he can cook breakfast.

Ramon Ramirez notices a wisp of smoke beginning to rise from the chimney. Soon it's puffing away as Woolsey has the stove heated and is cooking up some bacon. The smell makes its way into the back rooms and its enticing aroma awakens the other two cowboys staying at the station house. They dress and join Woolsey at the table.

"Good morning," Woolsey says to them, "coffee's on the stove."

"Good morning, boss," replies William Colvig. "Thanks, boss," adds Tim, the other cowboy, as he reaches for the coffee pot.

"Breakfast is almost ready," Woolsey announces. "After we eat, Tim and I are going to ride out to the ranch. My wife, Mary is due back from Agua Fria today." That's Woolsey's other ranch up above Wickenburg. "Bill, I want you to stay close to the station here for a few more days, just in case."

Colvig thinks his boss is being overly cautious, but says nothing. He walks over to the window just in time to see the first rays of the sun, which is climbing over the mountains to the east.

Ramon sees the man in the window and gets the rifle in his stiff arms ready.

"I think I'll use the privy," Colvig announces as he opens the front door and steps out onto the porch. "Brrrr. It's cold," he thinks.

Ramon wastes no time. He puts the front sight of the gun into the notch on the rear sight, lowers it to the man's chest, and pulls the trigger. Ramirez would usually make a shot like this; he's brought home many a rabbit for the family's cooking pot with just one shot. But on this bitterly cold morning, his hands waver a little, just enough to miss his mark. The bullet whizzes over Colvig's right shoulder and slams into the thick adobe wall of Stanwix Station, hitting Colvig with chunks of adobe and dust.

Colvig ducks and spins and leaps back inside. Before he can speak, a fusillade of shots rings out, battering the front of the building, shattering the windows and peppering the far back wall. Colvig kicks the door shut with his foot and he and the others dive behind the thick adobe walls and reach for their rifles.

Woolsey douses the lantern and the three men take positions under the windows and begin to return fire. Not wanting to stick his head up and risk getting hit, Colvig fires his gun blindly, just sticking it up far enough to shoot out the window. Bullets are flying, tearing up the cabinets and breaking the china, knocking everything off the shelves.

Then, just as suddenly as it started, the shooting stops. Woolsey, realizing that the bushwhackers must have retreated, opens the front door and fires off several shots up the wash to where he thinks they went.

"Come on back, you scalawags!" he yells. "Shoot up my station, will ya!" He fires off a few more shots for good measure.

Colvig and the other cowboy slowly come out of the building. "Holy cow!" Tim exclaims, shaking the glass out of his hair from the shot-out windows.

Colvig sits down on the front steps quaking with fear. "Who … who was it?" he asks his boss.

"Well, there were at least six of them," Woolsey

replies, “and they were all Mexicans as far as I could tell. So, Bill, I think they were after you.”

Colvig shudders as the words hang in the air. “So, it’s just like Mr. Baker said,” he says to himself. “I’m going to have to watch my back the rest of my life.”

Chapter 25

The Raggio brothers and Harry Roberts meet Doc Loring at the coroner's office at 10 a.m. as instructed. "Is it ready, Doc?" Luis asks after they close the door and step into the back room.

Doc Loring has his back to the men, but says, "Yes, it is," and turns around, holding a large pickle jar containing the severed head of one Clodoveo Chavez. Roberts is a bit startled at first as the expression on the bandit's face can only be described as gruesome. And the head is so large, he thinks, magnified by the glass jar. He can only imagine how imposing a figure Chavez was in real life, having seen him for only a brief moment before Colvig killed him, and he was standing in a trench to boot.

Luis Raggio's brilliant idea was far from original. He had remembered how as a boy he had heard the stories of the severed head of Joaquin Murrieta being displayed at a side show around San Francisco in a pickle jar filled with alcohol after Capt. Harry Love had collected the reward money.

That's what Raggio had wanted to talk to Doc Loring about in the courthouse yesterday after the verdict was read. Sheriff Werninger was right; the bloated, badly decomposing body of Chavez would have been impossible to bring to Los Angeles. The head was all they needed and Loring agreed to do the job for $25.

"That'll be fifty dollars please, gentlemen," Doc Loring says to them.

"Fifty dollars!" exclaims Harry Roberts. "You told Luis you'd do it for twenty-five!"

“Yes, that was for the head,” Doc Loring replies. “The other twenty-five dollars is for burying the body. Or do you men want to take care of that yourselves?”

Roberts is agitated. He knows the longer they hang around Yuma, the more likely that some of Chavez’s friends might pay them a visit.

“Luis,” he says, handing five $10 gold pieces to the doctor, “this is coming out of you and your brother’s cut. And you owe me five dollars for the telegram I sent to Los Angeles to let Sheriff Rowland know we’re on our way.”

“You know, Harry,” says Luis, “if you’re so worried, me and Vincente can take the head to California and you can just ride back to Stanwix Station.”

“Not on your life!” Harry Roberts fires back, not trusting the Raggios to return with the reward money. “Wherever that head goes, I go!”

Luis follows the other two out the front door to their waiting horses. Roberts looks up and down the street. “All clear,” he says. Luis pulls a burlap sack out of his saddle bag, slides the jar inside it and ties the top of the bag off with a piece of rope. At the other end of the rope he ties a loop and slips it over his saddle horn. The three mount up and hurry down the street, heading for the ferry at Yuma Crossing.

***

The following day, Rafael and Alonzo meet at the spot where they left their guns two days before. It’s about an hour before noon. “Buenos dias,” Alonzo calls out as Rafael rides up. “Hello, Alonzo,” Martinez says back to him with a sullen expression.

"So, Rafael, how'd it go at your girlfriend's house?" Cota asks.

"Okay, I guess," Martinez says. "I told Maria's father that I got a job working on a ranch down in Ensenada. I think that he believed me, but he sure stared at me a lot."

"And what did you tell Maria?" Alonzo prods further.

"The same thing!" Rafael replies. "What was I going to tell her? I couldn't tell her what really happened, could I?"

"No, no, of course you couldn't," Cota replies. "Who would believe you anyway?"

"No one," Martinez agrees. "Alonzo, we've gotten ourselves into a real fix and I don't see any way out of it."

"Me either," replies Cota. "I tried to lie to my sister too, but she already knew that we had ridden off with the gang. She cried and begged me not to go with them again, but I told her I had to. I told her we would try to escape if we could."

"What do you mean, 'She knew we rode off with them?'" Martinez asks, horrified.

"I don't know how she found out, but she did," Cota answers.

"Well, I hope that Maria doesn't find out!" Rafael says. "She would never marry me if she knew I lied to her and her father."

"Well, Rafael, you lied to protect them," Cota offers.

"You and I know that," Rafael says, "but she won't understand."

"You're right, Rafael," agrees Cota, "but we've got to get going if we're going to meet up with the gang by noon."

The two climb behind the rocks and emerge with their guns and little pouches of gold. Cota puts the gun in his waistband, but Martinez would be happy never to see his gun again. He puts it and the gold into his saddle bag. Seeing this, Cota can only imagine the torment going through his friend's mind.

The two mount up for the short 10-minute ride to the cantina, where they see a bunch of horses tethered to the hitching post out front. They take their horses around to the back so they won't be seen and tie them off there.

As they walk in, the gang is mostly in the back where they always are. Cruz Lopez, Jose Alvijo, Fedoro Vasquez, Poncho Alvitro, Francisco Albitrio and Romulo Gonzalez are all there. Cruz is sitting at the table and Vasquez, Alvijo and Alvitro are standing, looking like they're ready to leave.

"So, you hear what I'm telling you?" they overhear Lopez say to the three men.

"Yes, yes, Cruz," replies Poncho Alvitro. "We go back to Horsethief Canyon and see if we can find the four missing horses."

"That's right," Lopez says. "I told you to do that last week, but you stayed here and got drunk instead. Don't disobey me again. They probably didn't go far and are just up in a side canyon or something."

"Sure, Cruz," adds Vasquez, not liking being talked down to. "We'll find them and be back by Friday as you say."

"No later than Friday afternoon," Lopez quickly reminds them. "We have business to attend to on Saturday morning and I want everyone ready."

"Okay, jefe," they say as they leave the cantina.

Lopez now turns to Albitrio, having yet to notice the arrival of either Martinez or Cota. "Now, Francisco," he says, "you say you have some friends who might want to ride with us?"

"Si," says Francisco, "at least two men, maybe more."

"Then I want you to ride out and get them and bring them back to me," Lopez instructs him. "And don't tell them anything about what we're going to do. I don't want word to leak out about this. So wait a couple days before you bring these men to me."

"Si, jefe, I will," replies Albitrio as he turns and walks out the door.

That settled, Lopez looks up and finally sees Martinez and Cota lingering by the bar. "Amigos, come on over and have a seat," Lopez says to them and they do as he says, sitting at the two empty chairs. "You probably haven't heard yet, but Chavez is dead."

"Dead?" exclaim Rafael and Alonzo simultaneously. "How did it happen?"

"He was gunned down by bounty hunters in Arizona," Lopez says.

"That's right," Gonzalez adds with disdain in his voice. "They laid in wait for him and shot him in the back unarmed."

Cota and Martinez don't know what to say. They look at each other wondering if the same fate awaits them.

"It is terrible news, no?" Lopez says to them. "But we will ride over there in a few days and take revenge on those dogs, just like we took care of Sosa."

The thought of this brings mixed feelings to Martinez. He doesn't think he can stomach another killing like that, but he'll be glad to be getting out of town before he's seen with the gang and someone tells Maria.

"So, did you two have a nice visit with your loved ones?" Lopez asks them. They both nod. "Good, then," he says. "We have another little job to do soon."

"What is it?" Cota asks, knowing he's not going to like the answer.

Lopez looks around the cantina to make sure they're alone. They are, of course, as business at the cantina has been almost non-existent since the bandits arrived in town.

"We're going to rob the town of Campo," Lopez announces.

"Campo!" Martinez exclaims. "We're going to rob a whole town?"

"That's right!" Lopez replies proudly. "We need supplies to take with us to Sonora and Romulo says Campo has all the stuff we will need. It should be easy enough with all the men we have. There's only two brothers there and we can kill them real quick; it's not like they're expecting us or anything.

"Then we'll load up some wagons and be back across the border before anyone knows that we were there."

"But Campo?" Martinez repeats. "They know me there and I will be recognized …"

"You *know* these two Gaskill brothers?" Lopez jumps in.

"Yes," Rafael replies. "Not well, but they know that I live in Tecarte."

"Hmmm," says Lopez, the wheels turning quickly in his devious mind as he scratches his beard, "that might be just what we need. Yes, that will be perfect. You're going to ride in ahead and scout it out for us. Make sure that we're not riding into a trap. What do you think, Romulo?"

"Si, it is a good idea," agrees Gonzalez. "No sense taking any unnecessary risks and Rafael wouldn't raise any suspicions since they already know him."

"But … but I couldn't," insists Rafael. "If I'm seen in Campo, then Maria will find out and then she will never marry me!"

Lopez and Gonzalez look at each other and then break out in uncontrollable laughter at this hopeless romantic.

"How can anyone tell her if they're all dead," Lopez roars, still laughing.

"Dead?" Rafael replies. "I … I can't do it."

"You *will* do it!" growls Lopez as he leaps out of his chair and leans almost all the way across the table, so close that Martinez can smell the chorizo he had for breakfast. "And you will *not* give us away. You will go into Campo and look around and if there's more than three or four men in town, then ride back and tell me. If not, then you stay in Campo until we arrive and you will help us with the attack."

"But, senor," Rafael begins to say again, but Lopez cuts him off.

"Amigo, remember what I told you," Lopez warns. "If you cross me, I will take it out on your girlfriend and her family. And from what I hear, I will enjoy her very much."

"But, Cruz, please," pleads Martinez.

"No, Rafael, I have made up my mind," Lopez says, the veins bulging on his dirty neck, "and that is what you're going to do! Comprende?"

Cota sees his friend is on the verge of tears and

tries to calm him down. "It will be all right," he tells Rafael. "Better that the gringos get killed than us or Maria."

Alonzo turns to Lopez and says, "He will do as you say, jefe. We will both do as you say."

***

Things are beginning to return to normal in Campo. By Thursday, the town looks like it had before the scare. As it almost always does in the back country of San Diego County, the sun rises in a cloudless sky. The temperature is rising quickly, turning a cold morning into a nice warm day.

John Williams is riding into Campo on his large, black quarterhorse mare named Sally with his five-year-old daughter, Ella, on the back. Ella is ecstatic; she's never ridden into Campo before on the back of her father's horse and she can't wait to play with Walter.

John reaches back and picks Ella up and swings her around so that they both can slide smoothly off the horse. Ella giggles as she hits the ground.

Lumen Gaskill looks out the open door of the Campo store. "Walter, you got company!" he yells to his son, who is playing up in the rocks.

"What, Pa?" Walter yells back.

"I said you've got a visitor!" his father yells back. "Get on down here!"

Walter scrambles down from the rocks and sees Ella standing beside her father.

"Walter!" she yells, and runs over to him.

"Hi, Ella," he says. "Watcha doin' here?"

"I rode in with Pa," she replies. "We got to get Ma

some things."

"You wanna catch a frog?" Walter asks her.

"A frog?" Ella responds, making a contorted face.

"Sure, the creek's got frogs!" Walter says, all excited. "C'mon, I'll show you."

"You two be careful playing by the creek," Lumen says. "Okay, Pa," Walter yells back as they run off toward the creek. "They'll be all right," Lumen says to John Williams. "Creek's only a foot deep in that spot."

"I know," says John, but he yells after Ella anyway. "You stay out of the water, Ella, you hear?"

"Yes, Pa," she says as they turn the corner of the store and disappear from sight.

Satisfied, Williams turns back to Lumen and asks, "Have you heard anything new?"

"A little," Lumen replies. "On Sunday, a telegram came through from the sheriff in Los Angeles with evidence for the inquest in Yuma. And then Monday, another telegram came through from Yuma that said the inquest had determined that the dead man is indeed Chavez and the prisoners were let free. They're headed to Los Angeles to collect the reward now."

"Good, good," replies Williams, nodding. "That's what I wanted to hear. So, you think it's over?"

"I don't know," Lumen says. "We pulled Captain Billy off the hill up there on Monday and he left town, so it's only me, Silas and Jack Kelly still in town. The word is that the gang is still somewhere around here, but I don't think anyone knows for sure. You know how rumors are; spread like wildfire."

"Yeah," John says, "you can't put a whole lot of stock in 'em."

"That's what we're thinking," Lumen replies.

"We've got some guns ready in case something happens. We're not going to let this run our lives. If they show up, I think we'll give them a show."

***

The Valle de las Viejas ranch is situated in a small valley nestled at the foot of Viejas Mountain northwest of Campo. It's a nice, peaceful place with good water and fine soil. It's also dotted here and there with tall, old oak trees that provide shade during the hot summer months. Most of the valley is covered with grass and prized as pastureland.

It's a good place to rest and that's what James Johnson has been looking for. He's been on the trail now for over three weeks, riding all the way from the San Joaquin Valley up in the central part of the state. He's a beekeeper by trade, and has built up a few hundred hives on his small ranch near Madera' California' over the last ten years.

Riding up to the ranch house on a cream-colored horse, his arrival at Valle de las Viejas is announced by several barking dogs. The front door opens and a man steps out onto the porch with a shotgun leveled at the rider.

"Howdy," says Royal Barton, owner of the ranch and 160 acres of the surrounding valley.

"Howdy," replies James, staying on his horse, not wanting to get down until he's invited.

"Can I help you?" Barton asks the traveler, still pointing the shotgun in Johnson's direction. "Yes, maybe," he says. "I'm on my way to Campo...."

"Campo?" interrupts Barton. "Where'd you come

from?"

"Up north," replies Johnson. "I left Julian this morning and I'm not sure if I'm going the right way or not."

"Well, if you're going to Campo," Barton interrupts again, "then you needed to turn east about four miles back. That would've taken you into Pine Valley and then on down the grade to Buckman Springs. There you turn back to the south and follow the creek down to Moreno Valley. Follow the road and it will take you right to Campo."

"I see," Johnson says, remembering the trail to his left that he passed up about two hours back. He takes out his pocket watch to check on the time. Three in the afternoon it reads.

Barton notices the watch immediately and lowers the gun, calculating that a man dressed like him, with such a watch is probably no desperado. It's a gold watch, and a nice one too. He can see a row of silver hoops in the middle of its bob chain. "With a watch like that," thinks Barton, "this man should be well off." And seeing how he boards guests at his ranch, this man might want to stay the night given the lateness of the day. "Always good to make an extra dollar or two," Barton is thinking.

"Well," Johnson says after a moment, "is there another way to get to Campo from here without riding all the way back to the fork?"

"There's an old Indian trail," says Barton, pointing off across the valley. "It leads east over yonder. Follow it up and over that hill and then you'll drop down into the Sweetwater River Valley. It's not much more than a creek, you'll see, and if you follow the trail upstream a spell it will take you to a small meadow. You turn south and it will take you to Horsethief Canyon. From there it's an easy ride down the creek and then turn east up the Cottonwood Creek. It's the one near the end of the valley. Go upstream through Hauser Canyon to the Campo road. Then you turn south and you're almost there.

"But if I were you," Barton adds, "I'd go back and take the long way around."

"Why's that?" Johnson asks as he puts the watch away in a pocket on the inside of his coat.

"Because they don't call it Horsethief Canyon for nothing!" Barton quickly exclaims. "You might run into someone down there you'd rather not meet."

"Bad characters?" asks Johnson.

"Real bad," answers Barton. "We shy away from there because we never know who we're going to run into."

Johnson doesn't seem worried. "That's okay," he says, "I've been in many a bad place before," pulling a lever-action Henry rifle from its scabbard as he gets down from his horse. "Do you put up room and board?" he asks Barton.

"Sure do," says the rancher. "A dollar a night for you and a dollar a night for your horse. That includes feed for both of you."

"That sounds a little high-priced," deems Johnson, "but seeing how it's the best deal I can find, I'll take it." He ties his horse off at the post.

"So watcha going to Campo for?" the curious Barton asks.

"I'm a beekeeper," Johnson explains. "I've got a ranch up near Madera and I'm doing pretty well, but I keep hearing about how San Diego County has the best climate for raising bees."

"That it does," Barton interrupts yet again. "Why, John Harbison has a lot of hives around here. I'd say he's the man you want to talk to."

"I've heard his name," Johnson acknowledges, "but I've also heard that the Gaskill brothers down in Campo keep a lot of bees too."

"That's true," Barton admits. "They're probably the second-largest producers of honey in the county."

"Good, then," Johnson says, interrupting Barton for a change. "How far is it to Campo again?"

"Well, if you go back around like I told you, it's about twelve hours more or less on that fine horse you're riding," Barton says.

"And if I go through Horsethief Canyon?" Johnson interrupts again.

"I don't suggest you do that," Barton replies, "but if you insist on that path, you could shave about three or four hours or so. If you don't run into no trouble."

"Okay," decides Johnson. "I will stay the night and be gone at sunup." He gets out a money pouch and removes two silver dollars. Handing them to Barton, he instructs, "Give my horse enough feed tonight to hold him over until I get to Campo."

"Okay, mister," Barton replies.

"Oh, and where do I bunk?" Johnson asks his host. "In the house," Barton answers. "I got a room in the back for travelers. Dinner's about an hour after sundown."

"Good," Johnson replies, taking his Henry rifle in hand. Looking around, he can see the nearby creek where it flows west into a large grove of willows, where it spreads out into a wide marshy-looking area thick with the trees. "You mind if I stroll around a bit? I've been in the saddle quite a spell lately and the walk would do me good."

"That's up to you," Barton says, "but I wouldn't wander off too far if I were you. Neighbors around here are a might trigger-happy."

"Thanks; see you at dinner," Johnson replies, taking the rifle and walking down toward Viejas Creek.

Chapter 26

It's an hour before sunup, James Johnson notices as he lights a match and holds it close to his gold pocket watch. He blows the match out and puts the watch back in his coat pocket. He lights another match for the lantern on the dresser, grabs his clothes off the back of the chair and gives them a good shake in case any spiders or scorpions took up residence in them during the night.

He does the same to his boots too before pulling them on. He puts on his coat and hat and grabs his saddle bags and quietly makes his way to the front door. He opens it, blows out the lantern and leaves it on a little stand next to the door, which he silently closes behind him.

He makes his way through the frosty morning air to the stables and saddles up. It's just getting light enough to see as he gets on his cream-colored horse and sets off in the direction of the approaching dawn to find the old Indian trail that leads down through Horsethief Canyon.

***

Cruz Lopez wakes up in a bunkhouse behind the cantina to find that he's not hung over.

"That's nice for a change," he thinks to himself as he gets up and gets a drink of water from the olla hanging on a hook on the wall. He pours a little in his cupped hand and splashes it in his face.

"Get up!" he yells to the other men still sleeping, then realizes he's only got Gonzalez, Martinez and Cota with him. The others he sent on errands a couple days ago, he remembers.

"Let's go to the cantina and see if Pedro can get us something to eat," he says to them as they slowly roll out of their bunks and put on their boots, coats and hats. "I'm so hungry I could eat my boots," Lopez adds as they step into the chilly street.

"Si," they all reply as they open the cantina's front door and shuffle up to the bar.

"Pedro!" hollers Lopez and almost immediately the barkeep emerges from the door leading to the kitchen.

"Buenos dias, amigos," says Pedro to the men. "I have some hot food for you if you are ready to eat."

"Yes, we are," Lopez answers. "You are making yourself very useful, Pedro."

"Oh, thank you, senor. It is no problem," Pedro beams. That's good to hear; he's heard what happens to people Lopez no longer finds useful. "I had my wife cook up some ham and a skillet of huevos rancheros," he says. "And there are plenty of tortillas. They should be ready now." He turns and disappears back into the kitchen.

As they walk to the back of the bar and their usual table, Lopez says to no one in particular, "A smart man, that Pedro. He knows enough to mind his own business."

Gonzalez sees the opportunity he has been waiting for. "And that's exactly what I'm going to do too," Romulo tells the leader.

"What do you mean?" Lopez asks, turning to the one member of the gang that has his respect.

"I'm not riding with you to Campo tomorrow," Gonzalez tells him flatly.

Lopez looks at him for a moment and sees he means it. "Well, amigo," he says, "for you I will give you your choice, but I was certainly hoping you would go."

"No, amigo," replies Romulo, "this is your quest, not mine. Clodoveo asked me to help you with the horses and with Sosa and I have done that. I have a nice place close to here and I don't need to get involved with any of this business. I hope you understand."

"Si, amigo, I understand," Lopez says to him, "but I had hoped you would ride with us to Sonora and become a wealthy man."

"I have given that a lot of thought these past few days," Romulo replies, "but I have had enough of hiding from posses and the law."

"Well, amigo, you certainly have earned the right to leave the gang," Lopez tells Gonzalez, then looks toward Martinez and Cota, who are sitting across the table from him, "but don't you two get any ideas over there. You're going with the rest of us!"

"We know," Cota says, secretly wishing he and Rafael could get out so easily. Just then Pedro and a couple of old women emerge from the kitchen with four heaping plates, four glasses and a pitcher full of fresh goat's milk, plus a stack of warm tortillas wrapped in a basket.

Lopez grabs a tortilla, folds it, and using it like a shovel, begins to devour his breakfast. He pauses only once, addressing Martinez as he reaches for another tortilla. "Rafael!" he says louder than he needs to. Cruz Lopez likes to hear himself speak. He likes it even better when those spoken to respond in obvious fear.

"Si, jefe?" answers a startled Martinez, almost spilling his glass.

"After breakfast, you get your horse ready for the ride to Campo," Lopez says to him. "We will follow tomorrow early in the morning. Now, if you see more than four men in Campo that could put up a fight, then you ride back first thing in the morning and meet us on the trail. But if there's only three or four, then you stay put and help us with the fight when we arrive."

"Si," Rafael says.

"And you go straight to Campo," Lopez adds. "You do as I say Rafael, or you know what I'll do."

"Si, jefe," Martinez repeats. "I know. I'll do as you say. Don't worry."

"Worry?" says Lopez. "Me worry? Ha. It is you who had better worry, amigo."

***

Fedoro Vasquez boxes a mare into a small rocky alcove in a narrow gully where a little stream trickles into Horsethief Canyon. He manages to throw a lasso over its head and after being subdued, the horse decides to give up the fight. It follows him peaceably as Vasquez leads it back down the trail.

Once back at the campsite, Vasquez can see that both Jose Alvijo and Poncho Alvitro have recovered a stray as well. "You seen the other one?" Fedoro asks the others. "No," Jose replies. "Tracks say it went south, so maybe we'll find it on our way back."

"Okay," replies Vasquez, getting off his horse and tying the lasso on the mare to a stout branch. "Coffee still hot?" he asks.

"Si," says Poncho, who has let the fire burn out already, but has kept the pot in the dying coals.

Fedoro pours himself a cup. "Nice day," he says, "but cold as hell last night."

"Sure was," replies Jose. "I hardly slept a wink."

"We almost ready to head back?" Poncho asks the others.

"Sooner the better," answers Jose.

"Yeah," adds Fedoro, "just let me finish this coffee and take care of my morning business and then we'll get going."

"Can't you hold it until we get back to Tecarte?" ribs Jose.

"No, I can't," Fedoro replies. "I've already been holding it since I caught that mare back there." He drains his mug and walks up the trail and finds a nice bush to squat behind.

***

James Johnson so far has had a nice ride through Horsethief Canyon. The cold morning has now turned into a warm, clear day. He's been on the trail now for about four or five hours and has descended into the pretty little canyon. Heeding the advice of Royal Barton to a degree, he has his Henry rifle out across his lap in case he runs into any trouble. But so far he hasn't seen anyone along the trail, or even a single track that looks fresher than a week or more old.

He crosses a small creek and stops to let his horse drink. "What a pretty spot," Johnson says to himself as he looks around. "And all that wild buckwheat growing everywhere. What a great place to put an apiary."

Going on, he spots a large, dark bobcat prowling on the edge of a clearing. It sees him at almost the same instant and quickly disappears into the dense brush. The trail crosses the stream again and then meanders on downstream through some thick underbrush.

Suddenly, he sees a shadow whiz by and hears the telltale screech of a hawk soaring overhead. He looks up and spots it high above, floating gently on the warm thermal air currents rising up from the canyon bottom. As he tracks its path, he inadvertently looks straight into the sun and is momentarily blinded.

Vasquez hears the hawk too, and looks up from his compromising position just as a cream-colored horse and rider walk past on the trail mere yards away. He quickly finishes his business and pulls up his trousers and silently slides a pistol out of its holster, which is hanging in the bushes beside him.

Jose and Poncho also hear the hawk, but at the same time they spot the horse coming around a bend in the trail with its rider looking at the sky. Quickly sizing up the situation, the two bandits instinctively spread out a little so as to block his path. Johnson doesn't see them until his horse suddenly checks up, but by then it's too late. Standing in front of him are two men, one wearing two pistols, the other a pistol and a bayonet.

"They look like rough characters," Johnson thinks to himself. "I've got a bad feeling about this." His gun still in his lap, Johnson slowly eases back the hammer on his Henry rifle without drawing attention to it.

The two bandits see Vasquez creep out of the bushes behind the stranger with his gun leveled, and immediately drop their defenses. "Amigo!" Poncho exclaims, suddenly smiling. "How nice to see you this morning." Jose quickly gets in on the act. "Si!" he adds, "we thought we were all alone down here. Come down and join us for some coffee. It's still hot."

The diversion allows Vasquez to sneak up directly behind the traveler.

Poncho presses forward. "This is a fine horse you have here," he says, near enough to grab the reins. Johnson is perplexed. He's not sure what to do. He can't get around them because they've got him boxed in, and if he turns and makes a break for it, he'll probably get shot in the back. But James Johnson's dilemma is about to be resolved.

Suddenly, he hears the distinctive clicking sound of a Colt pistol right behind him. His eyes grow wide as saucers as he realizes what is about to happen. Vasquez squeezes the trigger and puts a bullet straight through the back of James Johnson's head.

The hawk screeches again somewhere overhead, but Johnson does not hear it. He doesn't hear anything. He doesn't feel anything either. His only sensation is a bright flash going through his head – the brightest flash he has ever seen. He doesn't feel himself falling forward and doesn't feel the hard ground as his body crumples upon it. He dies instantly.

His horse tries to bolt, but Poncho grabs it by the reins, steadying it. The body falls almost at Alvijo's feet. He bends over and reaches down to grab the Henry rifle. "What a prize!" he is thinking when suddenly he hears the distinctive clicking sound of the Colt pistol right behind him.

"Get away from that, Jose," he hears, turning to look straight into the wild eyes of Fedoro Vasquez and into the business end of his still-smoking revolver.

Frozen in his tracks, Alvijo has to think quickly.

"But, amigo, I was only going to pick it up for you," he professes to Vasquez.

"Sure," Fedoro says. "Get away from my gun."

As Alvijo backs off, Vasquez reaches down and

picks up the gun and puts the hammer down. Seeing as Fedoro has laid claim to the gun, and Poncho is already leading the horse away, the only spoil left for Jose is Johnson himself. He rifles through the man's pockets and quickly finds the gold watch, with its shiny silver hoops. He slyly slips it into his own pocket before the others can see.

He then pulls out a billfold and finds a large amount of cash. "Folding money!" Alvijo announces, holding up the bills. "Hundreds of dollars, looks like."

"Split it up three ways," Vasquez says, not wanting to wait until they return to Tecarte where Lopez might decide more shares are warranted.

"Si," agrees Alvijo, quickly dividing up the money into three piles.

He hands the other two their takes and then checks to see what else the generous traveler has for him. He pulls off the man's coat and wipes the blood off it the best he can. "It'll need a wash, but what the hell," he thinks as he sheds his old one and tries it on.

Vasquez is very happy with his new gun. He sees the hawk make another pass overhead and takes bead on it, pretending to take a shot. He checks to make sure it's fully loaded, and then goes through the saddle bags looking for spare ammunition.

They take everything they want and leave the body about half-stripped. Poncho even pulls off the man's boots and tries them on, but they're far too big for his feet and he has to settle for his own worn-out pair. They drag the body off the trail and flop it into a dry gully, tossing the boots and the other things they don't want into the gully with him.

"Let the coyotes have him," Fedoro sneers as they

gather up their growing herd of horses and start off down the trail toward Tecarte.

***

Rafael Martinez saddles up and heads northeast on the road toward the tiny settlement of Campo, ten miles and a world away across the border. Once out of Tecarte, he stops and waits, checking to see if Cruz Lopez might have sent someone after him to make sure he did as he was told. But Martinez has no intention of going straight to Campo as ordered; he has one thing to do before he leaves. He has to see Maria one last time.

Rafael begins to cry as he thinks about her. He still can't believe how quickly things went so horribly wrong. He knows this is going to be the last time he'll ever see the woman he so desperately loves.

He wants to tell her everything and beg her for forgiveness, but he knows he can't. In all her beauty and innocence, she could never understand. She's a good Catholic girl insulated from the mean world that surrounds her. No, she could never understand the ruthlessness of a man like Lopez, and it must stay that way.

He is nearing her house now. He knows that he'll have only a few minutes to be with her; maybe not even that long if her father catches him. What will he tell her? He doesn't know, but he'll think of something.

He rides around to the side and looks the small house over. No dog, he sees. It must be inside, he thinks, or maybe off digging up some squirrels or something. He hides his horse in the bushes and quietly makes his way toward the barn. His heart jumps. He can see Maria in one of the stalls, milking a goat.

"Maria!" he says quietly so only she can hear. She turns quickly at the voice and yells out, "Rafael!" and drops the bucket and runs straight into his arms. "Shhh," he says to her, holding his finger in front of his lips for emphasis. "I don't want your father to know that I'm here."

"Oh, Rafael, what are you doing here?" Maria implores, overjoyed to see him but a bit confused. "I thought you had left to go back to work in Ensenada."

"I was, sweetheart," he says, "but I had to see you first."

"Why, Rafael?" she asks. "Is there something wrong?"

"Well, yes, Maria," he tells her. "I've got to go somewhere for a while and I don't know for how long and I just wanted to let you know how much I love you."

"I love you too, Rafael," she answers back, "but where are you going?"

"I can't say, dear," he says, "but I just need you to know how much I love you."

"Oh, Rafael, there *is* something wrong, I know it," Maria replies, starting to cry. "I could see in Father's eyes at dinner the other night that he thinks something's wrong. Tell me, Rafael, tell me!" she pleads as she tucks her head into his arms.

Rafael is now starting to cry too. "It will be all right," he tells her. "I will be back as soon as I can."

"No, Rafael, don't go!" she begs of him. "You can't go and leave me here. I will go with you!"

"No, that is impossible!" Rafael says sternly. "You have to stay here with your father and when I can, my love," he adds, wiping tears from his eyes, "when I can, I will come back to you and we will be together forever." Oh, how he wished those words were true.

Maria is becoming inconsolable. "No, Rafael, you can't leave me!" she cries.

"I love you," he says, kissing her on the top of the head. "I love you more than you could ever know."

Then he pulls himself away from her and turns and hurries out the back door of the barn. He hears her shriek as he runs across the small clearing and into the bushes to get his horse. He can still hear her crying loudly and, as he mounts his horse and turns, he yells one last time, "I love you, Maria!!!!" and is gone.

As he rides off, he can see the front door open and Maria's father looking out and then running down to the barn.

***

In the Tecarte cantina, Francisco Albitrio has just returned with two men who want to join the gang. He introduces them to Cruz Lopez, who now has only Cota at his side at the back table. "These are my two amigos I told you about, Juan and Demarra," says Francisco. Lopez nods and says, "Mucho gusto," but fails to offer either a handshake. Albitrio excuses himself. He has to get the wagon ready to take to Campo.

"So, you two want to join the Cruz Lopez gang?" says Lopez to the men. "Si! Si!" they say. "Yes, we want to ride with the famous Cruz Lopez," adds Juan.

There's nothing Cruz Lopez likes more than a little flattery. Except killing, of course.

"Good, good," he says to the pair. "We are going to ride to Arizona to avenge Chavez's death."

“Si,” the new recruits say. “We would be proud to help avenge the great Chavez,” Demarra says. “It would be an honor.”

“You are the right men for me,” Lopez says with a smile and a forced laugh. “Cota,” he says, “show these new recruits where they’re going to bunk tonight.”

“Si, jefe,” Cota replies. He gets up from the table and says to the two new men, “C’mon, follow me.”

“And no drinking tonight!” Lopez yells after them and they turn back to face their leader. “We’ve got an important job to do in the morning. We’re going to rob the town of Campo. Either of you got a problem with that?”

They look at each other, then back at Lopez. “No, no, jefe,” they reply.

“Good,” he says, “then put your things away and come back later for dinner.”

“Okay,” the two say as Cota leads them out the door and down the alley to the bunkhouse.

Cruz Lopez is now alone in the cantina. Not too many patrons come into the bar nowadays. Just about everyone in town knows they are there. That means it’s about time to get moving, he thinks.

“Too many people know that I’m here,” he reasons. “We’ll rob Campo tomorrow, come back here to regroup, then pack up the wagons and get out of here.” Gonzalez has told him that there’s a place south of Yuma where a boat can bring them across the Colorado River, so they should be able to get to Sonora without going north of the border. He knows the ferry crossing at Yuma is out of the question since everyone there will be on the lookout after hearing the news of what they’re about to do in Campo.

Lopez is alone with his thoughts for a moment. "Gaskill," he says to himself over and over. "I wonder if this is the same man who sold my silver saddle so many years ago. Either way, it won't matter after tomorrow." He lets out a little chuckle at how foolproof his plan seems.

His thoughts are interrupted when the cantina door bursts open and Alvijo and Vasquez stride into the room. They are all smiles and Lopez can't help but ask what's happened.

They tell him about the gringo traveler and Vasquez shows him his new rifle. Lopez nods approvingly.

"Very good, amigos," he says to them. "And how many horses did you find?"

"Just three," Jose replies. "Poncho is putting them in the stable now along with the one he took from the gringo. The last one must have gone up a side canyon and we didn't have time to go find it."

"Okay," Lopez says. "Three is better than nothing. We will need them when we go to Sonora."

"When's that?" asks Albitrio as he has just returned from the stables.

"As soon as we get done with our business in Campo, we will return here and then pack up and ride east," Lopez tells them. "But I'll tell everyone my plans tonight at dinner. And I don't want any of you drinking tonight, you hear?"

"Okay, Cruz," Alvijo says. Vasquez and Alvitro simply nod their affirmation.

"Tonight we will have a grand dinner," Lopez says. He's as upbeat as any of the three have seen him. He's always upbeat when killing is in the forecast. "And then we will get to bed early," he adds. "I want everyone fresh and ready to ride first thing in the morning."

***

Manuel Estrada closes the door to his daughter's bedroom. "Is she okay?" his wife asks, looking up from some sewing she's doing in the main room of the small adobe house. "She has stopped crying, but she would not tell me what Rafael said to her," Sr. Estrada replies. He has never seen his daughter so upset before, and she has never disobeyed him before by refusing his questions. But now is not the time to press her, he feels. He has never seen her so fragile.

Just then he hears the dog barking, announcing a visitor. "It had better not be that boy again," he thinks to himself as he quickly opens the door to see who is coming. But instead he sees his neighbor, Carlos Ruiz, approaching the house with an unusual sense of urgency in his step that alarms Estrada.

"I must talk to you, Senor Estrada!" announces Ruiz in a rushed voice as he reaches the door.

"Come in then, my neighbor," Sr. Estrada politely replies.

"No, I must talk to you alone, senor," Ruiz tells him. "I have heard something in town just now that I think you will wish to know."

"One moment, por favor," he tells him as he turns and excuses himself from his wife, steps outside and shuts the door. "Let's walk," he says.

When they're out of earshot of the house, Sr. Estrada asks his neighbor what he's heard that is so urgent.

"Well, I can not tell you this with any certainty," Ruiz begins, "but I can tell you what I have heard in town. As you probably know, there is a gang of bandits in town, real desperados, the worst kind of men."

"Yes, I have heard," Sr. Estrada says, "but what could this possibly have to do with me?"

"I am afraid," Sr. Ruiz says, looking down at the ground, "that the boy who is courting your daughter has joined up with them. I was told that he has been seen at the cantina with these men."

It all begins to make sense to Estrada now. The horse … the lie about the job in Ensenada … not being able to look him in the eye. And his unannounced visit earlier in the day.

"What else did you hear, Carlos?" asks Sr. Estrada calmly.

"That they are planning some sort of robbery somewhere and are preparing to leave town," Ruiz replies. "And that all their men are going, including Rafael. I am so sorry to bring you such terrible news, my friend."

"No, thank you," Estrada says to him. "It is good that you did. I knew that something was wrong when the boy came to dinner the other night. And I saw him ride away from here this afternoon and Maria has been hysterical ever since. It is all beginning to make sense to me now."

***

It's now about an hour after dark and the bandits have just finished a feast. Pedro, the cantina owner, had to have his brother-in-law slaughter another one of his best cows to feed all the hungry men. Once Pedro and his helpers have removed the last plate and retired, Lopez gets up, pats his belly and then walks over and locks the front door of the cantina – not that anyone would dare enter anyway.

Then he walks back and sits down and addresses his men. "Here is my plan for manana," he begins. "We will leave early. I have already sent Martinez ahead to scout Campo out for us. I will take four men into town with me – Jose, Fedoro, Poncho and Alonzo. You other three will bring the wagon behind us. I don't want no one seeing a large group together at the same time.

"Anyways, you three bring the wagon in as soon as the shooting stops," Lopez continues. "It shouldn't take too long to kill the gringos. Then we'll load up the wagon with everything we can find. Maybe find another wagon and load that one up too. Then we'll ride back across the border. We'll be gone before a posse even knows that we were ever there."

He lays out the rest of the plan, to return to Tecarte and then to pack and leave for Sonora as soon as possible.

"Si, jefe," Poncho says. "Is there more?"

"Yes," Lopez goes on. "Now everyone listen closely. We'll ride into Campo real slow. Fedoro, you and Poncho hitch your horses off to the side somewhere. Me and Jose and Alonzo will ride up to the store and hitch our horses in front. We will take the one in the store. I'll stand in the doorway and give you a signal, Fedoro, and you take that new gun of yours and kill the blacksmith. You go with him, Poncho, and take Raphael with you if he's outside the store, and if there's anyone else about, you kill them too.

"And we'll take care of anyone else we find in the

store too," Lopez continues. "You men outside will guard us as we pillage the store and then the rest of the town. By then you men in the wagon will ride in and we'll load up and get back across the border."

"Si," all the men say, except Cota, who is standing in the back a few feet behind the others. He can't believe they're going to murder everyone they find in town. He wants to ride off and hide, but just like Martinez, he knows there's no way out. It's too late for that. He's got to go along.

***

Not long before, Vi Price was clearing off the table at the Campo hotel much the same as Pedro was doing ten miles away in Tecarte, – except the men she was serving were a bit more respectable. In addition to the two Gaskill brothers and Jack Kelly, a traveler by the name of Livingston had checked into the hotel. He rode the stage into town earlier in the day and liked the looks of the place – especially after having spent a fitful night at a bawdy establishment in Yuma a few nights before where the ruckus from the saloon downstairs kept him up most of the night.

Now it's nearly dusk, and Lumen, Jack and Mr. Livingston are enjoying a drink and a cigar on the front porch of the hotel. The only sound is the peepers in the creek. Silas would like to join the men on the porch but he's got some tidying up to do in the blacksmith shop and heads down the street.

On his way, he sees a lone man with his hat pulled down a bit walking a sorry-looking horse up the street. The man looks up and Silas can see he's Mexican, but that doesn't alarm him as he promptly recognizes the man as a lowly sheepherder he's seen in Campo from time to time. "Works for a man named Cenac or something like that," Silas says to himself.

Martinez sees Silas walking toward him and would like to spill his guts. But he doesn't dare. Instead, he asks if Silas would mind if he threw his bedroll out among the rocks for the night.

"Gonna be another cold one tonight," Silas says with a shrug, "but if that don't bother you none, I reckon it'll be all right. Just don't light no fire."

"Gracias, senor," Martinez replies. In addition to Silas, he sees only the three other men sitting on the porch. "Only four men," Martinez says to himself.

Sitting down on the porch, Lumen is trying to find out more about this interesting visitor named Livingston, what with his British accent and all. But all he knows so far about him is what the man divulged at dinner – that he rode in today from Yuma on his way to San Diego on some sort of business. Jack Kelly is the problem. He won't shut up about his impending marriage.

"Less than three weeks now!" he says excitedly. "It's going to be a grand wedding, Mr. Livingston. Her name is Annie McNaley and she comes from one of the finest families in Boston."

"You don't say?" Mr. Livingston offers politely.

"Yes, and if you're still in San Diego on the twenty-first, you should come to the wedding," Kelly adds. "All the important people in town will be there."

Lumen rolls his eyes. He's heard enough. Plus, it is now getting dark and the only thing dropping faster than the temperature is Lumen's eyelids. It's been a long day … a long week. He snuffs out the end of his cigar on the side of the arm of the rocking chair he's sitting in, tosses back the rest of his glass of whiskey and excuses himself.

"Goodnight, gentlemen," he announces. "Getting too cold out here for me."

The two men say goodnight in return and Lumen walks inside and shuts the door.

"Did you know I operate the Army telegraph station in Campo?" Jack Kelly says, "I was trained in the Signal Corps!"

"Pardon me," interrupts Mr. Livingston, looking at the door and then back at Kelly. "I do think Mr. Gaskill is correct. It is getting bloody cold out here. Please excuse me, sir, as I must be retiring for the evening as well."

Chapter 27

DECEMBER 4, 1875, THE DAY OF THE CAMPO GUNFIGHT

Rafael Martinez wakes up from a fitful sleep, if you could call it that. Really, he didn't sleep much at all. He found a place to roll out his blanket in between two large rocks that provided some shelter from the wind. And it got real cold last night. He can see there was some frost in the low-lying areas.

But it wasn't just the cold that kept him awake. He couldn't stop thinking about what he was doing here. How did he get into such a mess?

"God," he says, looking heavenward. "Forgive me, Lord, I'm sorry for what I'm about to do today. But what choice do I have? I must protect Maria at all cost. I will die before I let something happen to her."

He gets up and shakes the leaves and twigs out of his unkempt hair. He sees his horse is still tied to the scrub oak. The horse looks at him, and returns to nibbling some shrubs close by. Silas had said not to light a fire, Rafael remembers, but he'd sure like one right now. But, he figures, he'd better do as he's told so as to not draw any attention to himself.

He picks up his blanket and shakes it out, wraps it around his stiff shoulders and finds a rock where he can sit to await the coming of the sun's warming rays.

***

Just about the same time in Tecarte, Cruz Lopez wakes up in the bunkhouse. Unlike yesterday, this time it's crowded with men snoring and stinking up the place. "Must've been the beans," Lopez thinks, recalling the dinner they had last night in the cantina. He gets up and heads for the door; he can barely stand it in there.

"Get up, you smelly bastards!" he yells at them, kicking a few feet as he walks out of the room. He hears the men groan and start to come alive. He walks down the alley to the cantina and upon entering can see that Pedro is already up and has something cooking for breakfast. The bandit gets himself a cup of coffee and sits down at his usual spot.

Pedro hears the rest of the men begin to drift in and brings out a platter full of the usual stuff: huevos and tortillas. "Eat up, amigos," he says to them, "there's plenty more." He sets down the platter and goes back to the kitchen.

Alvijo comes in and sits down beside Lopez. "Buenos dias," Jose says to his leader.

"Yeah, good morning," replies Cruz with a mouthful of scrambled eggs.

"Looks like it's going to be a good day," Alvijo says as he fills his plate, "once the sun warms things up a bit."

Lopez takes a sip of coffee and says, "It sure is," thinking not about the weather but all the killing he's about to command. That good feeling is starting to flow through his veins already. "Sure is going to be a great day!"

Albitrio comes in and sits down as well. "Francisco," says Lopez, "as soon as you're done, you and the new hombres go out and saddle up all the horses and get the wagon ready. I want to leave as soon as possible."

"Si, jefe," he replies, and tells his new recruits to eat up.

"You ready, Jose?" he asks his lieutenant.

"Si," Alvijo replies. "I was born ready!"

"Ha, ha, ha," Lopez laughs. "I already knew that. You're a good friend, Jose, and I want you to stick with me." Cruz then leans close to his friend and says in a low voice so that the others can't hear, "I don't trust anyone else. If things go bad, we will kill anyone in our way and ride out together."

"You worried about Vasquez?" asks Jose.

"No," Cruz replies, "he will do his job. It is after we get back that he might get ideas. When today's business is through, I want to get that rifle from him. If I give you the signal, then we will kill him, okay?"

"Sure thing, jefe," replies Jose, remembering the wild look in Vasquez's eyes in Horsethief Canyon the day before. "I would love to. Just say the word."

Francisco comes back into the cantina and walks up to Lopez. "Jefe," he says, "some more muchachos, some friends of mine, wish to ride along in the wagon."

"You trust these men?" quizzes Lopez.

"Si," Francisco replies. "Two I know well and the other is my cousin, Felipe."

"Do they have weapons?" Lopez asks.

"No, but they can help us loot the town," Francisco offers.

"Okay, then," Cruz decides, "they can ride with us, but tell them that I am in charge and if any man doesn't do exactly as I say, I will kill him on the spot."

"It is okay. I have already told them," Albitrio

replies.

"Good," Cruz says, smiling. "Go back outside and make sure that everything's ready to go. I want to leave in ten minutes."

"Si, jefe," says Francisco and he turns and hurries back out the door.

***

The sun has risen in Campo and once again its rays are conquering the cool night air. Smoke from the woodstoves can be smelled drifting through the air. Silas Gaskill steps out into the street and looks the town over. "What a place to live!" he says to himself. "Me and Lumen really got lucky when we found this lovely valley."

Rafael Martinez watches Silas as he goes to the stable and gets out two horses. He ties them to a hitching post and gives them both a feed bucket. Next, he walks over to the blacksmith shop and throws all the doors open wide, letting the sun's warmth drift through the building. Stoking up the forge, he decides that he doesn't need any breakfast right now and starts to fix a wagon that he's been working on. Some of the boards in its bed have rotted and are coming loose; he'll need to replace them.

Lumen can hear his brother pounding something on the anvil. "I guess it's time to get up," he tells his lovely wife. "You know, Eliza," he says to her. "What, dear?" she replies sleepily. "I think you're getting more and more beautiful every day," he says. "Oh, stop that," she replies, blushing. "I'm almost thirty years old!"

Just then the bedroom door bursts open and Walter comes bouncing into the room. "Ma! Pa!" he exclaims.

"What is it, Walter?" Lumen says to his son with a chuckle.

"Auntie Price says breakfast is about ready," Walter announces.

"Okay, little man," Eliza says. "You go back and tell her that we'll be right down."

"Okay, Ma!" Walter exclaims again and just as quickly he runs back out of the room.

Lumen rolls over and hugs his wife. "What's that for?" she asks with a smile. "For giving me such a wonderful son!" Lumen replies. "I can't wait till we have more children someday."

"Why not start right now?" Eliza says with a wink as she gets up and shuts and locks the bedroom door.

***

Rafael Martinez finally warms up enough to shed his blanket and ties it on the back of his saddle. He looks through his saddle bags and finds a small bag of dried apples that he got in the market in Tecarte before he left. He also finds the small bag of gold and pulls out the pistol that he took from the drunken vaqueros on that fateful day when he met Chavez and Lopez.

Now he wishes he'd lost that fight. Then he wouldn't be in this fix now. He looks at the deadly instrument and then quickly puts it back into the saddle bag. He can see that life is stirring in the small village and that he should get ready for the arrival of Lopez and the gang.

Last night, he saw only four men in town, so he guesses that he should stay in Campo. "Cruz said that if there's no more than four men, I should stay," he says to himself, reworking it in his mind so that he's got it right. He shudders at the thought of what Lopez might do if he should mess up.

Now he wishes that a bunch of men would come riding in and then he'd have to ride out to warn the gang and maybe Lopez would call off the attack. Then he could ride back to Maria's house and take her away with him. Far, far away, where Lopez would never find them.

Thinking about Maria brings tears to his eyes again. Oh, how he must have hurt her yesterday when he rode off. "She doesn't understand and probably never will," he says to himself, "but I did it for her."

He wishes that he knew how to write so he could send her a letter. Maybe when he rides off to Sonora with the gang he can find someone down there who knows how to write and he could send her one then.

After pondering this for a while, his mind drifts back to the mission of the day. He figures it will be some time yet before the gang arrives and he'll look suspicious if he hangs around town all morning, so he decides to ride his horse down the creek a ways and wait a while. Then in a couple hours he can ride back into Campo and be ready when the gang appears.

For some reason, Lumen opens the store unusually late this morning, but it doesn't matter because he hasn't got a customer yet. Like his brother, he opens up the doors and windows to let a warming breeze flow through. He can hear Jack Kelly in the telegraph office in the back. He goes over and pounds on the door.

"Morning, Jack!" he says loudly through the door and then hears a similar reply from the other side. Lumen slides the bolt back on the store side of the door; he notices that it's still locked on the other side and walks back to the counter.

A wagon rolls in from the west and an old Mexican couple gets down from their buckboard and comes in for some supplies. Lumen speaks to them in Spanish, as he is learning to speak the language much better now that he's been in the area for so long. The couple is headed for Yuma and needs some things that they could not find in Tecarte. Lumen sells them tea, salt and other staples and they're quickly on their way.

Silas is busy working on the wagon. When he's working, he doesn't pay much attention to anything else that's going on in town. He saw the old Mexican couple roll into town, but gave them no mind. Stripping off the rotting boards from the wagon, he sets about cutting some new ones to replace them with.

***

The gang has started out on the road to Campo, with Lopez riding in the lead of his growing force. He can't think of a time when he has felt more in control than right now. He has twelve men at his command. This is the opportunity he's been waiting for. He's going to be the most famous and feared man in all of California. And Mexico too. More famous than Joaquin Murrieta or Tiburcio Vasquez.

He laughs to himself. With his small army, he will plunder towns, rob stages and hold up mining payrolls everywhere they go. "No one can stop me now," he says to himself.

He turns in the saddle to address the men following him. "My muchachos," he says, "today we will pay back the gringos for all the bad things they have done to us. We will be heroes to our people and you can tell your grandchildren that you once rode with the great Cruz Lopez!"

"Ole! Ole!" all the men cheer. "Viva the Lopez gang," someone yells and the men all cheer again.

Jose looks at Cruz and he can see that Lopez is loving every minute of it. He can see that Lopez's head is swelled with his newfound power. For the first time, Jose Alvijo wonders if he should look for another line of work.

***

Rafael Martinez rides slowly back into Campo. He leaves his horse off to the side in some shade. He opens his saddle bags and reaches in, pushing the gun aside as he reaches for the smallest of the gold coins. He finds a five-dollar piece and puts it in his vest pocket. He thinks about the gun he's got in the saddle bag. To wear a gun now would raise suspicion, he thinks. Better to leave it right where it is. That way, he might not need to use it.

He walks over to the side of the store and sits down on a stump that's been left there for that purpose. He's sweating and his heart is beating wildly. What's he to do now, he thinks, except wait?

Jack Kelly walks by with a washcloth and a pail of water he lugged up from the creek. He looks at Rafael, and says, "You're sitting on my stump! I've got to wash my feet!"

Rafael obliges and gets up. Not knowing how long it will take Lopez and the gang to arrive, he slowly meanders over to the front of the store. Kelly sits down on the stump, takes off his boots and starts to wash his feet.

Rafael looks over the town. "So peaceful," he

thinks to himself. "How can something so horrible be about to happen to such a peaceful place?" There's a lump in his throat the size of a lemon and he tries hard to swallow it as he walks up the steps to the front door of the store.

"Hello, Senor Gaskill," he says as he walks up to the counter. "Uh, hi there," Lumen replies, recognizing the man, but forgetting if he ever knew his name or not.

"I'd like some bacon and beans," Martinez says to him. "Okay," Lumen says and starts to get the items together. "And some of this candy here," Rafael adds, noticing a jar of hard candy on the counter top and helping himself to a piece. Lumen sees this and thinks to himself, "I hope he's got money to pay for that!"

***

Cruz Lopez stops his band when they get to an old sign nailed to a post that says, "United States Border." He knows what it says even though he can't read the words. In fact, it's almost impossible to read even if he knew how, it's been shot so full of holes.

"How far is it?" he asks Cota. "Only a little over a mile," Alonzo replies. "Okay," Lopez says, and turning to his men, lays out the plan. "I don't want all of us to be seen at the same time, so, Francisco, you wait here with the wagon and the rest of us will ride on ahead. When we get to the top of that hill over there," turning back and pointing to a rise about halfway to town, "you start in and when you get to the top, you stop and wait."

Lopez rides his horse around to the side of the wagon so he can address all of the men riding in it. "You all wait there until the shooting stops. And it won't take long. Then you drive the wagon on into town and we'll load it up with everything we might need. If you can find another wagon, fill that one up too. Saddle any horse you can find and ride it back."

"Si, jefe," they all say.

"And while you're waiting," Lopez adds as an afterthought, "find yourself some sticks and make some clubs. You might need them to finish them off."

"Okay, jefe, we will," they say, most of them thinking that they weren't expecting to do any of the fighting.

"Vamonos!" Lopez orders and the five senior members of the gang ride off into history.

***

Silas Gaskill is working on the wagon. He's pulled off the rotten boards and has the replacements all cut to length and ready to install. He can't locate his wood drill, so he's going to have to burn holes through each of the boards where the bolts are going to go through. He has marked each board and has one of them on his workbench inside the blacksmith shop with five pokers glowing in the forge.

He is using one poker at a time, keeping them red hot and then when the one he's using cools, he changes it with a hot one and gives the bellows a little pump to provide air for a hot fire. It's hard work to keep all this going at once and he's already got sweat dripping from his brow.

Jack Kelly has finished washing his feet. He puts his torn socks back on and then pulls on his boots. He picks up the bucket of filthy water and flings it out into the street. He yawns, knowing that it's going to be a quiet day since it's a Saturday and not much telegraph traffic is expected. "I guess I'll go back inside," he thinks. He's got some recent newspapers that Lumen gave him, so he might as well read them because he has to stay close to his office just in case.

He opens the back door to the telegraph office and closes it behind him. Setting the bucket down, he picks up the editions of the San Diego *Union* and sits down at his desk and begins to read.

Mr. Livingston walks out of the Campo hotel. It's getting a lot warmer now and he thinks that he'll take a little stroll around the village to work off his breakfast, and maybe climb the hill to look at the scenery. "What a quaint little town," he thinks, "and peaceful too." He remembers how Lumen told him at dinner last night how nothing exciting ever happens around here. He likes that.

He walks past Silas and sees that he's engrossed in his work and decides not to disturb him. There's two horses tied to a hitching post beside the barn and he walks over to have a look at them.

***

The five bandits come around the corner and can see the small village. Cruz looks it all over very carefully. "There's the store," he guesses, spotting the building. It looks like the front door is on the other side, he observes, and they'll have to ride around to get to it. He also can see a house farther back, built into the side of some large rocks. And another building farther back even still.

As they ride closer under the tall oaks he can now see the blacksmith shop and notices the smoke rising from its stovepipe. He also can see the barn and stables and another building. "Nice," he thinks, "all peace and quiet." He knows he's got the edge, the element of surprise.

He slows almost to a stop and gives Vasquez his instructions. He and Alvitro are to go over near the blacksmith shop and wait for his signal. Then he holds up to let them ride in first before telling Alvijo and Cota to follow him.

Rafael looks up and through the open doors can see Lopez and the others riding in. It feels like his heart has stopped. He's sucking on a piece of candy while he's chatting with Lumen, but now picks up his sack of supplies and says goodbye. Lumen doesn't even look up, but says, "So long, now."

Rafael walks out into the street just as Vasquez and Alvijo come riding around the store. He passes them without looking up. Lopez sees Rafael walk out of the store and takes it as a sign that everything is working according to plan. A smile creeps to his lips.

Silas is still busy burning holes in the board. He looks up and sees Vasquez and Alvijo hitching their horses to a post rail off to the side of the store. "Two vaqueros," he thinks. "Looks like they've been on the trail a while." Silas goes back to work never seeing Lopez and the others.

Rafael walks to his horse and puts the sack into his saddle bag. Then he walks around to the other side and opens the other saddle bag that has the gun in it. Looking to make sure no one is watching, he reaches in and unwillingly removes the pistol. He puts the gun in his belt and conceals it with his coat, then ties off the saddle bag. Meanwhile, Lopez, Alvijo and Cota have dismounted and he watches them walk toward the store's front door.

"This is it," Martinez thinks to himself. "It's really

gonna happen."

In the store, Lumen is sweeping dirt down through the open trap door behind the counter. He looks up and sees Cota and Alvijo come in. The first man he has seen before, but he doesn't think he knows the second one. They walk up to the counter and with a smile, the man he doesn't know says, "Good day, senor."

Lopez then walks up to the open door and looks in and sees Lumen still sweeping away. He can see that the storekeeper doesn't have any suspicions yet. Lopez looks down the street and sees that Vasquez has his Henry rifle out of its scabbard and is looking at him for a signal.

Lopez looks back inside as he hears Alvijo ask if Lumen has some hemp rope. As Lumen puts the broom down and turns toward where he keeps the rope, he sees Lopez standing in the doorway. He also sees that Lopez has one hand up as if to signal someone and is starting to draw his pistol with the other one.

Lumen instantly realizes what is happening and yells at the top of his lungs to warn his brother: "Murder!!!"

Chapter 28

Silas hears the blood-curdling scream of "Murder" coming from the store. Looking up from his work, he instantly sizes up the situation, realizing he should have paid more attention to the activity he saw in the street moments before.

If Silas Gaskill has a fault, it's that he gets so absorbed in his work that he doesn't pay much attention to what's going on around him. Despite the heightened tensions of the past week, people are always going in and out of Campo and Silas had been too wrapped up in the wagon to give the two riders a second look. And he hadn't even noticed Lopez and the others ride in after them and enter the store.

After finishing burning the holes in the boards, he was in the process of bolting them to the bed of the buckboard when he heard Lumen's shout.

Quickly looking up, he can now see another man in the doorway of the store dropping his hand as if to give a signal. Silas turns and sees Vasquez, one of the men in the street, little more than 60 feet away. He's raising a rifle in his direction.

Silas ducks as the man's shot whizzes by only inches from his head. He jumps up and as he hears the clicking sound of the lever-action rifle chambering a fresh round, Silas lunges for cover behind the wagon. But he knows he has to get to the shotgun he has cached just inside the blacksmith shop's door, so he makes a run for it.

Vasquez can't believe he missed with his first shot, but he doesn't with the second. He snaps off another round when he sees Silas break for the opening, catching him in the shoulder and spinning him into the door. Silas disappears inside, but Vasquez can see the blood he left behind on the door jamb and the bandit runs around the wagon toward the open door thinking he's dropped his man. Alvitro is right behind him, pistol in hand.

Silas, though, never even realizes he's been shot, as the bullet finds only flesh, slicing a nice, deep gash through the meaty part of the shoulder. He grabs the shotgun and in a single whirling motion cocks one of its hammers and points it out the doorway just as Vasquez steps around the side of the wagon.

"Boom," roars the shotgun and thick, gray smoke blocks Silas's vision, forcing him to duck back into the shop. Vasquez is struck full square in the chest as nine .12-gauge buckshot pellets rip through his body, sending him flying backward into the street. Vasquez dies instantly and his coveted Henry rifle lands on the ground almost at Alvitro's feet. Under cover of the thick smoke, Alvitro quickly picks it up and runs around to the side of the blacksmith shop. Seeing a stack of lumber, Alvitro ducks behind it to get away from Silas and the shotgun.

Like his brother, Lumen Gaskill also reacts instantly to the situation. When he sees the man in the doorway leveling a pistol at him, Lumen follows up his sound of alarm by diving behind the counter and scrambling for his own parked gun. But before he can get to it, the other two men – Alvijo and Cota – jump over the counter and grab him one on each arm, pinning him down.

Lopez quickly comes around the counter and is already grinning when a terrified Lumen looks up from his predicament and finds himself staring straight down the muzzle of the bandit's pistol. Lopez steps closer and coolly cocks the hammer as his grin widens. The bandit is almost laughing now at the thought of such a clean shot and slowly drops the barrel straight at Lumen's chest and without saying a word, squeezes the trigger.

To Lumen, it all seems surreal, everything moving in slow motion. But even though Cota has him by the right arm, Lumen has managed to grab a post that supports a shelf and just at the same moment Lopez squeezes the trigger, he pulls hard on the post and jerks his body. It wasn't much. Just a few inches, but that's all that's needed to make the bullet miss its mark. Instead of going through Lumen's heart, it passes above and to the right, cutting cleanly through the top of the left lung and coming out his back.

Lumen recoils as the bullet passes through him and then thick smoke from the black-powdered pistol fills the air, burning and blackening his face. Lopez is momentarily blinded by the smoke, but it quickly clears and he can see bright red blood gushing from Lumen's mouth and chest as he lies dying on the floor.

Alvijo cocks his pistol and is about to fire another round into Lumen to finish the job, but Lopez stops him. He knows no man can survive such a shot for long and he sees that Lumen is already drowning in his own blood.

"No, amigo!" Lopez says, reaching out to lower Alvijo's outstretched arm. "It only takes one bullet to kill a man. Save all your bullets; you might need them."

Satisfied, Lopez and Alvijo turn their attention to the store, searching for the cash box and any other items of value. Cota, though, can't take his eyes off the near-lifeless body. "This is it," he says to himself. "If I survive this, I'm never doing this sort of thing again."

Jack Kelly is in the back office reading the society pages, daydreaming about when his and Annie's names will grace this section. He's counting down the days to their wedding. Suddenly, he's snapped back to reality by Lumen's cry of murder. "What the hell?" he thinks as he gets up and hurries to the door separating the telegraph office from the store. Before he can slide the bolt on his side of the door so he can see what's going on, he hears a shot coming from outside, and then another. Then a loud shot rings out inside the store and then he hears someone yelling something about a cash box. Then another shot from outside.

Realizing what is happening, Kelly does what he does best: he panics. He quickly runs to his desk, fumbles through the top drawer, and finds his pistol under a pile of papers. Grabbing it, he races out the back door, tripping over the doorstep and falling to the ground. The gun goes tumbling into the bushes. Kelly scrambles to his feet, but wastes no time bothering to look for the lost weapon. Instead, he climbs under the corner of the building and jumps down into the creek, hiding under the store.

Rafael Martinez stops as he sees the shotgun blast tearing through Vasquez. He, too, has the sensation of slow motion as he stands there stunned and watches the body slump to the ground. He pulls out the gun tucked under his belt, but he doesn't know what to do with it. But he knows that if he stands there, Silas may come back out with his shotgun, so he runs around to the back of the building looking for a place to hide.

But at the same time, Silas comes charging out of the back door, and seeing Martinez with a pistol in his hand, snaps the barrel in his direction and shoots from the hip toward Rafael. The rushed shot is a little wide of its mark as Silas pulled the trigger a little too soon and of the nine balls of buckshot that flew out of the barrel, only three found a home in the body of Martinez. One passes through the side of his neck and the other two lodge in his side, spinning him around and to the ground. Silas, his gun now empty, runs back into the blacksmith shop looking for another.

Livingston is behind the barn when he hears Lumen's yell, but can't make out what he's heard. The next thing he hears is gunfire, and some commotion going on in the street. Walking quickly around the barn, he sees a Mexican with a rifle hiding behind a pile of lumber. "What's going on here?" he thinks as he walks out into the center of the street.

***

Back in the store, Lopez is getting frantic. "Find that money box!" he yells, still unable to locate it. "And grab any guns or anything of value. We don't have all day!"

Cota is scared now. He sees Lopez ranting like a lunatic and waving his gun around. "Cota!" Lopez yells to him from behind the counter. "I'm talking to you! Let's move!"

Cota quickly realizes that the best thing he can do is to simply appease Lopez, so he starts looking around for something to steal. After fruitlessly searching, they don't find much and Lopez orders them out into the street, which is momentarily quiet.

Just as the three bandits emerge from the store, Frenchy, the sheepherder, comes galloping into town. He was sent to Campo by his employer, Senor Ynda, again to fetch his mail, but when he heard all the gunshots, he spurred his horse and came riding into town fast. Looking around, Frenchy sees the bandits, jumps off his horse and begins firing his revolver at them.

Alvijo and Cota instinctively duck for cover, but Lopez stands firm and draws down on the new threat. His hurried shots miss their mark, but the third shot from Frenchy's pistol strikes Lopez, tearing a hole through the muscles in his neck. Lopez falls backward, slamming against the side of the store, and then slumps face-forward off the porch onto the hard, dusty street, knocking him senseless.

Alvijo, steadying his gun over Jack Kelly's stump, fires a shot at the Frenchman, the bullet going deep into his chest and bringing him down.

The blast from Silas's shotgun only momentarily stuns the wounded Martinez. He struggles to his knees, and hearing gunshots coming from the street, he crawls up into the rocks behind the blacksmith shop to hide. He finds a small nook under a rock and crawls into it as best he can. The painful burning in his side is more than he can stand and he passes out.

Silas is unable to locate another gun in the blacksmith shop, so he runs back into the street, where he sees Frenchy shooting it out with Lopez. As he looks around, he notices Livingston standing in the middle of the street looking bewildered. He runs up and hands him the empty shotgun. "It's empty, but it's better than nothing," he yells to the Englishman in passing while on his way to the barn to look for another gun.

Not finding one there either, Silas notices the two horses tied to the rail and quickly ushers them into the corral and shuts the gate. "No sense making it easy for them," he says out loud. Coming back into the street,

Silas sees that Livingston hasn't budged and then catches some movement by the lumber pile as Alvitro finally summons the courage to step out and rejoin the battle. Seeing this, Silas rushes over and grabs the empty shotgun away from Livingston and levels it at the bandit. Alvitro, not knowing it's empty, immediately jumps back behind the lumber pile.

Silas hands the shotgun back to Livingston and advises him to find a place to hide and returns once again to the blacksmith shop in search of the backup gun he knows he left somewhere handy. But where? He folds his arms as he tries to think and that's when he finally notices that he's bleeding. He quickly grabs a clean rag off his workbench and ties it snugly around the wound.

***

On the hill outside of town, the men in the wagon have been listening to all the shooting. "I thought he said it was going to be easy?" Demarra remarks. "Yeah," Juan replies, "it don't sound like it's going easy to me." More shots echo off the surrounding hills.

"What do you think?" another man asks Francisco. "I don't know," Albitrio answers. "Lopez told us to wait here...."

Another series of shots ring out.

"Well," Demarra says, "I'm not taking a stick into a gunfight, that's for sure." He looks at the thick oak branch in his hand that was supposed to be the club Lopez told him to find. Throwing it aside, he says, "I say we get outta here."

"No, we have to wait for Lopez to come back," Francisco says. Then the sound of more shots can be heard.

“I don’t think he’s coming back,” Juan replies. “I say we go.”

“Si,” all the other men agree as Albitrio is overruled.

“Okay,” he finally says, “let’s get the hell out of here.” He slaps the reins on the horses’ backs and turns the wagon around so quickly that two of the men almost fall out. “Ya!” he yells, and slaps the reins as hard as he can and the horses bolt into a run, jerking the wagon back down the road in the direction of the border.

***

The floor of the Campo store looks like it’s been painted red. Lumen Gaskill gasps and coughs up blood all over the front of him. He’s surprised to find that he’s still alive. But he must be, he reasons, because he’s in a great deal of pain. And even though he can’t move a muscle on his left side, it hurts like hell. Groaning, he tries to move his left arm again. A finger twitches, and then another. Slowly, his paralysis starts to go away.

He hears more shots coming from the street. “Silas!” he thinks. “I’ve got to help Silas!” Lumen reaches deep down inside for all the power he can muster, and pulls himself into a sitting position. He can see his shotgun still in its hiding place under the counter. He slides over and seizes it and slowly drags himself to the front door. The shooting has stopped for the moment and there’s a lot of smoke in the air. Through the haze it looks like a war just took place.

There are bodies lying all over the street. There’s only one man standing and through the haze he can see that it's one of the bandits that had come into the store. Lumen strains to pull back one of the hammers on the gun and lifts it slowly up. Balancing it on his left arm, he aims it at the unsuspecting Alvijo, who is standing over Frenchy's body to make sure the sheepherder is out of the fight.

Lumen steadies his hand the best he can and pulls the trigger. At a distance of about 55 feet, the charge spreads out and buckshot riddles Alvijo's body – three in the right side, two in the upper abdomen and two in the right arm. As the smoke clears from the blast, Lumen can see his man lying motionless on the ground.

Cruz Lopez opens his eyes. He's lying on the ground in front of the store. He heard the loud shot which came from the doorway and he saw Alvijo go down. "Not a good time to get up now," he thinks to himself and decides to play dead.

Silas is looking everywhere for a gun. "Damn," he says to himself. "Damn. Damn. Damn. How did I let myself get into this predicament?"

Alvitro pokes his head over the lumber pile after not hearing a shot being fired for a minute or so. Seeing no one in the street, he decides this is a good time to make a run for it. He sneaks out of his hiding place, crosses behind the blacksmith shop and stops in the street in front of the store. There's still a lot of smoke in the air, but he can see what looks like nothing but dead people lying in the street. He unties the cream-colored horse he took from the beekeeper and leads it out into the street.

Lumen sees Alvitro and points the gun in his direction and pulls the other trigger. The buckshot hits him hard as he is much closer than Alvijo was. Taking most of the charge in the left side of the gut, Alvitro goes down, writhing in the street. The bayonet he always carries falls out of his belt and lands on the street in the dirt.

Lumen now has an empty gun and he knows he has to get to the house to get another one. The best way to do this, he thinks, is to drop down through the trap door into the creek and crawl up the culvert under the store and then make his way to the house. He drags himself across the floor and reaches the trap door. Painfully, he drops down into the creek.

A shivering Jack Kelly nearly jumps out of his skin at the sound of the splash behind him. Turning, he's relieved to see that it's Lumen and not one of the bandits, but he's horrified at the sight of his condition. "Lumen!" he yells. "Are you all right?"

"Quiet, you fool!" replies Lumen in a hushed voice. "You trying to get us both killed!"

"You mean they're still out there?" Kelly exclaims, the fear showing in his voice.

Lumen has no time for questions. "You stay put," he says to Kelly. "I'm going to crawl up the tunnel and get my needle gun and finish them!" Lumen crawls to the upstream end of the tunnel that runs under the store and, popping his head up, sees no one around. He crawls into the bushes and makes his way toward the house.

"Pa!" he hears as he gets close to the house, and he looks up to see Walter running toward him from the rock he's been hiding behind since the shooting began. Walter runs up and hugs his father around the legs and Lumen leans on his young son.

"Good boy," Lumen says to his son. "Help me get to the house." Although Walter is only six years old, he knows that his father's life depends on him getting him inside. With all the strength in his little body, he helps his father make his way the remaining few yards to the front door. Throwing it open, they stumble in and Lumen falls to his knees on the floor.

The women come out of the back room and Eliza doesn't even recognize her own husband at first. Lumen is soaking wet, blood is everywhere and his face is covered with powder burns from Cruz Lopez's six-shooter. "It's me," Lumen says weakly.

Momentarily relieved that Lumen is alive, Eliza then looks at her little son Walter covered in blood and lets out a scream. "They've shot poor Walter!" she yells.

"No, they haven't," realizes Vi Price, putting down the needle gun. She's seen this before, but not since she left Mississippi following that awful war. "The boy's not been hurt," she reassures Eliza, "he's covered with his *father's* blood."

Lumen grabs the needle gun and crawls over to the door with it.

Cruz Lopez hasn't heard or seen anything in a while now and lifts his head again. Now's his chance, he thinks, and holding his hand on his bleeding neck, gets to his feet and looks around. Cota sees him and comes out of his hiding place too. Lopez walks over to the fallen Alvitro, writhing in pain. But he ignores the cries of his compadre and instead picks up the coveted Henry rifle lying on the ground beside him.

"Cota!" barks Lopez, "we need to get out of here!" It's the best news Cota has heard all day. "But we need that cash box first!" Lopez adds, deflating Cota again. "But I couldn't find it!" Alonzo pleads.

"Then go back in there and look some more!" orders Lopez, pointing the rifle at Cota for emphasis.

"And don't come out until you find something of value!"

The last thing that Alonzo Cota wants to do is go back in that store. Last he saw, two shotgun blasts came out the front door, taking down two of his cohorts. But with Lopez waving that rifle around like that, he knows he has no choice. Reluctantly, he goes back in, not knowing if death awaits him from the front or the back.

Cruz looks at his amigo, Jose, lying in the street, apparently dead. "Too bad for you," he says out loud. "You, my friend, I will miss." Untying the reins of his big bay, he pulls himself up into the saddle and looks over the streets of Campo, wondering how it all went wrong.

Lumen Gaskill crawls to the open front door of his house and, leaning on the jamb, can see Lopez sitting on his horse. With the needle gun in his hands, he tries to take aim at the bandit. Normally, this would be an easy shot for Lumen, but he is too weak from loss of blood. Try as he might, he can't get the gun up. Struggling with all his might, he raises the barrel nearly level, but then drops it to the floor, passing out in the doorway.

Vi Price pulls him back inside and shuts the door.

Silas can see Lopez sitting on his horse too. But he can't do anything either, not without a gun. Silas looks at the body of Vasquez lying not far way, with a pistol tucked in his holster. "I've got to get that gun," Silas says to himself, but then reconsiders this foolhardy plan as he can plainly see that with the Henry rifle in his hands, Lopez has full command of the street.

"Hurry up in there!" roars Lopez again as he can hear Cota rummaging around inside the store. Then suddenly he's surprised to notice movement beside him. It's Alvitro. "Help me, amigo," Poncho calls to Cruz. Looking down at the gut-shot man, Lopez replies coldly,

"Not much I can do for you now."

Cota then comes out of the store apologizing that he couldn't find the cash box, but he did discover some pistols in a drawer, handing them to Lopez. Cruz isn't pleased, but he knows they've got to ride now and tucks the pistols in his belt. What he does not know is that the pistols are all broken, in need of repair. Alvitro is now up and tries to climb onto the Frenchman's horse; but he can't do it, so Cota runs over to help him into the saddle. The wounded bandit can't sit up, but he leans over and holds on to the horse's mane.

"Let's go!" yells Lopez, spurring his horse, and Alonzo mounts his too and the three of them ride out of town to the east.

Once they're gone, Silas comes out and secures Vasquez's pistol. "Lumen!" he yells as he runs to the store. "Lumen!" he yells again when he hears no answer and rushes inside. The place is ransacked and blood is everywhere, but Silas can follow its trail past the counter to the trap door. Crouching down to look through the hole, he sees Jack Kelly standing in the water shivering uncontrollably.

"Where's my brother?" Silas demands sharply. "He w-w-went to the house," Kelly says through chattering teeth, "to g-g-g-et another gun."

Silas leaps up and runs out the door toward Lumen's house, not bothering to tell Kelly that the danger has passed and he can come out now.

Looking up at the hole, Kelly asks, "Is-s-s it ov-v-er?" But there is no reply.

Chapter 29

Jose Alvijo, left for dead in the middle of the street, suddenly comes to and tries to sit up. He hurts all over. With seven buckshot wounds in him it's a wonder that he can move at all. He looks around at the street, empty except for the body of Vasquez lying dead not far away and that of the Frenchman next to him.

Alvijo knows if he doesn't do something fast, he'll be captured or killed on the spot. With all of the effort he can muster, he drags himself to his feet and staggers down the road toward the border.

Jack Kelly finally summons enough courage to come out from his hiding place. He's dripping wet and shivering from being in the cold stream for so long. He climbs out from under the store and the warmth of the sun's rays is welcomed like a long, lost friend. Kelly reaches into his pocket and pulls out his tobacco pouch, his hands still shaking a little from the cold. He hopes he can keep them steady enough to roll a cigarette, but he finds it doesn't matter. The tobacco is spoiled.

Suddenly, he spots his gun underneath some bushes. Picking it up, he looks around quickly to make sure no one is watching, and tucks it under his belt, where it's been all along, as far as he's concerned.

Kelly walks into the street and surveys the carnage. Blood everywhere. Two bodies lying lifeless in the street. The only noise he can hear is coming from Lumen's house as the front doors are still wide open. As he approaches, he calls out Silas's name.

"In here," Silas calls back and Jack rushes inside to see Lumen lying on the floor and Silas helping Vi Price clean and patch his wounds. Silas tries to pick his brother up and take him to the back bedroom. “Just let me lay here,” Lumen says weakly. “I can’t last long and there’s no sense in getting the sheets all bloody.” Even in what he fears is his final moments, Lumen’s thoughts are on Eliza and his family.

“Help me, Jack,” Silas says and they pick up Lumen anyway and bring him into the bedroom.

Out in the street, one of the lifeless bodies suddenly stirs. “Sacrebleu! Where am I?” Frenchy says to himself as he sits up, his eyes and his head not quite focusing clearly. Then he remembers the shootout with the bandits. He winces sharply at the excruciating pain pounding throughout his chest. He can’t see Silas or Lumen anywhere, and assumes the worst. “Everybody must’ve been killed,” Frenchy thinks to himself. “I better get out of town before the bandits come back and finish me too.”

Same as the others before him, Frenchy struggles to his feet and staggers out of town.

“What can I do to help?” Jack Kelly asks Silas. “Here,” Silas says, “cut some more of these sheets into bandages.” “Okay,” Kelly replies, taking the shears from Silas, who turns his attention to his wounded brother.

“Just rest easy, Lumen,” comforts Silas. “You’ll be all right once we stop this bleeding.”

***

Cruz Lopez is also in danger of bleeding to death. A little ways out of town, he stops to tie his bandana tightly around his neck wound. Just then, a man on a horse, with another one trailing behind him, comes down the road.

Simon Miller sees the three men on their horses but doesn't realize who they are until he's ridden right up to them.

"Oh, my God," Miller thinks as he looks over the scene. He can see that one man is shot badly in the gut and can barely hold onto his horse's mane to keep from falling off. Another man is holding his right hand over a neck wound that is bleeding profusely. And in his left hand he sees a drawn gun. Simon thinks he's about to get shot.

"Get down off that horse," Lopez orders Miller, who quickly dismounts. "You got any money?" Cruz demands. Miller takes out his billfold and hands it to Lopez, who takes it and puts it in his pocket.

"Vamonos!" Lopez yells. "Let's get out of here." Giving the lead rope of one horse to Cota, Cruz grabs the reins on the other one and spurs his own horse. It jumps forward and they continue their escape with Alvitro barely able to keep up. Simon Miller lets out a deep breath.

***

"Come on, Kelly," Silas says to Jack after they get Lumen's wounds dressed up as good as they can. "Follow me." Silas pulls his gun out of his belt and Kelly reluctantly does the same as he wonders what he's being asked to do. Out in the street, Silas is surprised to see only one body now, that being the bandit he killed with his first shot. Amazingly, all the others have vanished. He picks up a bayonet and puts it in his belt.

Silas walks over to the dead man and puts his gun away, then bends over the dead body and pulls a folded piece of paper out the man's vest pocket. He can't read the Spanish words, but he sees the name signed at the bottom. "Fedoro Vasquez!" he says to himself, recognizing the surname instantly.

Quickly looking around the store, Silas sees that it's been ransacked, but is relieved to discover that the cash drawer has been left untouched. Kelly is still following him like a puppy dog when Silas turns around and almost laughs at the sight of Jack still holding his gun like it was a hot potato or something. "Jack, put that thing away," he says. "I need you to go and send a telegram to San Diego. Tell the sheriff what happened and tell him we need Doc Millard to ride out here on the double."

"Okay," Jack says and runs toward the telegraph office door. But he bounces hard off the door and sprawls backward, his gun sliding across the floor. He forgot the door was still bolted from the other side.

Silas would normally have thought this was funny, but not on this day. With the door still locked, he quickly realizes that Kelly failed to come to Lumen's aid when the alarm was sounded. Silas picks up Kelly's gun and can tell it hasn't fired a shot.

"So just what *did* you do during the gunfight?" Silas asks him, already knowing the answer.

"Well," says Kelly, his eyes darting around real quickly, "I … well, I … heard Lumen yell and I heard several men in the store, so I went out the back." Silas can see he's making it up as he goes. "Then I ran around the store and saw one of the bandits – the leader, I think it was – standing there, and he and I shot at each other a few times … and then … and then I ran out of shots and had to find a place to take cover. That's where you found me under the store."

Silas looks at the gun again and can plainly see it's fully loaded. Kelly can see the disgust in his expression and knows that Silas does not believe a word of his story. But Silas Gaskill is too big a man to upbraid Kelly. Why, he'd just be wasting his time on such a coward.

"Here's your gun," he says instead, handing the Colt back to Kelly. "Now go send the telegram."

"Yes, Silas," Kelly says sheepishly and heads out the front door and around to the back. Silas hears him slide the bolt open and then the telegraph starts clicking away.

Silas steps back to the door and looks out and what he sees next is a pleasant surprise. "Well, well," he says as he sees Mr. Livingston walking toward him still carrying the empty shotgun. "I was wondering what happened to you," Silas says to him as he gets closer.

"I was hiding up in those rocks," a visibly shaken Mr. Livingston says, but he's thinking something else. "Nothing exciting ever happens around here," he remembers Lumen saying just last night at dinner. "Balderdash!"

He hands the gun back to Silas. "I believe this belongs to you, sir," he says.

***

Staggering down the road toward the border, Jose Alvijo finds a nice place to hide. It's a small cave up on a hillside a little ways above the road. He's very careful not to leave any blood or tracks on his trail that would give his position away. He pulls some bushes in front of him and drifts off into unconsciousness.

Meanwhile, Poncho Alvitro is trying to keep up

with the others, but he's hurting real bad. "Cruz … amigo," he manages to say. "I … I can't keep going."

"You must," Lopez tells him. "We can't slow down and wait for you."

They don't get much further before Poncho loses his grip on the horse's mane and topples from the saddle.

"Cruz!" yells Cota to Lopez, who is riding slightly ahead. "Poncho has fallen off his horse!"

Lopez pulls up the reins and turns back. He stops and looks down at the helpless Alvitro lying on the ground moaning in pain. "Help me," Alvitro pleads, "help me, please."

"I will help you," Lopez says, climbing off his horse. Cruz knows that it's all over for Poncho; with a gut wound like that he will never survive. He drags Alvitro over to a small tree and props him up against it.

Cruz Lopez has always enjoyed killing, but he's not enjoying what he knows he has to do now. He can't leave Poncho here to be found by the gringos and possibly give them away. He knows where they're going. And he sure can't take him with them as he's only slowing them down.

For the first time in his life, Cruz Lopez uses his gun for mercy. He pulls out his pistol and shoots Alvitro in the side of the head. Just like that.

All the killing Cota has seen in the past few days has left him so emotionless that he's not shocked at all to see Lopez blow the brains out of one of his own men. He just looks at the lifeless body with a blank stare.

"Let's go," is all Lopez says as he climbs back onto his horse and gallops off down the trail. Cota just looks away, kicks his horse, and follows after him.

***

Sheriff Nicholas Hunsaker has received the telegram from Campo. He sent word out to Doc Millard to ride for Campo immediately to render assistance to the wounded. Since then he's been busy gathering up some men and getting supplies together for the long ride. They may be on the trail for days and he wants his men to be prepared.

His 21-year-old son, William, comes into the sheriff's office and tells his father that Doc Millard has left for Campo. "Good," he thinks, "at least he's on his way." He knows it'll still be a while before he and his posse are ready to ride out.

"William," he says, "take this over to the telegraph office for me." He hands him a piece of paper which reads, *"To Cline, justice of the peace at Campo. Authority is given you to organize force at once to pursue bandits."*

***

People are now riding into Campo from every direction. Word has filtered out to the area ranches and everyone is grabbing their guns and hurrying in to see what they can do. Silas is trying to organize a posse from among the gathered men. But for the moment, they're busy looking over the body of the dead man after Silas told them he was kin to the infamous Tiburcio Vasquez, the former leader of the gang who was hanged up in San Jose earlier in the year.

Moments later, a tired Simon Miller walks into Campo and tells everyone that he has just been relieved of two horses and $20 by the bandits on the Yuma road just east of town.

"Let's get on their trail, boys," announces John Williams, already in the saddle. "They've got a two-hour start on us already."

But Jack Kelly hustles out of the telegraph office and hands Silas a piece of paper.

"Hold on a minute, now," Silas says to the men. "A telegram has just arrived from Sheriff Hunsaker that says Charlie Cline is to head the posse."

"But he's not even here!" someone yells. "Yeah!" adds another, "we've got to get going before they give us the slip!"

Silas holds up his hand to silence the men. "They've already crossed the line, I expect," he says. "Are you going to follow them down into Mexico? Charlie is the justice of the peace and it'll be his job to decide, soon as he gets here."

"How long will that be?" asks a frustrated Thomas Cameron, itching like the others to get riding.

"Should be any time now," Silas responds. "I sent one of the Elliot boys out to his place."

Before Silas can finish his sentence, Zach Elliot gallops into town and announces that Charlie Cline is on his way and should arrive shortly.

***

Eliza Gaskill is holding her husband's hand with young Walter by her side. "I'll be all right," Lumen weakly whispers to her. "I know," she says, squeezing his hand and starting to cry. "Don't cry, my love," Lumen says. "If the good Lord is willing, I'm going to see it through." But Eliza can't help it. She starts breaking down, crying uncontrollably now.

Vi Price comes in and places her hands on Eliza's shoulders, trying to comfort her. She had come in to check on Lumen. "Can I get you anything, Mr. Gaskill?" she asks. "No, Vi," Lumen whispers, "just take care of Eliza and Walter for me please." "Sure thing, Mr. Gaskill," she replies solemnly, giving Eliza a comforting squeeze.

***

More people are coming into town, among them Charlie Cline. He quickly picks out a posse of ten men, and instructs them to quickly get their horses, guns and some provisions together. "We ride in twenty minutes," he announces.

Not long after the posse rides out, young Andy Elliot yells from up in the rocks behind the blacksmith shop. "I found one!" the 16-year-old hollers and everyone left in the street comes running up into the rocks. Andy has a rifle trained on Rafael Martinez. "Don't move!" Andy tells the bandit. If the situation wasn't so dire, Martinez might have laughed. If he could move, he would've done so long ago. He knew his hiding place wasn't a very good one, but he was too weak to look for a better one.

The men all congratulate Andy, slapping him on the back and saying, "Good work, son!" But the Elliot boy has his eyes fixed on Martinez. "Why, he's not much older than I am," is all he can think.

The men grab Rafael roughly and haul him out of the rocks and down into the street. "Is this one of them?" someone asks. "Must be," says another, "why else would he be hiding up in the rocks all shot up like that?"

But coming out of the telegraph office, Jack Kelly sees the prisoner and hears what the men are saying. "Uh, I don't think he's one of them," Kelly pipes up. "Why not?" Simon Miller asks. "Because he was in town before the attack," Kelly remembers. "I saw him over there," pointing to the stump sitting in front of the store. "I think he might know Lumen."

For one fleeting moment, Rafael's spirits are lifted. Maybe he *will* see Maria again.

But just then Silas comes hurrying over from the house, having heard the commotion. "Let's ask Silas," says John Williams. "Ask me what?" Silas says as he reaches the others. "Well, Andy here discovered this Mexican hiding up in the rocks," Williams explains, pulling Martinez forward so Silas can see him, "and he's all shot up. But Jack Kelly says he's not one of the bandits, but a friend of Lumen's."

"Jack Kelly?" exclaims Silas. "How the hell would he know what a bandit looks like?"

Silas takes one look at Martinez and says, "Yeah, that's one of 'em, all right. I shot this one out behind the blacksmith shop. Take him over to the grist mill and chain him to the floor until the sheriff gets here."

"Say, Silas," one of the men says as some others lead Martinez away, "how's Lumen doing, anyway?"

"He seems to be resting peacefully at the moment," Silas says. The men notice that Silas, too, is still bleeding from his arm wound. Silas pays it no never-mind. "It'll be alright," Silas replies, thanking the men again for their concern. "And Vi Price is working real hard to put a hot meal on the table for you all."

***

Sheriff Hunsaker left San Diego with his posse at 2:30 in the afternoon and has been on the trail for a few hours now. With him are H.H. Wildy, the San Diego County district attorney, Deputy Miller, his son William, another youngster named Jimmy Keys, and two others. After a quick stop to let the horses drink and to break off some jerky for dinner, Hunsaker has them in the saddle again. "Let's pick up the pace, boys," he says. "It's twelve hours to Campo and we ain't gone but three of 'em so far." They give their horses a slight kick, picking up the pace a bit.

***

Meanwhile, Jack Kelly sends another telegram to San Diego detailing the full particulars of the gunfight. He sends a pretty good description of the battle – except for the part about him running and hiding under the store. "I can't say that," Kelly thinks. "I'm supposed to guard the telegraph office, not hide under it!" So Kelly solves his little dilemma by telling a little lie. He includes in the dispatch a brief account of how he and Cruz Lopez shot it out in the street, how he took three shots at the gang leader and that the outlaw fired back each time. Neither of the men hit the other, he writes.

"That should do it," he says to himself, pleased with his work.

The gunfight is already big news in San Diego. The *Union,* upon being delivered a copy of Kelly's lengthy and detailed telegram, puts out a special edition, hitting the streets in the late afternoon. The newspaper heralds the Gaskill brothers as heroes and the headline even mentions the courage of the town's "plucky" telegraph operator.

***

When Frenchy doesn't return at a reasonable hour with Senor Ynda's mail, the sheep rancher goes looking for him and finds his employee barely alive and staggering down the road. Putting him carefully in the back of his wagon, Ynda can see that Frenchy needs a doctor as soon as possible, so he turns the wagon toward the road to San Diego. "Hang in there, Frenchy," Ynda tells him. "I'm taking you to Doc Millard in San Diego."

Unfortunately, Ynda has no way of knowing that Millard is on his way to Campo at this very moment and they will miss each other, as Millard has wisely taken the horse's trail that stays above the border, while the road Ynda is on dips through Tecarte before turning northwest toward the coast.

***

Just before sunset, a bunch of Indians ride into Campo from the east, momentarily causing a stir among the men guarding the town. When they report that they saw a dead Mexican propped up against a tree about two miles outside of town, it causes an even bigger stir. The townsfolk speculate that Charlie Cline and his posse found the body too, but kept on the trail after the other two bandits.

***

Once the sun goes down, it's another bitterly cold night. Sometime well after midnight, Jose Alvijo wakes up to discover he's got a more pressing problem than being shot up – he's freezing to death. Shaking uncontrollably, he knows that he's only got a matter of hours to live if he doesn't find someplace warm. Numb from the cold, he barely realizes what he's doing when he gets up and staggers back toward Campo.

He sees a light on in the Gaskill house and knocks on the door. Doc Millard, who arrived around midnight himself, is treating Lumen when he hears the knocking. "Who can that be? It must be 4 a.m.," Millard thinks as he walks to the front room and opens the door to find a shivering Mexican covered with blood and dirt standing there.

Millard leads the injured man in and places him on a cot next to the fireplace, and goes to wake up Silas. Flying down the stairs wearing just his long johns, Silas recognizes Alvijo as one of the bandits. But seeing that the man is no threat in his present condition, Silas allows Doc Millard to dress his wounds and lets Alvijo drift off to sleep. "I don't think this man will last until morning," Millard says and, satisfied with the prognosis, Silas goes back to bed.

***

By early morning, Sheriff Hunsaker and his posse have arrived and Silas informs him of the two prisoners and about the dead Mexican seen outside of town. Hunsaker gives Alvijo a hard shake and they're both surprised to see that he's still alive. The sheriff tells Deputy Miller to take Alvijo down to the grist mill to be held with the other prisoner.

As they stand him up, Jose Alvijo immediately starts begging. “Please, Mr. Gaskill!” he says to Silas, clutching his arm. “Please don’t let them take me. Please!”

Silas pulls his arm away and turns a cold shoulder.

“No, don’t take me!” Alvijo continues. “Please, Mr. Gaskill. I will work for you for twelve years! Twelve years for free if you don’t let them take me!”

Silas walks away without even answering him. “The gall of this man,” Silas thinks as he walks into the back bedroom and looks down at his brother’s pale face. “We’ll get them,” Silas says to the sleeping Lumen. “We’ll get them.”

Chapter 30

It's early Sunday morning the day after the gunfight and once again Carlos Ruiz has just left the Casa de Estrada. Maria's father, Manuel, can't believe what he's just been told.

The bandits who were in town were members of the same gang who rode with Tiburcio Vasquez and Clodoveo Chavez, but since Chavez's death less than two weeks ago, the gang was being led by a cutthroat by the name of Cruz Lopez. They had ridden into Campo yesterday morning intent on robbing the town and were met by stiff resistance.

But the worst part of the news was that the young lad Rafael had been in on the raid and had been wounded and captured.

"Oh, my Lord," he says as he looks at the sky. "What am I to tell my Maria now? She is so distraught that she hasn't come out of her room for two days. Give me guidance, God, and please help my daughter through this terrible time."

He bows his head to pray.

***

In Campo, Sheriff Hunsaker is busy organizing another posse to pursue the bandits. He puts H.H. Wildy, the San Diego district attorney, in charge of it. Joining him will be his own son William and five Campo citizens he has sworn in as deputies. Once they gather enough supplies, they head out east on the Yuma road.

Silas Gaskill comes out of Lumen's house and

walks up to the front of the Campo store, where Hunsaker is rolling a cigarette. "I just want you to know," Hunsaker tells him, "that I'm terribly sorry about what happened here."

"Well, that's all just fine and dandy," Silas retorts. "You had a chance to send forces to help us out and you chose not to."

"I couldn't!" replies an agitated Hunsaker. "We had no solid evidence when or even if the bandits would cross the line and you know I have no jurisdiction in Mexico. So what could I do?"

"You don't have to do nothing, sheriff," Silas replies. "We can handle it ourselves."

Doc Millard comes out of the Gaskill house and walks up to Silas and the sheriff. "Lumen's resting peacefully," he says. "I've done about all I can do for him for now."

"We're much obliged," says Silas, shaking the doctor's hand. "We really appreciate all that you've done."

Millard then turns to Hunsaker and hands him a gold watch. "What's this?" the sheriff asks.

"I took it from one of the bandits," replies Millard, "the one who turned himself in early this morning."

"It's a nice watch," says the sheriff, "and look at this chain. It's got silver hoops in the middle. I guess it's safe to say that it's stolen."

"That's what I thought too," Millard replies. "That's why I took it and am giving it to you."

"Good," Hunsaker says, "but I'll need you to sign a statement to that affect, Doc. I'll put it in with the other evidence."

"Let me know when you need it," says Millard,

adding, "I presume there are still prisoners who need my services? Where are they being held?"

"Over there," the sheriff says, pointing to the grist mill.

"Patch them up if you want, Doc," says Silas, "but as shot up as they are, I don't think either of them's gonna live long enough to see a trial."

"It's not my job to judge men," says Millard. "My job is to save their lives." With that, the doctor walks toward the mill clutching his medical bag.

***

The sheriff then holds an inquest into the death of Fedoro Vasquez. It only takes a few minutes to decide that Silas's shooting of the bandit was justifiable and the body is put in a makeshift wooden casket and buried on the south side of Campo Creek.

That done, Hunsaker and his deputy head for the mill to check on the prisoners. Doc Millard is still patching up Alvijo, who has been drifting in and out of consciousness but had quickly passed out again when the doctor started pulling medical-looking things from his bag.

Hunsaker asks for a report on the condition of the two prisoners.

"This one's wounds are much worse than the other's," Millard says of Alvijo.

Rafael Martinez is sitting a few feet away, but his mind is miles away … about ten, to be exact. He at first doesn't hear Hunsaker addressing him.

"I said, 'Do you know this man?'" Hunsaker repeats. But Martinez does not answer him, looking away instead. "Yeah, you know him all right," the sheriff concludes. He steps closer and grabs Rafael by his smooth cheeks and forces his head around so he can look him in the eye. "He's one of your amigos, isn't he?" Hunsaker says in a raised voice.

Martinez shrinks back as he thinks the sheriff is about to strike him.

"Easy now!" Doc Millard says. "I'm trying to patch them up here."

"That's all right. We're not going to hurt them none," Hunsaker says, giving Martinez a little pat on the head. "But we do have some hard questions to ask these men and we need some immediate answers."

"These men will not be assaulted while in my care," replies Millard sternly.

"I'm not saying we're gonna hurt 'em, Doc," the sheriff replies. "I just want to ask them some questions."

"Go ahead," Millard says, "but I don't think they're going to tell you anything."

Hunsaker knows that Millard is probably right. He looks at Martinez and then at Alvijo and a dejected look comes over his face. "They going to live, Doc?" he finally asks.

"That one might," Millard says, pointing at Martinez, "but I'm surprised this one even made it through the night. He's shot up pretty bad."

Hunsaker mulls this over and then says, "Thanks, Doc. Finish patching them up if you want, but I've got to have them ready to put on the mud wagon in the morning."

"You can't transport these men so soon!" replies Millard excitedly. "Neither one of them could possibly make the trip to San Diego alive."

"That's not your concern, Doc, it's mine," Hunsaker answers. "I'm going to leave Deputy Miller here to guard the prisoners." Turning to Miller, the sheriff adds, "I'll have Jimmy Keys relieve you after sundown."

"Okay, sheriff," the deputy replies as Hunsaker turns and walks out the door.

***

"We caught two of them," Silas says to his brother, who is now awake and learning all the details of the previous day for the first time. Still very weak, Lumen can only nod his head in approval from time to time. Silas places his hand gently on his brother's chest and can feel a good strong heartbeat. He smiles. "You'll get better," he says. "Just hang in there."

Eliza Gaskill and Doc Millard come into the room to check on Lumen's condition, glad to see he's awake. "He's just resting, Doc," Silas tells him and then gives Eliza a hug for support.

"Good. Good," the doctor replies, "but he'll need lots of rest to recover from this. You know, I'd say only one man in a hundred could've survived these wounds. Go on Silas, we'll watch him for a spell."

***

At the Estrada residence, Maria is hysterical. "No! No! It can't be. No!" she screams at the top of her lungs. "It can't be Rafael!"

"I hope not," says her father, "but it looks like it's true."

Maria breaks down in more tears. Her mother is

holding her, consoling her. "But why, Father?" she exclaims. "Why would Rafael do such a thing?"

"I don't know, my child," her father explains, feeling her pain. "I cannot tell you why."

***

Sheriff Hunsaker is giving Jimmy Keys instructions for the evening. "The prisoners are well-shackled," he tells the 20-year-old, "so you just keep an eye on them until morning."

"Sure thing, sheriff," says the young deputy and he heads over to the Campo mill to relieve Deputy Miller.

It's almost sundown and Silas is sitting on the front porch of the Campo hotel with some of the locals – all of them men he has known for years. But lots of other men have come through town today too, Silas has noticed, mostly out of curiosity, and he makes mention of it to the others.

"Some are cowboys," someone says, "driving a herd through to the north."

"They came in to see what all the ruckus was about," says another.

"Well, I hope they get a notion to leave fairly soon," Silas adds. "I don't want no strangers hereabouts tonight."

Jimmy Keys puts a log in the woodstove. He's not going to freeze tonight, he thinks, opening the vent to put some air to the fire. It was a mighty chilly ride from San Diego the night before and he doesn't want to have to face another long, cold night. It doesn't take long before the drafty mill warms up.

After stacking plenty of wood by the stove, he

checks to make sure the shackles are indeed fastened securely as the sheriff had said. They are both chained around the ankle and to iron rings protruding from the floor, with bolts securing the chains on both ends. Alvijo is sleeping on a cot and the other prisoner is sitting up in the corner just staring off into nothingness.

"It's like he doesn't even know where he is," thinks Keys to himself as he watches Martinez. He quickly bores of this and looks around to see if there's anything to do to pass the time. He lights the lantern on the table and the growing flame immediately illuminates a nearly full bottle of whiskey. Jimmy Keys' eyes light up. "Ha! It won't be so cold after all!" he says out loud. He pops the cork and takes a quick pull. "I'll just drink a little," he says to himself.

Rafael Martinez has already accepted his fate. He knows he won't survive this, and even if he does, he knows he'll never see Maria again. Not in this life anyway. "God, take care of her," he prays. "I know that I must pay for my sins. But, please, God, don't make Maria pay for them too."

Jimmy Keys puts another log in the woodstove. "Them prisoners ain't goin' nowhere," he says to himself, rationalizing another pull on the bottle. He puts his feet up on a wooden box and thinks this isn't going to be so bad. He pops the cork and takes a long drink.

It's a cold night in Campo once again. The thermometer is dipping close to freezing. The small community has folded up the sidewalks for the night. Everyone has turned in.

Jose Alvijo is awake and now sitting up. He asks Jimmy Keys for some water. "I'll get you some later," Keys replies. Jose looks at Rafael. He's still sitting there staring off into space. Alvijo turns back to his young jailor. "If you won't get me some water," he says, licking his dry lips, "then how about some of that whiskey you got there?"

"I ain't wasting no good whiskey on the likes of you," Jimmy replies with the hint of a slur. "You just sit there and keep quiet or I'll give you a lick, but not of this," Keys says, taking another pull from the bottle to tease Alvijo, and then, after wiping off his chin, adds, "but from this!" He holds up an ax handle he found suitable for just that purpose.

Alvijo settles back down and tries to figure out another tactic. "Amigo," he says a few minutes later, "you know I have lots of gold!"

This gets Jimmy Keys' attention. "What?" he says a bit drunkenly. "What are you blabbering about?"

"Gold!" Alvijo replies. "I have gold in my saddle bags and you can have it if you help me."

"If you do got some gold, then I can just take it anyways," Keys announces.

"That is true," Alvijo agrees, "but if I give it to you, then you can keep it. Your boss will never know."

"You're not going to trick me!" exclaims Keys as he gets up with the ax handle raised as if to strike the bandit. "You shut up or I'm going to give you some of this!"

Alvijo sees that this idea isn't going to work either and he leans back on the cot trying to think up another plan. He watches as Keys gets up, nearly trips over the wooden box and walks over to put another log in the stove. Keys stumbles back to the desk, sits down and takes another drink from the bottle. He puts his feet up to get more comfortable and it isn't long before Jimmy Keys is fast asleep.

***

A few hours later, the door to the Campo mill opens silently. Just a crack at first, but then all the way as several shadowy figures file quietly in. The lantern, now almost out of fuel, has burned down to a weak flame that can no longer penetrate the darkness. Martinez and Alvijo are awakened by a rag being stuffed into their mouths and a bandana being tied around their heads to keep the gags in place. At the same time, a couple of other men are using a wrench to unbolt the shackles.

Alvijo starts struggling wildly for someone in his weakened condition, but he is quickly restrained and they are hastily hauled away.

The door is silently closed and the only sound is the snoring of Jimmy Keys. The only light is the last flickering flames of the lantern which is on the table next to a near-empty bottle.

Alvijo and Martinez are carried and dragged some distance and then they feel their hands being bound behind their backs. In the waning moonlight, they can see before them a tall oak tree and two horses.

"Let's get this done with," they hear a voice say. "Yeah, before anyone hears us," another voice says.

A rope is brought forth – the same rope that Alvijo had asked to see in the store yesterday. It's tossed over a stout branch and the nooses on each end are placed over the bandits' heads and pulled tightly around their necks. Then they are hoisted onto the backs of two waiting horses and a man pulls on the rope, tying it to a lower branch, taking up the slack.

Alvijo is thrashing around; he knows he's about to die and he isn't going to go quietly. Martinez, on the other hand, sits calmly in the saddle and can't wait for it all to be over. He is crying – not for himself, but for Maria. "The pain she must be going through," he thinks. "Please, God," he prays one last time, "please let Maria get over this. Please let her live a good life." The life that he now realizes wasn't for him to live.

Struggling, Alvijo finally gets the bandana loose and spits out the rag. "Please! Please don't do it!" he begs the voices. "I didn't shoot anyone! It was that boy there that did the shooting!" he says, implicating Martinez.

"It's time to take your medicine," one of the voices replies.

"No! No! Please don't kill me, amigos!" Alvijo continues, now crying uncontrollably. "Please, I'll do anything! Please, no…."

A man lays a switch on the backs of the two horses simultaneously. The horses immediately bolt and the two bandits drop at the same time, slamming together as the rope comes taut. The twisting bodies struggle for a moment, kicking wildly until the tightening noose snuffs the last breath out of each of them.

When it's over, the man with the switch says with disdain, "I can't stand a man who begs for his life."

"Yup," says another, "it's a sorry thing to die like a coward."

The shadowy figures look over their handiwork.

"I'd say our job is done," someone says. "Yeah," replies another, "let's get out of here before someone sees us." The men disburse and all is quiet. Somewhere, a coyote yips. In the dim moonlight, two bodies can be seen swinging in the frosty night air.

***

Jimmy Keys' feet go flying off his wooden box and he tumbles out of the chair onto the floor of the mill.

"What the hell do you think you're doing?" bellows Sheriff Hunsaker. Keys hadn't heard the door slam open as Hunsaker stormed in and he didn't see the sheriff give him a swift kick that sent him flying. He can't see much of anything; his head is groggy and the brilliant sunlight streaming through the open door is blinding him.

"What do you mean, sheriff?" Keys replies sluggishly. "I, I, I'm watching these here prisoners!"

"What prisoners?" demands Hunsaker.

"Why, these two right here!" Keys says, gesturing with his hand and turning his head to look at the prisoners that are not there. As he does so, he knocks over the near-empty bottle with his hand and it lands at the sheriff's feet.

"So, you got drunk!" says the sheriff, more as a statement than as a question.

"No … well … I," stammers Jimmy.

"You son of a bitch, Jimmy Keys! You got drunk and lost my prisoners!" Hunsaker yells at him.

Shaking his head trying to clear his foggy mind, Keys replies, "Where … where did they go?"

"Oh, not far!" Hunsaker booms. "They're hanging from that damn tree over there!"

"What?" Keys says incredulously, jumping to his feet and looking out the door in the direction in which the sheriff is pointing.

"Lynched, Jimmy," the sheriff says. "Someone took them from you while you were passed out and lynched 'em."

"Well … I … I," stammers Jimmy again, just as Silas comes running into the mill followed by Deputy Miller.

"What the hell happened, sheriff," Silas demands.

"What's it look like?" exclaims the sheriff, pointing to the dangling bodies. "Someone lynched them!"

"They sure as hell did," Silas says looking at the two bodies, then adds, "Weren't you supposed to be watching them?"

If the hair on the back of Sheriff Hunsaker's neck wasn't up before, it is now. "I left Jimmy here guarding them and he got drunk," says a disgusted Hunsaker.

"Sorry, sheriff," Jimmy says meekly, holding his head, which is throbbing from all the yelling going on.

Silas sees the whiskey bottle and adds it all up real quickly. "Well, that was convenient, sheriff," he finally says.

"What are you implying, Silas?" Hunsaker demands.

"I think you can figure it out," Silas replies.

"You saying that I had a hand in this?" the sheriff says angrily.

"It's just convenient how you left this boy here with a bottle of whiskey!" Silas answers right back.

"The hell with you, Gaskill!" shouts Hunsaker. "You had just as much of an opportunity to do this as I did. Where were you last night?"

"Over at Lumen's, sleeping on the sofa," Silas says.

"And you had lots of witnesses, I bet," replies the sheriff sarcastically.

"Lots, sheriff," Silas replies.

"Yeah, I'll bet you did," Hunsaker fires back.

The two hard men stare at each other suspiciously for a moment, and then Hunsaker announces, "Well, I'd say my job is done here now. The prisoners are dead and my posse is out chasing the others. Deputy Miller, would you be so kind as to saddle our horses?"

Deputy Miller is still a little bit in shock by what he's just observed, but finally says, "Ah, sure, sheriff," and heads for the stable.

***

The news of the hangings travels like wildfire through the area. And it doesn't stop at the border. Soon, Carlos Ruiz is back at the Estrada residence with the grim news. This time, Maria is at the window eavesdropping on their conversation and hears everything.

"Father!" cries Maria as he steps back inside, his face ashen. "It's Rafael, isn't it?"

"I think it is, I'm afraid," he says solemnly.

"Nooooo!" she wails. "No, please God, no. Not Rafael!" She sobs in her father's arms. He's always been the one who has comforted her ever since she was a little girl and he's not about to stop now in the worst moment of her life. Being so much older than her brother and sister, Maria has always been his special child and he would do just about anything to remove this pain from her heart.

***

The wagon wheels creek as they wobble into Campo. Maria had begged her father to go and claim Rafael's body so they could give him a proper Christian burial. Looking into the imploring brown eyes of his daughter he knew his answer even before he spoke. "Yes, my child," he had said, "we can try."

Manuel Estrada hopes that by burying Rafael, his daughter might be able to put him in her past and in time be able to go on and lead a normal life. But as the little cart is led into Campo by its lone burro, even he is shocked to see that the bodies are still hanging in the tree, twisting in the breeze.

Maria sees them too. "Rafael!" she screams as she leaps from the wagon before her father can stop her and she goes running over to him and, crying hysterically, hugs him around the legs. Her father, close behind, pulls her away and Maria's mother rushes over and comforts her, leading her back toward the wagon.

Sr. Estrada pulls a knife out of his belt and cuts the rope, dropping both bodies to the dusty ground. He carefully removes the rope from around Rafael's neck and sees that Carlos Ruiz is now standing beside him with the blanket they brought with them. The two men silently wrap the body in the blanket and gently place Rafael into the bed of the wagon. The burro lets out a little bray as the cart turns around and heads back to the border, the only sounds coming from the rickety wheels and from Maria, sobbing in her mother's arms.

Epilogue

SUMMER, 1896

"And that's about it," says Silas, wrapping up his lengthy narration.

Ed Aiken is dumbstruck. Although he'd heard bits and pieces of the saga during his few months in Campo, he'd never heard the whole story straight from the horse's mouth, so to speak.

"That is truly amazing," Aiken finally says.

"Yeah, I guess today you could call it that," says Silas, still leaning on his hoe. "It's been twenty one years this December, but I remember it like it was yesterday. Back then, that was just one of many episodes that took place when us pioneers were settling the Western frontier."

"So, what happened to Frenchy, the sheepherder?" asks Aiken, still full of curiosity.

"He was wounded pretty bad," Silas says. "He lost a lot of blood when he tried to walk back to Ynda's ranch and he was pretty near dead when his boss found him on the road. Frenchy was so badly wounded that Ynda took him immediately to San Diego, but he had no way of knowing that Doc Millard was already on his way here at the time.

"When he got Frenchy to San Diego, it was decided that he needed a surgeon and they put him on the next steamer to San Francisco," Silas continues. "But we heard sometime later that he had died up there from his wounds."

"And what about Jack Kelly?" Aiken inquires. "Did he really shoot it out with Cruz Lopez like it said in the papers?"

Silas kind of chuckles and raises his eyebrows as if to tell Aiken he should know better than to ask a question like that. "No, of course not," he says. "Jack claimed he shot it out with Lopez in front of the store … that he took three shots at the bandit and that Lopez fired back three times with his six-shooter. But I saw Jack's gun in the store later on and I could see it had never been fired.

"And I saw Lopez when he rode out of town and he wasn't holding no six-shooter … he had that Henry rifle in his hands," Silas adds. "But Kelly made no mention of this, because he was hiding in the creek underneath the store!

"After Lumen recovered, I asked him about it, and he said he didn't hear no shots coming from the side of the store either," Silas goes on. "So that's six shots fired and nobody heard a one of 'em. So, about what Jack put in his telegram, well I think he was just trying to cover his ass. Being the only military personnel in town, it wouldn't look good in the newspaper if he said that he just ran and hid."

Aiken surmised as much.

"Anyways," Silas continues, "Jack got married in San Diego about two weeks after the fight and ended up being transferred out a few months later. I never forgave him for not helping Lumen, though, and we didn't have much to say to each other afterwards. He knew I knew the truth."

"Speaking of the military," Aiken interjects, "did they ever show up?"

"About a week after the battle was over, I sent a letter requesting military assistance as tensions were still high on both sides of the border," explains Silas. "Some of the folks down in Tecarte weren't too happy about the hangings and there was talk that we might be raided again.

"So, sometime around the middle of January a detachment of about ten soldiers was sent down from San Francisco to San Diego and rode out here," Silas adds, "but by that time everything had pretty well settled down and they weren't needed."

Then Silas lets out a laugh as he remembers what happened next. "This lieutenant named Storey was in charge of the outfit and became the final casualty of the Campo gunfight," Silas recalls. "He was on his horse and didn't have his pistol fastened down properly and it fell out of his holster. Everyone knows the only safe way to carry a Colt six-gun is to have the hammer down on an empty chamber, but he had six rounds in his pistol instead of five. Well, he paid for his carelessness because when the pistol hit the ground it went off, and the ball cut a nice chunk out of his backside!" Now Silas and Ed Aiken are both laughing.

"He rode a little high in the saddle on his way back to San Diego!" Silas manages to add between laughs.

"And what about the bandits, I mean the two that got away?" Aiken says. "Did they ever catch Lopez?"

"No, but he probably wished they had," Silas says. "That way he could've gone out with some dignity, because he ended up probably getting it the worst of all."

"What do you mean?" asks Aiken, his curiosity piqued.

"That neck wound Frenchy gave him was a lot worse than he thought," Silas says. "The ball went through the collar of his coat before hitting him in the neck and took a lot of fabric in with it, I reckon. Anyways, it got infected and Lopez couldn't exactly stop and clean it out properly, what with being on the run and all. It didn't take long for gangrene to set in. We heard from a Mexican who came through town a few months later that his whole face swelled up and he died a horrible death down in Sonora somewhere."

"So there was never any proof that Lopez died?" Aiken asks.

"No," Silas replies, "but we expect that he did die from his wounds, but *quien sabe,* who knows. Charlie Cline's posse couldn't cross the line, so they collected the body of the one they called Poncho on their way back to Campo," Silas continues. "Lopez must've shot him because he was wounded so bad he was slowing them down."

"And the other young one?" inquires Aiken.

"Oh, Cota, yeah, he was the only one who really got away," Silas says. "He wasn't even wounded. I don't even remember seeing him in the fight, but Lumen said he was one of the bastards who held him down while Lopez shot him in cold blood.

"We got a telegram about a year later from the sheriff in El Paso," Silas recalls. "Said he had Cota in custody and would escort him here all the way from Texas if we would pay him a thousand-dollar reward. But we told him to keep him. We weren't interested in him anymore. And certainly not for a thousand dollars!"

The sun is now sinking low on the horizon. Catharine walks over to the two men and says to her husband, "Silas, dinner's on the stove and will be ready in a few minutes."

"Okay, dear," he says, "Ed and I were just finishing up anyways."

"So," says Ed Aiken, "that was quite a story."

"Yup, Ed," says Silas, "it sure was. There's been a lot said about all those other shootouts you always hear about, but the one we had right here in Campo, well, that's how the West was *really* won."

With that, Silas leans his hoe against the pear tree and follows his wife up the street to his house. Ed Aiken watches this giant of a man walk away.

Then he just sits there on his rock and enjoys the final rays of sunshine as he replays Silas's story in his mind. Out of the corner of his eye, he catches some movement over by the blacksmith shop where the dead gambler's body is still propped up against the wall.

A young Campo cowboy is riding slowly into town and stops his horse directly in front of the body. The dead man's hat is still on his head. Its eyes stare blankly into nothingness.

The cowboy pulls a cigarette out of his pocket and strikes a match. He takes a few puffs as he just sits there looking at the body. The sun begins to sink below the horizon. The young cowboy takes a long drag off his smoke and leans over and puts the cigarette into the corner of the dead man's mouth.

He then straightens up in the saddle, gives his horse a little kick and rides slowly into the sunset without saying a word. A wisp of smoke drifts slowly in the breeze.

THE END

Afterward

Many readers of this book probably thought that California's history began the day James Marshall yelled, "Eureka! I have found it!"

Standing in the tailrace of a sawmill he had been building for Captain John Sutter on the South Fork of the American River, Marshall discovered something on the morning of January 24, 1848, that was arguably the defining moment in California history and perhaps even the most important event in the history of the United States since the Revolution itself: Gold.

The news did not reach Washington for nearly eleven months, but when it did, the Gold Rush of 1849 was on. Within a year, the non-native population of California sky-rocketed from less than 10,000 to over 100,000, and by the end of 1851 it had burgeoned to more than 225,000. By 1870 – a scant 20 years after its creation – San Francisco was the tenth-largest city in America with almost 150,000 residents.

California achieved statehood in virtually the blink of the eye, entering as a free state – after much wrangling in Congress – on September 9, 1850, having bypassed the usual interim territorial status. Its admission as the 31st state threatened to upset the balance of power back East, where the issue of slavery was dividing the country and would culminate with the Civil War little more than a decade later.

But it also represented to the American people the realization of Manifest Destiny, the expressly stated God-given right to expand the still-new nation westward. That movement had picked up speed in the 1840s with the admission of Texas as a state in 1845 and with the Mexican War that followed from 1846-48. When the war ended with the signing of the Treaty of Guadalupe-Hidalgo on February 2, 1848, ceding all lands north of the Rio Grande to the U.S., Washington felt justified as it suddenly found itself in possession of a nearly unfathomable expanse of land that truly could be said to "stretch from sea to shining sea."

A champion of Manifest Destiny, Thomas Hart Benton of Missouri, the Democratic leader of the Senate for more than 30 years, had been negotiating with the native Mexican population of California, numbering less than 10,000, for much of the 1840s. Benton had hoped for a peaceful annexation of the northernmost department of a Mexico whose government had been struggling to maintain control of its vast country since being granted independence from Spain in 1821.

Benton's desires were dashed when war with Mexico broke out, and his own son-in-law, John C. Fremont, lieutenant of the U.S. Mounted Rifles, led a regiment of 300 men that squelched the final resistance of the native *californios,* as they proudly called themselves, with the surrender of Mexican general Pio Pico and the signing of what became known as the Capitulation of Cahuenga on January 13, 1847. The U.S. military ruled over California for the remainder of the war and immediately afterward.

Fremont was even appointed the military governor of California by Commodore Robert F. Stockton, but President James Polk had other ideas. In fact, when Fremont refused to resign his position, he was arrested and court-marshaled, nearly putting an end to what was to become an illustrious career. But he returned to California to begin a political career that saw him voted in as the first-ever U.S. Senator from the Golden State.

Had the U.S. not taken California by force, it is debatable whether that would have changed anything that was to follow. It likely all became moot that fateful day in January 1848, when gold was discovered at Sutter's Mill. When news of the gold strike reached the East, the Great Gold Rush was on, and thousands of fortune-seekers headed west any way they could get there. Many were recent immigrants to the quickly expanding U.S., as the country's population had exploded from only five million in 1800 to about 23 million by mid-century. But all the newly arriving "Anglos," whether from the East, Europe or Australia, were considered "Americans," and the central tenet of Manifest Destiny, which can be traced all the way back to the Monroe Doctrine, was that "America is for the Americans."

Unfortunately, that was nowhere more spelled out than in the goldfields, where greed, racism and the lawlessness inherent in a male-dominated new frontier combined to give rise to an impassable culture clash between the arriving prospectors and the local native population, almost entirely Hispanic and Indian. Even worse, the native *californios* had beaten the gringo invasion to the gold camps, thanks to their proximity, and they were for the most part also the ones who taught the arriving greenhorns how to search for the gold.

But they were soon shut out of the mines by laws enacted by the legislature of the newest state, which labeled the pre-existing native population as "foreigners" on American soil. Though there was an incredible wealth of gold to be found – $594 million worth of the yellow metal would leave California for the East Coast in the first ten years of the Gold Rush – the newest arrivals sought all the bounty for themselves.

One of the very first laws enacted by the California Legislature was a license tax of $20 a month for all "foreigners" in the goldfields, and even though this law was repealed a year later in 1851, it is estimated that as many as 10,000 Mexicans were driven off their claims for failure to pay the tax. It was reported that there were as many as 200 lynchings in the mining camps between 1849 and 1853, and the overwhelming majority of the victims were Hispanic. And despite the repeal of the shameful law, the mistreatment of the Mexican population did not cease. They were still all-too-routinely rounded up, beaten and driven from the diggings, or even killed on the scantest of pretexts.

Not to be outdone, the U.S. Congress in 1851 seemingly reneged on the terms of the Treaty of Guadalupe-Hidalgo, which had guaranteed the land rights of the *californios.* The creation of the Board of Land Commissioners to decide the issue of land ownership in California was seen as another betrayal by the gringos. Even though the board upheld the claims of 604 of the 813 cases brought before it, those who won their cases more often than not had to sell off large tracts of land to pay the court costs incurred to defend their birthrights. It was seen as little more than the legalized theft of their land.

It was out of this oppression that emerged some of the most notorious bandits of the Wild West, forced by the circumstances of racism and social and economic inequality into a life of crime and vengeance, or as freedom fighters, depending on which side of the issue you stood.

An article in *Overland Monthly* in August 1888 summed up the pervading social climate that gave rise to these outlaws:

"The native californios had seen their peaceful, pastoral homes overrun by a horde of greedy foreigners who were bringing innovation and change. Little by little, their lands were passing into the possession of strangers, their institutions were disappearing, and their ancient supremacy becoming a thing of the past. Accustomed to lives of idleness and ease, the grim specter of work presented itself as the only alternative to starvation if they hoped to hold their own with the bustling stranger, who, besides injury actually inflicted, added insult thereto by terming them 'greasers' and treating them with contempt. To these considerations were added the bitter feelings engendered with the war with Mexico. It was the old story of animosity, taken advantage of by the less responsible and more desperate members of the community to excuse and justify their warfare on society."

And there seemed to be no end to those willing to take up such a cause. "Mexican or *californios* bandidos," some of whom achieved virtual mythical status, ran rampant up and down California from roughly 1850 to 1875, when the last major gang of desperados was surprised during its raid on Campo.

The first of these was unquestionably the most famous of them all, the legendary Joaquin Murrieta, who took out his revenge on gringos in the gold region until he was supposedly caught in 1853 by the posse of Capt. Harry Love. A transplanted Texan, Love had been commissioned by the governor to eradicate this impediment to California's efforts to overcome the growing pains of its rapid statehood.

In actuality, there were five Mexican bandits by the name of Joaquin operating at the time, and no one seemed to know what any of them looked like. One would strike in one town, and the same day, hundreds of miles away, there would be reports of another robbery by "Joaquin." On May 11, 1853, Gov. John Bigler put a bounty of $1,000 on the head of "any" Joaquin that Love and his men, known as the California Rangers, could bring in during the next 90 days.

Love and his posse scoured the desolate canyons and valleys of the region, but after two months and with time running out, they had located none of the Joaquins. Then their luck changed when the party came upon a group of Mexicans camped near Panoche Pass not far from Tulare Lake and present-day Bakersfield. Before they could ascertain any information, a gun battle erupted and the stated leader of the gang, who hadn't even had time to identify himself, was killed, along with many of the other Mexicans.

One, Manuel Garcia, was easily identified, because he had only three fingers on one hand, and was known as "Three-Fingered Jack," a reputed thief and murderer who had been wanted for some time. His signature hand was cut off and preserved in a pickle jar for later confirmation.

So, too, was the head of the leader, suspended in a jar of alcohol and brought back to the governor to collect the reward, despite the fact that no one knew his identity. Newspapers at the time simply reported that one of the "Joaquins" had been killed, even though there was no way to confirm that. Regardless, not only did Love collect the $1,000 reward and 90 days' pay for his men, but a grateful California Legislature approved a $5,000 bonus!

Somehow, it became accepted knowledge that the head belonged to Murrieta, but no one could confirm this. In fact, one newspaper, the San Francisco *Alta,* steadfastly maintained that the head was "absolutely not" that of Murrieta, but perhaps belonged to Joaquin Valenzuela, one of the other wanted "Joaquins."

Wrote the newspaper in a story on August 7, 1853, *"The head recently exhibited in Stockton bears no resemblance to that individual (Murrieta) and this is positively asserted to by those who have seen the real Murrieta and the spurious head."*

Even Murrieta's own sister, it was reported, went to see the bottled head and was overheard telling a companion, "That is *not* my brother!"

So how was it that Joaquin Murrieta became so famous that by the end of the century he was regarded as a hero of the Mexican people and immortalized around the world as a sort of Robin Hood? He was even called that in a book about his life entitled, "The Robin Hood of El Dorado," by Walter Noble Burns in 1932 that was made into a Hollywood movie four years later.

It was pure fiction. At a time when the oppressed *californios* needed a glimmer of hope, it was given to them in the form of a wildly sensational book by a part-Cherokee author named John Rollin Ridge, who published a short work entitled, "The Life and Adventures of Joaquin Murrieta, Celebrated California Bandit," in 1854. His book, which he purported to be the "true story," maintained that Murrieta had turned to his life of crime only after having witnessed his wife, Rosita, being raped, seen his brother hanged on a trumped-up charge of horse-stealing, and himself whipped mercilessly while tied to a tree – all at the hands of gringos.

He vowed vengeance on his American oppressors, swearing, as Ridge wrote, an *"oath of the most awful solemnity that his soul should nevermore know peace until his hands were dyed deep in the blood of his enemies."*

The *californios* and Americans alike ate it up. Though Ridge sold very few copies of the story, due mainly to an unscrupulous publisher, others retold and reprinted his version and it didn't take long for Murrieta to make his way into California folklore. It didn't hurt that perhaps California's greatest early historian, Hubert Howe Bancroft, used Ridge's story as "factual evidence," forever giving authenticity to the legend.

It was under these same circumstances that another poor Mexican who grew up in the Bay Area turned to a life of crime. This time, however, most everything surrounding the treacherous exploits of Tiburcio Vasquez is substantiated by a series of newspaper articles that is a veritable paper trail used by historians to elevate this diminutive *californio* into the authenticated legend he would later become.

Vasquez rode unchecked through the remotest regions of the northern goldfields to the rugged outskirts of Los Angeles for much of his 22-year reign of terror, a notorious highwayman who served three terms in San Quentin before finally being captured in 1874 and hanged in San Jose a year later.

The outlaw was convicted and sentenced to death in January 1875, for his role in the killing of three men at Tres Pinos, a dusty little town just south of Hollister, on August 26, 1873. Until that fateful day, Vasquez was seen as little more than a thorn in the side of authorities, a two-bit common criminal who had served a five-year prison term for horse-stealing interrupted by a seven-week "furlough" in 1859 when he was part of a successful escape from San Quentin. A few years later, he was again caught trying to run off a sizable herd up in Sonoma and found himself back in San Quentin for another three-and-a-half-year stint, paroled on June 4, 1870.

During his freedom, Vasquez was feared and admired, depending on whom he ran into. Even though he was only 5-foot-7 and barely 130 pounds, Vasquez was extremely intelligent and apparently had a certain charm about him that made him popular with the ladies. Ultimately, that would be his downfall, but in 1870 he had yet to assemble a gang of any significance and was not hounded by the law as he would be three years later after the Tres Pinos Tragedy, as it came to be known.

Thus, he often reportedly slipped undetected in and out of Hollister to visit his many lady friends, and when the constable was alerted and sent men looking for him, the local Mexican population would deceive the authorities so he could make his escape. However, he reportedly had an affair with the wife of a friend, Abelardo Salazar, in the town of San Juan (now San Juan Bautista) and the two men argued on the street. Salazar pulled out a pistol and shot Vasquez from point-blank range, but the bandit was able to dodge the bullet enough to take it through the neck and not in the face. He was many months recovering.

Another time, after holding up a stage near Soap Lake, he was shot in the chest by Santa Cruz County Sheriff Charles Lincoln, but escaped, though his accomplice, Narciso Rodriguez, was captured and sentenced to San Quentin. While recovering from that wound, Vasquez showed flair for the dramatic when he was alerted that three pursuers were housed for the night just down the road. Supposedly, he slipped out under cover of darkness and stole their horses, foiling the gringos and boosting his growing image among the Mexicans even more.

Even after Vasquez recruited the imposing figure of Clodoveo Chavez, then just a poor vaquero without a criminal past scratching out a living on a ranch in the dry hills outside Hollister, in the spring of 1873 and finally put together a first-rate gang, it is doubtful that he became the blood-thirsty killer as he was portrayed at his trial.

Vasquez's *modus operandi* had always been to tie up his captives and then rob them, leaving them unharmed. This all changed at Tres Pinos, which began not unlike most of his other robberies. Vasquez and his men entered the store of Andrew Snyder and proceeded to tie up everyone they found. But during the robbery, a Portuguese sheepherder entered the store and when he failed to halt, was shot dead on the spot, reportedly by Vasquez. Two teamsters loading a wagon nearby, heretofore unaware a robbery was in progress, turned upon hearing the shot and they were immediately ordered to lie down too. But one of them, a deaf man named Redford, ran for it instead and was likewise gunned down, supposedly either by Vasquez's nephew, Fedoro, or Romulo Gonzalez, two other members of the gang.

Then Vasquez was reported to have grabbed a rifle from his horse and, firing through the door of the local hotel, killed a man named Davidson.

But did Vasquez really commit these murders? He swore from his jail cell and during his trial that he had never murdered anyone, but that argument was no defense, since he was certainly an accessory to murder that day, even if he didn't pull the trigger. Either way it was a hanging offense, so Vasquez's adamant denial seemed aimed solely on clearing the blemish of murder from his record. Vasquez contended that it was one of his henchmen, Abdon Leiva, who was responsible for the two deaths attributed to him, which just might have been true, for two compelling reasons.

First, Leiva found out soon after the Tres Pinos Tragedy that Vasquez was having an affair with his wife, catching them together in a compromising situation. Leiva reportedly pulled a gun on Vasquez intent on killing him, but the ever-watchful Chavez drew on Leiva and backed him down. Leiva, however, immediately left and surrendered to authorities and gave up the gang, turning state's evidence on his leader. It is interesting that the warrant under which Vasquez was later extradited to San Jose for his trial listed Chavez, Gonzalez and Moreno as his accomplices, but not Leiva,

But more credible evidence comes from Snyder himself. When Chavez stated he was going to kill Snyder, the storeowner said that it was Vasquez himself who intervened and saved his life. Wrote Snyder years later, *"(Chavez) told Vasquez that I knew them and would be the cause of their arrest sometime, (but) Vasquez told him, no, that I had submitted and had been a friend to their people and the first man that undertook to harm me he would shoot the top of his head off."*

And had Vasquez indeed suddenly turned killer at Tres Pinos, he certainly would have had no hesitation in doing the same later in 1873 when on the day after Christmas the gang descended upon the small village of Kingston on the Kings River and committed their biggest act of bravado yet – they robbed the entire town and tied up at least 35 people!

But others in town that day, led by rancher John Sutherland, arrived in time to chase off the bandits, who had to make a run for it as they had left their horses on the other side of a new toll bridge built across the river, replacing a ferry. During their escape, Chavez was shot in the knee by Sutherland, a wound that would cause the bandit to walk with a limp for the short remainder of his life.

By now, legendary Sheriff Harry Morse of Alameda County, who had made a name for himself catching many of the notorious bandits of the day – both Hispanic and Anglo – was closing in on the gang. Under public pressure after the Tres Pinos Tragedy, the California Legislature appropriated $15,000 to finance Morse's efforts to bring Vasquez to justice, the first public expenditure to fund specific police action since Harry Love and his California Rangers supposedly vanquished Joaquin Murrieta in 1853. In addition, Gov. Newton Booth offered a $3,000 reward for Vasquez, which was raised to $8,000 before he was finally captured.

Morse, who had become a legend himself because of his daring exploits to capture such dangerous criminals as Juan Soto, another notorious highwayman of the day, had developed a reputation among the elusive bandits that he was invincible. They called him El Diablo – the Devil – because it seemed no bullet could find him. "A man had better have the devil after him than Harry Morse," the Oakland *Daily News* quoted an unnamed bandit after the lawmen captured him in late 1873.

Morse's posse painstakingly tracked Vasquez and his gang south toward Los Angeles, covering a reported

2,720 miles in the saddle over 61 days, scouring every side canyon along the way. When he arrived in Fort Tejon, Morse was informed that Vasquez was holed up in Alison Canyon in the Cahuengas in a house owned by a former camel driver known as Greek George. Not wanting to infringe upon the jurisdiction of Los Angeles County Sheriff William Rowland, the honorable Morse risked letting Vasquez escape by taking the evening stage the 110 miles to L.A. to pass on what he'd learned.

But Rowland, perhaps seeking the fame of catching the vaunted Vasquez and wanting to pocket the $8,000 reward himself – which is exactly what he did – dismissed Morse's information as unreliable and told him to return to Alameda County. Morse obligingly did so, and Rowland immediately formed a posse headed by one of his deputies, Albert Johnson. The next day, May 13, 1874, a party of six descended upon the house of Greek George concealed in the back of a wagon driven by two local Mexicans they had forced to assist them.

Caught in the middle of lunch, Vasquez leaped through the kitchen window and ran for his horse, but was halted by the shotgun blast of George Beers, a reporter from the San Francisco *Chronicle* who was only brought along to be a witness to the capture. About an hour later, Vasquez was recovering from his eight buckshot wounds in Rowland's jail, where he sat nine days before being transported on the steamship *Senator* to San Francisco and then whisked off to the San Jose jail.

While in jail in Los Angeles, Vasquez granted three interviews, maintaining his innocence in each, vigorously claiming never to have murdered anyone. While that is debatable, one thing is not – his womanizing had finally caught up to him. Warned by his gang that he was lingering too long at Greek George's – Chavez and the others had all left – Vasquez remained behind solely to continue a dalliance with a woman who lived there.

No one is sure how word reached Morse as to Vasquez's whereabouts, but one version says that Greek George's sister-in-law, Modesta Lopez, did it out of jealousy over the woman the outlaw was carrying on with at the shack. Another version maintains that Vasquez's own brother, Francisco, turned him in after Tiburcio had seduced and impregnated Francisco's 15-year-old daughter. And still another version claims that Greek George, a native of Cypress who came to the U.S. in 1855 to be a driver in the recently organized U.S. Army Camel Corps, had secretly worked out a deal with Rowland himself for a share of the reward money.

Asked later why he stayed so long so close to Los Angeles – Greek George's home was located in present-day West Hollywood – Vasquez could only shrug his shoulders, smile sorrowfully and reply, "I see now that it was a bad mistake."

While in jail he was also visited by his loyal right-hand man, Chavez, who daringly got past Sheriff Rowland's deputies by wearing a disguise of some kind. Considering that Chavez was nearly six feet tall and weighed almost 200 pounds, this must've been extremely risky. In a story he later retold to Luis Raggio, his boyhood friend – one of the same men who killed him for the reward on his own head – Chavez offered to round up the gang and break him out, but Vasquez told him not to risk it, that he was confident he would beat the charge.

After learning that Vasquez had been placed on a steamer bound for San Francisco, Chavez came up with another scheme, however. Gathering his men for the long

400-mile ride to San Jose, they planned to ambush Vasquez's escort somewhere between Gilroy and San Jose. But they arrived too late; Vasquez was already housed in the San Jose jail and Chavez could plainly see a breakout attempt would stand no chance.

While in jail, Vasquez became a celebrity. His capture not only made headlines in every paper in California, but was front-page news around the country. When the *Senator* docked at the San Francisco wharf, a large crowd of admirers turned out despite its 7 a.m. arrival, yelling, "Vasquez! Vasquez!" as he was taken away. From jail, he promptly issued an appeal for funds, and raised a big enough purse to hire a pair of reputable lawyers. He was visited constantly by well-wishers and reporters seeking interviews. Visitors often brought flowers, fine wines and other gifts for the prisoner.

In one day alone, he received 673 visitors, including 93 women, many of them high-society types. So besieged by those wishing to view the infamous bandit, Santa Clara Police Chief Theodore Cockrill even considered putting a couple of imposters in other cells to get the lines moving faster!

Newspapers questioned what "the elite and respectable" ladies of the city saw in a man who was barely 5-7 and 130 pounds, "with a retreating forehead and sullen look."

In the interviews he gave, he blamed the oppression of the Americans for determining his life's course. "The Americans heaped wrongs on me in Monterey (where he grew up), and the officers of the law hounded me," he was quoted as saying. "I have been persecuted and driven from point to point."

Vasquez went to trial on January 6, 1875, and

despite the fine efforts of his lawyers, their portrayal of their client as a victim of a society that was prejudiced against him fell on deaf ears. The jury needed only a couple hours to deliberate his guilt, and he was sentenced to hang on March 19. It was reported later that even Judge David Belden did not believe his guilt, but that was not evident from the harsh words he bestowed on Vasquez at the sentencing hearing on January 23. "(Your) life has been one unbroken record of lawlessness and outrage, a career of pillage and murder," Belden told him. "(You are) a synonym for all that is wicked and infamous."

While Chavez couldn't break his leader out of jail, he didn't give up hope. During the intervening two months before the hanging, Chavez admitted to dropping several letters in the Wells Fargo Express letterbox in Hollister taking credit for the Tres Pinos murders himself and that if Vasquez was hung for murders that he didn't commit, then "I will show you I know how to avenge the death of my captain." On the night of the hanging, Chavez was reportedly seen drunk in the streets of Hollister "tearfully mourning the death of his chieftain."

But Chavez's own reign of terror as the new leader of the gang didn't last long. He was gunned down for the $2,000 reward on his own head later that year.

Vasquez faced his impending death stoically. When his appeal to the California Supreme Court was denied on March 12, his fate was sealed and Santa Clara County Sheriff John H. Adams went so far as to have 300 invitations printed for the hanging, which attracted an immense crowd that jam-packed the courtyard in front of the jail.

The day before the execution, Vasquez asked to see the coffin he would be buried in and it was brought to his cell. Feeling the soft, satin lining, Vasquez was reported to have replied, "I can sleep here forever very well!"

That night, while guarded by Sheriff Adams' son, Vasquez reportedly would make an oft-repeated comment as to whether he believed in life after death. "I hope so," he is said to have replied, "for in that case tomorrow I shall see all my old sweethearts together!"

Vasquez carried a small crucifix with him on his escort to the gallows, looking at it intently the entire time, reports stated. He requested to make a speech to the overflowing crowd, but was denied. He even was said to have removed his collar so the noose could slide more easily over his head. Then, as the executioner sprung the trap door at 1:35 p.m., Vasquez uttered the final word of his life: "Pronto!"

***

Chavez, of course, kept his word, taking over the gang and heading east over the Sierras into the Panamint district. It was here that the legendary Morse followed him, having publicly stated that the ruthless Chavez was next on his round-up list after Gov. Booth placed a $2,000 bounty on the outlaw's head. Like every bandit that Morse tracked down, Chavez was well aware of the threat of "El Diablo," but what he didn't know was that Morse had used virtually all of the $15,000 allotted to him by the time he had tracked Vasquez to Los Angeles.

Only $500 remained when he saddled his posse to begin pursuit of Chavez and that quickly ran out; Morse guessed wrongly that Chavez would return back over the Sierras to his old haunting grounds in the Coast Range around Hollister and gave up the chase. As the readers now well know, Chavez instead headed south into Mexico and there split up with the rest of the gang and headed to Arizona, where he met his fateful demise for the reward on his head, just as his mother had predicted.

The political climate had changed greatly in the East Bay area during Morse's long tenure as sheriff, and he soon saw the writing on the wall. With a voting population now overwhelmingly Democratic with the influx of new immigrants to the West, Morse anticipated that he would not be reelected as Alameda County sheriff in the next election. Instead of mounting a futile campaign, he announced his decision not to seek another term, and instead moved his efforts across the bay to San Francisco where he started the Morse Patrol and Detective Agency, the first of its kind and the model for those to come.

After the inquest in Yuma that confirmed the death of Chavez, the bandit's head was taken overland to Los Angeles by Harry Roberts and the Raggio brothers. However, upon their much-heralded arrival, Sheriff Rowland could not ascertain without a doubt that the head belonged to Chavez and the State Legislature refused to pay the reward without further proof. The bounty hunters were told to take the head to Hollister, where Chavez's mother then resided, in order to positively identity it. It seems only Harry Roberts made this trip, as the Raggios understandably did not wish to show their faces around their hometown where Chavez was a hero to the *californios.*

Roberts obtained affidavits from Chavez's family that it was indeed the bandit, but even still the California legislature was not forthcoming with the $2,000 reward

… it didn't have the money. Roberts had to wait nearly two years until the next elected legislature could appropriate the funds, and Roberts finally returned to Arizona with $2,199.42, the additional amount presumably interest.

As for the Gaskill brothers, after selling off all their interests in Campo to Ed Aiken, they relocated in San Diego, then undergoing a boom. Silas and his wife, Catherine, had a house built on the corner of 16th and F streets, where they indeed did have two children. Lumen and Eliza, meanwhile, purchased a home on the corner of Third and Elm where they raised six children. Both brothers became staunch members of the Republican party, though neither ran for office, intent instead to invest heavily in real estate in the burgeoning city. Silas owned several residences, foremost among them the old Shoate house on Horton Plaza. Lumen's prize property was a 55-acre ranch in Mission Valley.

During this time, it is virtually indisputable that the Gaskill brothers, revered as heroes of the Old West among the residents of San Diego, would have met and shared stories with the legendary Wyatt Earp. The former U.S. Marshall, who had it out with the Clanton gang in the famous Shootout at the OK Corral in Tombstone, Arizona. Earp had lived in San Diego in the late 1880s and early 1890s and owned four saloons in the Stingaree District (now the Gaslamp Quarter) even after he and his wife Josie began their travels that took them eventually to Nome, Alaska, at the height of the gold rush there.

They might well have been introduced by the son of Sheriff Nicholas Hunsaker. William, who more than likely rode with his father to Campo following the famous gunfight, went on to become one of the most successful early era lawyers in California. He even spent a year in Tombstone, where he teamed up with the famous Tom Fitch, defending the Earp's in several of the Southwest's most infamous cases. The younger Hunsaker moved his practice to Los Angeles in 1892 and would eventually become president of the California State Bar Association.

Both Gaskill brothers died in 1914, Silas at the ripe old age of 85. He is buried in Mount Hope Cemetery in San Diego. Lumen, who miraculously survived the Campo shootout, died just six months prior to his brother at age 70 in Whittier, and is buried in Los Angeles.

Wyatt Earp, who lived out his latter years in Los Angeles where he became friends with many of the early Hollywood actors, died at the age of 80 in 1929. Among his pall bearers were Tom Mix and William S. Hart, the famous early Western actors, and also one William Hunsaker, perhaps the only man who knew that Earp's famous exploits at the OK Corral were eclipsed probably by only one other shootout in the history of the Old West: The Forgotten Gunfight in Campo.

Bibliography

BOOKS

Boessenecker, John; Lawman: The Life and Times of Harry Morse, 1835-1912. University of Oklahoma Press, Norman, Okla., 1998.

Burns, Walter Noble: The Robin Hood of El Dorado: The Saga of Joaquin Murrieta, Famous Outlaw of California's Age of Gold, Coward-McCann Inc., 1932.

Jackson, Joseph Henry; Bad Company, University of Nebraska Press, Lincoln, Neb., 1939.

MacGill, Ruth S.; True Tales from Historic Campo, self-published, second edition, 1998.

McCain, Ella; Memories of the Early Settlements: Sulzura, Portreo and Campo, self-published, 1955.

Munz, Philip A.; California Mountain Wildflowers, University of California Press, Los Angeles, 1963.

Pourade, Richard F.; The History of San Diego: The Glory Years, 1865-1898, Copley Press, La Jolla, Calif., 1964.

Ridge, John Rollin; The Life and Adventures of Joaquin Murieta, University of Oklahoma Press, Norman, Okla., new edition, 1955.

Secrest, William B.; California Desperadoes: Stories of Early California Outlaws in Their Own Words, Word Dancer Press, Clovis, Calif., 2000.

Secrest, William B.; Perilous Trails, Dangerous Men, Word Dancer Press, Clovis, Calif., 2002.

Wilson, Neill C.; Silver Stampede, Ballantine Books, New York, 1937.

Starr, Kevin; California, A History, The Modern Library, New York, 2005.

PERIODICALS

Aiken, Ed T.; "Wild Times at Old Campo," The Southern California Rancher, 1947.

Reed, Harry; "The Six Guns at Campo," *The West,* date unknown.

Richardson, D.S.; "Duels to the Death," *Overland Monthly,* Aug. 1888.

Secrest, William B.; "The Return of Chavez," *True West,* Jan./Feb. 1978.

"Great Campo Gunfight," *Butterfield Express,* Dec. 1964.

GOVERNMENT DOCUMENTS

California Supreme Court Reports, People vs. Vasquez, 40 Cal. 560 (Jan. 1875).

Report of Coroner E.J. Smith, inquest into the death of Clodovio Chavez, Yuma, Arizona Territory, filed Jan. 12, 1876.

NEWSPAPERS

Daily Alta California (San Francisco)

Inyo Independent (Independence, Calif.)

Los Angeles Times (Los Angeles)

Mendocino Herald (Mendocino, Calif.)

San Diego Union (San Diego, Calif.)

San Dieguito Citizen (Encinitas, Calif.)

San Francisco Chronicle (San Francisco)

UNPUBLISHED MATERIALS

Collins, Tom; "Fort Whipple's First Telegraph: A Turning Point in Prescott History, Sharlot Hall Museum Days Past, May, 2008.

Crawford, Richard W.; "Stranger Than Fiction: Vignettes of San Diego History, San Diego Historial Society, 1995.

Jaspar, James A.; "California History Makers: The Battle of Campo," undated.

Keenan, Ed; "Shootout at Campo Creek," published online, 2007.

Kimball, Russell F.; "Campo, California: A Brief History," San Diego Historical Society, 2000.

Klauber, Allan S.; "Ninety Years in San Diego: The Story of Klauber Wangenheim Co.," The Journal of San Diego History, July 1959.

MacGill, Ruth S.; "Campo Stone Store," undated.

MacGill, Ruth S.; "The Gunfight in Campo – 1975;" Mountain Empire Historical Society, Summer 2000.

Mills, James; "The Great Campo Gun Fight," undated.

Robinson, John W.; "The Bandit's Last Hurrah: Tiburcio Vasquez in Southern California," published online in the Dogtown Territorial Quarterly, date unknown.

Smythe, William E.; "The History of San Diego, 1542-1908," San Diego Historical Society, 1962.

Swisher, John; "Area Historian Previews Part of Helendale History," Keepsake (Vol. 1), undated.

Thrall, Will H.; "The Haunts and Hideouts of Tiburcio Vasquez," The Quarterly, Historical Society of Southern California, June 1948.

Watkins, Lee H.; "John S. Harbison: San Diego Pioneer Beekeeper," The Journal of San Diego History, Fall 1969.

"Historic Old Campo," Mountain Empire Historical Society.

"Shootout in Campo," Mountain Empire Historical Society, 2003.

Interview with Isola Derrick Hook, by Edgar F. Hastings, in Campo, Calif., Aug. 19, 1959.

Interview with Nancy Martha Webb McCain, by Edgar F. Hastings in Bostonio, Calif., Feb. 19, 1959.
Interview with Lois Ruth MacKechnie, by Bob Wright in Fallbrook, Calif., Sept. 12, 1972.
National Honey Board Fact Sheet.

Also, numerous web sites were consulted during the research of this book, including sandiegohistory.org, wikipedia.com and explorehistoricalif.com, among others.

About The Author

Bryon Harrington has been a student of the Old West for as long as he can remember. Growing up in a small town in Vermont, he spent his childhood reading the western tales of Louis L'Amour and Zane Grey and watching his Western heroes on television and on the silver screen. It was inevitable that he would end up living in the West. His first Western adventure was hitch-hiking cross-country at the young age of 21. Seven years later, he drove west again and settled in the backcountry of San Diego County near the Mexican border. It didn't take long for him to join the "Gaskill Brothers Gunfighters," an Old West reenactment team. Soon, he became a noted Western actor, quick-draw artist, bullwhip expert and gold prospector, among other talents. More than twenty years later, he is presently the skit director for the "Hole In The Wall Gang," another reenactment group. He knew immediately that the Campo Gunfight was a significant event in the history of the Old West, but no one had ever written a book about the December 4, 1875 shootout and Hollywood passed this one by. After more than ten years of research and nearly two years of writing, the amazing story is now complete. This is a story that most Western history buffs have never heard of but one that they won't soon forget - Campo: The Forgotten Gunfight.

Made in the USA
Charleston, SC
24 April 2011